BY NANCY THAYER

The Guest Cottage

An Island Christmas

Nantucket Sisters

A Nantucket Christmas

Island Girls

Summer Breeze

Heat Wave

Beachcombers

Summer House

Moon Shell Beach

The Hot Flash Club Chills Out

Hot Flash Holidays

The Hot Flash Club Strikes Again

The Hot Flash Club

Custody

Between Husbands and Friends

An Act of Love

Belonging

Family Secrets

Everlasting

My Dearest Friend

Spirit Lost

Morning

Nell

Bodies and Souls

Three Women at the Water's Edge

Stepping

THE GUEST COTTAGE

BALLANTINE BOOKS
NEW YORK

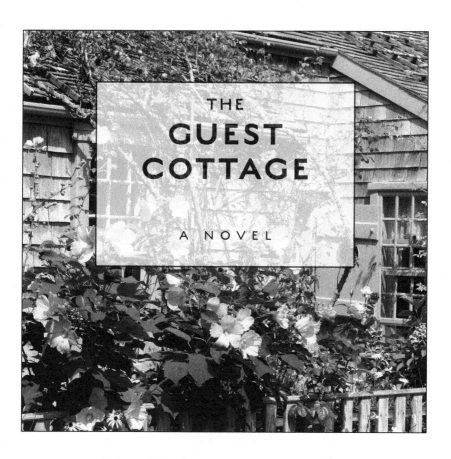

THE

GUEST COTTAGE

A NOVEL

NANCY THAYER

Copyright © 2015 by Nancy Thayer

All rights reserved.

Published in the United States by Ballantine Books, an imprint of Random House, a division of Penguin Random House LLC, New York.

BALLANTINE and the HOUSE colophon are registered trademarks of Penguin Random House LLC.

Library of Congress Cataloging-in-Publication Data
Thayer, Nancy.
The guest cottage : a novel / Nancy Thayer.
pages ; cm
ISBN 978-0-345-54551-0 (hardcover : alk. paper)—
ISBN 978-0-345-54571-8 (ebook)
I. Title.
PS3570.H3475G84 2015
813'.54—dc23
2015000879

Printed in the United States of America on acid-free paper

www.ballantinebooks.com

246897531

First Edition

Book design by Karin Batten

Title page photograph: Patrick Morrissey @ istockphoto.com

For Sofiya Popova, *С любов*.
One day I will read your books.
Nazdrave!

ACKNOWLEDGMENTS

I lift a glass of champagne—not just my beloved Prosecco, but real champagne, let's say Perrier-Jouët—to people I will call "the connectors," the people whose hard work and special joie de vivre make the connections that make a book possible.

I send enormous thanks to Hristo, Zarko, Ivan, and Valentina of the *River Beatrice* on the Uniworld Danube Cruise of August 4, 2013. You truly make it a Uniworld. Thanks also to Deborah Beale, who helped me learn a few words of Bulgarian, and who also helps me remember what a universal language music can be, not to mention how quickly she responded when I asked her for the first five notes of "Greensleeves."

Many thanks to Tharon Dunne of the Literacy Volunteers of Nantucket, for all her good work and for her genius instincts in introducing me to a female Bulgarian journalist.

Thanks to my Facebook friends, who have opened up the world to me, made me laugh, and kept me sane. Okay, as sane as they are. Really, I love you all.

Thanks to my extremely talkative family—talk about connectors!—my grandchildren, Ellias, Adeline, Emmett, and Anathea Forbes, who attach me to constant joy, and to their parents, Sam and Neil Forbes, who inform me of fascinating spiritual and scientific worlds, and to Josh Thayer and David Gillum, who share their mesmerizing, if occasionally incomprehensible, work with me.

Thanks to my ebullient and literate friends Jill Hunter Burrill, Jean Mallinson, Charlotte Kastner, Julie Hensler, Toni Massie, Tricia Patterson, Jan Dougherty, and my sister Martha Foshee. Great thanks to Dr. John West, who knows everything—and connects everything—and his wife, Mary West, who cooks the best dinners in the world.

A deep curtsey of thanks to my agent, Meg Ruley, who has connected me with so much great pleasure through the past decade. Thanks to all at the Jane Rotrosen Agency, especially the invaluable Christina Hogrebe.

And a forehead-to-the-floor full bow of gratitude to my editor, Linda Marrow, who can connect so well she knows what I meant to say even when I've said it incorrectly.

It takes so much work to put out a beautiful book. I send a bouquet of gratitude to Libby McGuire (I hope you and your husband make many trips to the island!), Gina Centrello, Dana Isaacson, Kim Hovey, Elana Seplow-Jolley, Christine Mitkityshyn, Maggie Oberrender, and Penelope Haynes.

And thank you again and again, Charley.

THE GUEST COTTAGE

Outside her daughter's bedroom window, the apple tree was a cloud of white blossoms in the soft glow from the front porch light. Here on the second floor of their stylish suburban Boston house, Lacey slept with her nightlight on and her arms around one of her stuffed animals. At ten, Lacey clung to childhood, and Sophie was glad.

Because it helps me believe we're still a happy family? Sophie wondered.

She left Lacey's door fully open; Lacey liked it that way.

Jonah had left his door to the hall slightly ajar, so Sophie slipped quietly inside. Her fifteen-year-old son was sprawled on his bed, wires hanging from the earbuds he wore even as his steady breathing told her he was sound asleep.

These children, she thought. *This generation will all be deaf by thirty.*

His backpack leaned against his desk. He would have done his homework and packed it up for tomorrow. Jonah was good that way. His computer screen was dark. She flirted with the idea of checking to see what he'd been doing last but decided against it. She didn't want to wake him, and besides, one of his video games lay blinking on the floor next to the bed. He'd probably spent the last hour vanquishing monsters. She smiled at the thought as she gazed at her firstborn, her precious boy. He was growing up, growing away from her, often gaping at her as if he thought she was hopelessly out of her mind for suggesting he put on a sweater or take his rain gear.

Jonah wore pajama bottoms and no top. His bony ribs pressed against his skin like staves of a boat. He ate constantly and gained inches, but the rosy plumpness of his childhood was gone.

She wanted to lean over and kiss his forehead but was afraid she'd wake him. Instead, she pulled a light blanket up over him. In response, he made a snuffling noise and rolled onto his side. She left the room, closing the door behind her.

This was her favorite time of day, seeing her children tucked safely in bed, sleeping, dreaming, while the house itself seemed to yawn and calm and sink into its own satisfied state of rest.

Then why, Sophie asked herself, *am I so increasingly uneasy—so mentally itchy?*

Padding barefoot down the stairs, she thought, as she had so many times, how she never would have chosen to buy this particular house. To Sophie, it was too angular, too spare. But Zack was an architect. He had designed it. He called it clean, fresh, Zen. Over the years, Sophie had managed to soften and cozy it with deep and comfy armchairs, cracked antique wooden wardrobes placed to make hidden niches, colorful fat vases of flowers, and wooden cases of well-read books. The only room Zack would call state-of-the-art now was the kitchen, and she supposed she was happy enough about that. All the newest gleaming chrome and plastic technology that he gave her for her birthdays and Christmas did come in handy. She loved to cook, and Zack appreciated complicated, unusual food. The children, not so much. On the nights when Sophie knew for certain that Zack wouldn't be home, she let them have cheeseburgers, pizzas, meat loaf with mashed potatoes.

She glanced at the clock. It was after nine. Where was he? He had promised to be home for dinner tonight. He hadn't even phoned.

She fretted, mildly. This happened a lot, was happening more and more these days. Zack's clients were some of Boston's youngest, wealthiest, and most demanding, and if they wanted an evening consultation, they got it. When she knew he was working late, she enjoyed it, sharing an easy meal with the kids, then curling up with a good book. But he always told her when he wouldn't be home for dinner.

With a slight sense of anxiety, she went into his study and woke up his computer. She wanted to know: had he told her he was coming home, or had she forgotten that he wasn't? She did not want to believe she hadn't remembered. It wasn't that she and Zack had become adversaries in their marriage; it wasn't that she prided herself on getting everything right all the time—or it wasn't all that, *only* that. She needed to know he was okay.

The family had computers all over the house. Hers was at the desk in the nook in the kitchen where she kept the calendar of the family's doctor appointments, the kids' sports schedules, school conferences. Lacey used that computer, too. At ten, she still needed supervision, and she wasn't as addicted to the technology as Zack was. Jonah's computer was on his desk in his room—he had to have it to do homework. Their agreement was that he would leave his bedroom door unlocked so that Sophie could stick her head in and make spot checks. She feared he would wander onto porno sites, but so far he spent all his free time on video games.

Zack's desktop hummed. Sophie settled in his massive leather chair and searched until she found his calendar. The tempestuous winter was finally over and builders could get out on ladders and scaffoldings and return to work. All his clients wanted everything done at once.

More and more Zack shared less and less of his work life with Sophie, but she had been married to him for sixteen years and this was a fact that didn't change.

Today, April 10. Zack had typed: *Remember L bday.*

L? Probably Lila, his associate. Lila was twenty-eight, a pretty career girl with an unfettered life and her own BMW convertible. She had no children, a fabulous wardrobe, and an adorable laugh. She considered Zack an architectural genius, unlike Sophie, who considered him a man who should spend more time with his family.

Yes, he should remember Lila's birthday. Lila was an important colleague, young, bright, and energetic. Sophie wasn't uneasy or jealous—she herself had worked as bookkeeper for Zack when he first started out. She knew only too well that when he was working he often lost his charismatic charm and often lost his temper, too. He could be bossy, dictatorial, critical, and a social climber. He was a perfectionist—well, she was afraid she probably was, too—and single-minded in his ambition. Sophie wouldn't want to work with Zack now. Being married to him was quite enough.

She focused on the calendar. Nothing there for tonight.

For tomorrow, April 11, Zack had typed: *Discuss Div with S.*

Div.

Her heart banged. She sat back in the chair, unable to take her eyes away from those three letters.

Div? The first word that leapt to mind was *divorce*, but not even ultra-organized Zack would enter a discussion about divorce on his calendar. Would he?

She closed her eyes. She controlled her breathing. She forced herself to be here now, in this quiet house with her children safe and asleep.

Div. Could he mean diversifying stocks? Maybe, but Zack handled all that without Sophie's input.

Div. Diversion? Maybe he wanted them all to go on a trip together.

Certainly the family needed to do something like that. It had been far too long since they'd done anything together as a family. But really, that was a stretch; Zack wouldn't ever call a vacation a diversion.

Dividend! Ah. Maybe a dividend, a windfall, had come in on one of Zack's stocks and he wanted to discuss how to spend it with Sophie.

Right, that was it. *Div* meant anything but divorce. Who was she kidding? All marriages had their ups and downs, but in the past year or so, the Anderson marriage had been on a steady slide toward a new low. Sometimes she thought she was hanging on only for the sake of the children. She found Zack less and less appealing, more—

The front door slammed, making her jump guiltily. She heard the familiar sounds of her husband dropping his briefcase on the hall table, his footsteps toward the kitchen, veering off to his study. Apprehensive but determined, she stayed where she was.

"What are you doing in here?" Zack asked, loosening his tie as he stood in the doorway.

Sophie studied her husband. Blond hair, blue eyes, former high school football hero, this year he had turned forty. He'd started using Grecian Formula. He bought a vintage Mustang convertible.

"Hello to you, too," she said, cocking her head, smiling to take the edge off her words.

Zack's voice was cool. "Sophie."

"You didn't call," she reminded him.

Zack made an impatient sound and turned away.

Her fingertips were tingling. She was angry, frightened, and oddly eager, as if she were about to dive into a strange lake whose depth she didn't know. *The children*, she told herself. *Take care of the children.*

"Are you hungry? I could—"

"I'm tired. Going to bed." Zack stepped into the hall, still not looking at her, and all at once Sophie was trembling.

She went to the doorway and took hold of his arm. "Zack. Zack, please, wait. What does *div* mean?"

"*What?*"

Now she had his attention. As she felt her husband's eyes on her, a fast and familiar sense of being judged swept over her. Okay, she was in jeans and a T-shirt, barefoot, and she didn't know when she'd last combed her hair, but she kept her blond hair short so that it was always more or less tidy. She was four years younger than Zack, she was slender, she was pretty enough.

Sophie repeated, "What does *div* mean?" She gestured to his desk. "I found it here on your calendar. 'Discuss *div* with S.' "

"Oh, Sophie, do you really want to get into this now?" Zack sagged, signaling his exhaustion.

She knew he was not *that* tired. "I do, Zack. I don't think I'll be able to sleep or even remain sane until you tell me." She gazed at her husband, trying to read his expression.

He shook off her arm, came into the room, and sank into an armchair. "Fine. Let's do this. Sophie, I want a divorce."

In spite of her suspicions, she was shocked. "But what about the children?" she asked. Jonah and Lacey had no way to shield themselves from pain. Lacey was still sweet and cheerful, but recently, Sophie had noticed changes in Jonah that concerned her. His grades were still good, but he was crashing in soccer and baseball, sports he'd always played. His coaches were all over him. If he had to deal with his father's desertion . . .

"Hey, I'm not divorcing *them*," Zack responded, his tone very nearly amused. He was stressed right now, but in his eyes, in his posture, was an obviously smugness. He knew something she didn't know.

"Are you divorcing *me*?" She'd done it: the words, those life-changing words, were out in the air between them. Flashing. In neon.

Zack shook his head impatiently. "Come on. Admit it: you haven't been happy, either."

Was that true? At this moment, Sophie wasn't sure. She was a good mother, an efficient and creative housewife, a good friend . . . but happy? The palms of her hands went damp; she rubbed them on her jeans.

"Is it Lila?" she asked. She sat on a chair across from her husband. If he wanted to, he could reach across and touch her, he could tell her he was sorry, she could suggest they start over . . .

"Does it matter who it is?" Zack countered.

"You could fire Lila, and we could start over," Sophie offered.

Zack flinched. "I don't want to fire Lila. I love her. She loves me."

"Wow." Sophie recoiled, trying to absorb his words. He was so very far ahead of her in this situation. "Wow, Zack. I don't know what to say."

Zack snorted with impatience. "You see how it is with you? Why can't you cry? Call me names? Throw a book at me?"

Sophie grimaced. "So it's my fault."

Zack slumped. Ran his hand through his thick, sandy hair. Leaned toward Sophie, his elbows on his knees, a pose she'd seen so often, the honest man trying to close a deal. "Look, Sophie. I'm not trying to be a monster here. I know Lila's young. She's new. You and I have been married for sixteen years and the—the passion, or whatever you want to call it—has faded. You know I don't want to break anyone's heart. I don't want to be the villain."

"And yet you're screwing Lila." Sophie studied her husband's face, seeing the charm, the force, the concentration he could focus like a raptor on its prey, all of this aimed at her. Once she had admired him for this, adored him for his power. He had changed—or she had. "You say you love her."

Zack gave Sophie a pleading look. "She makes me feel young again."

Sophie nodded. "I can understand that." After a moment, she said, "I don't want the children hurt."

"Christ, Sophie, do you think I do?"

No, Sophie thought, Zack wouldn't want to hurt the children. On the other hand, he never thought of his children unless she prompted him. He had never been a natural family man. She took a deep breath, gathering herself. If Zack was the hunter, Sophie was the mother lion, shielding her cubs. Protecting the family.

This was humiliating, but maybe the right thing to do.

Sophie forced a pleasant tone. "I was planning to discuss this with you—Susie Swenson called yesterday. An old friend of mine from college. She has a summer home on Nantucket she wants to rent out for July and August. They call it the guest cottage, because the main house was next door, but they've sold that off and subdivided the land. Whatever, this place sounds like a mansion: six bedrooms, three baths, everything furnished from linens to lobster crackers. I thought it might be good for you and me—and the kids, of course, but especially for you and me. We could walk on the beach. Drink margaritas. Get in touch with each other again." She watched her husband as she spoke. His eyes did not light up; his face did not brighten.

"How much?" Zack asked, avoiding her eyes.

She named a sum and Zack snorted. "Nantucket." He shook his head. "No. No, I'm not paying that kind of money."

"Do you *want* to go?" She reached across and touched his arm. "Would you like to try again?"

He patted her hand, as if it were the morose muzzle of a clingy old dog, and drew away. "No. And I don't think it's fair for you to expect me to spend that much for you and the kids. You and the kids can stay in the house. I'll move in with Lila."

"For how long?"

"Well, for good. Now that we've gotten it out in the open, I think we should proceed. First, a separation. I'll move in with Lila while you and I make the arrangements for the divorce." She observed his eagerness. He was ready to jump out of the chair and leave the house this very moment.

"No, Zack, wait. Give us some time. We're a *family*. Maybe—things—will change." The idea of the house on Nantucket shimmered like a beacon in the dark confusion of her marriage. She'd been dreaming about it ever since Susie called. She wanted this. She *needed* this. "I'm going to take the kids to Nantucket for July and August."

Zack bridled. "Where are you going to get the money for that kind of rent?"

Sophie smiled. It was the first time she'd smiled during this conversation. "Aunt Fancy," she said.

Aunt Fancy's motto had been: "If I've gotta go down, I'm gonna go down in style." She used the last of her inheritance to buy a new wardrobe and have her hair colored red when her husband left her in 1970 when she was just twenty-four. These changes promptly attracted the attention of Fred Lattimer, a wealthy divorced man twelve years older, who wooed Fancy, married her, and gave her the four children for whom she'd been longing.

Sophie had always admired Aunt Fancy, who lived with so much more flair and gusto than Sophie's own mother, Hester. Hester's idea of dressing up was putting on her white coat and stethoscope. Hester could save lives in the emergency room, but she had no sympathy for malingerers. If you wanted a bit of wickedness and fun, you went to Aunt Fancy. For Band-Aids and a healthy meal, you went to Sophie's mom.

Sophie wished she could now run to Aunt Fancy, who'd probably suggest they go out to a bar together and pick up some men. "If the horse throws you, climb right back on" was another motto of Aunt Fancy's. She had a lot of mottos.

Fabulous Aunt Fancy had died on her sixtieth birthday while parachuting from an airplane. On the up side, it was exactly the way Fancy

Lattimer would have liked to go. But Sophie had counted on her aunt having a long life, serving as a role model and a playmate for Sophie as she got older.

In her will, Aunt Fancy left most of her money—and there was a lot of it—to her four children. But she also left a nice big chunk of money for Sophie to use for what Aunt Fancy called "mad money."

When Sophie started dating, or what passed for dating at age fifteen, her mother sat her down to discuss birth control. Aunt Fancy had given her a pretty quilted coin purse with a flower-shaped clasp. Inside were tucked two ten-dollar bills.

"When I was growing up," Aunt Fancy told Sophie, "my mother made certain I carried mad money. All the girls carried mad money, which came in handy if some guy had us out in a car and thought he had us trapped, or if he got fresh during a movie and tried to put his hand up our dress. We always had money for a taxi and a way home back then. It gave us independence."

Mad money. Sophie was certainly mad at Zack. She was also mad in general—demented, flustered, heartbroken, mentally blitzed, psychologically wacko. Sophie had always been a cautious person, a good girl. The idea of spending her inheritance to rent a house, sight unseen, on Nantucket, a resort island she had only visited on day trips, was downright *epic* for her.

"I'm going to do it," Sophie said aloud, to herself as much as to Zack. She left him standing in his office and went off to find her cell before she changed her mind. She phoned Susie.

"Susie, I want the house."

"Really?" Susie squeaked with surprise. She hesitated. "Look. I have to be honest with you. One of the reasons I don't want to go through a rental agent is that they will take a big chunk of money for a commission. This year I need all the money I can get, and I don't want to share it with my spendthrift cousin Ivan. But we can talk about that another time. Another reason I'd like to do this privately is that not many people would rent a place with a family member stuck in the apartment attached to the house."

"A family member," Sophie repeated.

"It's my grandfather, but not the one who bought the property on Nantucket. The other one, Connor Swenson. He moved in this winter after our grandmother died. He's a nice old guy, perfectly harmless, I promise, but he's kind of let himself go in his grief. Plus, he was a farmer in Iowa and he totally doesn't get the whole island thing. I've been out to visit him a lot, but he pretty much keeps to himself. He's not crazy, I swear on my life," Suzy continued, "but he's sad and perhaps a bit confused. He's sort of holed up in the apartment. I can't ask him to move out."

"Do you want us to do anything to help him?" asked Sophie. "Buy him groceries, drive him to the library, that sort of thing?"

"Not at all. He brought his old pickup truck. He buys his own groceries, cooks his own food, and as far as I can tell, spends his time watching television, doing jigsaw puzzles, and whittling."

"Whistling?"

"*Whittling*. You know, carving."

"I didn't know people still whittled. Does he whistle while he whittles?" Sophie's mind was all over the place; she was light-headed with excitement.

"So you don't mind if he's hanging out back there?" Susie asked.

"I don't see why," Sophie said.

Sophie and Susie were friends, so there was no need for any kind of legal contract. Sophie agreed to send Susie a check and Susie said she'd send Sophie the keys and a map to the house.

Aunt Fancy would have approved.

2

As Trevor Black sat in the waiting room, his knee jiggled up and down with anxiety. Was he doing the right thing, talking to a child psychologist about his four-year-old son? In a way, he felt he was betraying Leo; he knew at Leo's preschool the teachers told the children not to "tattle." But Trevor was a parent, the only parent, and he was concerned.

Before Trevor could change his mind, the receptionist showed him into Dr. Warren's office. Dr. Warren rose to shake his hand. A pleasant older man, he wore a suit but no tie, which oddly made Trevor feel more comfortable, less *judged*. Trevor ran his computer business from his home and only wore suits when he had face meetings with certain clients.

The therapist gestured to a chair. "How may I help you?"

"It's about my son," Trevor said, and all at once he was on the verge of tears. "Leo. Leo is four. He's a really good little guy. But his mother, my wife, Tallulah . . ." Trevor took a deep breath. "She died in November."

"I'm so sorry. Was she ill?"

Trevor hesitated. "It's all confidential here, right?"

"Of course."

"I wouldn't want Leo to know. He wouldn't understand. And I don't want to disrespect Tallulah. She was an actress. She got a lot of roles in local Boston theaters, and in suburban ones, too. She loved acting. Her whole world was acting. When I first met her, she warned me, she told me, 'The only thing you need to know about me is that I'm an actress.'"

Trevor paused, remembering when he met Tallulah at a party in Cambridge. She took his breath away. Tallulah had silky red hair that fell in a curtain past her shoulders and was parted to drape enticingly over one eye. She had a figure that wouldn't quit. She had a deep, husky voice that she later told him she had achieved by smoking, talking, and singing when she had a cold so that her vocal cords were slightly damaged. That was proof, she reminded him, that all she cared about was being an actress.

"I'm warning you," she'd said. "Don't get serious about me."

Of course Trevor, being the kind of not-arrogant but pretty damn self-confident guy he was, took Tallulah's words as a challenge. Trevor had been twenty-four years old then, a good-looking, clever, laid-back guy who pretty much always got what he wanted. All his life, things had come easy for him: good grades, high school quarterback, any girl he wanted, entrance to MIT, and a computer business that kept him busy and rich. Tallulah made their relationship even more stimulating by not responding to his charms as easily as most women did. He had to pursue her. That was kind of fun. He didn't understand her and he enjoyed a puzzle. So his brain was as attracted to Tallulah as his body. Okay, maybe not quite as much as his body.

How arrogant he'd been back then! How young!

"Mr. Black?" Dr. Warren said quietly, pulling Trevor out of his reverie.

Trevor cleared his throat. "Okay. Okay, here it is. Tallulah never was into the whole housewife/mommy bit. Still, she was Leo's mommy. She was my wife. We loved her, and even though she was unusual—demanding, not nurturing, I guess you could say—we all made it work." This was harder than Trevor had known it would be, this talking business.

"How did she die?" Dr. Warren asked.

"Um. Tallulah, you see, wasn't around a lot normally. Rehearsals, auditions, buying clothes—I don't know, we were used to it. Recently she'd seldom been home. I thought she was at rehearsal. But then—" The memory made Trevor stumble over his words. "In November—it was morning—Leo was at preschool, the police knocked on my door—I have an apartment in Cambridge. Okay. They told me—and they were respectful—they told me Tallulah was dead. She had died of an overdose of heroin she'd been smoking at the apartment of another actor. Tallulah had always said that Wilhelm was one of the most gifted actors of their generation. But, um, the thing is, both Tallulah and Wilhelm were naked when their bodies were found."

"How difficult for you," Dr. Warren said, with no judgment in his tone.

Trevor bit his lip. "Right." He was having trouble breathing. "So, anyway, I had to figure out how to tell Leo. I mean, he was used to his mother being gone for hours and even days at a time. I'd always been the main parent for him, right from the start. Tallulah had never been keen on discussing preschools and play groups or Christmas presents and birthday parties, that sort of thing. Still, she was Trevor's *mother*. He loved her. He *adored* her." Trevor swallowed back a sob.

After a moment of silence, Dr. Warren urged, "Go on."

"When I told Leo that afternoon—" Trevor had been much more reserved telling the other parents at the school, the teachers, and his friends about this. He hadn't wanted it to get back to Leo. Now he was afraid he was going to cry. "When I told Leo, we were at the apartment after school. I had given him juice. We sat on the couch. I said it as gently as I could, that his mommy had died. He knew about death from animals in school, television. We had talked about it. He kind of understood. So I told him." Trevor swallowed. "Leo said, 'No, Daddy, *please*.'"

Trevor cleared his throat. Dr. Warren waited.

"I hugged Leo. We cried together. I told him Mommy lived in heaven now, a beautiful place where Mommy was always happy. Mommy had been sick, I told Leo—" He glanced at the psychologist. "Really, in a way she had, right? I told Leo it had happened suddenly, she had just gone to sleep. Well, that was probably true. I said Mommy would always be looking down on him with love. Leo wanted to know where she was, and I said up in the sky, and Leo jumped up from the sofa, raced to the balcony door, and stepped up to the railing. He, um, Leo *waved at the sky*. He yelled, 'Hi, Mama!'" Trevor brought his hands to his face and forced himself not to cry. Embarrassed, he said, "I thought I'd cried myself out."

"It's fine," Dr. Warren told him. "It's good. Take your time."

Trevor reached for a tissue from the box on the coffee table and blew his nose. After a moment, he got himself back together.

"So we went on. We made a small shrine to Tallulah in Leo's room. Gradually, when Leo was at preschool, I removed some of Tallulah's less conspicuous stuff—the shoes, cosmetics, wigs, secondhand clothes—so the apartment opened up a bit. We have three bedrooms—one is my office—I have a computer business. One bedroom is Leo's, and for the first couple of months I slept with him." Trevor thought of the nights in Leo's room, curled around him on the small twin bed. He could only hope they brought as much comfort to his son as they did to him.

Dr. Warren rose, went to a side table, and poured Trevor a glass of water.

"Thank you." The cool water revived him. Setting it on the table, he began again, more in control now. "So that's why I'm here. Leo. I'm troubled about Leo."

"Go on."

"I mean, at first, Leo was sad, quiet. He dragged his feet when we went to the park and didn't even want to get ice cream. He spent less time painting and drawing and more time curled up on his bed with his arms around Tubee, his pet giraffe. Other times, the slightest problem—a broken cracker, dropped soap—sent him into tantrums. I spoke with his preschool teacher, who said Leo was quieter and less playful but in general seemed happy enough. I talked with other parents. They told me Leo was young and children are resilient." He glanced at the psychologist for confirmation.

"Yes," Dr. Warren agreed. "That is usually true."

"*Usually?*" Trevor shifted on the sofa. He was glad he had come. "Okay, then, here's what bothers me. In January, Leo started doing things that disturbed me, but I also thought maybe they were signs of, well, moving on. That's why I wanted your advice."

"What kind of things?"

"Well, at night, before Leo goes to sleep, he takes out all his clothes for the next day and arranges them on the floor of his bedroom in an absolute unchanging order. Briefs, jeans, T-shirt, socks, sneakers, sweatshirt. He'll eat his lunch only if I pack the same thing day after day: a cheese and mustard, not mayonnaise, sandwich on whole-wheat bread, a banana, yogurt. One day I was out of bananas and put an apple in the lunchbox. When Leo got home that afternoon, I opened the box and saw Leo hadn't touched any of the food."

"Anything else?"

"Well, he's gotten kind of obsessed with Legos."

For the first time, Dr. Warren smiled. "He'd be unusual if he weren't obsessed with Legos."

"Good," Trevor said, relaxing a bit. "That's good to know." He waited.

After a moment, the psychologist said, "I think Leo is dealing with the loss of his mother by trying to take control of his own small universe."

Trevor nodded, listening hard.

"Leo has to do something," Dr. Warren said, "and these are actually not worrisome actions. If they continue, or become worse, then I'd like you to bring him in. He could have OCD. Obsessive-compulsive disorder. OCD is an anxiety disorder related to the transmission of serotonin in the brain. But I think it's too soon to be concerned about that."

"What can I do?" Trevor asked.

"Summer is almost here. Perhaps you could take him on a vacation, somewhere the child has never been with his mother. A new environment might provide a break for the boy's grieving. Is that a possibility for you with your work? Financially?"

"Yes, sure," Trevor said, nodding. *God*, it felt great to have an expert advise him.

"It's good that you built the shrine," Dr. Warren continued. "Good to talk about Leo's mommy, try to get him to talk about his feelings. It would help if you found a way to deal with your own grief, too. Children are remarkably sensitive to their parents' emotions. Leo is very young. *You* are not so very old—how old are you? Thirty?"

Trevor nodded.

"You both have a great deal of life before you. I'm sure you will find a way to make it a happy life for your son and yourself."

Driving home after the appointment, Trevor thought about the psychologist's advice. There was so much Trevor hadn't said, he felt guilty. For months before her death, Tallulah had been all over the place emotionally, staying out all night, losing weight, having rages, shrieking at her puzzled son to leave her alone. He'd suspected she was using some kind of drug, but heroin? If he'd even suspected, he would have tried to help her. If only he had tried to help her!

Trevor parked in his driveway and sat in the car, thinking. Leo was going to a playdate with his best friend, Cassidy, after preschool and wouldn't be back for a couple of hours. He scrutinized his apartment building. It was kind of a dump, although the neighborhood was safe. An old three-story, three-family house, he'd first rented it back when he was a graduate student at MIT. After Leo's birth, Trevor had suggested buying a house in one of Boston's many suburbs—he had the money. This freaked out Tallulah. Maybe they needed a bigger condo, she said, so the crying baby could have his own room, but no way was she going to become a suburban mom. The city was where the action was.

Tallulah treasured the location, so near theaters, shopping, and the T. She hadn't cared about interior decor—hell, she hadn't even cared about comfort. Tallulah's basic needs were, in order of importance, a closet for her many clothes, a bathroom with a shower and a large mirror so she could put on her intricate makeup, and some kind of bed to flop on at the end of the day or the long night. They had turned the sun porch into Trevor's office, and turned what had once been his office into a bedroom for Leo. His son's room held the only new furniture in the apartment. It never occurred to Tallulah to suggest replacing Trevor's ancient sofa and chairs with pieces that didn't sag or list.

Tallulah was not a monster. She'd cuddled her son, and even though she didn't nurse him because she didn't want to ruin her breasts, she learned to give him a bottle. As he grew older, she discovered he was the best audience she had ever had in her life. She tried out for *Shear Madness*, a long-running comedy, and won the part of the ditzy beauty shop assistant. For a long time, she was happy. She taught Leo songs from Broadway musicals; she taught him to say a few time-honored lines. The line that stuck was: *To be or not to be, that is the question.* At two, Leo pronounced "To be" like "Tubee," as if it were a person. He named his favorite stuffed animal, a giraffe, Tubee.

"You're going to be an actor like me!" Tallulah had crowed when he told her, and kissed him.

When Tallulah was around, Leo went manic, always trying to catch her attention by singing songs, making silly faces, doing somersaults, taking off his clothes and putting them on in silly ways—anything to get her to look at him, even if the response was irritation on Tallulah's part. Once he tried to put on her makeup. Tallulah screamed at him and screamed at Trevor, too, for not watching the boy more carefully. Her reaction had been so over the top it had scared Leo and made Trevor vow secretly to himself to be more cautious and watchful. It had also made Trevor immensely sad. By then, he was thirty, and beginning to understand the long-lasting consequences of his infatuation with the beautiful actress.

Trevor sighed. That was all in the past. He had to find a way to move into the future with optimism.

He checked his email and answering machine—nothing urgent— and flopped down on his sofa, thinking. Should he take Leo to visit his mother? Audrey had never claimed to be thrilled about housekeeping or raising Trevor. She liked traveling, cruises, five-star hotels, entertainment, and she got bored easily. Now on her third husband, she seemed fond enough of Leo. She seldom visited, though, and possibly she was on a cruise right now. It was spring, a good time to travel.

Who else? Where? He was wary of talking to the other parents about this; several of the young mothers, divorced and married, had made it clear they would be only too glad to console him. He wasn't ready for anything like that.

When his cell buzzed, Trevor checked the name: Ivan Swenson, an old college friend. Curious, Trevor clicked on.

"Hey, Ivan, what's up?"

"Dude! Have I got a deal for you!"

Trevor rolled his eyes. Ivan was a blissed-out, pot-smoking, follow-the-sun kind of guy who was always phoning from Guatemala or Portugal.

"How would you like to spend the summer in a great big old house on Nantucket?"

Trevor sat up straight. "What's the catch?"

"I need some cash quick. I'm going to India with this awesome girl. Look, the house is fully furnished, close to the beaches, completely wired for cable and Wi-Fi. Let me tell you, when you see the girls in their bikinis, you'll think you've died and gone to heaven."

"Ivan, I'm thirty years old and have my own business and a four-year-old son."

"Well, hey, your kid would love it there. He could play on the beaches, plus they've got cool day camps for kids. Look, I can't talk long—I'm phoning from London. Are you interested?"

Trevor knew Ivan would call this karma. And maybe it was.

"Actually, Ivan, I am."

3

ophie sent Susie Swenson's photos of the house to her children's phones. She studied them on her computer, scanning the details.

The Nantucket house was three stories high, with a two-story wing off each end. The house looked British, like something out of an old black-and-white mystery involving butlers and Bentleys, except shingled with gray wood instead of built with brick or stone. An ancient, thick wisteria vine drooped its violet blooms over the front door. Trellises covered with climbing pink roses framed the doors of the two wings.

A brick driveway circled in front of the house. Another brick driveway ran down to the left of the house past a long enclosed passageway and the attached apartment. More pink roses densely quilted the walls of the addition. By the blue door to the grandfather's quarters stood pots of old-fashioned peppermint-striped geraniums. A small stone patio had been laid at the end, complete with wrought-iron furniture and urns bright with pink petunias. The Swensons obviously liked pink.

Photos of the interior displayed a warren of rooms as worn and welcoming as a fairy-tale grandmother's lap, and as rumpled. A front hall divided the living room from what looked like a library, both rooms crowded with comfortable sofas, chairs, and cases of books and games. Behind, a dining room and a family room. A long, modernized kitchen ran the width of the back of the house, opening onto a patio laid in a herringbone pattern with urns spilling with flowers at each corner. A large gas grill, a long wooden table, and wooden chairs turned the area into an outdoor dining room. From there, perhaps thirty feet of well-kept grass flowed in a lush green carpet before sur-rendering to scrubby beach grass and shrubbery.

Upstairs, six bedrooms were packed with old spool beds, bunk beds, double beds, and twin beds, plus bureaus, wing chairs, standing mir-rors, and more bookcases spilling with books and games.

What a perfect summer house! It wouldn't matter if Sophie never dusted, if the kids tracked sand in, if it rained for days in a row. And guests! They could have so many guests! Jonah and Lacey could each have a friend for as long as they wanted, and Sophie could invite her mother (out of duty), and her friends Angie and Bess, and perhaps a couple of her other friends, too.

After Sophie pleaded with Zack, they presented a united front to the kids, presenting the plans as *their* plans, saying that Zack had so much work, he didn't know when he'd be able to get to the island. Jonah and Lacey didn't question it; they were used to their father being too busy to be with them.

So on the last day of June, her green SUV packed with luggage, a cooler of food, and last-minute additions—first aid cream, a few more paperbacks—Sophie drove down Route 3 in the crowded parade of summer people headed for the Cape and islands. Determined to be cheerful, she blasted the music she loved, upbeat '80s songs like Cyndi Lauper's "Girls Just Want to Have Fun," while her children in the backseat nodded along to their own favorite music on earbuds.

Once they boarded the car ferry and began the two-hour trip to the island, the kids came out of their shells. They bought hot dogs and ate them leaning on the railing, staring out at the endlessly blue ocean. Jonah helped Lacey load photos on Instagram and they texted their friends at home.

By the time the Andersons were driving off the ramp and onto Nantucket, even Jonah, who had become unusually quiet the last few months, was talking.

"This is cool," he said. "No skyscrapers, no traffic lights."

"The streets are so narrow!" Lacey shrieked.

Jonah pointed, laughing. "Look, the traffic's stopped for a bunch of ducks crossing the road."

"I want to take a picture," Lacey cried. "Oh, they're so cute, the way they waddle. I think it's a family."

Smiling, Sophie waited for the last duck to hop up onto the grass, then continued, heading over to Surfside Road. Susie's house was hidden in a labyrinth of streets between the high school and Surfside Beach. Only the beginning of driveways, mailboxes, and stones painted with street numbers announced the presence of houses in what seemed like a primitive forest. Sophie turned on her GPS to find her way through the maze to Susie's house. Finally they arrived at the right driveway, bordered by thickets of wild roses. Sophie drove through a small tunnel of green, breaking through to a slight rise in the land. There was the house, massive, shabby, and enchanting, its windows sparkling in the sunlight.

"Wow," Lacey exclaimed. "That's enormous."

Sophie stopped her car in front of the house and took a deep breath. It was the last day of June, hot but not too hot, breezy but not windy. *Here we go,* she thought. *Stick with me, Aunt Fancy.*

In the few moments Sophie paused, her kids unsnapped their seat belts and exploded from the car.

"Hurry up, Mom," called Lacey. "I want to see the inside!"

Sophie walked to the front door beneath the clusters of thick violet wisteria, inserted the key, and unlocked it.

The kids burst into the house, racing through the rooms, screaming and shouting. When Jonah was around other people, he treated his ten-year-old sister like an indulged pet. But when they were alone, Jonah became a kid again. Sophie paused, standing in the doorway with her eyes closed, reveling in the sound of her children together and happy. So maybe it would be okay.

She entered the house. It was hot and stuffy from being closed up all winter. A center hall led straight through to the back, dividing the house. She walked to the right, the room Susie had called the library, and began opening the large windows. Whoever had been here last had left a paperback of *Great Expectations* open on the sofa. She smiled.

Footsteps thundered as the children raced up the stairs to the second floor. More shouts filled the air—happy shouts.

"Aunt Fancy, you clever old dear." Sophie squeezed herself as her heart began to fill just the tiniest bit, perhaps one-eighth in a large cup, with hope.

She crossed the hall into the large living room and opened the door to the addition extending between the main house and the apartment. Susie had said the connecting room was built especially for her aunt, a rather eccentric relative who was obsessed with the piano (*thank heavens for eccentric aunts*, Sophie thought). Because of her, this music room existed, an elegant chamber that seemed to have been lifted from a Viennese music hall. *Zack*, Sophie thought, *would have called it old-fashioned*. Thick Turkish rugs gleamed like satin against the dark wooden floors, a sparkling crystal chandelier hung from the ceiling, and gilt-framed paintings of concerts and pianists covered the walls. A long, deep-cushioned sofa, covered in pink roses strewn over an icy white background, sat against one wall.

In the middle of the room was a Steinway baby grand.

That the piano was here astonished Sophie—and cracked open the firmly shut door on her memories and on an enormous and profound part of her most essential self. She hadn't played piano for sixteen years, but how could she not play again here?

4

R iver Ford—yes, his parents had named him that—was Trevor's
second-in-command and only full-time employee. Trevor paid
River well, but River was what he called *relaxed* about the way he
spent money and seldom had a stable place to live. When Trevor suggested that River live in Trevor's apartment for the months of July and
August, rent free, with only a few small domestic duties, River had
jumped at the chance.

The day had come for Trevor and Leo to make the trip to Nantucket. Trevor was slightly nervous about leaving his stuff in the care
of his brilliant but absentminded friend. Before he left, Trevor sat
River down and made him look at the list that would be attached to
the refrigerator door, and to the bathroom wall next to the mirror, and
to the desk next to the motherboard.

"Read it aloud," Trevor ordered.

"Oh, man, come on!" River had a high-pitched voice and a ten-
dency to giggle.

Trevor glared at him.

River sighed. "'One. No smoking weed in the house. Two. Phone me every morning at ten a.m. Three. Clean aquarium once a week. I mean it, River.'"

Trevor's red-haired employee made a face at him. "Dude. And you think your *son* is anal?"

Trevor folded his arms over his chest. "Do you want a free place to live for two months or not?"

"Yes, and you know why? Nestra's going to move in with me. It's serious, man. This will be our trial live-together thing. I won't mess up."

Trevor ran his hands through his thick, dark hair. He had met Nestra—short for Clytemnestra, which she had renamed herself from the more pedestrian Ann—did these kids even read mythology? Did they not know the original Clytemnestra murdered her husband? Still, the current Nestra was a good influence on River. She loved living creatures. She would see that the aquarium was cleaned even if she had to do it herself.

"I'll count on that." Trevor rose and went down the hall to his son's bedroom. Leo was trying to cram more Legos into an already bulging duffel bag. "Okay, kid, time to hit the road."

"Okay, Daddy." Leo's innocent, trusting, unmarred face was like a spear to Trevor's heart. How did parents survive such responsibility? How did the world even manage to carry on?

River helped Trevor and Leo load up the Volkswagen Passat. River and Leo performed their complicated hello/goodbye hand ritual. Trevor strapped his son in his car seat with Tubee and a pile of books to look at for the ride down to the Cape. He filled his go-cup with iced coffee, handed Leo his go-cup filled with milk, and began the drive.

It was the last Thursday in June. At the first of the month, when the summer rentals started, Trevor knew the traffic to the Cape could be atrocious. Since no one lived in Ivan's house, no one would care that Trevor would beat the traffic by arriving a day early.

And once he got to Nantucket? Trevor couldn't get a clear picture in his head. Ivan had told him the house was large. Was that a good thing? Leo was familiar with the small rooms of their second-floor apartment in Cambridge. Maybe a spacious place would freak him out. Trevor might have to do some kind of damage control.

He began a to-do file in his mind. Walk through the house. Let Leo choose his own bedroom; then Trevor would choose the bedroom closest to Leo's. Go to the beach—a brave new world for them both. Trevor could imagine the blaze of sun on water, the vastness of the blue sea and sky. Their minds would widen, their hearts would lift with possibility. Later, they'd unpack. Organize a Lego room. For now, Legos seemed to be his son's antianxiety magic.

Once Leo had his Lego room under way, Trevor could set up his computer room. River would be able to handle much of their website business but Trevor needed to be online as much as possible, responding to clients, performing triage, and following up on possible new business leads. After that, he would go through the house, checking on the condition of the beds and linens. Ivan wasn't the kind of guy to know or care how many decent towels or what sorts of cooking paraphernalia the house had. Trevor had invited a couple of the families with children who played with Leo to come down for a few days of Nantucket sun and fun. His theory was that the more his son was around people he knew, the more comfortable he would be. He daydreamed of long, sunny days on the beach with Leo building sand castles with friends his own age or walking through town eating ice-cream cones, and slowly but surely allowing the thought of his vagabond mother to fade from his mind.

They arrived at the car ferry precisely when Trevor planned to arrive. The big old ship was a monster. Trevor hoped it didn't frighten Leo. He was delighted when the boy reacted with wide eyes and laughter at the sight of the enormous container trucks growling up the ramp into the hold.

Once they were on board, Trevor lifted Leo onto his shoulders and hauled him up the shaking metal stairs to the main deck. Sometimes he wondered if he was treating his son like a baby, carrying him on his shoulders, but the shuddering, rumbling ferry was a literally unsettling experience. They found a booth next to a window. Trevor pointed out yachts, docks, sailboats, sand bars, and gulls as the ferry left the harbor. The trip took over two hours and once they were out on the open water, the window lost its appeal. Leo watched the other children chasing each other up and down the aisles. Trevor opened his laptop and caught up on some email. After a while, Leo opened his iPad and began to play a game.

Finally, the island appeared, low and steamy on the horizon, like a mirage. The ferry drew closer, and houses appeared on the shore; boats sailed past on flashing blue water. It seemed to Trevor that the short Brant Point lighthouse on its rounded spit of land was an uncommonly welcoming sight—here was *safety*. The harbor was dense with sailboats, motorboats, kayaks, and windsurfers. Leo pressed his nose to the window as the town and island came into view. Nothing urban, nothing strange, everything storybook—piers and dogs and leafy trees. Pastel banners waving over shops. Gulls perched on the top of pilings, grooming themselves as if this were simply another day. Church steeples gleaming in the distance. Leo grinned.

It was going to be okay.

They returned to their car on the lower deck, Trevor buckled Leo in, and they bumped over the ramp onto dry land. Trevor turned on his GPS and followed it out of town and toward the house near Surfside. It was three o'clock in the afternoon.

He was glad he had GPS on his car dashboard because the roads to Ivan's house were poorly marked and obscured with shadowy stands of trees. Finally, he saw the name *Swenson* painted in white on a rock almost hidden by wild roses. He turned into the drive and headed forward. Here it was. A huge, slightly shabby old house that had once been the guest cottage for an even huger house that was now hidden by fences and hedges.

A large green SUV was parked in front. That was a surprise. Maybe Ivan had paid someone to come clean the house. Trevor parked behind the SUV.

"We're here, buddy!" Trevor told his son as he lifted him out of the car.

"Daddy, what's that pretty noise?"

Holding his son's hand, Trevor listened. "Someone's playing the piano," he told Leo. "Let's go see who it is."

5

Sophie slowly stepped into the music room and stood in front of the piano. She raised the lid and gazed down at the ivory keys. The keys were moonstones to her, gleaming pearls, black diamonds, a wealth of romance and desire.

Could she remember even how to play?

Sliding onto the piano stool, she placed her hands on the keyboard. Instinctively, her fingers chose the spot, the notes: G, B-flat, C.

"Greensleeves."

Without thinking, her hands found the keys, the chords, the rhythm, and she sang as she played.

"Alas, my love, you do me wrong, to cast me off discourteously . . ."

So courtly, so melancholy, the ballad written hundreds of years ago in England told of heartbreak experienced then, and now, in Sophie's own heart. It was universal, being cast away; it surpassed time and space. It was said that Henry VIII composed the song for Anne Boleyn. Another discarded wife.

At least Zack couldn't shut Sophie in a tower.

She hit a few clinkers, but it was a surprise how it all returned at once, how good Sophie still was. She played, her hands spontaneously embroidering the simple tune with evocative chords. As she played, her heart broke open. The tears she'd been holding back streamed down her face.

"Mom?"

Sophie flinched. In one awkward move, she rose, turning to see her son and daughter standing in the doorway of the music room, both her children staring at her as if she'd turned into green cheese.

A man stood there, too, holding the hand of a little boy.

What?

For one frightening moment, Sophie thought she was hallucinating.

"Hello?" the man greeted her, tentatively, carefully, as if she might start foaming at the mouth.

"Sorry," Sophie said, wiping the tears away. "Sorry. Got carried away. How can I help you?"

The man smiled quizzically. "Um, well, not to be rude, but, uh, you can tell me what you're doing in my house." He was tall and incredibly good-looking, with thick black hair and green eyes with such dark lashes it looked as if he'd used eyeliner.

"*Your* house? This is *our* house."

The man was young, younger than Sophie, and his clothes gave him an adolescent air, especially his rumpled T-shirt printed with the slogan *Geeks Do It with More Ram*. Politely, he inquired, "This house is the old Swenson guest cottage, right?"

"It is. I'm renting it from Susie Swenson."

"Ah. Now we're getting somewhere. I'm renting it from Ivan Swenson. Susie and Ivan are cousins. And not particularly communicative with each other, it seems."

Sophie stared speechlessly. Her unexpected piano tsunami had flushed away her usual, Capable Mommy persona. It didn't help that the young man was jaw-droppingly handsome. She had to turn her eyes away from him in order to think. Her children frowned at her. "Maybe I'd better join you in the living room. We need to sort this out."

"Good idea." The man approached Sophie with his hand held out, his small son clinging to his leg and gawking wide-eyed at Sophie as if she might explode at any moment. "I'm Trevor Black. From Boston. This is my son, Leo."

Trevor Black was relaxed, easy in his body, present but not pressing. Zack always came on strong—the blazing smile, the hearty greeting. Trevor's hand was a bridge, not a rope to jerk her into Zack's realm. She lightly touched his palm, and her heart leapt in her chest. Oh, good. She was physically attracted to some random young guy right in front of her children. Nice.

She knew her cheeks were scarlet. She withdrew her hand and summoned up any dignity she could find. "Sophie Anderson, also from Boston. This is Jonah and Lacey. Come on, kids. Let's all sit down and talk." She gestured toward the living room like Vanna White, feeling silly.

They sat on facing sofas. Lacey was almost on top of Sophie while Jonah, obviously embarrassed by his mother, sat at the end. Across from them, Trevor sat with his son squeezed next to him, leg to leg.

"Where should we start?" Sophie asked.

Trevor said, "I guess the first question to ask is whether or not you have some kind of legal contract."

It was as if the man had thrown a glass of ice water in her face. "Legal contract?"

From his end of the sofa, Jonah muttered, "Mom."

"Mommy!" wailed Lacey. "We haven't even been to the beach."

Trevor held up his hands, palms out, reassuringly. "Hey, it's okay—I don't have a legal contract, either. Ivan phoned me from London and we made a verbal agreement for me to rent the house for two months this summer. All I have is a copy of the wire transfer of the money I paid him."

"All I have is a copy of the check I sent Susie," Sophie admitted.

Trevor frowned. "It looks like it's up to us to come up with some sort of compromise. Like, you could have the house for July and I could have it for August. Except I've kind of given my apartment to someone for both months."

Sophie went numb. She didn't want to discuss the sordid details of her marriage with this stranger, especially not in front of the kids.

Leo whispered in Trevor's ear. Trevor nodded.

"We need to use the bathroom."

"I'll take him," Lacey offered.

"Thanks, but I think I'd better do it. Can you tell me where it is?"

Like a good miniature tour guide, Lacey announced, "There's a bathroom off the kitchen on the first floor, and a cute one squeezed into the space beneath the staircase, but if you want more privacy, there are lots of bathrooms upstairs."

Trevor smiled. "Thanks." Holding his son's hand, he left the room.

"Mom, what are we going to do?" Lacey asked.

Jonah had sunk into himself, chewing on a thumbnail, staring at the floor.

Sophie thought aloud, remembering the lie. Renovation work was being done. Daddy would be staying in a house he was working on. "Daddy's having the interior of the house painted, every room, and the floors all sanded and stained. Everything will be topsy-turvy, sand dust everywhere. We can't go back."

"We could live with Grandmother," Lacey offered.

Sweet Lacey. "Do you want to live with Grandmother?" Sophie asked. Sophie's mother was widowed. Hester continued her work as an emergency room doctor at Emerson Hospital in Concord, and lived in a small house she kept as sharply neat as the corners on a hospital bed. Grandmother—Mother—Hester—firmly believed in striving to do one's best every day. No slouching allowed.

Lacey's mouth turned down.

"No," Sophie agreed. "I don't want to, either." She looked around. "Plus, this place is great. I was looking forward to spending lots of time at the beach."

"Uh, excuse me?" Trevor and Leo Black were back, standing in the entrance to the living room.

The child looked frightened. He stuck his thumb in his mouth and squeezed next to his father. The poor kid was scared and miserable, and Sophie's heart went out to him. She could stand for it not to be okay, but she could not stand for it not to be okay for this little boy.

"I'm sure we can work something out," she said, and was glad to see Leo's face light up. "This is a big house."

"We could share it," Trevor suggested.

Sophie met his eyes. He *seemed* normal enough . . . "If there were some way we could, I don't know, exchange references," she said. She checked her watch. "It's almost too late now for any of us to get off the island, and it's probably too late to find a hotel room we can afford, at least one that *I* can afford."

"We could stay here tonight," Trevor Black said. "You all can stay in one wing and we'll stay in the other."

Sophie hesitated. "Yes, and maybe we could try it for a few days while we work on other possibilities. I mean, I'm taking it on trust that you're not a—" She glanced at his goofy T-shirt. She didn't want to call him a hopelessly lame dork in front of his son.

Trevor's shoulders loosened and he smiled. "Good idea. And I'll take it on trust that you're not a constant singing-off-key-while-playing-the-piano kind of woman."

"Mom wasn't singing off-key!" Lacey insisted, insulted.

Sophie laughed, and the tension in the room broke. "If only we could get references, or I suppose I mean reassurances—talk to someone who knows us. You live in Boston, right?"

"In Cambridge. Hey, I helped set up the website at a local church. You could phone Linda Logan—she's the secretary. She'd vouch for me."

"That's a good idea. And—" Sophie shook her head. "I should just hand you my cell phone and let you punch in the numbers of the heads of all the committees I serve on for the schools the kids go to."

"That's not a bad idea."

Leo interrupted, tugging on his father's shorts. "So can we go to the beach?"

"Yeah, Mommy," Lacey chimed in. "Let's go to the beach!"

"I don't know, Lacey. I should make some inquiries . . ."

"We could take our phones and laptops," Trevor said.

"Swimsuits." Sophie chewed her lip. This was all going so fast. She felt out of control. She *was* out of control. "I don't think we should unpack yet."

"We don't have to swim," Trevor pointed out. "We can kick off our shoes and wade. We can at least stick our feet in the water and get sand between our toes."

"Yeah, Mom, he's right—come on," Jonah urged.

Jonah was a good judge of character, a sensible guy, and protective of his younger sister. Since he seemed to feel Trevor was an okay guy, Sophie felt strengthened in her own judgment. Still, she needed to be in charge. "All right, sure. Let me find Susie's map to the closest beach . . ."

Trevor said, "It's Surfside. You all can ride with me and Leo."

"Beach towels," Sophie said weakly.

"I'll get them!" Lacey piped up, racing from the room.

6

Sophie scanned the living room. "Will I need my purse? I could hide it somewhere . . ."

Lacey ran up, clutching so many towels she could scarcely see over them. Jonah relieved her of them and nodded toward the door.

Jonah said, "Mom. Put it in the car. Lock the car. Let's go." Taller than his mom, Jonah was a lanky boy not yet comfortable with his height—boy, did Trevor remember those days.

Leo buckled himself into his car seat in the backseat of Trevor's Passat. All their stuff was in the rear hatch, except for a bunch of books, snacks, and car toys. Trevor swept them onto the floor to let Lacey and Jonah squeeze into the backseat. Sophie sat in the passenger seat, snapping her seat belt immediately.

Trevor shot her a look. "I'm not going to speed. I've got a child in the car."

"Of course. Sorry. I—sorry."

In the rearview mirror, Trevor saw Jonah roll his eyes.

It took only five minutes to make the drive to Surfside Beach. By the time Trevor pulled the car into the parking lot, he found a lot of empty spaces. People were trudging up the path from the beach, lugging baskets and beach chairs, their skin fluorescent from a day in the sun.

"No lifeguard on duty, dude," one guy told them as the group headed down toward the ocean.

Trevor nodded and gestured thanks. Leo held on tight to Trevor's hand and his eyes were all over the place, checking out Jonah and Lacey and the view at the bottom of the dune where the beach stretched to the end of the world and the blue waves rolled in.

"Look, Mommy!" Lacey shot ahead of the group toward the water.

"Don't go in the ocean! There's no lifeguard!" Sophie shouted. When her daughter paid no attention to her, she pleaded, "Jonah."

The long-limbed teen covered the ground easily. He took his sister's hand, bent down, and spoke to her. She kicked off her flip-flops and rolled up her pink flowered trousers.

"Your son's a good guy," Trevor told Sophie.

"He is," Sophie agreed. Glancing up at Trevor, she asked softly, "Do you think a boy can be too good?"

Trevor looked away, tilting his head as if he were reflecting on her question. In fact, he was dealing with the electricity that zapped him when their eyes met. So much was going on inside that woman's head and he was a man who loved complications. Still, that had gotten him into trouble with Tallulah.

"I mean, Jonah has friends and everything. He's not weird or odd, I'm not saying that. It's, well, I don't know how to explain it—he's been acting different lately." Sophie shook her head, laughing at herself. "I must sound a bit demented, sharing intimate details with a stranger like this. But you're a man. You might have some insight."

"Maybe just a little," joked Trevor, before saying, "It's hard to be a teenage boy." He mentally kicked himself for such a lame statement.

"I'm sure you're right." Sophie ran off to join her children.

Trevor tore his attention away from the way her butt looked in her jeans and knelt down next to his son. "Let's take your sandals off and we can wade in the water." Seeing fear flash across his son's face, he added, "I won't let go of you, I promise."

The sun was still high in the sky; they were only a few days past the longest day of the year. The sand beneath Trevor's bare feet was soft and hot from the day's sun. Warm water frothed up around his ankles. Plenty of people still populated the long stretch of beach, dozing face-down on beach towels or reading or lounging in beach chairs, sipping bright-colored drinks in plastic glasses. Tallulah would have loved this, Trevor thought cynically. She would have put on her skimpiest bikini and sauntered along the water's edge, allowing everyone to get a good look at her in all her voluptuous glory.

Up ahead, Lacey shrieked with delight. She showed something to her mother and brother, then raced back with full hands to Leo.

"Look, Leo, look!" she shouted.

Leo clutched his father's hand tighter and recoiled slightly as the larger child came charging toward him.

"It's a toenail shell," Lacey informed the little boy, holding out her cupped hand. "It's not really a toenail—it just looks like one except prettier. See how this one sort of shines? Isn't it pretty?"

Leo looked down at the shell. Cautiously, he nodded.

"Would you like to have it? Here, it's for you. I'm going to see if I can find another one. Mom says we can make a fairy house in the backyard and we need all sorts of shells and rocks to build the house in the paths and make their dishes. This shell could be a dish, maybe— we'll have to see how big the house will be." With that, Lacey raced away back down the beach.

"She's energetic," Trevor remarked to his son. Leo was studying the shell as if it were something remarkable. Trevor realized that for his son this shell *was* remarkable. He squatted down next to him.

"It's like orange sherbet," Leo said, holding the shell up for Trevor to see.

Trevor smiled. "Yeah, it looks like orange sherbet but you better not eat it."

"Daddy," Leo giggled at Trevor's silliness.

My God, Trevor thought, when had he last heard Leo giggle?

Jonah waded along down the beach. Lacey knelt to build a sand castle, near her.

Leo industriously packed sand into walls.

Sophie spread out the beach towels and sat down. "Okay," she said to Trevor. "I'm going to make some phone calls." *Don't be rash*, she told herself, *you've paid for two months in this house.* She used what ammunition she had. "One of my best friends," she continued, "Angie Clift, is a trial lawyer in Boston. I'll have her check around while I call your church reference."

Trevor sat down on the beach towel close to her—but not too close. "Great."

"Do you want to phone any of my contacts?"

"Nah." Trevor opened his laptop. "I'll Google you. Check out your Facebook page."

Sophie rolled her eyes. "It's all flowers, recipes, and cute animal videos," she confessed. She focused on phoning Angie and was sent— as always, how could she forget this?—to voicemail. She left a message, Googled the church number, and phoned the office.

The phone rang and rang, until suddenly a laughing woman said, "Oops, hello! I was just going out the door." Her voice was warm and maternal.

"Sorry to bother you, and I won't take much of your time," Sophie said. She introduced herself and explained the unusual circumstances, finally asking, "Do you think it's safe for us to share a house with Trevor Black?"

Linda Logan sounded warm and wise. "Oh, my dear, of course! He's a lovely man and the most wonderful father," she said. "I can give you a long list of people who know him and adore him—preschool teachers, mommies, our minister."

"That's so helpful. Could you give me maybe one mother's name? I'll feel better with another reference . . ."

"I understand. I'll give you Candace Hall's number. Her daughter Cassidy is Leo's best friend in preschool."

Sophie wrote the mother's phone number in the sand. "Thank you so much."

"You're welcome. Tell Trevor and Leo hello."

"Linda Logan says hello," Sophie told Trevor. "She spoke highly of you."

Trevor, tapping away on his iPhone, only nodded.

"I'm going to phone someone named Candace Hall now."

"Fine," Trevor mumbled, his attention still on his phone's screen. "She's nice, kind of long-winded, but a good mom."

Sophie dialed Candace, who answered and listened to Sophie's explanation of the odd situation. When Sophie paused, Candace said, in an oddly hostile voice, "I'd give anything to have your problem. Trevor Black is the nicest man on earth, plus he's responsible, reliable, honest, and kind."

"Oh," Sophie said, surprised. "Well. That's good to know. I mean, that you can vouch for his character."

"Yeah, well, I hope you're ugly," Candace sniffed, then laughed feebly. "Sorry, sounds like I'm jealous. Maybe I am."

Well, that's blunt, Sophie thought, but again, it was reassuring. "I'm married," Sophie said, as if she needed to offer a defense.

"Still, hands off," Candace said, adding humorlessly, "Ha, ha. Anything else?"

"Um, no. Thank you so much." Sophie clicked off and sat staring at the ocean, letting her thoughts settle.

"What do you think?" Trevor asked. The sun was sinking lower, the ocean's silver fading to gray.

"Everyone gave you a glowing report," Sophie admitted. "Especially Candace Hall."

"Oh, Candace, yeah. They'll be coming to visit this summer. So, you're feeling okay about sharing the house tonight?"

"I can't think of any other solution."

Trevor nodded. "I'm glad. It's a huge house and our kids seem to get along. I'm sure it will be fine."

The sun was low when they drifted up the dune to the parking lot. They kicked the sand off their feet, buckled themselves into the car, and drove back to what was probably going to be their summer home.

At the guest cottage, they sat around the kitchen table eating the snacks, sandwiches, fresh veggies, and fruit that both parents had packed in the car for the trip. Trevor and Sophie set out the food, encouraged their children to eat apple slices even though they had gotten brown during the day, and wiped up accidental spills. The two smallest children were too tired to talk and Jonah kept checking his cell, as if anything there was preferable to the action around him.

"I've got to put my guy to bed," Trevor said, looking at Leo, who was almost falling asleep on his plate.

"Let's go up and organize our territories," Sophie said.

The second floor was divided by a large hall around the stairs, with a window seat beneath long casement windows. Long wings on each side of the house held three bedrooms and a full bath.

"You could have the left half and we could take the right," Trevor suggested. "Or vice versa."

Sophie nodded. "Yeah, that would work. I mean, we'd have to make some rules about not walking around naked."

"*Mom,*" Jonah muttered.

Why had she said that? Sophie thought. Her mother would bark:

Get your mind out of the gutter. "Except the kitchen," Sophie continued, as they all trooped downstairs. "No way to divide that."

"Do you like to cook?" Trevor asked.

Sophie chewed her lip. Did she want to make the meals for two extra people? It wouldn't be so different from cooking for the family, back when she had a family with a husband in it, and she'd be happy to get that poor, thin little boy plumped up . . .

"I do like to cook," she admitted cautiously.

"Then I have a suggestion. What if I went into town and got all the food—which is a pain, let me tell you, with all the congestion and people and not enough parking places and so on. And you cook, but I clean the kitchen."

"You can clean a kitchen?" Sophie asked doubtfully. She didn't think Zack knew where the dishwasher soap was.

"I can." Trevor held up his arm and made a muscle. "I'm kind of fanatical about cleaning, to tell the truth. In the best possible way, of course. Aren't I, dude?" He looked down at his son.

Leo gave a tiny nod.

"Are you vegetarian or vegan or lactose intolerant?" Sophie asked, wondering if she was making a big mistake.

"Nope. We'll pretty much eat anything, although Leo eats only one thing for lunch. I'll make his lunch."

Sophie glanced at her kids. At home, they alternated nights cleaning the kitchen. They'd be thrilled with this arrangement.

"Let's try it for a week," Sophie suggested. "The whole living together, cooking, cleaning thing. Let's try it for a week and then evaluate."

"It's a deal," Trevor said, and held out his hand.

Sophie extended her hand to shake. Again, Trevor's grip was warm and firm, not too hard, not too soft. Like *Goldilocks and the Three Bears*, she thought irrationally: just right.

Trevor hefted his son in his arms and carried him up to bed. Sophie herded her own two children upstairs, let Jonah choose his room, and agreed to allow Lacey to sleep with her in the big queen bed for this first night. They dragged up their luggage, did a minimal bit of unpacking, and then Sophie supervised Lacey brushing her teeth and nagged Jonah to do the same.

She returned to the kitchen after tucking her daughter in and calling good night to Jonah through his closed bedroom door. Trevor was already there, feet up on the table, a beer in his hand.

"Wow," said Sophie, looking around the tidy kitchen. "You're fast."

"Yeah, it was really hard to put all that stuff in the trash or the fridge." Trevor held up a bottle. "Have a beer. They're cold."

Sophie hesitated. She never drank beer. She preferred wine, or a vodka tonic on a hot summer day. But she hadn't brought any liquor with her and she could use a drink right now. "Thanks." She took a Heineken from the refrigerator.

"Your kids asleep?" asked Trevor.

"Lacey is. She was wiped out from all the fresh air and sunshine. But heaven only knows when Jonah will go to bed. He'll stay up tapping away at his cell phone or his computer until the middle of the night and then he'll sleep until two in the afternoon."

"Typical teenage boy."

"And Leo?"

"He was asleep before his head hit the pillow. I didn't even make him brush his teeth or use the john. I hope I don't regret that tomorrow morning." Trevor quickly added, "He doesn't wet the bed anymore, but this is an unusual day. And I'll do all our laundry, of course."

"He's a sweet kid."

Trevor leaned his forearms on the kitchen table—he had nice, muscular arms, broad shoulders, and long legs, all in all a spectacular package, Sophie thought. She felt herself blush at the word *package*. When had she gotten so self-conscious, so prudish?

"Right." Trevor announced, "Cards on the table. True confession time." Seeing the confusion on Sophie's face, he clarified: "I'm not asking for salacious details. I just thought while the children are sleeping we should get a few things out in the open so we don't make some kind of giant blunder in front of them. I mean, you should probably know Leo's mother died last fall."

"She died?" Sophie's hand flew to her heart. "Dear Lord. I'm so sorry. Oh, your poor little boy."

Trevor nodded. "People keep telling me kids are resilient. Still . . . Anyway, that's why I brought him here. I'm kind of hoping summer on the island will help him heal." He shrugged. "That's the word the professionals use. *Heal.*"

"It's hard to know what to say," Sophie murmured softly. "It's a terrible situation. Heartbreaking."

Trevor shifted uncomfortably.

"That puts my problem in perspective," Sophie admitted. "I'm here because my husband's in love with another architect, the young and gorgeous Lila."

"Ouch." He blinked. "Are you two splitting up?"

"Probably. Jonah and Lacey don't know, by the way. I haven't told them—I'm not sure what to say. When Susie called me about this house, I jumped at the chance to put some space between me and Zack. We both have a lot to think about."

"Are you sad?" Trevor asked, rushing to explain: "I mean, sometimes people feel okay when someone breaks up with them."

Sophie looked out at the horizon. "It's complicated."

"Anyway." Trevor stood up and stretched. "So I guess we know the basics. Tonight went well, and tomorrow's another day, right? This house is huge. It's sort of like residing in a hotel but we have to supply the room service." He yawned openly. "Sorry, but I'm beat. There's nothing like sea air to make you sleep well."

"I'm tired, too." Trevor's yawn was contagious. Luxurious drowsiness swept through Sophie. "I'll make a grocery list in the morning and if you'd like, you can leave Leo with us while you go to the store."

"Thanks, but I'm not sure that he's ready for that yet. Let's see how everything is in the morning." Trevor took his empty bottle and rinsed it out in the sink. Over his shoulder, he said, with a smile, "I hope you're not planning to rise at the crack of dawn."

Sophie crossed the kitchen and set her own bottle in the sink, allowing herself to be sidetracked for a moment by the pleasurable sensation of standing so close to the tall young man. "If I do rise early, I promise not to bang a gong and force us out for an early morning march."

"Please, no." Trevor grinned.

"All right, then, good night." She forced herself away from that smile. When she was at the door to the hallway, she turned. "Thanks for insisting that we go to the beach tonight instead of unpacking. That was a really good idea."

As she walked up the wide central staircase, Sophie had the surreal feeling she was ascending into another, different world where she felt happy, content, relaxed, and also kind of turned on. She would have to drink beer more often.

She woke around eight the next morning. Late for her, but the house was quiet. Beside her, Lacey slept deeply, making sweet piglet snores. Sophie slipped from the bed and padded to the bathroom. The mirror reflected her typical night wear—a stretched-out, too large, ancient, dark green T-shirt hanging over boxer shorts. No wonder Zack went to Lila.

Downstairs, the cool morning air drifted in the open windows. She made coffee—she had brought her Keurig—and took it out to the patio off the kitchen. Settling in a large wooden deck chair, she folded her legs beneath her, sipped her coffee, and gazed around. A large yard stretched a good long distance, bordered by an unpainted wooden fence with a crisscross of lattice at the top. The grass needed mowing. At the edge of the patio, the geraniums and pansies in the two plaster urns needed watering.

To the left, the music room led straight to the private apartment. No sign of movement flashed in the windows. Sophie had told the kids about the grandfather living there. She'd warned them not to bother him. She would introduce herself sometime, but there was no need to rush.

Clouds drifted high in the sky and a slight breeze shivered the air. She would take Jonah and Lacey into town this morning and they could go to the beach this afternoon. They had to unpack, too. And she needed to make a grocery list for Trevor. She liked him, although he was so handsome it was almost embarrassing to look at him during normal conversation. He didn't seem to notice, though, and he was funny and easygoing, even though he'd been recently widowed.

What a summer of surprises this was. Susie's phone call, Zack with his announcement about Lila, this vacation house, complete with strange man and child. It was unsettling. She knew she was not good at spontaneity. She preferred routine, boundaries, organization.

Now all that was gone. She might very well become a single parent. Her husband of sixteen years was in love with a younger woman. The comfortable, even enviable home life she had spent her youthful years creating for her family was about to be shattered. She wondered if she was in a state of shock; if she had been since Zack's announcement. She thought she was doing pretty well, putting one foot in front of the other, keeping a cheerful face, being an optimistic, efficient mother . . . holding back a landslide, a flash flood, a geyser of emotion and desire. *Desire*. She had forgotten all about desire.

Okay. She was getting herself all worked up on this luscious Nantucket morning. She forced herself to return to the kitchen for more coffee, found a notepad and pen, and began making a grocery list for Trevor.

7

Trevor wandered into the kitchen barefoot and unshaven. He wore board shorts and a T-shirt with a picture of a horse's head on it and the words *Why the long face?* Little Leo followed, clutching a duffel bag to his chest. Like his father, he was fully dressed but barefoot.

"Try it under the table, Leo," Trevor told his son. "That won't get in anyone's way." He scratched his head, making his dark hair stand out in several directions. "Coffee! I smell coffee."

"Good morning," said Sophie. "Help yourself. Cups are on the counter."

Trevor's eyes darted around the room, landing on anything but Sophie, who wore a baggy T-shirt that couldn't hide the fullness of her breasts. When had a woman last greeted him with a smile? Or filled the room with such a clean, sweet fragrance that he wanted to rub up against her skin like a cat? Or made coffee in the morning? He poured himself a cup of coffee and took a large gulp. "Man, this is good."

Leo had obligingly crawled under the large kitchen table, where he knelt, unpacking his Legos. With great care, he began his routine, grouping them according to color: yellow, blue, red, green.

"Leo, want some Cheerios?" Without waiting for an answer, he poured some Cheerios into a bowl and set them on the floor next to his son.

Sophie looked concerned. "Doesn't he want milk?"

"He prefers to eat them by the handful. I'll give him some juice after a while." Sophie's eyebrows folded into a small frown. "Hey, don't worry, he gets plenty of milk."

"Glad to hear it," Sophie said lightly, adding, "It's a gorgeous day."

Trevor opened the sliding door to the patio and stepped out into the sunshine.

"Daddy." Leo didn't raise his voice, but the anxiety was there.

"Right here, kid. Not going anywhere." Returning to the kitchen, Trevor poured himself a bowl of Cheerios and added milk. He pulled out a chair and joined Sophie at the table. Nodding toward a bowl of fruit in the middle of the table, he said, "That looks nice."

"Help yourself," Sophie told him. "I keep a lot of fruit around for the children."

She wore no makeup. Her face glowed from yesterday's sun, accentuating the blue of her eyes. One eyebrow arched a fraction of an inch more than the other. No pencil darkened her brows. She was all natural, and healthy, and fresh.

Sophie looked puzzled. "Would you like a banana?"

Trevor jerked himself back to reality. He nodded toward the sheet of paper in her hands. "Is that the grocery list?"

"It is." Sophie's slid the paper across the table to Trevor, who took a moment to read it as he shoveled Cheerios into his mouth.

"Huh? Arugula? Salmon? Quinoa?" His mood flipped. Leo had never eaten these things, and in his fragile emotional state it would be a disaster to suggest it. "Excuse me, but I thought we were buying food for children, not for international CEOs."

Sophie arched an eyebrow, the slightly higher one. "Doesn't Leo eat fish?"

Protectively, Trevor said, "He eats tuna fish. Leo is four years old. He likes hot dogs, pizza, mac and cheese, cheese-and-mustard sandwiches, cheeseburgers, and French fries. I make him eat some cucumber, carrot, or edamame with every meal." Trevor looked down at the list again. "But linguine? Clams? First of all, how can he even eat linguine? I can hardly eat it. It falls off the fork. And clams? He's never had them before. I'm not a fan either. They taste like rubber." He knew he sounded unreasonable, but he didn't want Leo faced with unusual food that would frighten him into throwing a tantrum.

Was she being judged, insulted, found lacking in her judgment? Sophie went on the defensive. "So you're saying we *all* have to eat at the level of a four-year-old's palate?"

Offended on his son's behalf, Trevor snapped, "Well, excuse me, Nigella Lawson."

Sophie counted to ten and tried to be reasonable. "I'm remembering that when Jonah and Lacey were younger, I cooked *everything* and insisted they each try two or three bites. If they hated it, I made them a peanut-butter-and-jelly sandwich. But I think it's a good idea for children to learn to like all kinds of food."

"Okay," Trevor agreed uncomfortably, "I take your point. But sometimes it's best to stick with what's familiar."

Leo, Sophie thought. She'd been thoughtless. "Of course."

"'Sup?" Jonah, garbed like Trevor in shorts and a T-shirt, came into the room, his flip-flops flapping with each step. Pulling out a chair, he collapsed into it, sticking his long legs under the kitchen table.

"No!" Leo shouted from beneath the table. "Now you've ruined everything!"

Trevor half rose from his chair in alarm.

Sophie reached over and clasped Trevor's wrist. She whispered, "Wait."

Trevor gawked at her as if she had gone mad. Underneath the table, his little boy was crying.

"Dude." In one lanky coil, Jonah slipped out of his chair and onto the floor. "Sorry. Didn't see you there. Hey, this is cool. What is it?"

Sophie had no idea at all how fragile his son was, how upsetting the destruction of his Lego project would be for Leo, and how Jonah must seem like some kind of gigantic teenage transformer. And she had no idea of the thrashing, screaming monster Leo could turn into if something set him off. "Leo—"

Leo sniffed. "It's the Great Wall of China."

"Dude, that is totally awesome," said Jonah. "Want me to help you put it back together?"

Leo was quiet for a while. "I have to do it a special way."

"Got it," Jonah said calmly. He crawled out from under the table and stood up. He bent down and said to Leo, "But tell me if you want some help."

Sophie's hand was soft and warm. Her touch made the back of Trevor's neck shiver. He wanted to seize her, throw her on the table, and ravish her. At the same time, he wanted her to back off, to let him handle Leo. He didn't want his son upset, nor did he need her to see how helpless he was in the face of Leo's outbursts.

"Listen, Sophie," Trevor began.

Jonah snapped off two bananas and stepped out onto the patio to eat them. Under the table, Leo hummed to himself as he repaired his Lego wall.

"Yes?" She tilted her pretty face toward his, waiting.

What the hell was happening here? He didn't even *know* this woman who'd brazenly touched him as if they were somehow related, who walked around in boxer shorts with her pretty legs hanging out, who appeared before him all natural and braless, who made him feel so many things at the same time he was afraid he would explode. The intimacy between them was like a song he'd never heard before. At the same time, anger flared from his gut. Who did she think she was to intervene between him and his son? She knew nothing about what Leo was going through.

"Look, how can I say this? My little guy is special."

Sophie settled back in her chair and crossed her arms over her chest. "All kids are special."

"What I mean is, maybe you shouldn't tell me what to do with my own kid."

"I'm trying to help. I've raised two children. I know what four-year-olds are like."

Trevor stalked across the room and poured himself more coffee, giving himself time to think. "Okay, sure. But you don't know what *my* four-year-old is like."

"Trevor, maybe you should remember no man is an island. If we're going to live together for the next two months, we have to be comfortable talking to each other's children."

You haven't seen Leo's tantrums, he thought helplessly. But he didn't want to scare her off and ruin this arrangement. Cornered, he snapped, "So now you're Dr. Seuss?"

Sophie covered her mouth to hide a smile. "I think you mean Dr. Spock."

Trevor felt his eyes bug out. "From *Star Trek?*"

She couldn't prevent a laugh that made her head fall back, exposing her slender throat.

Humiliated, Trevor said, "Don't be so superior. I've raised my son all by myself while running a successful computer business out of my house. I haven't had time to read books or chat with mommies or find out about the latest authorities on children."

He saw he'd struck a nerve with Sophie. She sat up straight in her chair. "I get that, Trevor. I raised two children practically by myself." She glanced out at the patio, where Jonah stood, eating a banana while absentmindedly observing a robin. "Their father never changed a diaper or cooked a meal. In the early years, when he was starting his architectural firm, not only did I take care of the babies but I also did all the bookkeeping for him until Zack could afford to find someone else to do it. I'm not trying to act superior and I would never interfere with your disciplining of your son. But I've spent a lot of time with children. Okay, Jonah is not so young anymore, but Lacey is only ten and she loves babysitting. If we're lucky, these children will be relaxed together, and so will we."

As she talked, Sophie's tone changed from challenging to placating. She had an earnest expression in her eyes. She really was trying to be friendly. He'd been a jerk, lashing out like that, and he hated himself for it.

Trevor said, "I apologize. I guess I freaked out a bit about the food. But Leo and I have both been knocked off-kilter, by, um—" He gestured vaguely with his hand, not wanting to mention Tallulah's death with Leo nearby. "We sort of need to do what's normal. What's comfortable. I don't think we're up for any changes yet."

"I'm sorry, too," Sophie said. "I think I understand." She waited a beat, then two, for him to continue. "Okay, well, I'd better get organized." She hurried from the room.

That first morning, the Blacks and the Andersons went into town separately. Trevor and Leo did the grocery shopping. Sophie took Lacey to the library, where they got cards and checked out books while Jonah, not thrilled at the idea of hanging out with his mother and sister, loped off exploring the streets and wharves by himself, promising to meet them at the car at noon.

As Trevor had warned, the small town was packed with people and parking spaces were scarce, although the traffic was not as bad as it

would be in August. Sophie stopped at Glidden's Island Seafood to
choose salmon for dinner and then happily headed back down Surfside Road to the house.

After a casual lunch of sandwiches, everyone changed into bathing
suits and drove to Surfside Beach. Trevor and Leo sat in the backseats
of Sophie's minivan—it seemed silly to take two cars. Once on the
beach, they split up. Sophie established a beach chair beneath an umbrella and took turns playing in the surf with Lacey and reading. Once
again Jonah ambled off by himself, walking along the water's edge
toward the distant horizon. Trevor and Leo made sand castles.

Sophie became a bit restless after an hour or so. She wasn't used to
long periods of unscheduled time. The sea was calm today, lapping at
the shore in a lulling rhythm that made her want to close her eyes, but
she needed to stay alert to watch Lacey. All up and down the shore,
clusters of people on beach blankets laughed and talked and rubbed
suntan lotion on each other. Lovely young girls in bikinis strolled
past, pretending not to notice people looking at them in admiration.
Sophie glanced down at her black Speedo, her good old mommy bathing suit. She could still wear a bikini. She'd brought her red one. Perhaps she'd even wear it. But not today. The sky was high and blue, the
sun hot, the occasional breeze refreshing. Children screamed and
giggled as the waves nibbled at their knees. Sophie felt as if she were
encased in a glass globe called *summer*.

Back at the house, they all rinsed off the sand in the outdoor
shower, then raced inside for a real shower. They dressed and wandered away, sunburnt and content, to read or nap or tap on computers
or, in Leo's case, to work on the Great Wall of China. Sophie cooked
dinner—salmon, quinoa, salad complete with arugula, sliced carrots,
and cucumbers, and one cheese-and-mustard sandwich for Leo. To
the boy's credit, he tasted the strange food and said he really liked the
salmon. Sophie tried not to look too pleased.

After dinner, the sun was still high in the sky. The fresh air was inviting. They found a badminton set in the large hall off the kitchen. Jonah and Trevor staked the net in the backyard, which was flat and large enough for a good game. They decided to play, Jonah and Lacey against Trevor and Leo. Sophie carried a tall plastic glass of iced herbal tea out to the patio to watch.

A person could write a psychological study of people solely from watching them play badminton, Sophie decided. She was delighted to see her son racing to slam the birdie, fully engaged in the game, and shouting encouragement to his sister. Jonah was almost as tall as Trevor and almost as muscular. He was a good-looking boy, a smart student, and he'd always had plenty of friends. She couldn't understand why he'd become so withdrawn around her. During the past two months when she had tried to ask him how he was doing, he'd always shrugged and answered that he was fine, acting as if she were loopy even to ask the question. Zack, of course, never wanted to engage in a discussion about their son.

At least now, this evening beneath the soft blue sky, her children were safe and happy. She didn't want to think about her marriage. Not tonight. And she tried hard not to look at Trevor as he sprinted around hitting the birdie with his long, well-toned arm.

Suddenly, the peace of the evening was broken.

Lacey screamed. "A man! A man in the window!"

The game slammed to a halt. Jonah dropped to his knees, put his arms around his sister and talked to her. Sophie assumed he was reminding her about Susie's grandfather staying in the apartment.

Then the blue door of the apartment opened and Connor Swenson stepped out. In his seventies, he didn't fit the image Sophie had conjured up of a retired farmer. She had expected striped overalls and a baseball cap with the words *Carl's Cattle Feed* across the top. Instead, the man wore chinos, a clean white collared T-shirt, and a clean if rather beat-up pair of leather loafers. His hair was thick and snow white and his eyes were Icelandic blue.

Sophie walked down the lawn to greet him. "Hello, I'm Sophie Anderson. I'm renting the house for two months from Susan."

The man held out his hand. "Connor Swenson. Pleased to meet you. Didn't mean to give your girl a fright."

The rest of the group ambled over to introduce themselves.

"I hope all our noise wasn't bothering you," Trevor said.

"Not at all. I enjoy having people around." Connor smiled down at Leo, who stared back, wide-eyed.

"Would you like to play with us?" asked Jonah.

Connor shook his head with a rueful smile. "I'm afraid my badminton years have passed."

"Would you like to join me on the patio to watch?" asked Sophie. "I'll fix you a glass of iced tea."

"Thank you for the invitation, but not tonight. I've got a slight problem walking—nothing to worry about—oh, yes, and there is a TV show about to come on for me." With a wave of his large weathered hand, Connor turned back into his apartment.

Sophie noticed that with the few steps he had taken out of his home, he had limped a bit and grimaced with each step. Arthritis, she assumed—her mother was beginning to get it in her knees.

The game began again and Sophie resumed watching, thinking about Connor Swenson alone in his apartment. He seemed like a perfectly nice man. She wondered if he was lonely without his wife, on this island instead of his farm. Change is hard, she reflected, although if this day were any sample of her own transitional period, she counted herself lucky.

Twilight was falling by the time the badminton game ended. Sophie and Trevor herded the two smaller children into the house to begin the routine for bed while Jonah barricaded himself in his room with his various electronic devices.

Sophie hadn't failed to notice that Trevor had not cleaned the kitchen—she couldn't blame him for that; he had come out to play badminton. Lacey had decided to sleep by herself in the free bedroom tonight so that she could start arranging her special shrines of books and seashells, which allowed Sophie to have her bedroom to herself. She wasn't that tired, although she was relaxed and drowsy from the sunshine. It would be nice to go down and pour herself a glass of wine to take outside to the patio to drink while she listened to the night sounds. But she knew if she went to the kitchen and saw the dishes still there she would start cleaning the room, and then she would be mad at Trevor, and it was ridiculous that she was even thinking about this! For a moment she allowed herself to fantasize Trevor backing her up against the sink.

"Get a grip," she whispered, alone in the bedroom. "You are a thousand years older than he is. And you are not going to go do those dishes. We made an arrangement."

She busied herself with her laptop, answering emails and posting on Facebook. She left her bedroom door open, in case Lacey called out, but by nine thirty, Sophie shut her door and crawled into bed with a book.

When she got up the next morning and went downstairs to make coffee, she found the kitchen sparkling clean.

8

After the first couple of days, time began to blur for Trevor, in a really good way, as if he were on a cruise with no obligations except to enjoy himself. He checked in with River ten times a day in case some snag had snarled up that River couldn't handle—but no, all was cool, and as the days passed, Trevor texted him less and less. Domestic life fell into a pleasant routine revolving around food, the beach, more food, badminton, tag, or Frisbee, and television or a book.

Sophie's kids were heaven-sent. Jonah, a monosyllabic boy clumsily growing into his height and handsomeness, trudged along obediently wherever his mother took him, but moved like Houdini around eight o'clock, zapping into the family room to take possession of the remote control and turn on the Red Sox game before anyone else could claim the television. This allowed Trevor to watch the game, too. He was a huge Sox fan, even though they were playing poorly this year. Leo, tired after a day at the beach, would sit between Jonah and Trevor, asking endless questions about the game until he began to yawn. During a commercial, Trevor would carry his son up to bed and dutifully urge him through the ritual of brushing teeth, peeing, and washing hands.

After a few days, Leo stopped laying his clothes out for the next day. He was too sleepy, plus all he needed to put on was one of his two bathing suits. A little triumph, Trevor thought happily, a small step forward.

Lacey at ten was as talkative as Jonah was silent. Lacey talked *all the time*. She never seemed to have a thought she didn't announce aloud. A busy, cheerful, pretty girl, she shared her indecision about how to wear her hair that day—braids, pigtails, or ponytail, and did Leo prefer the mini-barrettes with the bows on them or the coated rubber bands with the sparkly round balls? One morning Trevor saw Lacey and Leo in front of the mirror in Lacey's room. Lacey was settling a headband with pom-poms on it onto Leo's head. Leo waggled his fingers like a bug and pretended the pom-poms were antennae, and Lacey shrieked and ran to hide behind her bed.

Trevor stepped back into the hall, closed his eyes, waited for his heart to calm, and tried to grasp his own over-the-top reaction.

Ah. After a moment's reflection he realized why all his alarm bells had gone off. That moment had been so much like the times Tallulah had spent playing dress-up with Leo. Trevor had wanted to yell: *Don't make him remember his mother while he's happy! Don't send him back into his lonely well of sorrow.* Leaning against the wall, he heard Leo and Lacey giggling and realized he didn't need to protect his son right now. Silently, Trevor said a prayer of thanks that his boy was playing.

But he knew that sometime Leo was going to blow, and the Anderson family would realize what a nutcase his child was. And then what?

The third morning they went to the beach, it happened.

They were in Leo's bedroom, getting ready for a day at the beach. Leo insisted on taking along Tubee, his stuffed giraffe.

"Tubee will get all sandy and gross on the beach," Trevor pointed out.

His son had clutched the animal—one of nature's less fortunate designs, in Trevor's mind—to his chest like a diva in an opera. "Want Tubee."

"Sorry, dude," Trevor said, trying to be brisk and natural, "no Tubee. Come on, let's go splash in the ocean."

"Daddy. I want Tubee to live in my sand castle," Leo explained reasonably.

Trevor knelt next to Leo. "Leo. Look. We can wash the sand out of your hair when we return from the beach, but sand and salt water will ruin Tubee. His fur would get all yucky—if he gets soaked, he might even fall apart."

Wrong thing to say. Trevor knew it the moment the words were out of his mouth. Leo didn't need anything else in his life to fall apart. Leo shrieked. Gripping Tubee even tighter, he ran into the closet and slammed the door shut behind him.

"Leo. Come on. Don't you want to go to the beach?" Trevor tried to keep his cool.

"NO! WANT TUBEE!"

Trevor opened the closet door. His son was huddled on the floor like a storybook character fearing the ogre. "Leo. Tubee can wait right here on your bed. Or even in the car, we can leave him on the seat in the car—"

"NO!" Leo began to kick and yell in protest, making such a racket that Trevor finally shut the door on his son, leaving him to have his tantrum in the closet.

Aware that the entire household could probably hear his son's freak-out, Trevor sat down on Leo's bed and forced himself to count to ten. Children held their parents hostage, he thought. They had no shame about screaming, while their parents had to act like adults.

For a moment, Trevor wished Lacey would come in and work her happy-girl magic on Leo, cajoling him to join them on the beach. Instead, Sophie stuck her head into the room.

"We're leaving now. Maybe we'll see you at the beach later." With a smile, she was gone.

Trevor heard the front door slam. *They've deserted me*, he thought sullenly, and then admitted to himself that probably they were trying to do him a favor, to get out of earshot of Leo's gale-force fit.

After a while, Leo's energy ran out and he went quiet. Trevor opened the door to be sure his son hadn't turned blue from yelling. "I'm going to work in my computer room," he said, and left the room, with the door open.

His hands were shaking too hard to manage the computer, but he sat staring at it, calming down, wondering what to do next. Sophie and her kids were so disgustingly normal it made Trevor and Leo look worse by comparison. Should Trevor forget about this and go back to Boston, or take Leo to a hotel in Maine or something, where no one could see what a loser he was? Plus, what about Sophie's family's reaction to having a screaming child in the house?

Leo came into the room, head hanging. "I want to go to the beach, Daddy. I put Tubee in bed for his nap until we get home."

Relief and something like joy flew up inside Trevor's chest. *They give us these miracles, these pardons, so generously*, he thought; *they crush our spirits like crashing boulders only to hold open their hands to give us jewels.*

"Good boy, Leo. Good decision."

Another crisis threatened one day when Sophie was preparing lunches to take to the beach. It had taken them a few days to develop a routine for getting all the paraphernalia to the beach: towels, beach chairs, sand toys, beach umbrella, cooler of drinks, basket of lunch or snacks, books, sunblock. Getting out the door was like preparing for a trip to a foreign and backward country, but once they'd lugged everything down to the shore, the world opened up in a blaze of blue sky and sunshine. It was worth it. Sophie and Trevor had decided to join forces until they got to the beach rather than duplicate the coolers, the lunches, the chairs.

Sophie was making sandwiches. "Do you want to try tuna fish today?" she casually asked Leo.

"No!" Leo said. "Daddy makes my sandwich."

Trevor was dumping ice into the cooler. "Leo," he began, hoping that his son would relent.

"Only Daddy," Leo asserted stubbornly.

"Fine," Sophie said easily. "I've put the bread out—"

"I want *Daddy* to make my sandwich," Leo insisted, and now his voice was more scared than bossy, as if in Leo's mind something bad would happen if each single detail weren't followed exactly as it always was.

Trevor put down the ice. What could he say? *Careful, or he'll blow?*

To his infinite relief, Sophie shrugged. "Okay. I'll give this to Jonah. He can always eat lots of sandwiches."

When they got to the beach, Trevor and Leo established their home base a few yards away from Sophie and her kids. After all, they weren't a family. Leo seemed to prefer playing alone, building walls out of sand or walking along the beach holding Trevor's hand. The few times Lacey had made overtures—bringing Leo more shells, asking if he wanted to throw the Frisbee with her—Leo had done his shoulder-shrug, head-dip movement in response. Lacey stopped visiting their camp.

Still, they all went home together. Trevor and Leo used the outside shower, then dressed in dry clothes. Lacey and Jonah clomped up to their rooms to shower and check their iPhones, and Sophie rinsed her feet with the hose, then ambled into the kitchen to begin preparations for dinner. She always set out a plate of chewies—carrots, celery, zucchini sticks, almonds—to keep the kids from digging the potato chips from their hiding place and devouring them. Everyone became crazed for salt.

By the end of the first week, when Trevor got ready to make his

shopping expedition to the grocery stores, Leo said he'd stay home
and work on his Lego wall. He didn't say he'd play with Lacey, or invite Jonah to help him, but he was willing to remain in the house with
the Andersons while Trevor was gone. That, to Trevor, was a success
of great magnitude.

And eating Sophie's fabulous cooking every night was a bonus he'd
never anticipated. They all sat together, eating and talking, and although Leo insisted that Trevor was the only one who could put food
on Leo's plate, he quite happily ate the food that Sophie, not Trevor,
had prepared. Small steps, Trevor thought. Inch by inch.

Sophie had forgotten how dazzling the world was. Sitting on her beach
chair, watching Lacey and Jonah splash in the waves, listening to the
laughter and chatter of other families, friends, and lovers floating like
balloons up and down the beach, feeling the warm gold of the sun on
her skin, staring far out to a horizon that seemed never to end, she remembered the grandeur of the world. It was like being a child again.

Yet her oldest offspring was leaving childhood. Jonah had been her
one true love, her pal, her pet, her honey bunny. Lacey, five years
younger, had both Sophie and Jonah (and Zack, of course, busy in the
background) to care for and be adored by, and Lacey had a different
personality. She was curious, people-loving, outward-bound. Sophie
and Jonah joked that Lacey would grow up to be the entertainment
director on a cruise ship. Jonah had always been quieter, slower to
react, more of a homebody. A smart, studious boy, he'd enjoyed baseball, soccer, and swimming, but he liked his private time, too, reading
or playing video games. He'd shared everything with Sophie, he'd
lean against her on the sofa when the family watched TV—and then
this year he'd turned fifteen and morphed into some version of Eeyore,
slouching directly into his room from school without saying hello,

shrinking away from Sophie's slightest touch, eating at the dinner table as if the rest of the family were invisible.

This was only normal, natural, Sophie knew that, but it was hard to be ignored by her son, and more than that, she worried about him now that he never shared the inner workings of his heart. What *could* he be doing on his iPad all the time? Was he happy? Were any adolescents *happy*? She found great consolation when Jonah, by the fourth day, started hanging out with some guys his age, body surfing up the beach from where Sophie and Lacey had established their camp.

Lacey lay on the blanket, reading with Sophie, or raced into the water, shrieking, playing with other children, some much younger, a few her age. Each day brought a new and different community. Some days Lacey built sand castles. Another day she helped a toddler wade in the cold water while the little girl's mother, bulky with another pregnancy, watched gratefully. Sophie kept her sunglasses on, not ready to meet anyone yet. The situation with Zack buzzed endlessly through her thoughts, agitating her so much she had to jump up and stride along the beach or throw herself into the cold waves. Was she doing the right thing to keep the present circumstances between Zack and her a secret from her children? She thought she was. Children didn't need to know everything about their parents. Besides, this was *vacation*, vacation for the three of them, paid for by fabulous Aunt Fancy's legacy. Sophie didn't want to ruin this magical time with a newsflash that would, at the least, complicate what should be a glorious holiday.

And so far it was pretty darned glorious. It was a treat to have Trevor buying the groceries and lugging them into the house. It was a real joy for Sophie to have five people to cook for, four of whom—Leo was still cautious about what he ate—devoured her meals with gusto. She enjoyed trying new recipes, and at home she had once cooked wonderful dinners, but as the years passed and Zack stayed out late on business and the kids had ballet practice or baseball games, dinners became casual, often catch as catch can, and Sophie really only cooked on the holidays. The scent of fresh herbs, the glory of a fat red tomato, the challenge of recipes she discovered on the Internet or on suggestion cards given out at the fish market, brightened her life. She liked it very much, too, sitting at the table watching the others savoring her meals. Somehow it made her feel warm with satisfaction.

Not to mention: the piano. It waited for her like a childhood fantasy, tempting her to return. She played it only when everyone else was out of the house, and that was rare. She almost wondered whether she *should* play the piano. She needed her friends, Bess and Angie, to come down. Bess was sweet and practical; Angie was no-nonsense and interfering. They'd known each other forever, the three of them. Bess and Angie had supported Sophie in high school when she gave up so much of a normal adolescent life in order to focus on her music. They would help Sophie decide what to do now.

But for now, this week, this period of sunshine, laughter, delicious food, and deep, refreshing sleep as cool salt air blew through the bedroom window, for now Sophie was astonished by the gifts of the world.

The seventh night, Trevor and Sophie sat on the patio after getting the kids to bed. The dark sky, the hush of the household, and a healthy sense of exhaustion after the bright, busy day made the moment feel intimate.

"First week's up," Trevor said. "What do you think?"

Sophie took her time to consider. She was happy. Her children were happy. Even Leo seemed less shriveled and nervy. The days had flown by as everyone slept late in the morning, went to the beach or into town, played badminton and croquet on the back lawn, and ate Sophie's delicious dinners.

Cautiously, she said, "You know, I think it worked. I think we could last two months. You?"

"Yeah. Yeah, it's been a good week. You and your family are very kind to Leo. Plus, you're a helluva cook."

Sophie smiled. "Thanks." It had been a long time since anyone complimented her cooking. From the maple trees at the side of the property, doves called out the arrival of night. Golden light glowed from the windows of the apartment where Susie and Ivan's grandfather lived. Sophie realized it was somehow comforting, having the kind old gentleman around. Somehow more—*complete*. "This is like a fantasy world."

"True, and I could use some of that. So let's agree to keep on like this for the next two months, and if any problems come up between us we'll find a way to sort them out."

"Agreed." After a moment, Sophie offered, "We'd be glad to include Leo when we go to the library while you're at the grocery store. Lacey is itching to play with Leo. She thinks he's adorable."

"Leo likes Lacey and Jonah, too, I can tell. Sure, ask him the next time you go and we'll see what he says. Sooner or later, I'm sure he'll accept."

This evening before dinner Leo's Great Wall of China, begun below the kitchen table, reached so high it almost touched the underside of the table. It was beginning to snake out into the room. Trevor hadn't been sure how to handle this. To his surprise, Sophie had announced casually, "From now on, we're going to eat in the dining room. Lacey, you will set the table, and Jonah, you will clear."

"I don't know what to do," Trevor admitted. "He wasn't always this way. He played with other kids. He went to their houses, and we had kids over to our place." After a moment, he added, "He's breaking my heart."

"Give him time," Sophie advised. "He's processing. You're good with him. You take care of him, he feels safe with you, but you don't baby him, you don't smother him."

Trevor's throat closed up with emotion. He nodded, unable to speak.

Next to him, Sophie made a noise between a cough and a laugh. "Listen to me, the great know-it-all. At least *your* son talks to you."

"Jonah's fine." Trevor glanced over at Sophie. Their eyes caught, snagged, and they both quickly averted their gaze. "Guys don't talk to their moms much, anyway."

"He used to talk to me. This spring he's become too quiet. He missed a lot of baseball and soccer practice. He used to build his *world* around those games. His grades are dropping, too." Her voice thickened when she confessed, "I can tell Jonah likes you."

It was the perfect moment, the perfect opening, for Trevor to ask, "And do you like me?" But he didn't want to come on to her like some kind of horndog. Still, he was rattled by her words. So he responded in a Mafia don accent, "Eh, what's not to like?"

"Jonah doesn't have a real grandfather," Sophie said thoughtfully. For a moment, Trevor was thrown by her words. What relevance did that have to this conversation? "My father died a few years ago and he never was involved with my kids. Zack's father lives in Florida, and gets a new girlfriend every year. He seldom comes to visit. I guess I was kind of hoping Jonah might strike up a relationship with Connor. I worry about him, too. I don't think it's good for the old man to be alone so often."

"You worry too much," Trevor told her. "It's summer. Let's give ourselves some time." He bit his tongue after saying ourselves. That implied the two of them were in this together.

Well, after all, they kind of were.

Next to him, Sophie nodded. "Good advice." She wasn't looking at Trevor now, but he could sense some sort of force field radiating from her toward him like the heat of the afternoon's sun. His throat went dry. He could pick up a woman in a bar, no problem. But this woman was older and classy and talking to him as if he were her friend. Probably she was all mixed up, what with her husband messing around with another woman.

Before he could think what to say next, Sophie stood up. "I think I'll go up and read. Good night."

"Good night." He sat alone for a long time, staring at the starry sky.

9

As July deepened, the heat intensified. Sophie met some of the surfer boys' moms and exchanged information and phone numbers, all of them checking each other out in a friendly way. After that, some evenings Jonah would meet his surf buddies to go into town to see the latest action movie. Other nights, he'd stay home, watching the Red Sox or playing video games on his computer in his room. Trevor and Sophie lounged on the back patio with cold lemonade while Leo and Lacey played at the side of the yard.

Lacey had made overtures to Leo, inviting him to help her build her fairy house from rocks and twigs from the yard and shells and seaweed from the beach. He had watched her carefully, not speaking, not helping, until the evening they went out to discover that during the day part of the house had fallen in. This had seemed to frighten him, certainly to worry him.

Lacey had noticed how the little boy's eyes had widened, how he had backed away, his chubby fists clenching.

"It's okay, Leo," she assured him. "I can fix it. I didn't make the corner strong enough."

"I'll get my Legos," Leo told Lacey. "I'll build my wall over here."

"Great," Lacey agreed. "Then our fairies can visit each other!"

So the children built their houses beneath the bushes on the side of the lawn, about three feet apart, one house whimsical, lopsided, and lovely, the other made of plastic Legos, not so organic, but less fragile.

Often in the evenings, Connor Swenson would sit on his patio when Sophie and Trevor came out to theirs. Connor would wave a greeting to them, but he sat facing the lawn, not the house, and he appeared content with his own company. Two or three times, Sophie or Trevor had walked over to the apartment to say good evening and ask Connor if he wanted to join them for dessert. Connor always politely refused, saying, "No, thanks. I'm all settled here." His response made them feel they were intruding on him, so the last time Sophie walked down, she'd answered, "If you ever feel like joining us, you know you're more than welcome."

"I thank you for that," he'd said.

During the long, sunny days at Surfside Beach, Lacey made friends with a girl named Desi. The moment the group arrived at the beach, she raced off to find her friend. Jonah hung with a pack of surfers of all ages. He was agitating for her to buy him a bike so he wouldn't have to leave the beach whenever his mom did.

Sophie kept an eye on her kids, but mostly she was free for long, sunny hours to read or drowse, or stare out at the blue horizon, thinking. It was a background perfect for remembering.

Zack would love it here. Not because of the natural beauty, not because he loved to swim, but because everyone on the island appeared to be blessed with wealth. As a young man recently out of college, Zack had been in a hurry to accumulate wealth and its signals. He came from western Massachusetts, where his father was a dentist and his mother was head of human resources for a large corporation. Jeanette, Zack's mother, doted on her only son. In her eyes, he could do anything, he could be anyone—he could be president of the United States, he could be the conductor of the Boston Symphony Orchestra, he could be a Major League Baseball pitcher, or perhaps a movie star with his beautiful, thick blond hair. Zack had two sisters who were older and clearly as infatuated with their spectacular younger brother as Jeanette was. His sisters never really welcomed Sophie into their family, but Jeanette had been warm and affectionate from the start, and over the years had become a good friend to Sophie and a doting grandmother to Jonah and Lacey.

Still, was Zack's ambition all about pleasing his mother and his sisters, the first females in his life, the women who believed he had hung the moon and could bring it down for them if they asked? When Sophie first met him, she had been struck by his unusual closeness with his mother and sisters, but she assumed her reaction was caused by the difference between Zack's family and hers. Like her mother, her father was a physician. He was fascinated by research on prostate cancer, and as more and more technological advances filled the field, he became less attentive to his wife and daughter and even more obsessed with work. Both parents had been gravely disappointed when Sophie showed no signs of liking or even comprehending biology and chemistry in high school. When Sophie married Zack, her parents had grown even more distant. They didn't think much of him. As it turned out, Sophie thought wryly, they were right.

The first years of Sophie's marriage had been both difficult and exhilarating. Jonah was born nine months after the wedding, while Sophie and Zack were renting a second-floor apartment in Lexington, Massachusetts. Not only did Zack work full time for an architect, he also insisted that they attend every party they were invited to and give parties on every possible occasion. "Making contacts," he called this.

"Building my list." One of Sophie's jobs was to catalog every person they met, their phone numbers and addresses, and any relevant information that would help Zack build a sense of familiarity with them.

He had worked hard, day and night. His life was all about work, really. Sophie, Jonah, and Lacey became "the family," another asset in building trust with his clients. By the time Jonah was eight, they were able to buy the large house in the posh suburb. By the time Lacey was ten, they belonged to a country club, took winter trips to the Caribbean, and attended charity galas as "Angels."

They were not as much a family as an enterprise. The children weren't aware of that, of course. Many young parents were working as hard as Zack. If Sophie wasn't happy, she was certainly "fulfilled," busy with her beautiful children and an active social life. But should a woman remain married to a man who no longer loved her—to a man, she had to admit to herself, she'd never loved—for the sake of the children? She knew she was not the first woman to ask this question.

It would be wonderful to have a friend to talk to about all this. Angie and Bess were coming to visit sometime this summer, but she had to be careful discussing her husband and her marriage with them because their husbands were friends of Zack's. Her best college friend, Marty, lived in California, was pregnant with her fourth child, and had, so she said, the perfect husband; she was far too busy with her own family right now to discuss issues like divorce with Sophie.

In the evenings, after the usual badminton and croquet games, after the children were in bed, Sophie and Trevor usually sat out on the patio with iced tea or beers, talking about their day and their plans for the next day. They purposefully kept their conversation light. So far this odd arrangement was working well for both of them. They didn't want to endanger it. Trevor would probably be upset if Sophie tried to get into a deep emotional discussion about marriage and divorce. He'd been widowed, and even though he intimated that Tallulah had been troubled and far from perfect, still she had been his child's mother.

Sophie sensed that he was attracted to her. But Trevor was young, at least five years younger than she was. Between an older man and a younger woman, this would seem like nothing, but it was different this way around. She didn't kid herself. She knew what men were like. They'd go to bed with almost anyone female. Sometimes, when he was making all the children laugh, Lacey and Jonah and Leo, Sophie watched Trevor with admiration and a rising sense of—yes, she would admit it—lust. This was a sensation she had strictly and sternly banned for years. She hadn't wanted to get into a series of reckless affairs with the daddies of her own children's friends or with the magnates who bought the mansions Zack designed. She had learned to live within a routine, a velvet cage of her own creation, which allowed her to appreciate the sensual pleasures of flowers, fabrics, and especially food. She took pride in being a loving and present mother and a helpful and efficient wife. Her life was not difficult. Her life was wonderful.

Well, her life *had been* wonderful. Her husband might become her ex-husband. Had Zack set her free by having an affair with Lila? Did that mean Sophie was free to go to bed with another man—with Trevor? The very thought made her so nervous she had to get up and move around, drink some water, do some laundry, search out recipes on her iPad—anything but think about what it might be like to press her lips against the lips of the tall young man she saw every day.

It would only be a *fling*. She had never had a fling. Her friends would tell her she really ought to have one, especially now. Maybe it would be nice, for both her and Trevor. Maybe they would find a summer's consolation in each other's embrace. Maybe it was karma, meant to be—why else would they have ended up together in this house?

But what if she hurt herself even more in the process? She had seen the picture of Tallulah on the bedside table in Leo's room. No way could Sophie compare with that goddess. Plus, she had only ever slept with Zack, and she never had been wild and creative that way. She could imagine going to bed with Trevor one time and having to live the rest of the summer in the same house with him meeting young women on the beach and either bringing them home or going out to their place at night while Sophie babysat. That was the more believ-able possibility.

10

One evening in early July, as Trevor and Sophie watched from their patio, Connor called out to the children, who ran to his small patio at the end of the apartment. Moments later, both children raced up to their patio with objects in their hands.

"Look, Mom, Mr. Swenson made me a table and four chairs!" Lacey held up a miniature dinette set loosely crafted from balsa wood.

"I got a bear and a dragon!" Leo yelled, opening his fists to show two tiny carved creatures.

"Wow!" said Trevor, bending to inspect them.

"These are adorable!" Sophie picked up the table and chairs; they were as light as air. "They'll be perfect in your fairy house." When the children ran back to their end of the garden, Sophie said to Trevor, "I'll get some of the blueberry pie I made today and take it to Connor."

"Don't do that tonight," suggested Trevor.

"Why not?"

"Let him enjoy the pleasure of being generous. If you take pie to him, that makes you as generous as he is, and sort of takes away from his generosity, if you see what I mean."

Sophie studied Trevor for a long moment. "That's very astute for someone so—" She hesitated, not wanting to insult him.

"So male?"

"I was going to say someone so young," Sophie told him and felt her cheeks grow warm under his gaze.

"I'm thirty. How old are you?" Trevor challenged.

"Thirty-six." Why did she feel so embarrassed? It wasn't as if she had lied on a questionnaire on Match.com. She hadn't come here to meet a man.

"And Jonah is fifteen? You married young."

"It's true, I did." Sophie looked away from Trevor at the yard, then at her hands.

"You must have been madly in love," Trevor said.

"I was, but not with Zack." Sophie closed her eyes, remembering.

"That's a cryptic statement if I ever heard one. Don't leave me hanging," Trevor said.

For the past ten days since they'd arrived at the guest cottage, the piano had been tugging at her. It was like a kind of hunger or thirst. Here on this island where she knew so few people, and those she knew would not judge her, she burned to touch the rose-white, petal-soft keys again.

She hadn't been drinking and yet she felt inebriated, high, as she rose from her chair. "All right," she said. "I'll show you what I was in love with."

Leaving Trevor on the patio, she walked into the house, through the living room to the music room. All the windows were open in the house. She sat on the stool. She placed her hands on the keys. She began to play a dreamy, soft Chopin étude. At first, she rushed, hit the wrong keys, could not get the rhythm right, but she continued, and as the music unwound like a silken rope from a magic skein, she entered that kingdom that art created, between reality and the possibility of other realities, between harsh life and shining beauty, between death and the possibility of eternity, that radiant realm that nourished her soul and made her understand why she lived.

When she finished, she bowed her head and simply breathed. It was there, it was all still there. This was a revelation. She was trembling.

"Mom, dude." Jonah stood there with his iPod wires hanging around his neck and an expression of amazement on his face.

"Mommy, you did it again," said Lacey with astonishment. "You never told me you could play the piano."

"I haven't played for a long time," said Sophie. She stood up. "We don't have a piano at home," she reminded them.

"Well, that's lame." Jonah shook his head at her as if she were beyond comprehension.

Trevor was holding Leo in his arms. "I'm not quite sure I understand," he said, referring back to their conversation. "But trust me, I want to."

His eyes were warm and soft and full of admiration, and something even nicer Sophie could not name.

"Thank you," Sophie said. "I'm glad you enjoyed hearing the music." She ran her fingers over her forehead. "I'm sorry, you all, but that sort of tired me out. I think I'll go on up to bed. See you in the morning."

She'd done this before, left her children to get themselves to bed. They were on vacation now. She could allow herself this selfish period of time to think, to feel, to recover—to *hope*?

Upstairs, she ran a hot bath, filled it with bubbles, and sank into its comforting warmth. Her heart calmed. Her mind slowed. There was no need to rush. She leaned her head back against the warm porcelain, inhaled the fragrance of lavender, and let her mind drift.

The amazing thing was that she could play the piano with her children and Trevor listening to her. She could play the piano even though she hadn't played for years, even though she knew she hit clunkers, forgot entire passages, and probably sounded like Liberace on sleeping pills.

They said that when one door closes in your life, another door opens. But what if the entire house comes down around you, exposing you to a universe of possibilities? How did you take the first step? How did you play that first note? Sophie smiled. Maybe she already had.

11

What was the deal with attractive women and their obsessions with art? Trevor punched his pillow hard. He really liked Sophie, and not just because she was easy on the eyes. She was smart and funny and good with her children, and she was flexible. She was capable. And she played the piano like a magician, sending cascades of music into the air, music he hadn't heard before, complicated music that lifted him up and dashed him down and made him breathless as if he'd been running. When she played, she moved his soul. But that wasn't why he had come to the island. That wasn't anything he'd wanted. He had enough on his plate taking care of Leo and trying to help his son recover from Tallulah's death. His poor soul had been moved enough!

But he wanted to go to bed with Sophie. He wanted to do a whole lot of things with Sophie. Yet she was still married, obviously confused, and there were children to consider.

"Grow up, Trevor," he muttered into his pillow.

Two of his friends, Kyle and Anne Manchester, were coming down this weekend with their son Gabe, who was Leo's favorite boy buddy. They would be great buffer people between him and the overintense Sophie. Maybe he and Kyle could slip into town, go to the Box, and he could find someone carefree and fun to date this summer.

The arrival of the Manchesters Thursday night was a gift to them all, Sophie thought. Anne was a yoga chick, mellow and generous-spirited, with great swaths of frizzy red hair and a slender body draped in batik. Kyle was quiet but friendly, and Leo lit up when he saw Gabe. The boys hurried to what had been called the Lego bedroom, where the Manchesters would sleep during their stay, and spent every free moment in construction.

Friday everyone went to the beach, although Sophie took her kids to Steps Beach on the other side of the island to give Trevor and his friends some breathing space. Jonah complained—Steps was "lame," without the surf—but Lacey loved the gentle lapping water of Nantucket Sound, even though she missed seeing Desi. That night Sophie took her kids out to dinner and to a movie at the Dreamland—one of those "the world is coming to an end but Tom Cruise and the newest skinny starlet will save it" mega-action flicks.

Saturday was the beach in the morning. Trevor asked Sophie and her kids to join them, so they all went to Surfside, swimming and playing with a beach ball and falling around laughing in the surf. It was a good way to get to know each other. When they returned home for lunch, Sophie and Anne had bonded. Lacey was allowed to invite Desi to spend the night. Jonah had a sunburn and planned to lie low with his iPod. The men were eager to watch a Red Sox game and the little boys built Legos in the backyard.

Anne asked to check out the organic vegetable gardens in the area, so Sophie drove her around, and by dinner the two women were cooking together, drinking wine, and laughing. It was like old home week for Sophie, lots of kids of all ages bumbling around hungry, the men out on the patio grilling steaks, steam rising from huge pots for corn on the cob, Sophie making her special salad dressing.

After the kids were in bed, the men said they thought they'd try out one of the bars, if the women were okay with that. Sophie and Anne glanced at each other. The women were okay with that.

The night had grown moist with fog, so they opted for the living room, where they sat at either end of the sofa, their bare feet up on the cushions.

"So," Anne said, "how lucky is Trevor to fall into an arrangement like this with you? You're a great cook."

"He buys all the groceries *and* cleans the kitchen," Sophie said.

"I'm sure he does. He's always been a good boy, our Trev. I'll bet he tries extra hard since he's got a crush on you."

Sophie rolled her eyes. "Please."

"I'm serious."

"A, I'm older than he is. B, his wife just died."

Anne rolled *her* eyes. "Tallulah was all about her acting, which for her had the extracurricular appeal of screwing around and doing drugs. I'm sorry, don't speak ill of the dead and so on, but Tallulah was trouble. Beautiful, but vapid. Incredibly narcissistic, totally centered on Tallulah. I tried to like her—I honestly did work at it. But there just wasn't much there to like. She was seldom around, and she'd been doing drugs for a while. I was anxious for Leo. I may sound harsh, but that sweet boy is better off without her. Trevor has always been the real parent." Anne shifted to pull her knees to her chest. "Anyway, tell me more about you."

Sophie tilted her head, staring into her wineglass. "As I said in the car today, my husband, Zack, is in love with a younger woman. He's not sure what he wants to do and as each day goes by and he doesn't phone his children, I'm becoming more and more sure that a divorce is in our future."

"You don't seem messed up and heartbroken about it," observed Anne.

"I guess I hide it well," Sophie said with a smile. "No, that's not quite right. I *was* messed up and heartbroken and I still am for the children—they don't deserve a shattered family. But this summer on Nantucket has made me think that possibly what I've thought was a charming, cozy, well-furnished home is in fact a kind of cage." She shook her head impatiently. "That sounds too dramatic and is not quite what I mean. I'm just seeing things differently here, realizing I have options in life."

"You certainly do. This is your time to play around a bit, girl, while you're still young."

"Play around? Do you mean sleep around? I don't know if I could. I've never been with any man except Zack." She paused, then added, "And it's been a long time since I've gone to bed with him."

"Well, that's just sad. Sex is one of man's greatest pleasures in life and you shouldn't miss out. Why not have some fun with Trevor? He's adorable, and he blushes when he looks at you."

"I think *you* have a crush on Trevor," said Sophie, trying to turn the conversation away from herself.

"Of course I have a crush on Trevor! I also have a crush on Johnny Depp and Ryan Gosling and the UPS man, but I'm not going to do anything about it. I intend to be faithful to Kyle for the rest of my life, but I can do that because I had a lot of fun before I met him. So did he. But as they say, I'm married, not dead. I like to look, and I like to feel. When Kyle and I watch the Red Sox games, I talk to my girl-friend on the phone about which new player is the cutest. We have a saying: *PILF*, Player I'd Like to—and Kyle sits right there ignoring me. He talks to the television. 'That was a strike, you dumb-ass umpire!' And I'm saying to my friend, 'That new Holt boy has one fine ass!'"

Sophie laughed. "I feel like a Puritan, listening to you."

"You can always change. I'm not saying go to a bar and pick up any guy. But Trevor is a good man. He's devoted to his son, he's a great friend, and he deserves happiness in his life."

"You think if I go to bed with him that will bring him some happiness?" Sophie asked skeptically.

"I think it will bring you both some pleasure, and probably happiness, as well."

Sophie reached to the coffee table, picked up the bottle of wine, and poured them each another glass. "Tell me how you got so wise."

For the rest of the evening, Anne talked about her difficult childhood and young adulthood, finding yoga, committing herself to the yoga life, studying at Kripalu, becoming a certified yoga instructor. Sophie listened carefully. The Manchesters were a happy family and she wanted to learn how they managed that.

Monday morning, the Manchesters left. Trevor and Leo went into town grocery shopping. Sophie surrendered to Jonah's insistent pleas, and she took him and Lacey to Young's Bicycle Shop to buy Jonah a bike. It was a relatively inexpensive used ten-speed, not cool, but in good working condition. They drove back to the house with the bike loaded into the back of the minivan. The day was turning out hot and muggy, and Sophie and her family weren't in the mood to go to the beach again.

High-pitched screams assailed them the moment they stepped out of the car. Jonah and Lacey turned to their mother, dismayed and confused.

"Perhaps Leo has an ear infection," Sophie said, rushing to the house.

Inside, they found chaos. Cushions had been pulled from the sofa and chairs and rugs were flipped upside down. Sophie and her children hurried upstairs, toward the noise.

Trevor was with Leo in the child's bedroom. The mattress had been half dragged to the floor, which was littered with clothing and toys. In the middle of it all, Leo lay in the throes of a full-force tantrum. His small face was swollen and red. His father knelt next to him, helplessly repeating his name.

Trevor looked up at Sophie. "Tubee's missing. We've looked everywhere. I don't suppose you know where he is?"

"I saw him yesterday," offered Lacey, trying her best to be helpful.

"Sorry, man," said Jonah. "Did you look outside?"

"We looked everywhere." Trevor's T-shirt and hair were damp with sweat. He was on the verge of tears himself.

Sophie closed her eyes and envisioned the way the house had looked last evening. "Could the Manchesters have accidentally packed him?"

"Sophie, you're a genius! Did you hear that, Leo? Maybe he's with the Manchesters!"

"No! No! Want Tubee now!" The child lay on the floor roaring, hitting the floor with his fists, kicking it in a furious rhythm.

Trevor jumped up, dug his cell phone out of his pocket, and walked into the hallway where he could hear himself speak. He punched in a number. A moment later, he said, "Anne, is there any chance Tubee is with you? We can't find him anywhere here." After waiting a moment, he said, "That would be amazing, and I'd be so grateful." Returning to his son's bedroom, he knelt next to Leo. "Hey, guy, the Manchesters are almost home. The moment they get in the house, they're going through all their luggage to see if Tubee's there."

It was as if Leo hadn't heard. He continued to howl like a maddened beast. Next to Sophie, Lacey began to cry quietly, tears sliding down her cheeks. Jonah slunk off to his bedroom and quietly shut the door. Trevor attempted to gather his furious son into his arms, but Leo fought him off, hitting his father's chest and arms, shouting, "No! Want Tubee!"

Sophie felt like a voyeur at a terrible catastrophe. Wrapping her arm around her daughter's shoulders, she guided Lacey downstairs and into the family room. "It's going to be okay, I don't want you to worry. Leo is having a tantrum. All kids have tantrums when they're young. It's not nice to see but it's not dangerous. If we could do anything, we would. But right now Trevor is the only one who can help Leo."

"It's so scary, Mommy," Lacey whispered. "His face is so red."

"I know, honey, I know. Many children have a special toy or blanket that gives them security. You had your pink blankie when you were a toddler, remember? You carried it around until you were three years old and it was almost transparent from so many washings. You had tantrums like Leo's if you misplaced it. One day when you were three, you left it in your bedroom and never needed it again. But Leo has . . . lost his mommy. We have to remember that. Sadness comes out in different ways. I think Leo is crying for his mommy as much as for Tubee."

Lacey's tears intensified. "That hurts my heart."

Sophie cuddled her daughter next to her on the sofa. "It hurts my heart, too, sweetie, but you know what? Sometimes crying is a kind of cure. Sometimes that's what the body and the heart need to do. It's hard to watch, but it's not always a bad thing."

"Can't we do anything to help Leo?"

"I'm afraid not, although I might go upstairs with a glass of ice water for both Leo and Trevor to drink. For us, I think it's time we watched some television, something really stupid." Reaching for the remote, Sophie clicked until she found the cartoon channel. "I'll be right back."

As she headed up the stairs with the ice water, she heard Trevor in the hallway talking on the phone. She saw him go into Leo's bedroom.

Trevor knelt on the floor next to his wailing son. "Anne found

Tubee, Leo. He was in the pillowcase with their laundry. He was tucked away in a nice, soft place. Anne is going to package him up and mail him back overnight express mail. He will be here tomorrow. For sure."

At these words, Leo's rage gradually subsided. His sobs diminished to whimpers. Trevor gathered his son in his arms and sat on the floor, hugging the boy against him, rocking him.

"Want Tubee." Leo cried, his bony body shuddering with exhaustion.

"Tubee went on a quick trip with our friends. He'll be back tomorrow."

Sophie tiptoed into the room, set the two glasses of ice water on the floor within reach of Trevor's hand, and quietly left.

Trevor took a sip of the cold water and was surprised at how it revived him—he could almost feel the clear energy spread through his system, calming him. Holding Leo's glass, he coaxed his son to take a sip, and then another. The hot flush of Leo's skin slowly faded. The boy's breathing slowed. He relaxed against Trevor.

Trevor rocked Leo in his arms, humming softly until the child's trembling eased and his eyes closed. He laid Leo in his bed. He removed his son's sandals and smoothed his hair, pulled a sheet over him, then simply stood watching for a while. Leo folded into a fetal position and sank into a deep sleep.

Downstairs, Lacey was in the family room watching television. Sophie was sitting on the back patio with a book in her lap, her head resting against the pillow of the lounge chair.

Trevor went outside to sit on the chair next to her. "Well, that was awful."

"I've seen worse when a child didn't get the candy he wanted in a grocery store," said Sophie comfortingly. "But, yes, it was awful, for you and for Leo. And yet, possibly not the worst thing that could happen. I was telling Lacey how sometimes it helps to have a good tantrum. Often the immediate problem isn't the real cause."

"Catharsis. Yeah, I know." Trevor stretched out on his lounge chair and closed his eyes. "I feel like my heart has been squeezed so hard it's as limp as a rag."

"Kids will do that to you," Sophie said. "I don't want to interfere, Trevor, but you *have* talked with Leo about death and about losing people, right?"

"Of course I have. And I talk to Leo about his mother every day. You've heard me." Trevor rubbed his forehead, remembering the advice of other parents and the therapists he had visited. "I really don't want to put Leo on medication."

"I think you're right. Although, there have been times in my life when I've wished I could share a nice slug of vodka with my kids to ease their pain over a crisis like Leo's. I'd never do it, of course. I suppose growing up is partly about learning how to handle loss."

Trevor barked a low laugh. "Some of us never learn how to handle that." Glancing over at Sophie, he remarked, "You and your kids don't seem to be freaking out over this separation from your husband."

Sophie shifted in her chair, turning her body toward Trevor. "Well, the kids don't know why we're apart this summer. Plus, we're used to being without him. He's always working. He's never cared much for the whole soccer/ ballet recital/family camping trip kind of thing. He loves his children—" Sophie stopped talking and chewed on a fingernail. After a moment, she continued, "He *does* love his children, but now that I think about it, he has never gone through with either one of them what you just went through with Leo. I'm afraid Zack would find it all far too unpleasant. Not to mention unprofitable."

"Not to be rude, but he sounds like a jackass."

"I think he is. Believe me, I've given our situation a lot of thought in the past few weeks. Sometimes I wonder what we ever saw in each other that made us wild enough about each other to marry. Even when I look at the early photographs, I can't recall a feeling of ecstasy. He was challenging and exciting. And I looked good back then."

"You look good right now," Trevor murmured, but Sophie didn't seem to hear.

"Sometimes I think nature makes us marry the closest—in proximity—person to us simply to propagate the species."

"It was certainly that way for me with Tallulah," Trevor admitted. "What I mean, I guess, is for me it was all about sex. For her, too. Tallulah had healthy appetites—what am I saying? She certainly had some unhealthy appetites, too. But I think she got into the drug thing quite recently. I'm sure she did, in fact. I never noticed any signs when she came home. No glazed eyes, no mania, just her normal narcissistic self. I have that to be grateful for, that Leo never saw his mother drunk or high or unable to function."

"That is good. Leo's memories of his mother will all be happy ones."

"I hope you're right," said Trevor. "When she was there, she cuddled and kissed him and sometimes read him stories. She acted for him, too. She fascinated him; his face glowed when he watched her. He would sit on the sofa while she acted out a scene in her current play and even though he couldn't understand all the words, he was mesmerized. She must have seemed magical to him. I was the boring old disciplinarian who forced him to brush his teeth and take baths and eat his vegetables."

"Someday, when he's older, much older, Leo will appreciate you. Right now, of course, he can't understand the kind of good luck he has in having you as his father. I would pay money to have Zack spend a fraction of his time and charm on the children that you do. He does support us financially, and he does do that well. I have to admit that. We've never lacked for anything. He's never been mean to the children and he's always been there at night, which I'm sure gives the children a feeling of security." Sophie chewed her fingernail again, thinking. "Jonah used to adore his father, but now he doesn't seem to. Both kids know something's going on. I'm not sure what to do." Sophie laughed. "What am I saying? Zack wants a divorce. I've got to suck it up."

Trevor's brain had stuck on her words about the good luck Leo had in having him as his father. That meant Sophie liked him. Maybe even admired him. Much of the lowering weight of gloom and despair from Leo's tantrum lifted from his heart. "Really," Trevor joked, "we are a pathetic pair."

"For now, we are," Sophie agreed, taking his comment seriously. "But it's the beginning of the summer. I have a feeling things will change." She stood up and stretched. "The humidity is getting to me. I think I'll take a nap."

For the rest of the afternoon, Trevor worked on his laptop. He checked on Leo regularly, and found the boy still sleeping. In the evening, Leo refused to come downstairs to eat, so Trevor brought him up a sandwich. Leo took a few bites, then turned to face the wall and closed his eyes. Trevor went to bed early, hoping the express mail would be there when they awoke in the morning.

12

Of course the mail didn't work that way. Leo sat on the front step, watching for the delivery truck all morning. Trevor worked on his laptop in the dining room, keeping an eye on his son through the window. Sophie went to the beach with her children, and Trevor, like a total hopeless case, missed her. He reminded himself of Kyle's words:

"She's older, man, and she's got two kids. One of them is a teenage boy. Plus, she's not even divorced yet, and for all you know she'll go back to her husband. She's nice, and she's good-looking—oh, I can see the attraction. But you're still recovering from a major shock, a big, fat life trauma. Don't be looking for any more complications at this time in your life."

In the early afternoon, a FedEx truck rolled into the driveway and a man brought Leo a package. Trevor stood next to his son, watching him rip it open.

"Tubee!" Leo squeezed the stuffed giraffe so tightly it would have been suffocated if it had breath. "Dad, Tubee's back!"

Trevor wondered if there were a way to permanently attach the thing to his son's body. Handcuffs? Too weird. Trevor would simply have to be more observant.

When the Andersons returned, Sophie prepared a feast, concluding with strawberry shortcake in celebration of Tubee's return. Afterward, during the long, bright evening, Trevor sat on the patio watching Leo busily working on his Legos and chatting with Connor. He hoped his son wasn't bothering the older man, who clearly enjoyed his privacy. Rising, he strolled over to join the conversation.

"Hi, guys, what's up?" Trevor asked.

"Connor's making a chair for Tubee!" Leo cried with excitement. "Then Tubee can sit out here with me without getting dirt on his bottom."

"That's really nice of you, Connor," Trevor said. "I hope it's not an imposition."

"Heck, no, I suggested it," Connor replied. "I've made a lot of miniature furniture for my grandchildren. I enjoy doing it. It's sort of restful for the mind."

"Maybe I'd better take it up, then," Trevor joked.

Connor looked up at Trevor, who was leaning against the outside wall of Connor's small apartment. "Maybe you should. Your generation does everything so fast I think you've forgotten how to enjoy the pleasures of going slow. Not to insult you personally—I don't mean it that way."

"I know what you mean," Trevor said, but silently he thought, *Yeah, but you're old, you've lived your life, you've got it all figured out, and I feel like I'm on the spin cycle of the dryer.* He watched in silence for a few moments while Connor carved and Leo arranged his Legos, but the heat and humidity of the day pressed on him. "Hot day," he remarked.

"Not like in Iowa," Connor replied. "This is mild compared to Iowa. The apartment has an air conditioner, but it makes the rooms feel like an icebox. I like sitting out here, hanging out with your boy."

Trevor studied the older man. "I hope all the noise we make doesn't bother you."

"Heavens, no. My hearing's shot. I wear these—" he tapped his ears, indicating small hearing aids—"if I want to hear anything. Without them, I'm deaf as a stone."

Trevor shifted uncomfortably. "Too bad."

Connor gave him a sweet smile. "Not really. With them, I'm good. They're like my glasses, part of the stuff that old age requires."

"Well, hey, I'm going to make some iced tea. Can I bring you a glass?"

"No, thanks. I'd just have to go pee."

Leo giggled. "Connor said 'pee.'"

"I'll be in the house, then. Okay, Leo?"

"'Kay," Leo responded, preoccupied with his building.

Back in the house, Trevor made a big pitcher of iced tea—a mixture of Darjeeling and herbal raspberry that Sophie had showed him how to make. He could hear Sophie moving through the house, gathering up laundry, using the washer and dryer, folding towels. He wished she would come outside and sit with him. Later, he heard laughter. He peeked into the family room. Sophie and her kids were watching a movie starring Adam Sandler and howling with laughter. *Probably inappropriate for a four-year-old,* Trevor thought, trying not to feel hurt that she didn't ask them to join their group.

The next morning, they all went to the beach. Jonah ran off to find his surf buddies while Lacey sprinted through the sand to greet her new friend. The two girls squealed at their reunion as if it had been years since they'd seen each other, then settled down at the edge of the waves to construct fantastic sand castles. Sophie set up her private beach lair with its striped umbrella to shade her as she reclined in her beach chair, engrossed in a paperback novel. Trevor had brought a thriller along. Up the beach, not far from Sophie, he lay on his beach towel, trying to read while watching Leo construct his own sand fort. Leo didn't seem to want to interact with any of the other children, which made Trevor deeply sad. But what could he do? Bribe someone to play with his child? Leo seemed happy enough, anyway.

A good-looking guy cut his way through the crowds of beach umbrellas and blankets and stopped, to Trevor's surprise, next to Sophie. He said a few words, and Sophie smiled up at him. They shook hands and the man sat down on the blanket next to Sophie. Trevor snorted: the man talking to Sophie resembled a hero in one of the shield-wielding, chest-beating *Clash of the Titans* movies. Probably forty, tanned and taut, with an expensive haircut that made his graying dark hair stand up in bristles. Sophie was too far away from Trevor to hear their conversation, but because he was wearing sunglasses he was able to watch her surreptitiously. They talked. Sophie laughed. Probably the man was a friend of Sophie's husband, Trevor decided, and he didn't like the guy.

Later that afternoon, the house filled with the tantalizing aroma of tomatoes and cheese. In his room with his computer, Trevor imagined a delicious meal and afterward sitting on the patio talking with Sophie. He was sure she would want to discuss Leo's meltdown over Tubee. Trevor certainly did.

He found Leo in his bedroom constructing his Lego universe, and took him downstairs, expecting to see Sophie in the kitchen and Lacey setting the dining room table.

The downstairs was empty. Leo went under the kitchen table to his Legos. Trevor took another beer from the refrigerator and wandered around aimlessly. It was six o'clock, their ordinary dinnertime, not that he was all anal about it. Dropping down on the living room sofa, he took his cell from his shorts and was checking for messages when he heard female giggling and saw Lacey and Sophie coming down the stairs.

Lacey wore a madras sundress and her toenails were painted the green that matched her sandals. "We're going out to dinner," she announced to Trevor.

"We are?" he asked in surprise.

"No, silly, Mom and I are going to dinner at Desi's house."

Sophie wore white flip-flops and a simple white cotton sundress with a thin blue belt. She wasn't what Tallulah would have called "dressed up," but she still looked drop-dead gorgeous. Her blond hair had gotten becomingly shaggy and streaked by the sun with flecks of silver and gold. Her only lipstick, a pale gloss, emphasized her tan and her large blue eyes.

Trevor stood up. "I didn't know you were going out to dinner." He felt betrayed, jealous, and irrationally angry.

Sophie smiled. "Desi's father invited us when we spoke on the beach today. I made a casserole for you and Leo and Jonah. It's in the oven, ready anytime. I've knocked on Jonah's door and told him to come have dinner. You all can have fruit or whatever you want for dessert." She didn't look at Trevor but searched around the table in the hallway for her purse, her car keys, and her sunglasses.

"When will you be home?" Trevor demanded, mentally smacking his forehead the moment he spoke. He wasn't her husband, her boyfriend, or her father! He had no right to this information.

"Who knows?" Sophie's whole attitude was carefree and cheerful. Obviously Trevor was only a gnat at the periphery of her vision. "Come on, Lacey, we don't want to be late." Taking her daughter's hand, she went out the door, turning back to say, "Jonah has my cell phone number if you need me for anything."

Trevor watched out the window as Sophie and her daughter got into the minivan and drove away.

13

Of course she thought of Zack. Not constantly, not even as much as she feared she would, but often and in ways she hadn't expected.

Tonight, dressing for dinner at Hristo Fotev's house, she'd winked at her tanned and glowing reflection in the mirror and thought: *You ought to see me now, Zack.*

More frequently, she remembered moments of their marriage, both good and bad. Sometimes she searched for signals she should have caught that would have predicted his infidelity, other than his good looks and winning ways. She never found any. Occasionally, she allowed herself to remember why she had married Zack in the first place, back when she was so young, but the memory was uncomfortable, painful, maybe even shameful, and she shied away from it.

She hadn't heard from Zack since she'd been on the island. Both children had cell phones but she tried not to spy, although she did keep an eye on Lacey's Facebook account. As far as she knew, Zack had not called either child. This infuriated her. He could leave *her;*

fine, she could almost understand that. But he shouldn't ignore his children, as if they didn't matter anymore.

Tonight she swallowed her anger. It became a fireball inside her, and like her summer tan, it made her glow. She knew she looked pretty. Trevor's reaction when she came down the stairs seconded her opinion. But she had gone out of her way not to look seductive. She wore flat sandals, not heels. No eyeliner, just a touch of mascara and a pale Burt's Bees balm. Her only jewelry was her watch, and because she knew Lacey would notice, her wedding ring.

Lacey assumed, of course, that this dinner tonight was so Sophie could get to know Desi's parent. That happened all the time at home. Lacey probably had no idea that Desi's father was divorced, thrillingly wealthy, and could easily double for Gerard Butler. And she absolutely didn't notice how Hristo had gazed with his deep, mysterious eyes at Sophie when they chatted on the beach.

Jonah knew there was a casserole in the oven. He'd be happy watching a video or playing on his computer. There was no reason for Sophie to feel so nervous—so guilty. Guilty, and she hadn't done anything. Yet.

During the short drive to Hristo's house at Surfside Beach, Lacey chatted incessantly. "Desi speaks *three* languages, Mom. Could I start taking French lessons? She plays piano, too. Her mother lives in Sofia, Bulgaria—isn't that amazing? I Googled it; it's awesome. Desi likes castles and medieval stuff like I do. Did you see the sand castle Desi and I built on the beach today? Desi says there are castle ruins like that in Bulgaria—not made of sand, of course!" Lacey giggled at herself.

"Don't forget, Lacey, you're talented, too," Sophie reminded her daughter, hoping Lacey wouldn't feel inferior to such an accomplished girl. "You write wonderful stories and draw beautiful pictures."

Lacey hadn't even heard her. "And Desi has all these gowns of her mother's that we get to try on. I know we're too old for dress-up; this isn't dress-up, really, it's more like make-believe or maybe practicing to be grown-up. Have you ever had a *gown*? And jewelry, Desi's mother left *jewelry* at the Surfside house—"

Sophie interrupted. "Are you sure you should be going through her mother's belongings?"

"Her mother never comes here anymore—oh, MOM! Look at the house!"

Unlike most Nantucket houses, this one was modern and long, with walls of windows. Perched on a sand dune like a rectangular box of glass and wood, it was surrounded by the natural landscape: sand, wild roses, beach grass. Lights blazed from the house, illuminating the Belgian block drive and bluestone walkway.

"Hey, there." Hristo was at the door, with Desi next to him. His coral linen shirt accentuated the black of his thick hair and eyes. Desi's hair was lighter, her brows and lashes brown, her eyes a creamy caramel.

"Come *on*," Desi cried, taking Lacey's hand. "I want to show you my room. We don't have to be with them for half an hour."

"*Them*," Sophie intoned ominously as the girls ran off. "So we have become the dreadful, boring *them*."

Hristo laughed. "I've got some wine to help soften the pain."

He led her past the foyer with its spiral staircase straight into a large open room with an expansive sea view. To the west, the sun was sinking, casting a sheen of golden light on the mild blue Atlantic.

Sophie sank into a sinfully soft sofa and accepted the wine Hristo handed her.

"What an amazing house," Sophie said. "Such a beautiful view, and it all seems to be part of the landscape."

"Thanks. Yes, it's always good to be here."

"You said you're Bulgarian. I know nothing about Bulgaria."

Hristo shrugged. "I'm not surprised. It's been beaten down a lot recently. But it's an ancient, historical, and quite beautiful country."

"But you live in the U.S. now?"

"Yes, and elsewhere. I'm a dual national, American and Bulgarian. My companies are involved with transportation—building bridges, seaport docks, and railroads."

"Do you live on Nantucket all year?"

"No. My main residence is in Manhattan. But I get a lot of work done here on the island. Many multinationals enjoy vacationing here where it's relatively peaceful and isolated. And you?"

Sophie hesitated. She didn't want to blurt out that she'd drained her aunt's trust fund in order to escape an unfaithful husband. "I've rented a house here for two months this summer," she slowly began. "We live in Boston, my children and I and my husband." She swallowed more of the delicious wine. "When I return after the summer," she added lightly, "I think he'll become my ex-husband."

"Huh," said Hristo. "Might be a good thing. *I'm* divorced. My ex and I are fairly amicable." He grinned. "It helps that she and I live in different countries."

"I'm sure." Sophie smiled and sipped more wine. She noticed over Hristo's shoulder a baby grand at the other end of the room. "You have a piano."

"A souvenir of the years when I was in a rock band."

"Do you play?"

"If I'm in the mood to torture the seagulls. You?"

"I used to." Sophie put her drink on the coffee table and half rose. Was it the wine? The wine, yes, and the continuing sense of floating dreaminess that pervaded the air of the island. She was drawn to the instrument as if by some kind of mesmerism. "May I?"

"Please."

Sophie drifted across the room, seated herself on the bench, and put her hands on the ivory keys. What was there about this island that was bringing it all back to her, the longing, the fulfillment? A lilting

Strauss waltz seemed to drop from her fingers onto the keys, and as had happened in the guest cottage, the music carried her off, separating her from the room, from reality. Both joy and sorrow rose within her, tangling, caressing, and tugging her into memories.

"Mom! You're doing it again!"

Lacey and Desi stood on the stairs, gawking at her.

"Come down, girls," Hristo said. "I've got to throw dinner together. You two can set the table." He turned to Sophie. "You play beautifully."

Sophie said, "Thank you." She moved away from the piano. "Will you reward me with food?"

Hristo smiled. "Yes. Please join me in the kitchen."

Sophie leaned against the counter, watching as Hristo quickly stir-fried spring vegetables and tuna that he tossed over pasta. As they ate, Hristo focused the conversation on the girls, the events they might wish to attend this summer, and what sports they played. Afterward, Desi and Lacey were excused to make ice-cream sundaes in the kitchen while Hristo and Sophie went out to the deck to look at the night sky.

"Your daughter's nice," Hristo said.

"So is Desi. I'm glad they've met. It makes this summer so much happier for Lacey." Sophie was leaning on the railing, half listening to the waves.

"You've got a son, too?"

"Yes. Jonah. He's fifteen. I think he's beginning to grow up, and, I hate to say it, to grow away from me. We used to be such chums. Now he doesn't hang out with me or confide in me. It's to be expected, but I do worry about him, because he's changing so much."

"Do you think he'd like to go out with me on my boat?" Hristo asked. "We could all go. I have a small yacht docked at Great Harbor Yacht Club."

"Oh! Jonah doesn't know how to sail, but I'm sure he'd love to go out with you." She couldn't disguise the pleasure in her voice. "We all would. This is extremely kind of you."

Hristo moved closer to her, leaning his tanned, strong arms on the railing a few inches away from her. "Maybe I have an ulterior motive."

She felt his gaze on her like heat. He was *flirting* with her. She was sure that flirting was as easy for him as breathing, probably a natural talent he had polished to use in his work as well as in his private life. Sophie, on the other hand, hadn't flirted for years. She'd had sex with only one man in all her life: Zack, that massive skunk. She froze, desperate to come up with a clever retort.

"Oh, you must have heard about my paella." Proud of herself, she twinkled up at him. "I'll make it some night and invite you and Desi to dinner."

Hristo stepped closer to her. "I'd like that."

Sophie swayed. She was having trouble catching her breath.

Hristo was cool. "I have to go to New York for a few days on business. Could I take you out to dinner next Tuesday?"

"I think that evening's free," she said coolly.

"Great. I'll call you." He slid the glass door open and they returned to the bright lights of the house, where the girls sat giggling on the sofa.

"It was funny watching you, Dad," said Desi. "Kind of like watching an old movie."

"Well," Hristo responded without missing a beat, "we are old people."

"Time to go home, Lacey," Sophie said.

Lacey, as expected, protested, but Sophie was firm. Soon they were driving back from the beach to their summer home.

14

The three pitiful males ate their casserole in front of the television. The Red Sox were rained out, and even though they cruised through the channel guide twice, they couldn't find anything that would satisfy a four-year-old, a fifteen-year-old, and a grown male. Trevor's mood slumped until he had an inspiration.

"Jonah, do you know how to play poker?"

Jonah shook his head. "Not really."

"Come on then. I'll teach you."

They sat at the dining room table, Leo on Trevor's lap, Jonah waiting patiently as Trevor explained the face cards to Leo. They had a fresh deck of cards, but no chips, so they used paper clips from Trevor's office. It wasn't a great game with only two players—and Leo occasionally spontaneously yelping, "Look, Daddy, you got the king!"— but it was still fun. Trevor taught Jonah straight and stud poker and five-card draw. When Leo started yawning, Trevor stopped the game to take his son to bed.

"I'm gonna check Facebook," Jonah said, loping away up the stairs. Over his shoulder, he said casually, "Thanks, man."

When Leo was in bed and Jonah secluded in his room, Trevor sat in front of his computer and scanned his work log. Nothing urgent. He opened up a computer game but it couldn't hold his attention. Sophie going off for dinner with that guy had really gotten under Trevor's skin and with his analytical mind, he wanted to figure out why.

He'd only known the woman for a short while, for Pete's sake. She wasn't the most babealicious female he'd ever seen, but what he felt for her wasn't lust. Okay, it *was* lust, but there was a whole lot more going on, too. He liked the way she was in the world, genuine, engaged, easily capable. He really enjoyed hearing her play the piano, although she did it so seldom. He liked her cooking. He liked the way she gathered daisies from the roadside and set them around the house. He liked the way she received with optimism and a gentle acceptance what the world threw at her. She hadn't freaked out when the Manchesters came; she hadn't made a scene, shouting that she hadn't agreed to cook for a crowd. Instead, she'd made a great meal, including a blueberry and strawberry cheesecake, maybe the best dessert he'd ever eaten. He liked the way she sent Jonah or Lacey down to give Old Man Connor chocolate-chip cookies fresh from the oven or a bowl of fruit salad.

She was always doing mundane things naturally, without fuss. Like tossing the kitchen dish towels into the laundry and replacing them with fresh ones. Humming while she vacuumed. Her entire approach to each day made him reflect on his own values. Trevor was far from impoverished. He had some family money, and he did staggeringly well with his computer business. Yet he lived in a small apartment in Cambridge that he'd begun to rent when he was a grad student at MIT.

These two weeks with Sophie made him understand that he lived a pretty childish life in a rather slapdash manner. True, he hadn't had time to think about the niceties of life during the past five years; he'd been too busy taking care of his son and buying diapers, bottles, a crib, clothes, and then soft shoes, snow boots, sneakers, backpacks, lunchboxes—an explosion of necessities.

When Trevor's mother came to help him with the newborn baby, and many other times during Leo's life, she had never commented on the way Trevor and Tallulah chose to live. It had surprised Trevor that she was willing to admit she was a grandmother. In fact she seemed to dote on Leo and visited often, taking care of him, taking him to museums and parks, and cooking the food Leo liked: macaroni and cheese, hot dogs, cheese-and-mustard sandwiches. Tallulah and his mother got along all right, especially because Tallulah was rarely in the apartment; she was usually off rehearsing, acting, or auditioning. Audrey never mentioned the furnishings and Leo never noticed the decor; why would he? He was a child.

Sophie probably thought that Trevor wasn't much more than a child himself, with his stupid T-shirts with slogans on them that various computer companies sent him as gifts and that worked nicely as pajamas or shirts. No wonder she had gone to dinner with that European guy. What was his name? Trevor remembered: Hristo Fotev. Russian? Anyone who had a house right on Surfside Beach had to have a lot of money. Maybe, Trevor thought, hopefully, this Fotev guy was part of the Russian Mafia.

He went to his computer. He was going to check out the dude.

His fingers flew over the keyboard and he grew more and more miserable. This Fotev guy was a real multitalented, multinational master of the universe. He was CEO of his own company and sat on the boards of several major refugee aid organizations. His uncle had left Bulgaria before the Communists took over the country. He took the family fortune with him to England and later into the United States. When his brother, Hristo's father, was thirty, he and his wife moved to the United States, and Hristo was born there in 1970. After the Communists left the country in 1989, the Fotevs returned to Bulgaria to reclaim some of their property. When Hristo's uncle died, he left his fortune and his love of the country to Hristo.

He was still searching when he heard the front door open and Lacey babbling to her mother as they entered.

He couldn't help himself. He went downstairs, as eager as a storybook spinster to hear about the evening.

It must have gone well, because Sophie was glowing.

"Oh, hello, Trevor. Are you still up?" Sophie's laugh was like a tinkling of chimes. "Of course you're still up—you're standing right there."

Trevor narrowed his eyes, wondering whether Sophie was a bit buzzed.

Lacey cried, "Trevor, Trevor! Desi has the most awesome house! And they have—"

Sophie interrupted, "Trevor doesn't want to hear about all that."

"Yes, I do," Trevor said, biting the inside of his mouth for saying it so quickly.

"Desi has a room like a princess, and she has five American Girl dolls!" Lacey's eyes were shining. "And wardrobes for all their clothes, and—"

"Lacey, why don't you go up and write about this in your diary? And it really is time to go to bed. I let you stay up late tonight."

Like a slaphappy ballerina, Lacey twirled her way up the stairs, singing.

"I'd better go to bed, too," said Sophie, yawning.

"Did you have a good time?" Trevor folded his arms over his chest and leaned against the wall in what he hoped appeared to be a casual, inviting way.

Sophie's smile was almost smug. "I had a wonderful time." She did the thing with her shoulders she did when she was especially happy, sort of lifting them up and squeezing them toward her ears. "Everything here okay?"

"Fine," Trevor replied. What else could he say? *I spent the evening checking out your new boyfriend?*

"See you tomorrow, then," said Sophie, and she drifted away from him up the stairs as if invisible wings carried her.

15

During the night, the wind rose, whispering through the windows with cool scents of rain. Sophie left her bed still half asleep to close the windows in her children's room and pull the covers up over their shoulders.

When she woke in the morning, a heavy rain slanted down against the house, tapping on the walls and windows. Pulling on her light cotton robe against the sudden coolness, she went into the kitchen. It was after eight o'clock and no one else was awake. She made coffee and took it into the living room, curled up on the sofa, and picked up a novel to read.

It was sweet to be awake and alone even for a brief time on this rainy day. She wondered what Hristo and his daughter were doing. Clearly he was a good father. He was a fascinating man, and his foreignness gave him an almost dangerous exotic allure. Last night she had felt as if she were playing a game, trying on a different personality, performing a part in his spontaneous play. Was the real Sophie Anderson the woman in that glamorous house last night? She hated being such a cliché female, her tidy mind zooming from one delightful evening to the possibility of years together. But why kid herself? She was no cosmopolitan starlet. She'd forgotten the French she'd had in high school. She was only a suburban mom with two children and even though her marriage was rocky if not right on the rocks, for the time being she still had a husband. So she should stop trying to predict the future and enjoy the present. Wasn't that what everyone said? Be here now. She looked back down at her novel and forced herself to concentrate.

Later, when everyone else was up, the rain still thundered down, insistent and relentless. Sophie and Trevor decided to drive into town to visit the Whaling Museum with the children. Afterward, they went to lunch at the Downyflake. The restaurant was packed, as usual, but when they were finally seated, the food arrived quickly and all conversation ceased as they devoured blueberry pancakes and bacon, licking blueberry syrup off their lips. By unanimous vote, they bought a bag of the famous doughnuts to take home for later. *Later* for Jonah and Lacey turned out to be during the ride home. "Save one for me!" Sophie demanded as she steered through the rain.

Back at home, they ran from the minivan through the downpour into the house. Everyone scattered to his or her own place. It was the perfect day to read or nap, to enjoy some solitude after days of togetherness.

At the end of the afternoon, the rain moderated but the sky was still overcast, sending a slanting blue-gray light through the wet windows. Sophie stretched. As if caught in a spell, she drifted out of the living room into the opulent music room, where the piano waited in its grand isolation. She sat down on the bench, placing her fingers on the cool ivory keys, welcoming a gentle Brahms melody. Why could she play so readily at this house when she hadn't touched a piano for years? As she played she forgot to wonder. She lost herself in the music.

Exactly when Leo entered the room, Sophie didn't know. Only when she had finished one piece did she realize the small boy was standing just inside the doorway, watching her. When she saw his expression, she understood at once. In his face she saw both desire and fear.

"Would you like to come sit with me?" she invited Leo in a calm, almost indifferent tone.

Leo nodded. Slowly he approached her. Sophie lifted him up onto the bench.

"These are called keys. You press down like this to make the music come out." Gently she indented middle C. Next to her, Leo put his index finger on a key and pressed. "Harder," she told him. "Don't be afraid. You can't hurt it."

Leo punched the keys and burst into a smile when the notes sounded. Glancing up at Sophie for approval, he placed all five fingers on the keys, producing a cluster of noise. Excited by that, he put his other hand on the keyboard and pounded away.

"That was loud, but it wasn't very pretty, was it? Here, let me show you how to play a tune." She lifted Leo onto her lap, placed his right hand on the keyboard, and put her hand over his, pressing each finger slowly so that a rather warped version of "Twinkle, Twinkle, Little Star" floated into the air. Leo looked up at Sophie, eyes sparkling.

"Again!" he demanded.

Sophie hadn't taught piano before but Leo was such an attentive student, pleased by the slightest passage that sounded like a familiar melody, willing to sit quietly listening to her explain the names of the keys and how to play a scale. Like his father, he was tall and lanky and his small hand had long fingers. When he made a mistake, they both giggled.

Trevor heard the music from his second-floor bedroom/office. First, rhapsodic music, then a pause, then tentative one-note clinking. He quietly went down the stairs and stood at the door looking at his son sitting on Sophie's lap, determinedly pushing down the black and white keys. Over and over again. Hitting sour notes, without any rhythm. Sophie's arms were around his son, her graceful neck bent as she murmured so quietly into Leo's ear that Trevor couldn't hear her words. Leo pressed the keys over and over again, and then like a bird lifting off from its nest, "Twinkle, Twinkle, Little Star" emerged as a full-fledged tune into the air.

Trevor saw Leo look up at Sophie. "I did it!"

"You learn fast, Leo. I think you are a natural pianist."

Leo giggled. "That sounds like 'penis.'"

Sophie chuckled. "Silly. The word is *pianist*. Say it." She pronounced the three syllables slowly.

"Pi-an-ist," Leo echoed back, solemnly.

"Excellent. A pianist plays the piano. Do you want to try it again?"

Leo nodded eagerly. Trevor quietly slipped out of sight into the hallway, taking deep breaths to fight the tears in his eyes and calm the wave of emotion that had swept over him at the sight of his son sitting so happily on Sophie's lap.

Trevor returned to his office to work halfheartedly and absentmindedly, his ears practically aimed backward like a horse's to catch sound from downstairs. When it stopped, he heard his son running up the stairs and into his bedroom/Lego room. Should he say something? He didn't want to go all sentimental and gooey and ruin the experience for his son, so he forced himself to wait until they all went down for dinner and simply said, "Cool piano playing, Leo."

That night the entire household watched a funny Jim Carrey movie while eating popcorn. The next day dawned gray and thunderous, with ominous rumbling from the east and a persistent wind. After breakfast, Jonah biked off to meet his surf buddies in town. Lacey called Desi, but her friend wasn't available that day. Lacey slumped around the house for a while, bothering her mother, who was trying to read, insisting that she was bored and didn't like any of her books. After a while, Lacey went upstairs, returning with arms full of sheets and blankets, and began to construct a fort out of the dining room table. She put the biggest sheet over the table so that it hung down to the floor. When Trevor went down to get more coffee, he heard voices. Leo was in the fort with her and they were making plans in whispers.

Trevor carried his coffee to Sophie, who was still curled on the sofa. She wore leggings and a pale blue sweater. Her feet were bare and she had pulled a light blue cotton throw over them.

"Can we talk for a minute while everyone else is busy?" asked Trevor.

She stuck a bookmark in the pages of her novel and set it down. "Sure. What's up?"

Trevor settled in the chair across from her. "I don't want to make a fuss out of it, but it was an amazing sight to see Leo playing the piano with you. He's never shown any interest in it before."

"He learns quickly," Sophie told him. "I think he has a natural talent. He wanted to play first thing this morning, but I thought he should use up his squirming energy first. I told him we'd play this afternoon."

"You think he's really good?"

"I do."

"Do you think he could be, well, *talented?*"

The smile faded from Sophie's face. Reaching out, she picked up her coffee and looked down into the mug as if the answer lay there. "It's too soon to judge, Trevor. And I don't know if I'd wish that on him."

"Why not?"

"Playing competitively isn't for everyone. It's demanding, it's exhausting, and it steals your life."

"Whoa," Trevor said. "Tell me more."

From the dining room came peals of laughter. Lacey and Leo ran into the room, snatched up a few throw pillows, and carried them back to their fort.

Sophie sighed. "It's all so different here, isn't it? I mean, it's as if on this island we can look back at our lives as if we were looking at boats making passages toward the land."

"I kind of think you're evading the issue," said Trevor.

"Of course I am," Sophie laughed, bitterness tingeing her voice. "Look. My parents were both doctors. My father has passed away, but he did important research and traveled all over the globe. My mother's still working at the ER at Emerson Hospital. I'm their only child. They assumed I would go into medicine. I didn't want to, but I did like piano, and when my teachers told me and my parents I had serious talent, they thought, well, okay, then I could become a world-famous concert pianist."

"Ambitious parents."

"You have no idea. My father told me over and over again: *You're either a winner or a loser. No in between.* They paid for the best music teacher, bought me a Steinway baby grand, and didn't care about my grades in school. They set a strict daily practice schedule for me." Sophie smiled sadly. "My arms still ache, just remembering."

"From the brief amount I've heard you play, it sounds like you got pretty good."

"I did. Oh, I wasn't a prodigy, but I was *good.* In my high school and my town, I was a celebrity. My mother took me into New York to buy gorgeous dresses for me to wear at my concerts in competitions. I was admitted to the New England Conservatory of Music in Boston. But I didn't make it all the way."

"I don't know what you mean by that."

"Well, I'm not a concert pianist, that's for sure." Sophie paused. "Do you actually want to hear the whole grisly truth?"

"Sure."

"Okay. Well, when I was nineteen, I was chosen from all the pianists in Boston for a competition of New England young pianists taking place in New York. My mother accompanied me. My dress was perfection. My father didn't come, but before the trip he presented me with large diamond studs for my ears. It was like a fairy tale coming true. The hotel was five-star, posh, and crammed with people who loved music more than breath. I attended some of the competitions and was impressed, but not *dismayed* by the other students' virtuosity. When it was my turn to compete, I walked onstage with my head held high and my heart pounding. I felt like I was the sun, the center of the universe, the bright glowing heart of the world."

Suddenly Sophie rose, setting her coffee cup on the table, and walked to the windows, where the rain was just beginning to spill against the panes. With her back to Trevor, she softly said, "I choked. Don't ask me why. I don't know. I've gone over that moment a million times. It happens to everyone, but it had never before happened to *me*." Sophie began to pace, gesturing with her hands as she spoke. "Sometimes some slight thing will throw a performer. A disgusting cough from the front row. Or someone laughing—that's always distracting. Meeting a stranger's eyes as you walk onto the stage and seeing contempt, or even admiration. *Something.* I can't tell you what caused it, but when I sat down at the piano, I went blank. I put my hands on the keys and had no idea what I was to play. I waited, trying to make myself calm, but I *was* calm. Oh, I was nervous, too, you have to be nervous to give a good performance, but I wasn't anxious, I wasn't frightened. I cleared my throat, shuffled around on the bench, as if adjusting my dress, giving myself time to get back into my groove—but there was no groove. *Just play,* I ordered myself. If I could just begin, it all would surge back, I was sure. But I couldn't begin. I heard people whispering in the audience. The curtains backstage rustled as the master of ceremonies peeked out to check on me. I pressed one key tentatively, hoping the sound would spur on my mind—but no, nothing." Tears welled in Sophie's eyes. "It was *horrible*, Trevor—it was the single worst moment of my life." She twisted her hands together.

Quietly, Trevor said, "It must have been awful."

"Yes. Awful. I finally stood up without looking at the audience and walked offstage. I can still feel that walk in my bones and muscles. I held my head high. I could see other competitors in the wings watching me with wide eyes. The stage seemed to stretch out into eternity. The walk took forever. When I was behind the curtains, I heard a couple of girls giggling with their hands over their mouths, and I knew they were both thrilled at my failure and horrified. I just kept walking. My mother was in the audience. She rose and came to find me where I ended up, standing outside the backstage door, hugging myself, rocking myself, afraid I would shatter and fly apart."

"Was she nice about it?"

Sophie hesitated. "Yes. Yes, she was exceptionally kind that day. But she and my father were both devastated. They were furious with me when I told them I was through competing. My father's been dead for a few years. He died without forgiving me." She lowered her head and pinched the bridge of her nose.

Trevor was silent for a while, letting Sophie decompress before asking gently, "And then?"

Sophie nodded, once. "It was the end of the spring semester, so I didn't have to return to school. I went home—we lived in a Boston suburb—and stayed there for a couple of weeks, sleeping and watching television constantly. My parents pestered me, wanting me to get up and practice, but I refused." Sophie looked down at her hands, gently swiveling them palm up, palm down. "Then Zack phoned. He had just graduated from Harvard. We had met at a wedding about a month before. He asked me for dinner and I went." With a wry smile, Sophie held up her hands and said, "And that's the end of the story. I guess now I'm trying to figure out whether or not it was a happy ending."

"Are you saying you think you might have rushed into marriage?" Trevor asked.

"Rushed? I bolted. I *flew*. But to be honest, I was in love with him. Zack is a great guy—smart, articulate, charming, and handsome."

"Sounds like the perfect man."

"I thought he was, for a while. He had a vision and he needed me to help him fulfill it. He was a talented architect who wanted to run his own firm. I helped him in all the little ways a wife could. I kept his clothes immaculate. I haunted the sales for classy shirts and suits. We had rented one of the furnished houses on the market. When he invited clients home for dinner, I made gourmet meals. It was fun, actually, helping someone else achieve his dream. Then I had Jonah and we were a family and Zack was doing really well, so we bought our own house . . ."

"And what about the piano?"

"I never played again. Of course when Jonah was born and later when Lacey came along, music returned to my life in the form of children's songs, but it didn't bother me. It didn't hurt. I was happy to be simply normal. I never wanted to buy a piano for our home."

"And now?" Trevor prompted.

Sophie tapped her lip, thinking. "Well, now, first of all, I'm beginning to understand that a person can love playing music without tying it to ambition. I guess what started all this was you asking if your son could be *talented*. It's too soon to tell, I think, and I'm not the right person to make that decision. But I can say that I hope if Leo plays, he plays for pleasure, for the joy of it, not as some kind of goal. It's not necessary to be the *best*. Sometimes it's quite enough simply to be happy."

"I get what you're saying."

"Do you? Good. Because I hardly do." Sophie laughed and rose suddenly. "And now, Dr. Black, it's time for our therapy session to end." She hurried from the room.

16

ater that afternoon, Trevor sat at the top of the stairs listening to
his son learning from Sophie. He sensed that Leo would be braver
without his father watching, so he didn't go into the music room. But
even though Leo's attempt at melodic playing was hardly easy listening, Trevor was fascinated.

When would he have a chance for another intimate conversation
with Sophie? He had so much he wanted to ask her and so much he
wanted to tell her. He wanted also, fiercely, simply to be around her,
to watch her whisk eggs or brush her blond hair off her forehead or
kiss Jonah's cheek. He admired the easy communication she shared
with her children. Often if the kids were dawdling or arguing with one
another, Sophie had only to say their names in a certain tone—
Jonah—and the behavior would change. But she also took the time to
listen to their explanations if they were arguing for something they
really wanted: to go off biking with the other guys, to go back into
town for more books from the library even though they had been
there only two days ago.

Once again, he wondered if he was falling in love with her. *What a ridiculous thought*, he told himself, but over the years he had met plenty of attractive women, including gorgeous aspiring starlet friends of Tallulah's, and he'd never had this reaction. It wasn't mere lust, as it had been for Tallulah, although there was plenty of lust mixed in with the confusing jumble of emotions he felt when he saw Sophie. It wasn't simply that she was so kind to his son, helping him discover a love for music Trevor had never known existed within his child. Perhaps it was partly the complexity of the woman. She intrigued him.

But she was older than he was and more mature. He didn't want to come on to her like some pickup artist at a bar. She was elegant, and Trevor wondered if he could behave with enough elegance to be attractive to her.

The rain stopped. The sun came out. Monday and Tuesday were spectacular beach days with low humidity, clear skies, warm water, and mild surf. Monday night Trevor barbecued hamburgers on the grill while Sophie made a tomato-mozzarella salad, corn on the cob, and small red potatoes drizzled with butter and rosemary. *This is what a family is like,* Trevor thought, as they sat around the dining room table eating, chatting, laughing—even Leo was laughing. If only it could go on forever.

If only after the children were in bed Trevor could go up to bed with Sophie.

Tuesday when they came home from the beach, Trevor received a rude surprise. Once again they would have to have dinner without Sophie. She was going out with Hristo.

"Really? Where is he taking you?" asked Trevor casually as the two adults unpacked and rinsed out the sandy insulated beach coolers.

"To the yacht club, I think." The back of Sophie's neck was red and so were her shoulders. "I've got to get some lotion on my shoulders and nose. I got too much sun today."

Of course he belongs to the yacht club, Trevor thought snidely. "I'll put lotion on your shoulders," he offered.

Sophie was on her way out of the kitchen. "Thanks, Trevor, but I'll have Lacey do it after I have a quick shower." Then she was gone.

Trevor got himself a beer out of the refrigerator, slammed the door, and leaned against the kitchen counter. Why hadn't she told him earlier she had a date tonight with that Bulgarian dude? On the other hand, why *should* she tell him? He wasn't her father. He wasn't her brother. He was only some random man who through the unpredictability of fate ended up in the same house with her.

Screaming interrupted his thoughts. He went to the patio, where he saw Lacey and Leo running through the sprinkler. All that energy! Returning to the house, he wandered around aimlessly, trying to decide what to do with himself before dinner. Jonah was in the family room watching an action DVD.

"Jonah, I'm going to take a quick shower. Keep your eye on the kids for me, will you? They're playing in the sprinkler."

Jonah nodded. As Trevor showered, he reflected that he should be in a better mood. There his little boy was, running and laughing and playing, forgetting the loss of his mother in the immediacy of hot sun and cold water. This was a good thing and Trevor had to stop focusing on Sophie. The world wasn't about Sophie.

Dressing quickly, he went down to the kitchen to see what he could conjure up for dinner for everyone. The answer was easy: the refrigerator was filled with leftovers of every kind. He would simply set them out on the table and hand out fruit for dessert.

Sophie returned to the kitchen, this time wearing a skimpy blue dress that fit her far too nicely. She'd done something to her eyes so that they looked larger, and her lips looked pinker and puffier. Kissable.

Trevor cleared his throat. "You look nice."

Sophia laughed. "You sound just like my husband. I think that was the only adjective he knew, at least when it came to me. No matter what I wore, he thought I looked *nice*."

Horrified at being compared to her husband, Trevor's mind went blank. "I don't mean—I mean—"

"You look *nice* yourself, Trevor," Sophie told him. "In that ruby-red shirt, you look absolutely—" She blushed as red as his shirt and stopped talking.

"Absolutely what?" He took a step toward her.

For a long moment they stared at each other, hardly breathing. What could he say that would make her cancel this date with Hristo and stay here, with him?

Sophie broke the spell, moving away, digging in her purse, placing a piece of paper on the table. Her hands were shaking. Probably, Trevor thought, she was just excited to see Hristo. She was breathless when she said, "Here's the phone number where we'll be. My cell phone number is on the refrigerator door. Jonah can stay up as late as he wants. Actually, Lacey can stay up as late as she wants, too, as long as they are in the house when it gets dark." Before Trevor could answer, she said, "Oh! I think that's his car now." She did a twinkling thing with her fingers to say goodbye and practically ran out of the house.

"Have fun," Trevor said, not meaning it at all. She didn't hear him, anyway.

He gave the kids fifteen more minutes, then called them in for dinner. He knew that Leo would get exhausted and cranky if allowed to play too long.

"Connor says we can come watch him carve," announced Lacey around a mouthful of tomato and cold corn salad.

"That's nice," Trevor responded automatically. "When?"

"After dinner. He's sitting outside. There's still plenty of light."

"I'm going, too," Leo announced.

"Well," Trevor said, "be careful to stay away from the knife."

"Duh, Dad," Leo said.

Trevor opened his mouth and shut it. Leo had sassed him—a good sign of healing for sure.

After dinner, Trevor sat on the patio, working on his laptop and keeping an eye on Leo and Lacey. Connor sat in a lawn chair, carefully working on a block of wood, and speaking in a low voice to the children. Trevor didn't join the group. He didn't want to interfere. He liked it that Leo was so involved, so attentive.

After a while, Lacey drifted over to her fairy house, kneeling among the hostas and hydrangeas, arranging pebbles and shells. Leo remained by Connor's side. They seemed to be enjoying a conversation, a slow, unanimated chat.

He allowed Lacey and Leo to stay outside later than usual, oddly reluctant to put them to bed and be on his own on this soft summer night. It was Lacey who finally chose to come in, calling good night as she went upstairs to crawl into bed with one of her books. Trevor bathed Leo, read him a good-night story, and watched his son fall asleep at once. He wished his sleep could be as easy.

He didn't want to stand at the window watching for Sophie's return, so he ended up playing ridiculous computer games until one in the morning, when he finally heard the door open and close and Sophie's gentle tiptoeing up the stairs and into her room.

In her bedroom, Sophie simply slipped off her blue dress and let it lie where it fell at her feet. She kicked off her heels, removed her earrings, carelessly dropping them on the bureau, and collapsed into bed without brushing her teeth or doing anything else sensible and routine. She curled on her side, closed her eyes, and as if in a dream, replayed this evening with Hristo.

The yacht club was elegant, posh, and formal. They had a table by the window overlooking the harbor, a breathtaking view. At first their conversation was light, two friends sharing anecdotes of how their children had spent the day. Hristo ordered wine for them, and an appetizer of oysters Rockefeller. A group of teenagers ran up from the docks, still wearing their life vests, giggling, chatting, bronzed and ebullient after a day on the water. Sophie sensed a kind of melancholy pass over Hristo.

She said, "Tell me about your summers as a child. Did you go to Bulgaria?"

Her companion's melancholy lifted like a mist. He smiled. "Oh, yes, we were allowed to spend a great part of our summers in Bulgaria. This was in the Rhodope Mountains. You can see the Black Sea from there. The air is clear and fresh as ice."

"Did you stay in a hotel?"

"No, no, we stayed with family. Always. Our uncle had a small house on a large plot of land. Many cousins came; we all ran in a pack together. We used to pick wild strawberries and blackberries with my aunt. She made jam that would last the whole year. On rainy days we helped her. But on sunny days, we roamed like wild creatures. The land has such variety—there are caves, waterfalls, and strange rock formations. You see, this was the birthplace of the musician Orpheus. With his orphic music, he charmed all living things. Even stones could not resist him." As he spoke, Hristo's face seemed younger, less serious, less responsible.

"It sounds enchanting."

"Enchanting, yes. That is the word." Hristo fell silent. "The landscape remains. Someday I'll take Desi there."

The waiter appeared with their entrees. They focused on their delicious meals, commenting on the delicate flavors, enjoying a complementing wine. Hristo said, "Now you must tell me about *your* childhood summers."

Sophie laughed. "They were not as heavenly as yours, that's for sure. My parents were very busy, very important, so they sent me away to a series of camps from the time I was five."

"Day camps?"

"Oh, no. *Stay-away* camps, I used to think of them. They would pack me up with a sleeping bag and a duffel bag and I would be gone for a month or more at a time. We were allowed to write letters home and talk to our parents on the phone once a week, but that was the only contact we had. Not that it was terrible—it wasn't. I made some good friends and learned all sorts of skills." Laughing, she asked, "Would you like to see me start a fire with a stick and some leaves?"

"Thank you, no. I will trust your word." Hristo smiled. He prompted, "So you learned early to be independent."

"I don't suppose I ever thought of it that way." Sophie chewed her lip, remembering. "I still had my parents, and they were still together. That means something."

"You are thinking of your own marriage, now."

"I am thinking of my own *family* now," Sophie specified. "To be honest, I haven't been thinking much at all while I've been on the island. It's been so pleasant to focus simply on every day. To choose fresh new lettuces I've never tried before. To try new recipes with fish that my children might actually deign to eat. Of course, lying on the beach, swimming in the ocean—that has for me a kind of magic. As you felt in the mountains, I feel transformed."

Hristo nodded. "I understand."

"I've been reading light novels. Playing silly board games with my children. It's good to get away from real life."

The waiter appeared again to take their orders—coffee, no dessert— and went away.

"And what will you do when you return to your home in Boston?" Hristo inquired gently.

"I haven't thought much about that." Sophie shook herself as if waking from a dream. "I suppose I don't want to think about it, about the future. Also, I don't really have control of it. I've told you, my husband's in love with another woman. He moved in with her this summer. When we last talked, before I came here, before I even made the arrangements to come here, he said he wanted a divorce. For the children's sake, I'm hoping he'll change his mind."

"What do you want?"

Sophie looked at Hristo, seeing not only a handsome man but a person who was actually attracted to her. "I think I might want a divorce." She hadn't said that before to anyone. Perhaps she hadn't even known that before she spoke.

"Will you be okay financially?"

"Oh, I think so. If Zack doesn't offer to take care of us, I'm sure the courts will force him to do it." Suddenly she closed her eyes. "I can't believe I'm talking about this. I can't believe I am so calmly speaking about the dissolution of a marriage."

"You are also speaking about the beginning of a new life," Hristo reminded her.

Sophie nodded. "That's true."

His words echoed in her mind as she lay in her bed, listening to the night birds call. Hristo had walked her to the door when he brought her home, and almost ceremonially he had bent forward to kiss her cheek. Then he withdrew with a nod. Sophie felt dazzled, *enchanted*, by the man—his foreignness, his formality, his accent, his courtesy, and his attentiveness. He had listened so carefully when she spoke.

The beginning of a new life, he had said. She fell asleep easily, relaxed on good wine and sweet thoughts.

In the middle of the night, when the windows were black, she was startled awake by notes from the piano.

At first she thought she was dreaming. But only four notes sounded, over and over: DAH-dum-dum-dum. The last three notes were the same. She glanced at the bedside clock: three nineteen. Someone was downstairs, in the music room. An arrow of guilt shot through her. Did Lacey or Jonah want to learn piano but not want to ask? She slipped from her bed and hurried down the stairs.

As she entered the music room, she saw Trevor there, kneeling next to Leo, whose fingers were on the keys.

"Hey, buddy," Trevor whispered. "It's kind of late to make music. You'll wake everyone up."

"I know a song, Daddy," Leo said, but he seemed puzzled.

"Awesome, guy. Why don't you try it tomorrow when it's daylight? It's time for you to be in bed now."

"Okay." Leo surrendered, sagging against his father.

Sophie tiptoed back upstairs to her room. She heard Trevor come up the stairs carrying Leo, heard the doors shutting, and finally fell back asleep.

17

Three days later, in the middle of July, Trevor and Leo found themselves alone in the big house while Sophie, Jonah, and Lacey drove off with much ado to meet Sophie's gang at the boat. Trevor knew he and Sophie were not *together*. But as Trevor stood in the kitchen watching Leo eat his Cheerios, a sad thought occurred to him: he and Leo had probably spent more time in a family atmosphere, doing family kinds of things, *here* with Sophie than they ever had with Tallulah.

He had plenty of work to do, but instead he coaxed Leo outside for a game of Frisbee. The fresh air and exercise would do them both good.

Leo was sitting on his shoulders, straining to reach the Frisbee where it had landed on top of one of the privet bushes, when he heard the crowd arrive. Doors slammed, people laughed, and then Sophie called, "Trevor, Leo, come meet everyone!"

"I got it!" Leo yelled, clutching the Frisbee in his hand.

"Yay, you!" Trevor said. "Come on, Lacey's back."

They were all there: practical, no-nonsense Bess with her son Cash, who was just Jonah's age, and daughter Betsy, twelve years old and clearly Lacey's idol. And Angie, who came without her children because they were with her ex-husband for the month.

The women were easy to tell apart. Bess taught history in high school and was the least attractive of the three, bony and angular, with cropped hair and brusque ways, but Sophie said Bess and her husband were deeply in love. Angie was a trial lawyer and sexy as hell, with crazy black curls she tied back with a brilliant multicolored scarf. She wore a low-cut sleeveless slip dress she could have worn as a nightgown.

"You didn't tell me about Trevor," Angie purred, flashing a look at Sophie.

Sophie reddened. "Of course I did. And Leo, too."

"Mom." Jonah and Cash stood just outside the door. "I thought we were going to the beach."

"We are. Let's change into our bathing suits and load up the stuff." Sophie glanced over her shoulder at Trevor. "Do you and Leo want to come with?"

"Nah, you all have a good reunion," Trevor told her. "Leo and I have other plans." He was not going to trail after Sophie like a lovesick bull. He'd come up with a cool idea while playing Frisbee with Leo, and after they got their bathing suits on, he took Leo to Jetties Beach, rented a kayak and life vests, and took the boy out in the water.

The harbor was crowded with kayaks, sailboats, and windsurfers in a riot of Crayola colors that washed a childish happiness over the scene. From the water they could look back at all the people lying on their beach towels, or reading on beach chairs beneath umbrellas, or, of course, building sand castles. Great ferries glided past them to and from Hyannis. He had slathered both himself and his son with sunblock, and they wore T-shirts and scalloper's caps with large bills, but even so, after a couple of hours, he could feel the sun reddening his skin. He returned the kayak and took Leo up to the Jetties snack bar for lunch.

Leo fell asleep in his car seat on the way back to the guest cottage. Trevor carried him into the house and laid him on his bed to finish his nap. He took a hurried shower with the bathroom door open, listening for the sounds of Leo waking up, but when he was freshly dressed, he returned to find Leo still asleep.

He brought down his laptop and was checking emails when Sophie and her gang returned. They were giggling and chattering like a gaggle of geese. Betsy and Lacey ran up to Lacey's room immediately. The boys lumbered up to Jonah's room. Sophie, Bess, and Angie threw themselves down on the furniture around Trevor, exuding sunshine and silliness.

Trevor stood up, intending to take his laptop to his room, but Angie patted the sofa next to her and said, "Don't run away, Trevor. We won't bite. Unless you want us to," she added playfully.

"Stop that, Angie," Bess ordered. "He'll think we've been drinking."

"What a good idea!" exclaimed Angie. "I could use a drink right now."

"We're going to make a big salad for everyone, and we've brought cold cuts so the kids can make their own sandwiches," Sophie told him. She was wearing a red bikini with an open-cut white top over it. Her nose was sunburnt and her hair was messy. She was gorgeous.

"We're going to the Box after the kids are in bed," Bess told him.

"Why don't you come with us?" invited Angie.

Trevor stood there feeling like the odd man out, which, actually, was exactly what he was. "Leo—" he began.

"The older kids will be here," Sophie reminded him.

Without waiting for his decision, Sophie left the room, heading toward the utility room with an armful of wet towels. Angie rose and came toward Trevor, raising her sleek olive arms to catch her crazy curls and twist them behind her head. They immediately exploded back all around her head in a dark halo. She wore a gold bikini and, he couldn't help noticing, she had a tiny gold ring in her belly button. A long turquoise shirt covered her shoulder and arms, but she left the front unbuttoned so it exposed bits of her as she walked. In a way she reminded him of Tallulah, physical and earthy and fun-loving.

Just when he thought she was going to walk right into him, Angie veered to the side. "I'm going to make a cocktail. Want one?"

"Sure," Trevor answered. "I'm not sure if we've got the makings for one, though."

"No problem—I stopped by the liquor store on the way home." Angie sauntered into the kitchen.

Trevor headed up the stairs with his laptop. He was glad he was not being left out, but he wasn't certain he liked the way he was being included.

"How old are you?" he said to himself in the mirror. "Twelve?"

By the time he was downstairs, someone had put on music, light summer songs: "Surfin' U.S.A.," "Dancing Queen," "Flashdance," "Footloose." He checked on Leo, who was oblivious to it all as he worked on his Great Wall of China. In the kitchen, Sophie and Bess worked competently, washing lettuces, chopping vegetables, discussing movies, and sipping their drinks.

"Here," Angie said, holding out a fluorescent pink drink.

Trevor looked at it suspiciously. "What is it?"

Angie cocked an eyebrow. "It's my own concoction. I haven't named it yet. Just try it." With a clearly seductive look, she added, "I promise you it's not too sweet."

Trevor swallowed the drink, which seemed to include vodka and raspberry liqueur and something bitter with a tang. He had to admit he liked it. "It's good."

Angie took his arm and steered him toward the patio door. "Sophie and Bess have it under control in there. Sophie and Bess always have it under control. We might as well enjoy our drinks."

Once they were settled side by side in patio chairs, Angie glanced over at Trevor and remarked, "Weird, huh? The way you met Sophie. The two of you living together like this with your children. It's kind of like college. Or maybe a halfway house, not that I've ever been in one."

"True," Trevor replied. "I've tried to reach Ivan Swenson, but his number no longer responds. When I last spoke to him, he was planning to go to India. If he has gone there I don't expect to hear from him anytime soon."

"But it's working out all right, isn't it?"

"Did Sophie say that?"

"She did. She said you're really good about cleaning the kitchen." Angie threw back her head and laughed. "You can tell she's an old married woman, judging a man by how he cleans the kitchen." She threw a challenging look at Trevor, clearly giving him the go-ahead to ask how *she* judged a man.

Trevor's mind said: *Oh, man, do I really want to get into this?* Trevor's body said: *Let's go!*

"She's a champion at cooking," Trevor said. "And her children, Lacey especially, are really nice to my boy."

"Yeah," Angie said quietly, "Sophie told us you've lost your wife. How's Leo doing?"

"Okay, although he often has nightmares and tantrums."

"All kids have nightmares and tantrums," said Angie. "Few kids can focus for as long as it seems Leo can. He's really dedicated to his Legos."

"Yes, that's a new behavior, the obsession with putting Legos together. Plus he has to put his clothes out for the next day, in a certain order . . ."

"So do I, if I've got a busy day," Angie told him. "So you live in Boston?"

It took a moment for Trevor to switch gears, to stop thinking about his son's behavior and return to conversation mode. He took a sip of his drink. That helped. For a while he talked easily with Angie, telling her where he lived, what kind of work he did, and how he had kind of fallen into computers as a profession. In turn, she told him about her life. She'd been divorced for three years and had two children, nine-year-old twins, both girls. She was a partner in a Boston law firm. She liked her work and was good at it. She also liked her ex-husband and his new wife. She couldn't help it, she confessed to Trevor—she preferred to be happy in her life.

Bess called them in for dinner. Jonah and Cash got permission to take their enormous handmade sandwiches on a plate into the family room to eat while they watched a movie. Betsy and Lacey fussed around Leo, fixing his sandwich for him, asking him if he liked mayonnaise, cutting it into four triangles. After dinner, Trevor took Leo upstairs to bed. The little boy had had his bath and now he was droopy-eyed with sleepiness. Trevor started to read him a story, but Leo's eyes closed and he sort of melted into his pillow, in a luxurious deep drowse.

Trevor went down to start cleaning up the kitchen. He turned off the radio—the music was beginning to irritate him—and listened to the sounds in the house as he rinsed and stacked and carried. The three women had gone upstairs to get ready for the Box, which seemed to cause incredible hilarity. Trevor smiled to hear them. Tallulah had seldom brought girlfriends home. She hadn't particularly cared for other women, judging them as competition or criticism. It was men that Tallulah liked, men and acting, and, it seemed, heroin. It had never been the perfect marriage, but when Trevor thought of Leo, he never regretted a moment he'd spent with Tallulah.

He heard whispering and giggling. The three women were creeping down the stairs, holding their high-heeled sandals in their hands. They all wore sundresses that showed off their tans and tan lines from their bikinis. They were gleaming with mascara and lipstick, even the usually subdued Bess.

"We're going now," said Sophie, obviously unaware as she bent over to strap on her shoes how far down the front of her dress this position allowed Trevor to see.

Angie undulated over to Trevor and put her arm through his. "Please, Trevor, come with us. It would be such a favor to us if you would come. Then we'd look more like a party."

"The kids—" began Trevor.

"The kids are fine," Sophie told him. "I've given Jonah orders to keep an eye on the kids, especially Leo. He'll call me if Leo wakes up and needs you. Come on," she added with a mischievous smile. "You could use some fun in your life."

So he ended up driving the three women to the long, low rectangular building hidden on a side street near a pharmacy and a Stop & Shop. The Box was surrounded by people of all ages lounging against cars smoking and talking. Inside, the large room pulsed with music. Almost everyone was dancing to techno versions of the latest hits.

"I'll get the drinks," Trevor offered.

The women only nodded—no one could hear over the music—and deserted him to squeeze onto the dance floor. Trevor wedged himself between two overgrown boys who smelled as if they'd been landscaping all day. In a zoo.

He waited patiently to order their drinks. He kept his eye on the women. Clearly fueled by a day of sunshine and freedom from mommyhood, the trio danced with abandon, laughing, tossing their hair, waving their arms, shaking their booty. Angie had the body the most like Tallulah's. She had that kind of aura, too, her presence flashing in Times Square neon: *Look at me! Come and get me!* She would be some-

thing to get, Trevor realized. It had been a long time since he had
been with a woman, since he had comforted himself by sinking into
the softness of a curvaceous female.

When the drinks finally arrived, he managed to collect them and
squeeze through the crowd to a table at the far end of the room. Mango
Tinis for the women, just a beer for him. He was the designated driver.

"Thanks, Trevor," Angie cooed when he set the drinks down.

"I don't want to drink," Sophie said. "I want to dance. Come on,
Trevor." Sophie took his hand and pulled him to the dance floor.
Their linked hands made his blood flash. For a moment he was almost
paralyzed with surprise—that she was touching him, that he felt this
way, that when she turned to face him, her eyes were full of desire.

Sophie began to dance, lifting her arms and surrendering to the
music. She swayed, moving her hips but keeping her eyes locked on
his.

"Tre-vor," she said teasingly, laughing, almost taunting.

The pounding beat of the powerful bass filled him and he danced.
He wasn't a fancy dancer but he knew he had some good moves, a
slight tilt of the shoulders, a slow roll, starting with his feet, moving
through him. What was Sophie thinking? he wondered. Did she have
any idea of the effect she was having on him?

A massive blond surfer dude not much older than her own son slid
between Trevor and Sophie, facing Sophie, nodding at her, putting
his hands on her hips. He looked Scandinavian, the kind of muscular
contractor who could toss around beams without taking a deep breath.
The dance floor heaved with motion. Light flared over the crowd.
Trevor kept dancing, caught up in the music, not caring that he had
no partner—well, except for hating the Scandinavian—and suddenly
Angie was there, sliding next to him, undulating in front of him, turn-

ing her back and sliding her body against his, her sweet ass skimming his crotch.

He wasn't drunk. He wasn't an asshole. But he was a male who could read signals when they were sent to him as clearly as Angie was sending them. *This isn't a good idea,* he told himself. But Sophie wasn't a girlfriend—Sophie was barely a friend—or if she had become a friend it was only because of pure chance.

Searching, he caught sight of Sophie and her surfer. Trevor had to admit the guy was a great dancer in a crazy, floppy kind of way, but when he saw him catch Sophie by the waist and pull her to him, when he saw her reach up to put her arms around his neck, Trevor ripped his eyes back to Angie. *All right, then,* he thought. *All right.* When Sophie had pulled Trevor out to the dance floor, it had been only because she wanted to dance, nothing more. He got the message loud and clear. He kept dancing with Angie.

The bar closed at one, spilling people stumbling and howling with laughter out onto the road. They dispersed to their various cars, gradually becoming aware of the cop car parked at the end of the street. Trevor's three passengers piled into the backseat, falling on top of each other, snickering and snorting. With a great show of sober maturity, he sat in the front seat, fastened his seat belt, and started the car. He kind of hoped a cop would stop him and give him a breathalyzer test. He'd look like a hero, the designated driver who kept them all safe.

But they weren't stopped by a cop. Trevor drove home through the dark night, unable to avoid listening to the backseat conversation.

"Sophie, why didn't you go home with that big blond guy? He was a hunk." Angie dug through her purse as she spoke, suddenly and irrelevantly adding, "I don't smoke! I was looking for my cigarettes and I forgot I gave up smoking!"

The women howled with laughter. "Bess," Sophie said, "I think that Jamaican dude was hitting on you."

"I think he was, too," Bess admitted. "I couldn't help thinking—" She stopped suddenly. "Tell you later." In the rearview mirror, Trevor saw Bess's eyes flick warningly toward him. Clearly this was something not for his ears.

"I know what you're thinking." Angie pulled her friends' heads toward her in a huddle and they began to whisper.

Trevor tried not to roll his eyes. He wanted to say, *Sophie, why didn't you go home with that big blond guy?* But he kept his mouth shut all the way home.

"I'm going to have such a headache in the morning," wailed Bess.

"Drink lots of water before you go to bed," advised Angie. "Besides, I don't think we drank that much—we were always dancing."

"I agree with Angie," said Sophie. "Now that we're out of there, away from the music, I don't feel drunk, I feel limp."

"Me, too," Bess agreed. "Angie and I are sleeping on the family room pullouts, right?"

"Right," Sophie said, and yawned so hard she squeaked.

By the time they arrived home, the women were quiet. The giggling phase had given way to concern about not waking the children, and everyone went carefully to their beds. Trevor took the world's quickest shower and shampoo, glad to relieve himself of the beer/smoke/sweat stink of the evening. He checked on Leo, who was sleeping deeply. He dropped into his own bed like a felled tree.

It seemed he'd barely closed his eyes when he sensed movement in the room, a rustling noise, the door he usually kept open for Leo being closed, the lock clicking shut. Perfume drifted toward him, and he opened his eyes. Angie, in a scarlet lace nightie, slid down onto the bed next to him.

"Hello, big boy," she whispered, drawing her hand down his chest.

In spite of himself, Trevor moaned. Pulling himself up to a sitting position, he said quietly, "Angie, I don't think this is such a good idea."

"I think it's a very good idea." She sat up, too, allowing one of the straps on her nightgown to slip down her shoulder.

"Look, I'm in no shape to start a relationship."

Angie chuckled. "Who said anything about a relationship? I'm here for one night of pleasure." She ran her hand along his thigh toward his crotch.

His body responded. "My son's asleep in the next room."

"Are you asking me to be quiet? I can be quiet." Quietly, she slid around the bed so that she was sitting on top of him. She put her finger to her lips and whispered, "Ssssh."

He felt her sweet, alcohol-scented breath against his lips. Still, Trevor hesitated. He had never known any woman except Tallulah, no matter what she said *before*, not to expect more *after* having sex.

"I think you're in love with Sophie," Angie teased.

"I'm not in love with Sophie!" Trevor insisted.

Angie continued as if she hadn't heard him. "But Sophie isn't here. Sophie is getting all hot and bothered over that Bulgarian guy." As she spoke, she slowly rolled her body against his, smiling wickedly as she felt him respond. "I'm here now."

The summer moon filled the room with light. Trevor could see Angie's smile. She was a warm, luscious woman. He put his arms around her and pulled her down on the bed.

18

The next morning, it took Sophie about nine seconds to realize that Angie had slept with Trevor. It wasn't that Angie flaunted it, it was that Sophie knew her friend so well. When Angie had been made love to, she glowed like a firefly.

Sophie had risen late, feeling slow and lazy on this hot, muggy day. She could hear people bustling around downstairs, so she took the opportunity to catch a quick shower and wash her hair. In shorts and a tank top with her shaggy blond hair damp against her neck, she went down to the dining room to see what was going on.

Trevor was in the kitchen making pancakes. Jonah and Cash sat at the dining room table, eating a gigantic pile of them like a couple of drifters who'd been starved for days. Leo was under the kitchen table, sitting next to his Great Wall of China, eating Cheerios from a bowl by hand. Lacey and Betsy were outside, playing with the fairy house. Bess was in the living room talking to her husband on her cell phone.

Angie lounged at the dining room table, clad in a brilliantly flowered sarong that exposed more flesh than it covered. "Hey, sleepyhead," she greeted Sophie. "About time." Her smile was smug. "Sit down, sweetie, and Trevor will make you some pancakes."

Sophie sat down as invited, but Angie's proprietary air grated on her nerves. Who was Angie to tell her what Trevor would do? Meeting Angie's eyes, Sophie knew exactly what had happened.

Trevor turned from the stove with a plate full of pancakes. "Pancakes, Sophie? Want a cup of coffee?" He wouldn't meet Sophie's gaze and his face was crimson. Sophie was pretty sure it was not from the heat of cooking.

"No pancakes, thanks," Sophie said coolly, even though she was starving. "I'll get my own coffee." Rising, she brushed past him headed toward the coffeepot. She couldn't understand why she was angry with him. Did she think he had taken advantage of her friend? But no one took advantage of Angie. Could Sophie possibly be jealous? That was patently ridiculous. She had known him for three weeks. She'd never see him again after this summer. He was a boy.

Yet she felt herself on the verge of tears. She absolutely shocked herself when she heard herself say, casually, leaning against the kitchen counter, "Hey, guys, how would you all like to go sailing on a yacht today? Hristo has offered to take us out whenever the weather is right and today looks pretty nice. I could give him a call and see if he's up for it."

Jonah lifted his head. "That would be cool, Mom."

Next to him, Cash echoed, "Cool, yeah."

Bess strolled in, sliding her cell phone into the pocket of her jean shorts. "Good morning, Sunshine," she said to Sophie. "You slept late." Pulling out a chair, she joined them at the table. "Did you get any pancakes? They were delicious."

Good grief, could anybody talk about anything except the damned pancakes? "I was asking everyone if they'd like to go for a sail today." Out of the corner of her eye, Sophie noticed how Trevor's face had shut down. He put the plate of pancakes on the table and returned to the kitchen at the same moment Sophie carried her coffee in to the dining room. They passed each other like ships in the night and did not speak.

"Gosh, I'd love to," Bess said.

Angie sauntered into the kitchen and knelt down face-to-face with Leo, who crouched beneath the table with his Legos. "Want to go on a big boat today, Leo?" She sounded as if she were offering candy-coated cake.

She thinks it's more than a one-night fling, Sophie thought, *if she's trying to ingratiate herself with Trevor's son.*

Leo looked up at Angie with his huge green eyes. "I want to play the piano with Sophie."

Bess gaped at Sophie.

Angie, always the interrogator, asked, "Are you playing again, Sophie?"

Sophie shrugged. "Maybe. There's a piano here, an entire music room." She knelt next to Leo. "I want to play with you, too, Leo. Would you like to, now?"

Leo's hands were full of small round O's. "When I'm through with my Cheerios."

"That's fine. No hurry."

"In the meantime," Angie challenged, "let's hear *you* play, Soph. Can you remember how?"

"Kind of. If you want to know, you're free to listen. I'll leave the door open to the music room."

She took her time walking to the music room. Lifting the lid of the bench, she took out some sheet music she'd discovered there and chose Beethoven's "Für Elise," a quiet, gentle, almost melancholy piece that required delicacy and restraint. While she played, the others wandered into the music room and crowded onto the rose-covered sofa.

When she lifted her hands from the keyboard, Bess said, "My goodness, Sophie, that was luscious. You play as well as you always did."

Angie cocked an eyebrow. "Yeah, but can you play 'All You Need Is Love'?"

Sophie felt her shoulders tense at Angie's witticism. Something about this visit was bringing out Angie's competitive qualities. And, she had to admit, her own.

Sophie launched into "All You Need Is Love," embroidering it with chords and flourishes. She played it too quickly, without feeling, or rather with a feeling of spite, even revenge—not just on Angie; she loved Angie, she understood Angie—but on everything, on Zack, on her mother and father, on herself for letting this all go, for being a failure—and then she stopped.

"So." Standing up, she stretched her arms. "Leo, want to play with me now?"

Leo's glance flew toward Bess and Angie.

Bess said, "Come on, Angie, let's help Trevor clean the kitchen."

When they were alone, Sophie lifted Leo onto her lap. "Can you find Middle C? Good! Press it."

Leo pressed it and looked up at Sophie for more.

"Now, remember the scales?" She sang the notes aloud as she played them. "Eight notes. Eight notes make an octave. When we learn to play the piano, we learn to play the scales over and over again."

"Like learning to write my name," Leo said.

Sophie beamed. "Yes, Leo. Like learning to write your name."

When Leo's hands grew tired, he slipped off Sophie's lap and wandered out of the room. A moment later, Bess and Angie stormed in.

"We are so not going sailing today," Bess announced. "Trevor is taking the kids to the beach, and you are sitting here and telling us why you're playing again."

"Good," Sophie said. "I'd like that. I've been waiting for you two."

"Mom." Jonah stood in the hall, barefoot, beach towel in one hand. "Cash and I are going with Trevor to the beach. He's taking the girls and Leo, too. We'll be home this afternoon."

Lacey, holding hands with Leo, wiggled behind Jonah and sang to her mother, "Trevor's going to buy us lunch at the snack stand!" Lunch at the snack stand was always a point of contention between Sophie and her children because it cost so much money, so much more than the sandwiches and juice she prepared and took to the beach.

This time, Sophie didn't argue. "Have fun, kids." As Trevor walked toward the front door, beach bag in one hand, car keys in the other, she called, "Thanks, Trevor."

"Got it." Trevor waved without looking at her and the gang left the house.

Bess settled on the sofa, Angie at the other end. Sophie chose an armchair facing them.

Bess leaned forward. "When did you start playing again?"

Sophie smiled. "It's kind of funny. I started playing the moment I walked into this house and saw the piano. I've been playing occasionally when no one else is around. One time Leo heard me and wanted to learn how to do it." Thoughtfully, she added, "Oh, and I played at Hristo's house, too. He has a piano for his daughter."

"But *why?*" Bess probed. "Why did you start again? Why play for your children and Trevor and Leo and Hristo?"

"I've been trying to understand that myself. You know I was good back in high school. And you know I failed."

"*Once,*" Angie interjected. "You choked one time."

"At an important competition. I humiliated myself, my teacher, and my parents. I failed my parents."

"You didn't—" Bess began.

"In their eyes, I did," Sophie cut in. "I failed myself most of all. I wanted to be the best. I wanted, I guess, all or nothing."

"You're a perfectionist," Angie said.

"Am I? I suppose I am, in some ways. But I was both relieved and heartbroken when I gave up piano."

"Honey, you didn't have to give it up. You're so good," Bess urged.

"But I was *supposed* to be *the best*." Sophie waved her hand. "The point is, I did give it up. I was *done*. My parents were pretty much sick of the sight of me. When I met Zack, he gave me a new reason to live, a *way* to live. He was so energetic, optimistic, confident, outgoing— he was like a gorgeous towering wave that picked me up and carried me along with him." Leaning back in her chair, she allowed herself to remember. "Suddenly, I wasn't a failure, I was a *girlfriend*. You remember—I began to have fun. I saw movies, I read books, I went Rollerblading without being afraid I'd break my precious wrist."

"Did Zack know about your music?"

"Not much. I didn't want to talk about it much. So for him, I was a lovely blank page for him to write on. He was starting his firm. He needed a sounding board/bookkeeper/secretary. I could answer the phone, I could type, I could be charming."

"You devoted your own life to his," Angie said.

"True. But Angie, I loved it back then. I had so much fun; I learned about parts of myself I had never known existed. I gained so much self-confidence when I was with Zack. I learned to cook, I found plea- sure in keeping house, the world became so sensual to me—spreading clean sheets on a bed, the smell of rain on grass, and laughter, espe- cially laughter. When my children came, their sweet, small bodies—" Tears filled Sophie's eyes. "Once I had my children, I didn't even think about performing."

"All right," Bess said. "I get all that. But why did you start again, here?"

Sophie shifted on the armchair. "Well, there's a piano here, for one thing."

"Now *there's* an evasive response," Angie said.

"Okay. You're right. But it's complicated." Sophie took a moment to think. "The best answer I can come up with is that here on this island, without Zack nearby, I feel free. Especially free from the weight of judgment. You both know what I'm talking about—you live with it, too. We all live with it. Do our husbands still think we are pretty, sexy, exciting? Well, Zack has made it very clear to me that he's found someone prettier, thinner, sexier, and unarguably younger than I am."

"If you've lived your marriage basing its strength on Zack's opinion of you physically, then you've got a pretty sad marriage," Angie said.

Sophie didn't argue. "You think?"

They sat in silence, the three women, occupied with their own thoughts. After a while, Bess asked gently, "Do you think you'll keep up with it now, Sophie?"

"Not professionally!" Sophie answered, almost rearing back. "I'll never be that good again."

"Why does it have to be professionally? Can't it be just for yourself? For pleasure, for the love of it?"

"Right, Bess." Angie nodded sharply. "Bess is right. Play because you want to and don't worry about being a perfectionist."

"I'm hardly a perfectionist," Sophie argued.

Angie snorted.

Bess stood up. "I need to move."

"Me, too," said Sophie. "Thanks for listening to my true confessions. Now let's go to the beach."

19

As it turned out, Sophie didn't go to the beach. She was in the mood to cook. Partly, she told herself, it was to treat her friends for being so generous in their attentions to her, and to treat the kids, especially the big boys Jonah and Cash, for not fussing about all the seafood they were served while their guests were here.

On the spur of the moment, she phoned Hristo to invite him and Desi. Unfortunately they already had plans, which put a damper on Sophie's spirits, but only for a moment. She phoned Connor down in the apartment.

"Please come for a meal with us tonight," she said. "My two best friends are here, and Jonah's good friend Cash, and Lacey's friend Betsy. I'm making a huge lasagna, one of my specialties."

After a long moment of silence, Connor replied, "Why, thank you very much. I would enjoy that indeed. With one condition: that you will come here for dessert. I picked two quarts of blueberries from the wild bushes at the back of the property and I've been wondering what to do with them all. My wife taught me how to make a blueberry pie before she died because she knows that's my favorite dessert. If you could bring along some vanilla ice cream, it would go nicely."

"It's a deal," agreed Sophie, adding ice cream to her list.

She dropped Angie and Bess at Surfside and drove into town. She went to Moor's End to buy fresh lettuces, red and yellow tomatoes, basil, zucchini, onions, and spinach. She went to Annye's Whole Foods to purchase a large selection of olives and cheeses, figs, garlic, prosciutto, cantaloupe, marinated red peppers, artichoke hearts in olive oil, and baguettes shipped over from Pain D'Avignon. At the Stop & Shop, when she finally found a parking place, she bought the rest of the necessities: ground beef, lasagna noodles, lots of different chips and crackers, and of course the vanilla ice cream. One more stop: Hatch's Package Store, where she loaded up on an assortment of good red wines.

At home, she put on a CD of *Tosca* and sang along with it as she prepared the various layers of a large pan of beef lasagna and one of spinach lasagna. She roasted the red peppers and blended them in the food processor with garlic, goat cheese, olive oil, basil, and rosemary to make a dip to serve as an appetizer with the plate of antipasto she would put out. No fish or shellfish in anything; over the past three weeks they had had fish almost every day. When the lasagna was in the oven, she washed the lettuces and tore them into a wooden bowl, ready for dressing at the last moment. She took out the most colorful tablecloths she could find in the cupboards and spread them over the tables outside and in the dining room. At Moor's End, she'd bought several bundles of fresh summer flowers. She had put these in water when she first got home; now she arranged them in various vases and pitchers and set them around on the tables. Then she hurried to take a shower and dress before everyone arrived home from the beach.

She chose a cute blue-checked gingham sundress that might have been a bit too low-cut for her to wear except on the beach, but it was a hot night and she looked good in it. She ruffled her increasingly shaggy hair, clicked on hoop earrings, and took special pains with her makeup. She hadn't really cared what she looked like before except on her dates with Hristo, but tonight she felt playful and even daring. In the back of her mind—oh, what the hell, it was *her* mind after all—in the *front* of her mind, she thought: *Okay, Angie, you can look sexy; well, guess what? So can I.*

Her friends and the kids had caught a ride home from the beach with Trevor. Around five, everyone spilled into the house at once, hot and sandy, hungry and thirsty. They raced off to shower and came back downstairs.

"What smells so good?" asked Trevor. He wore board shorts and a clean T-shirt that said, *Never trust an atom. They make up everything.*

"I'm in an Italian mood today," Sophie told him. "I invited Connor to join us. He'll be up any minute. And we're going to his place for dessert!"

Trevor stared at her, squinting his eyes as if she'd become a problem to solve.

"I'd love it if you'd open some of the wine," she cooed, sending the subliminal signal: *You believe I'm jealous because you slept with Angie? Ha! Look how happy I am.*

"Sure," Trevor said, going into the kitchen.

"Mom." Jonah slumped into the kitchen, his freshly shampooed hair dripping on his shoulders, Cash behind him. "What smells so good?"

"Lasagna," she told him. "Go outside—I've set chips and a tub of iced drinks out there."

"Awesome." Jonah and Cash bumped into each other getting to the door to the patio.

Lacey and Betsy were next, shepherding Leo in front of them. "Mom, we're so tired from being in the sun all day. Could we watch some television?"

"I think that's an excellent idea," said Sophie. "Trevor, what do you think?"

"Fine with me," Trevor agreed.

"Here, take this in with you." She handed her daughter a plate of sliced carrots, cucumbers, and cheese and handed Leo a basket of chips.

The kids hurried to the family room, giggling. Bess came into the kitchen with her short hair still damp and her pretty face free of makeup. She wore a loose sundress and no jewelry.

"What can I do?" she asked.

"Help yourself to a glass of sangria and relax on the patio," Sophie told her. "I made lasagna. Connor Swenson, the old gentleman in the apartment, is coming up for dinner and we're going there for dessert. I'll be out in a moment."

"Fabulous," said Bess. "This is a perfect day."

It wasn't until Sophie and Trevor had joined Bess and the boys on the patio that Angie made her appearance. She had taken the time to blow-dry her curly black hair, which she wore loose and free. She wore a long, multicolored gypsy skirt with tiny bells on the hem that tinkled seductively when she walked and a skimpy white tank top with no bra so that her dark nipples showed clearly.

"Wow, Sophie! What a feast! I'm ravenous!" Angie slid a smile at Trevor as she spoke, making it clear exactly what she was hungry for.

As the group gathered on the patio, sipping drinks, selecting munchies from the table with its bright cloth, flowers, and abundance of food, Connor Swenson came toward them over the lawn, moving slowly, leaning on a cane. Sophie introduced him to her friends, noticing that the side of one of Connor's deck shoes had been cut open. She didn't remark on it, but quickly ushered him to a chair. Trevor asked the older gentleman what he'd like to drink and handed him a cold beer.

And then, as Sophie had thought it would, a perfect summer evening unfurled beneath the cloudless sky. She passed around the platter of antipasto. Trevor kept everyone's glass filled. Bess clicked photos of everything with her phone before subsiding into her chair. Angie, not to be overlooked, carried the chips and Sophie's red pepper dip to Connor, kneeling before him to hold the plate as he dipped a chip, her gypsy skirt swirling on the patio tiles.

After a while, they all went in for dinner. Sophie had put candles on the table, and now she lighted them and turned off most of the lights in the house. She called the kids to come join them, so it was a grand total of ten people of all ages gathered around the table enjoying lasagna, salad, and crusty garlic bread.

They talked about the island, the seals they'd caught sight of in the water, the great white shark rumored to be hanging out at Great Point, the fabulous variety of birds winging through the air—hawks, cormorants, crows, cardinals, and finches—as well as the snowy swans swimming in local ponds and the mallards who lived in shallow water at the end of the harbor and often stopped traffic on Orange Street as they crossed to visit local lawns.

Connor mentioned that he was carving a duck decoy and the conversation turned to him. Everyone, especially the children, was fascinated to hear that he'd been a farmer in Iowa.

"Oh, yes," Connor told them, "I was a real farmer. I had a herd of polled Herefords. You all probably don't know what polled means. It means that they've been bred to be hornless. Less danger, especially from the bulls."

"Did you have a bull?" Leo's eyes were wide.

Connor laughed and leaned back in his chair. "Yes, Leo. I had many of them."

"Were they scary?"

"Truthfully, yes, they were. Or could be. Cows—the females—are pretty mild-tempered, but bulls can be unpredictable, especially when the cows are"—he stopped to think of a euphemism—"ready to mate. And bulls are territorial."

"What does that mean?" asked Lacey.

Connor explained and went on to describe a time when his wife, Audrey, had taken a liking to a newborn bull she named Wooly Bully. He had curly white hair on his forehead and he loved for her to scratch it. Whenever Audrey came out of the house, Wooly Bully would run to the fence and bellow for her. But he grew up and moved to another field, and Audrey didn't see him as often.

"One day, after a spring storm had washed out a fence, Wooly Bully wandered over into a neighbor's field. How to get him home? By then he was three years old, in full possession of his male properties, and he weighed over three thousand pounds. He was not especially mean, but bulls and cows in general tend to butt one another with their heads to communicate. One hard knock with his head could send a human unconscious. Audrey, just a tiny thing weighing scarcely over a hundred pounds, insisted she could bring him home. So she walked right over into that field of fescue, walked right up to that great big animal, cooing his name the whole time. He snorted. He pawed on the ground. It had been quite a while since Audrey had scratched his forehead, and it was possible he had forgotten her and would consider her an invader." Connor paused to take a drink.

Sophie looked around the table as Connor spoke. The children were fascinated, even big Jonah and Cash. The adults were calm but engrossed, their lips shining in the candlelight with olive oil and wine. Everyone looked beautiful to Sophie. She thought she would always remember this moment.

"Hurry up! Tell us what happened!" cried Leo.

Trevor's face bloomed with a smile to hear his son interact normally. His eyes flew to Sophie's and they exchanged a quick nod of triumph.

"Well," continued Connor, "Audrey walked right up to that bull and reached up—he was a big one—and scratched his forehead. He blew out his breath, making a noise like this"—Connor created a huffing sound with a low bass rumble—"and snorted, and knocked Audrey for more scratching. But here's the thing: he didn't knock her hard. He did it just about as gently as any bull could. And there I was standing on the other side of the fence, my heart in my throat with fear for her, and what does she do? She reaches up and puts her arms around the bull's neck and hugs him and whispers in his ear." Connor took out a handkerchief and blew his nose. His eyes were shiny with tears. "That bull hadn't forgotten her. He was like Audrey's puppy dog. She fastened the lead rope around him and led him back to our field." Connor barked a short laugh. "I'd better add that I had to leave the battlefield sharpish. He wasn't so happy to see me."

"Do you miss your farm?" asked Lacey, a distressed expression on her face.

"Yes, I do, Lacey. But you know, I'm an old man now and I can't do what I used to do. Plus farms aren't what they used to be. A corporation bought my property and farms it with machines. They knocked down our hundred-year-old farmhouse and our barns. When we lived there, we had cats, dogs, chickens, a couple of horses, and of course the cows. Now no animals live on that land. Things change. That's just the way it is." A shadow passed over Connor's handsome old face, but then he resolutely brightened. "But change can bring good things, too. You children have seen my carving. I didn't have time to really enjoy it when I worked the farm. In fact, whenever you're ready, we can go on over to my house for dessert and I'll show you around."

Sophie was afraid the kids in their excitement would hurry to Connor's house before he could get there. "Connor, why don't you go with Bess, Angie, and Trevor, while the children and I wrap up some of this food for tomorrow?"

"Mom," objected Jonah.

"Mommy, that's not fair," Lacey whined.

"It won't take long," Sophie said cheerfully with a note of iron in her voice.

So the adults rose from the table and slowly ambled over to the apartment. Sophie blew out the candles and turned on the lights. She organized the kids to clear the table outside and in the dining room. She put the leftovers in Tupperware containers or wrapped them in foil. She loaded the dishwasher. She rinsed out the empty wine bottles and gave them to Jonah and Cash to put in the recycling bin. She told the kids to use the bathroom and wash their hands, and was pleasantly relieved when Leo obeyed her without question.

As they walked through the grass, light faded from the sky, and the stars began to flick on, one by one, as if someone were passing through rooms above, turning them on. A hawk—Sophie thought it was a hawk—shrilled in the trees. The night was muggy and still. Lacey's fairy house and Leo's Lego fort were black shapes in the fuzzy gray bushes.

Connor's apartment was almost too small to hold ten people. Sophie found it oddly thrilling to see the place, at last. It was very simple: one large room with a galley kitchen at one end. A door, always closed these days, connected to the music room. Stairs led to a loft bedroom and a bathroom. A recliner faced a large-screen television. An end table next to the recliner was stacked with books and magazines.

The surprise was that in place of a dining table, a long worktable stretched against the wall. A vise was attached to the table and on the wall next to it hung knives, chisels, clamps, hammers, pliers, and tools Sophie couldn't name. Each implement was outlined in white chalk so that the correct tool would always be returned to its proper place. Blocks of wood were stacked at one end of the table. Next to it were several tubes of paint, lacquers, and wood sealers. Jars of turpentine, containers of brushes, a basket of rags, and a dustpan and small brush sat at the other end of the worktable. It was a world unto itself. Sophie could imagine getting lost in the intricate creation of a wooden bird with all the exact markings and feathers of an actual bird.

"Awesome," Jonah said as they gathered around the worktable.

"I can't see!" cried Leo, and Trevor picked him up.

"Can I try?" asked Lacey, reaching for a block of wood.

"Absolutely not," Sophie quickly told her daughter. "Those knives are sharp."

"Perhaps you might help me soften this ice cream by putting it in the microwave," Connor said to Lacey. "I know how to use it, but I never can judge how long for what food and I don't want to turn the ice cream into mush."

Lacey, complimented by Connor's assumption that she knew such things, directed her attention away from the carvings to help Connor soften the ice cream and spoon it over the plates of blueberry pie he had already prepared.

It was too crowded in the apartment, so the group went outside and sat in a circle on the grass to eat their desserts. Light fell from the open door of Connor's apartment, illuminating their party. Behind them, the Swensons' house rose like a ship on a black-green sea, the windows glowing rectangles of light gold.

Trevor sat next to his son, helping him balance his bowl on his legs.

"This is delicious," said Sophie.

"My wife's recipe," Connor told her. "We used to pick the berries from wild bushes growing all around the farm."

While everyone else talked about recipes and berries, Trevor concentrated on helping his son spoon the food into his mouth without dropping it all over his clothes. He was grateful to have such a task so obviously require his attention. Angie had been shooting him sly complicit looks all evening, as if she wanted to make certain everyone around knew they were a couple.

They would never be a couple. Angie was fierce and controlling, almost gymnastic in her frenzy. As they made love, she pinched him, slapped him, and growled. On the side of his neck he wore an unattractive love bite she had given him during their session. That had been oddly arousing and repellent at the same time. He couldn't stop himself from thinking of vampire movies and ritualistic brandings, and no matter how he tried to pry her away from him, Angie was determined. He suspected she was trying to literally leave her mark for her friends to see. She was a beautiful woman but rather frightening. He had a feeling she thought she owned him now, and that was absolutely not true.

"Connor," Bess said, putting her empty bowl on the ground and leaning back on both arms, "thank you. That was scrumptious."

"And your carvings are amazing!" Angie added. "Why don't you try to sell them in town? I'm sure a lot of shops would carry them."

Connor chuckled. "I'm no master artist. Besides, trying to sell them would take all the fun out of it. I'd start comparing my carvings with those of other people and then I'd feel that I wasn't as good. If my carvings didn't sell, I'd really take a hit to my ego and I'd probably stop carving. My Audrey said to me when I started carving birds, *you don't want to let it get out of hand.*" He chuckled again at the pun. "Of course, she was probably referring to the mess of wood shavings that fell off my clothes when I came in from my shed."

Angie, appearing slightly miffed at having her brilliant idea rejected, scanned the area around them restlessly. Suddenly, she cried, "Oh, Leo! What is all this under the bushes? Legos?" Talking to herself—"They're plastic, I guess, so the rain won't hurt them"—she crawled a few feet to the bushes at the side of the yard. "What is all this? Honey, you have them arranged in *lines.* Hasn't anyone shown you what else you can do with Legos?"

Without waiting for Leo's response, Angie began to pick out certain Legos and move them around, saying, "You see, if you take a few pieces out *here,* you have the doorway and you can put the Legos up *here* so they make turrets. Now, start a wall of Legos here to make a rectangle which will end up being a castle, which is much more fun than just a straight line—"

"No!" screamed Leo. Jumping up, he ran to his Legos and threw his body down over them. "No, no! You ruined it. Stop it! Stop it! Daddy, help!" He continued shrieking, his small limbs flailing.

Shocked, Angie moved back immediately, flashing a horrified look at Sophie. "Sorry, Leo. I was only trying to help."

Her words were drowned out by Leo's hysterical cries as he frantically tried to return his Legos to their proper place. Seizing a turret, he knocked over several other Legos and dissolved into sobs.

Angie put her hand on Trevor's arm. "Oh, gosh, I'm so sorry. What can I do?"

"It's all right," Trevor told her. He felt bad for her. She had only been trying to be friendly. "He'll calm down. He's kind of touchy these days."

Sophie stood up. "It's getting late. I think everyone is sleepy. Connor, we'll take the bowls to the house and load them in the dishwasher. We'll return them tomorrow."

"Suits me." Connor had been sitting in a lawn chair just outside his doorway. Now he rose stiffly. "Thank you, Sophie, for that wonderful feast."

"You're more than welcome."

Angie followed Sophie. Trevor joined Leo beneath the bushes, clicking the Legos back into place. Leo was calming down and Trevor thought, *Thank God.* It was painful when his son freaked out like this, especially in front of a group. He had thought Leo was getting better, too. When Leo was finally satisfied that the Legos were in the right place, he allowed Trevor to lead him back to the house and went through his bedtime ritual easily.

Trevor tucked his son in, kissed his forehead, double-checked the nightlight, and left the room, closing the door behind him.

Angie was there in the hallway, leaning against the wall. "Trevor, I'm sorry for causing your son such misery."

She was lovely, and her apology, her own misery, seemed genuine. If he turned her away tonight, she would think he was angry with her, or sulking. Trevor embraced her, kissing the top of her head. "It's fine. He's fine."

She nuzzled his neck. "And you? Can I make you *fine?*"

He didn't want to hurt her feelings. Plus, she was a delicious woman. "I'd like that," he murmured, and with his arm around her, he led her into his bedroom.

In the dark of night, Trevor sat up in bed, heart pounding. His paternal alarm system was blaring through his body: something was wrong. Crawling over Angie's sleeping body, he dropped to the floor, pulled on his swim shorts, and hurried out to his son's room.

Leo wasn't there.

Then he heard it: notes from the piano, the same four notes played over and over again, gently, experimentally, and then with more firmness.

"Shit," Trevor murmured. He raced down the hall and down the stairs.

His son stood alone in the long music room, illuminated by moonlight, pressing the ivory keys.

"*Leo.*" Trevor didn't want to startle his son—was the boy doing some sort of sleepwalking?

Leo turned and smiled at Trevor. "Hi, Daddy."

"Leo, we talked about this. No playing piano in the middle of the night."

Leo hung his head guiltily. "I just wanted . . ."

"What, honey? What do you want?"

"I'm ready to go back to bed now," Leo said.

"Good. Night is the time to sleep." Trevor knelt to pick up Leo, who wrapped his arms around Trevor's neck.

Back in Leo's bedroom, Trevor tucked his son in gently. "Go to sleep now," he said.

Leo fell asleep at once. Trevor watched him for a while. His child looked peaceful in his sleep.

"Is everything okay?" Angie whispered from the doorway.

Trevor walked over to her. "He wakes up in the night, sometimes."

"Is he okay now?"

"I think so."

She held out her hand. "Come back to bed."

Trevor shook his head. "I think I'd better sleep in here with him tonight."

Angie hesitated. In the hall, lit only by a nightlight, he couldn't read her expression. After a moment, she said, "Sure, sweetie. I understand. Good night."

She kissed his cheek lightly and slipped away. Trevor closed the bedroom door and lay on the other twin bed, listening to his son's deep sleeping breaths. He wished sleep would come as easily to him.

20

The next day dawned hot and intensely muggy, like a bathroom after someone has taken a long, steamy shower. Angie, Bess, Cash, and Betsy had appointments and plans in Boston, so Sophie drove them to catch the morning ferry. Trevor volunteered to hang out with the kids at home.

Leo had had a good night's sleep after his musical interlude, and he woke happy and refreshed. But even the little boy was influenced by the heat and humidity. All he wanted to do was watch cartoons on television. Trevor didn't have the energy to argue. He didn't want to do anything much more intellectually strenuous himself.

After getting up to say goodbye to their friends, Lacey sequestered herself in her bedroom reading and Jonah slumped back to bed. The snores reverberating behind his closed door told of a deep adolescent slumber.

Trevor spent some time finishing the final cleanup from last night's party. He unloaded the dishwasher, wiped off all the counters and tables, and like a zombie janitor, slowly swept the patio, then swept and mopped the kitchen floor. As he worked, he wondered what Angie was telling Sophie about their nights together. He didn't want Sophie to think badly of him and he didn't want her to think that he had used Angie.

He heard the front door close.

"Great, Trevor!" Sophie stood there, dangling her car keys, in shorts and a tank top and flip-flops. "That floor so needed washing. Is there any coffee left?" Without waiting for him to answer, she checked the coffeepot, filled a glass with ice cubes, and made herself iced coffee. "It's brutal out there today. Hot as Hades and cars everywhere." She appeared completely friendly and normal, as if she had developed no new opinion of Trevor during the car ride. Was it possible that Angie hadn't said anything at all?

"Jonah is sleeping. Lacey is reading. Leo is watching cartoons. And I am subhuman." Trevor rinsed the mop and stuck it in the closet. "No beach today for me."

"Good. Nor for me, either. The best I can do today is lie around like one of those blubbery seals and digest." Sophie took her coffee into the living room.

Trevor went into the family room to check on Leo. He'd fallen asleep again, his hair damp with sweat. Trevor went to Sophie, who was getting settled on the sofa with a book.

"I vote to turn on the air-conditioning," Trevor said. "I'll pay the electric bill if it's too extreme."

"Yes, please," agreed Sophie. "I hate when everything I touch is moist."

Trevor found the temperature controls, and soon the soothing white noise of cool air began rushing into the house. He went back to join Sophie.

"Done." He dropped down onto a chair. "I never want to eat again in my life."

"I never want to move again in my life," Sophie replied, but denied her own words by curling up on her side to face Trevor.

Did she have any idea how sensual she looked lying there, completely relaxed, no makeup, messy hair, barefoot and serene as she snuggled against the pillows? Trevor wanted her to stay there so he could look at her and be happy. He started to ask whether her friends had had a good time but was afraid she would mention Angie. He didn't want to go there.

"Will you play the piano again today?" he asked, genuinely curious.

"You know, I think I will. I want to. And I hope Leo wants another lesson. He learns fast and seems to have a real aptitude for it."

"Another Mozart?" Trevor joked. Sophie obviously hadn't heard Leo toying around in the middle of the night, so he didn't bring it up.

"I don't think so," she answered, taking his question seriously. "But he doesn't have to be a prodigy. Perhaps he can just enjoy it. That might be more fun for him, anyway." She narrowed her eyes, observing Trevor as if seeing him for the first time. "Trevor, tell me about *your* work."

Trevor stopped himself from grinning like a kid and eagerly asking, *Really?* just in time. *Act like an adult,* he told himself as he faced the very adult Sophie. "*Don't Panic.* That's what my business is called. Mostly I build and maintain websites for large and small businesses. I have one employee, River Ford—I know, what can I say? It's what his parents named him. He looks like your typical slacker/hacker with tattoos and a soul patch, but he's a good guy and probably a genius. The CIA wanted to hire him, but he wouldn't sign a form swearing he'd never smoke pot, plus he didn't want to work in a cubicle."

"So you don't have cubicles in your office?" Sophie shifted on the sofa to make herself more comfortable. Her breasts moved slightly.

It took Trevor a moment to stop thinking about those breasts. "I don't really have an office. I have an apartment in Cambridge, the second floor of a tall, narrow, three-family unit. River and I use a closed-in sun porch for our computers. The rest of the place is average—my bedroom, Leo's bedroom, and an all-purpose room with kitchen and bath."

"What if you have to meet a client?"

"I take my laptop to their place or meet at a Starbucks. They don't really need to see me. They need to see the work."

"Do you like working at home?" Sophie asked.

"Yes, I do. First of all, I'm always there for Leo. I've set my office up the way I like it—efficient, easy, and not fussy. I can work in my boxer shorts, drink coffee, and not have to suck up to bosses or deal with annoying co-workers."

Sophie smiled. "You don't have any annoying clients?"

Trevor thought about it. "Well, my clients *are* human beings. It's not so much that they are annoying as that they are unintentionally unclear. For example, they'll tell me they want a website with completely light colors, so I'll do a design with pastels. But no, what they meant is a high-contrast site with lots of dark lines to highlight light sections. Plus, don't get me started on designing a website for two or more people, all with different opinions."

Sophie nodded. "Yeah, I can understand that. When Zack started his architecture firm, he had similar problems with clients who wanted modern, for example, when they meant absolutely and only Frank Lloyd Wright."

Not thrilled to hear Zack's name mentioned, Trevor forced himself to ask, "Tell me about working with Zack?"

Rolling her eyes, Sophie told him, "I'd say it was more a matter of working *for* Zack, never *with* him. When he started out, I served as his secretary and bookkeeper for the first year. After Jonah was born, he brought in a real bookkeeper but I worked with her on and off while Jonah was a baby, until he was a toddler and too much to handle in an office." Repositioning herself on the sofa—every time she did, Trevor's heart stopped at the sight—she continued, "I liked being a secretary. It was so restful after practicing, competing, *interpreting*."

"I get that. June seventh is always June seventh. No ambiguity, no misunderstanding. If you make a mistake, it's clear. I like working with the logic of computer puzzles, especially after dealing with the ambiguity of personal relationships."

Sophie sat up straight, pulling her knees up to her chest and wrapping her arms around them. "Piano requires math and mathematical analysis—measures, rhythm, beats, and so on—but after that it requires a kind of personal translation." She leaned her head against the sofa and lowered her eyes, looking drowsy. "You can play one piece of music many different ways, depending on your mood, even on your instrument. Some instruments are more responsive."

"More user-friendly," Trevor interjected with a smile.

"Right. And music is so emotional. It can be dreamy, or lighthearted and cheerful, or dark and ominous, or romantic. When you *surrender* to it, give yourself over to it completely, it can transport you to another world."

I'd like to be in that world with you, Trevor thought. Instead, he asked, "Do you think you'll continue playing now that you've started again?"

"I'm sure I will," said Sophie, nodding so that her chin knocked against her knees lightly. "I've been thinking about that a lot. Actually, Leo is a godsend."

"How so?"

"Because he's a child who wants to learn to play and I'm learning how to teach. I think when I go home, I might start offering to teach piano. I never knew how much I'd enjoy it. Well, maybe when I was younger and all about ambition I wouldn't have enjoyed it. But it hasn't gone away, you know, the love?" She looked questioningly at Trevor.

Trevor was struck dumb by her words and her look. His brain wouldn't work.

"I mean the love of music." Twisting around, she held out her hands imploringly. "How *could* I have gone for so long without playing? I don't understand myself. At first it was me, I know. I was traumatized and I felt guilty for making my parents spend so much money on my piano career. I was a failure. When Zack came along, it was like a rescue. I became a girlfriend, a helpmate, a wife." Laughing at herself, she settled back on the sofa, reclining sideways and pulling a pillow against her chest as if in protection, as if she felt she had revealed too much. "I'm such a whiner. Do me a favor, talk for a while."

"What about?"

"Tallulah. Tell me about her."

He shrugged. "I'd rather talk about you. You're more interesting."

"More interesting than the mother of your child? The woman you lived with for what, five years?"

Had he ever talked to anyone about Tallulah? Had he ever wanted to? "I'm not that dig-deep-into-the-tar-pits-of-my-mind kind of guy," Trevor joked.

Sophie simply looked at him. That was all. Her blue eyes contained something he'd seldom seen—perhaps it was pity, or possibly he had no idea how to differentiate between pity and attention. It wasn't a sexual, come-hither look and it wasn't maternal, either. It held curiosity but not the eager, give-me-the-good-stuff curiosity. It held warmth but not heat, and caring but not desire. It occurred to Trevor that possibly he seldom noticed the looks women gave him unless they were flirtatious.

"Really? You want to know about Tallulah, *really?*" He wriggled his shoulders, chewed a thumbnail, and considered a moment. *Remembered.* "Okay, well, she was beautiful, the most physically beautiful woman I've ever seen. Sometimes, even after we'd been together for years, I'd look at her and wonder if she were a real person. She was so physically perfect." He looked down at his feet. "But she wasn't perceptive or concerned about, say, the state of the world or global warming or who was running for president—I don't mean she was stupid, either. She hadn't had an easy childhood. I don't mean she was abused, nothing like that, but her family was poor. She had a lot of brothers and sisters, but I never met any of them. Never met her father or mother, either. I think she learned early on that the only way she could find a place in the world was through her beauty." Something inside Trevor was coming alive or beginning; he could sense it the way he knew when he was coming down with a cold or when the stomach flu first made its delicate rumblings. He felt helpless and resistant and slightly angry. He felt as if he were in a line at the post office and someone was crowding him, invading what people called "his personal space" and creating a sense of heat, like being pushed when trying to get on the subway.

Sophie was sitting quietly, one finger resting on her lips. Suddenly Trevor wanted to crawl into her deep, warm eyes like a kid crawling onto his mother's lap, and what kind of a bizarre thought was that to have? He realized he had tears in his eyes. He was so grateful to Sophie for not saying something goopy like, "That's okay, go ahead and cry." After Tallulah's death, Trevor had been surrounded by preschool mommies wanting to hug him while he cried. Their sympathy—which appeared to him like a kind of emotional greed, almost a ghoulish hunger—had caused him to close up like a clamshell, tight and inviolable.

"She had so many faults," Trevor admitted, and fuck it all, the tears were coming and he wasn't going to leave the room or make a joke or suck it up. "In many ways, she was simply hopeless. She had almost no time for Leo. She was totally, and I mean totally, self-absorbed. She'd go on these diets, she was always trying to lose weight, although she didn't need to, but she didn't use drugs—I mean at least when she was

pregnant with Leo she didn't use. I don't know when she started that."
Trevor shot a frantic glance at Sophie.

"Leo has turned out just fine. He's a wonderful little boy," Sophie
told him calmly.

"Right. True. Thanks." Trevor nodded, and the nodding moved
into a kind of psycho mini-rocking. "Tallulah *wanted* the baby when
she found out she was pregnant. I did, too, and when Leo arrived, I did
everything I could. I took care of him. I fed him. She didn't nurse him
because she was afraid it would ruin her breasts. She didn't like touching his diapers, or his throw-up when he got sick. She didn't have the
patience to do the necessary stuff like teaching him to brush his teeth.
Well, and I can't blame her—it's hard, thankless work. And Tallulah,
well, she was glamorous. Babies, children—they totally weren't her
thing."

So much raw confession made Trevor feel itchy with guilt. He
stalked across the room and peered down the hall, listening for a moment to hear any sounds that meant Leo was awake. When he returned to his chair, he looked at Sophie with a self-deprecating smile.

"Do you want more?" he asked.

"Sure," Sophie replied quietly.

"Okay. Tallulah loved acting. Her dream was to be in a New York
soap opera. When she wasn't rehearsing, trolling through the used-
clothing stores for a fabulous find, hanging out with her girlfriends
doing each other's nails and hair, or, although I didn't know it, doing
drugs with Wilhelm, she was at home watching TV shows like *American Idol* and *The Voice*. Oh, yeah, reality shows were a big hit with her,
too. She'd say, 'I can do that. I can do better than that.'"

"And with Leo?" Sophie prompted.

"She was kind to Leo. If she was home, she would hold him on her
lap and cuddle him. He loved that so much. Some days, especially
when she had a part in some play, she'd be all dizzy with joy. She'd try
on her different outfits and dress Leo up, too. He would stumble

around in one of her sequined tops, getting his feet caught in the hem, tripping and falling, and Tallulah would laugh and clutch him and fall on the bed with him, tickling him. Those were Leo's best times in his life. He was just a little kid. He didn't know what a perfect mom was supposed to do. In his eyes, Tallulah *was* perfect. And you know, in my eyes, she was kind of perfect, too." The powerful heat within him pushed its way to his throat and Trevor made an odd choking sound. "I had just started my business when I met her. I like my business. When I'm working at my computer, I get into a kind of zone and it's like the rest of the world disappears. And, it was so cool, the way she didn't care about the house. Like all my friends were getting married, and the wives wanted stuff like All-Clad cookware and silver and platters and throw pillows, and if Tallulah and I would ever go out to dinner with them, the wife would just go on and on about decorating. Tallulah never did that. She couldn't have cared less what the walls looked like. That really freed me up to work on my business."

Trevor forced himself to shut up. But after spilling his guts like this, he realized he still wasn't through, or rather it—his grief—wasn't through with him. "I had no idea she had started using. I knew she was excited about the new play she was in and she was always, more than usual, rehearsing with this guy Wilhelm. I didn't really pay attention. After the cops came, I just kept thinking, why didn't I notice, why didn't I do something? I walked all through the apartment, I tore through the medicine cabinet and all our kitchen cabinets, looking for something, I don't know what, a packet of white powder? I never found anything, not that I'd even know it if I saw it." When Trevor looked up at Sophie, tears spilled from his eyes. "I'm so angry at her. What was she thinking? I know she didn't do much with Leo, but she was there for him, I mean she *existed* for him, he could see her walking around. I'm so pissed off at myself, I could totally punch myself in the face. If I'd paid attention, I would have noticed the drugs, I would have tried to stop her. I'll never forgive myself for that." Trevor dropped his head into his hands and cried shamelessly in front of Sophie.

He cried relentlessly, unable to resist the powerful emotions shaking his shoulders and streaming tears down his face. He had cried before, of course, many times. But he had never spoken as honestly to anyone before, and the grief had never hurt as much.

Pretty soon, he heard rustling, and Sophie came over to his chair, sat on the arm, and simply stroked his hair. She said nothing, only stroked his hair.

"Mom."

Trevor didn't look up, he didn't have to—he could tell that Jonah was in the doorway.

"Go in the kitchen, Jonah," Sophie told her son quietly. "You'll find anything you want to eat in the refrigerator or on the counters."

Jonah's presence cooled Trevor off fast. He sniffed back his tears, making yet another disgusting noise in the room.

"Sorry, Sophie," he apologized. "Sorry. I'm a mess."

Sophie moved her hand from his hair down to the back of his neck and then gently ran her hands back and forth across his shoulders. "Don't be silly. It's kind of an honor. It helps me understand you. Plus," she added, with a lighter voice, "I'm sure you'll have the opportunity to return the favor."

Somewhere in the house the phone rang. *Forget it,* Trevor wanted to say, *don't interrupt this moment.* That pushing, angry sensation had disappeared, to be replaced by a kind of amazement at the gentle touch of Sophie's hand. He would never say this now, and he was thirty now, not a kid any longer, so he knew he needed to give himself some time and think about it all when he wasn't so emotional. But at this moment, he felt like he was in love. In real love for the very first time.

"Mom." Jonah ambled into the room with the phone in his hand. "It's for you. It's that guy." Jonah cast a baleful look at Trevor that said all too clearly he didn't think much of *that guy*.

Sophie removed her hand from Trevor's back and stood up. "I'll take this call in the other room."

Trevor was both upset and relieved when Sophie left the room. It allowed him to take out his handkerchief and give his nose a good honking. But he also wished Sophie had remained next to him with her hand on his back. He had a lot more he wanted to say to her.

It seemed to him she was gone for a long time. When she returned, she was all bright and shiny.

"Guess what! Hristo has invited us out on his yacht today. Do you think Leo would like to come with us, and you, too, of course?" She stood in the doorway, far away from Trevor.

He couldn't believe it. He could not *believe*, after he had opened his heart to her, that she would so frivolously skip off to play with Mr. Moneybags. He was insulted and in the primal part of his guts, he was furious.

"No, thanks, I'm sure Mr. Bulgarian would like to have you all to himself." Trevor knew he was behaving loutishly, but he thought she was being pretty insensitive, brushing him off after the way he had confided in her.

He stood up, tucked his handkerchief back in his pocket, and left the room, careful not to brush against her as he passed. "I'm going to check on Leo."

21

As Sophie prepared herself and her kids for an afternoon on the water, she was vexed by an irritating emotion right under her skin, like a developing rash. Guilt peppered her for leaving Trevor at such an intimate moment. She had probably hurt Trevor when she cut him off like that at the moment he was opening up to her about Tallulah, especially since she was leaving him to see "Mr. Bulgarian."

She hadn't wanted to hurt him. But as she sat next to him, meaning to offer him comfort as she stroked his wide shoulders, she realized she was way too strongly appreciative of his taut muscles, his clean masculine scent, his thick dark hair. Her mind had been screaming: *Not appropriate!* He was far too young for her. Not to mention he was a widower.

Okay, he had been with Angie, but she knew Angie's modus operandi. Angie didn't take no for an answer if there was something she really wanted. But to give Angie her due, she was not a tattletale. She was practical about satisfying her needs and she seldom bad-mouthed a man or even spoke about her experience with one unless she knew it would provide her friends with hysterical laughter. Angie had said nothing about her night with Trevor.

When Hristo called, Sophie had been on the verge of wrapping both arms around Trevor and pulling him to her in a consoling maternal embrace. She had struggled not to do this, well aware that she did not feel maternal and that consolation was not what she would like to give him. Hristo's phone call had been a saved-by-the-bell moment for her.

And she *had* invited Trevor and Leo, after all—even though Hristo had been reluctant in his agreement when she asked if they could come along. She was both relieved and disappointed that the Blacks didn't join them. Really, she decided, it was better this way. She had enough on her hands with the way Jonah was acting.

At first Jonah refused to come along. After she cajoled him, reminding him this might be a once-in-a-lifetime opportunity, he changed his mind and sullenly agreed, but he acted as if he was doing her a great big fat favor. Maybe Jonah was simply acting like a normal adolescent.

Lacey was thrilled to see her friend Desi, and Sophie herself was tingling with anticipation at the thought of being around Hristo again. She pulled white shorts and a loose linen shirt over her red bikini. Yes, dammit, she was going to wear that bikini. Whatever this thing was with Hristo, she knew it was a kind of make-believe relationship that wouldn't last beyond this summer and she was going to be as bold as she could, bolder than she'd ever been. Aunt Fancy was whispering, "You go, girl!" in her ear.

Hristo picked them up in his Range Rover and drove them to the yacht club. Lacey and Desi chattered away in the backseat like BFFs who hadn't seen each other for months, while Jonah stared out the window, his face as stormy as if he were being hauled off to an algebra test.

At the club, they found a launch waiting to take them out to the yacht. It wasn't as big as the impressive hundred-foot vessels that moored in Nantucket Harbor during the summer, bearing flags from Bermuda or Great Britain. It didn't have a helicopter pad or Jet Skis, but it did have—why was Sophie surprised?—a crew wearing white uniforms who helped them aboard. Hristo introduced them all as if they were friends, and probably they were, since they were all Bulgarian. He spoke to them in their language, then led Sophie and her children into the main cabin.

Decorated in dark wood with plush sofas of white leather and navy-blue pillows printed with gold anchors, the main cabin was luxurious. A vase of blue hydrangeas sat in the middle of the coffee table, amid bowls of nuts, figs, cherry tomatoes, and chocolates.

Noticing Jonah's expression, which to Sophie's relief had changed from anger to awe, Hristo said to him, "Feel free to look around. If you go down those stairs, you'll come to the master bedroom. There's a head if you need it. Desi can show you her quarters. We'll eat lunch later out on the deck. For now, may I offer anyone a cold drink?" Quickly, he added, "I suggest only water. It's easy to become dehydrated out here. The sun reflects off the ocean."

Lacey giggled as she trailed after Desi. Hristo showed Sophie and Jonah the bridge of the yacht and Jonah opted to remain there, fascinated by the various computerized instruments. Sophie and Hristo returned to the main room to settle in and enjoy the view of the island from the long windows.

Hristo studied Sophie's face. "You think I'm spoiled."

Defensively, politely, Sophie quickly replied, "No, not at all. I don't think you're spoiled. *Lucky*, yes."

"True. I would like to explain."

"Please."

"The money that bought all this was left to me by my uncle, who fled Bulgaria before the Communists came. My uncle invested wisely.

He requested I use my money to help Bulgaria. I, too, have invested wisely, and I am trying to help."

Sophie nodded, aware that he had more to tell her.

His face creased with worry. "I am Bulgarian. My country is in a time of dire crisis. I have the ability to help influence international businesses to base themselves in Bulgaria. I cannot go to them like a beggar with my hand out. The people I must deal with do not want to see a loser. When I bring them out on my yacht, our discussions are much more likely to go the way I want them to go."

"Of course," Sophie responded, as if she had any idea what he was really talking about.

Hristo was wearing navy-blue shorts with a white shirt that set off his tan and gave him a romantic, dark-knight aura. As he spoke to her, he leaned toward her on the leather sofa, gazing at her intensely, like a hypnotist. And she was hypnotized. She had never met anyone quite like him.

"I am a dual national," he continued, "but I am Bulgarian to the core. Desi is also a dual national and she spends several months a year in our country."

"And your wife?" Sophie inquired.

"My ex-wife. We are divorced. She will never leave Bulgaria. She is committed to it. She works as the assistant secretary of the Department of Transportation, which allows her to know much important information she wouldn't have access to otherwise. She's a brave woman and I admire her. A good mother? Not so much. We all do our best." A gentle smile stole across Hristo's face. "A good wife? Not for years. We are friends, colleagues, and of course the parents of our lovely daughter. We keep in touch. I take Desi to see her. But I admit it, I am a lonely man. Yes, I have all this, but I am a lonely man."

Sophie listened to Hristo with increasing wonder, both at his unimaginable life and at the fact of her, a typical American mother, hearing such things. Being on Nantucket, on vacation from her real life, was allowing her a freedom she'd never known, and she heard herself say, as if she said such things to men every day, "How can you be lonely? You are handsome, charming, and," she risked a carefree smile, "obviously wealthy."

"I'm not saying I couldn't be with one of the many lovely young Bulgarian women I know. But I am trying to help them, not use them. I am not so young. I am forty-five. I am weighed down with responsibility. I chose that responsibility. I am proud of myself and I do not want to act in an unseemly manner." He returned her daring smile. "Although, if I may be so bold, I find myself wishing very much to act in an unseemly manner with you."

Sophie knew she was blushing from the crown of her head to the tips of her toes, partly from embarrassment, partly from attraction. She managed to keep her eyes on his. She managed not to giggle like her daughter. It crossed her mind that the first thing she would do when she got home was to phone Bess and Angie to repeat this amazing conversation.

Hristo continued to look at her, his gaze growing warm. Sophie had stopped breathing. She thought he was going to take her in his arms and kiss her—and then one of the crew appeared to announce that they were going to anchor now, out in the sound within sight of Great Point.

"Shall we have a swim before lunch?" invited Hristo, smoothly changing the topic.

"Mom." Jonah came into the main cabin. "This is awesome. Zarko says we can go swimming now, but do these guys know about Genie?"

"Genie?" asked Hristo.

Before Jonah could reply, the uniformed man quickly said, "Genie is a great white shark. She has been tagged by OCEARCH. She comes to Nantucket in the summer because of the population of seals at

Great Point. That's why we have anchored out here. And our sonar shows no sign of a large fish."

"Thank you, Zarko," said Hristo. "Would you be kind enough to tell the girls?"

The group went to the stern of the boat, where a ladder down to the water was fastened. Hristo pulled off his white rugby shirt and dove into the water. Jonah followed.

Sophie cautioned, "Lacey, I think you should wear a life jacket to swim out here."

"Mom, don't be so lame. I've had swimming lessons forever." Lacey rolled her eyes at her mother and without waiting, dove off the boat, surfacing a moment later, treading water and giggling. Desi quickly dove in next to her.

"I am here," Zarko told Sophie. "I will watch and if I see any sign of trouble, I will help. I have taken lifeguard instructions."

Now there was nothing for Sophie to worry about except stripping down to her red bikini. Hristo was an attractive man. She was, at least for the summer, a free woman. She would probably never see him again. This summer she was learning to be brave. She removed her shorts and shirt and dove into the icy water. Blue bubbles surrounded her, the sun dazzled her, and the cold temperature woke her up. She felt effervescent with life.

After their swim, they sat around a long teak table on the boat's stern to have lunch. The crew served a selection of lobster and avocado salad with warm rolls, and lobster rolls with French fries and onion rings—something for both generations. The conversation was light, focusing on the waters between Cape Cod and Nantucket and the various sea creatures existing there. Lacey and Desi and Jonah, too, became animated during the discussion of the growing population of great white sharks in the summer. This led to talk about *Jaws* and other movies involving imaginary monsters swimming in the deep.

Dessert was fresh fruit over vanilla ice cream, and then the three young people were free to roam the boat or watch movies on the DVD player. Sophie, with sunblock on her nose, sat talking on the upper deck with Hristo as the crew turned the boat and they slowly made their way back to their mooring.

"It's wonderful to see the island from this perspective," said Sophie.

"Yes, you get a different understanding of the shape of the land and its relationship with the ocean."

The boat reentered Nantucket Harbor, slowing its speed as it threaded its way past other yachts and sailboats. Houses, wharves, and the town returned to view, wrapping around Sophie's sight: solid land after so much blue ocean.

"This is like returning from a dream," Sophie murmured.

"I would like to be part of your dreams," said Hristo. Reaching over, he lifted her hand in his. "I would like to be your friend. I would like to be more than your friend if you would allow me." He kissed the back of her hand.

Sophie was charmed. When had anyone ever kissed the back of her hand? For a moment she felt like a princess. Nearly breathless, she sighed, "I would like that a lot."

Hristo moved in, putting his hand gently on the back of her head, pulling her toward him, and pressing his lips against hers. Softly, and then not so softly. Foolishly, she thought, *I'm kissing a European.* She couldn't help being thrilled.

"Mom!" Jonah's voice was startled, his eyes wide.

Horrified, Sophie jerked backward from Hristo so quickly she almost lost her balance. "Jonah—oh, sweetie, what's up?"

"We're here," Jonah told her. "Ready to get off."

She rose, looking around for her sunglasses. "Thanks for telling me, Jonah. I'll be right there."

Jonah thumped back down to the lower deck.

She glanced guiltily at Hristo, who whispered, "He is young. He is a son." With the back of his hand, he gently stroked Sophie's cheek. "To be continued, yes?"

As the vessel slowed to a stop and a launch boat approached them, Sophie replied, "Yes," but her thoughts were tangled.

22

Trevor decided he was not going to behave resentfully about Sophie going off with Hristo, even though that was certainly how he felt. He knew he had no right to be jealous. Plus, Sophie had been cooking delicious meals night after night and it was about time he returned the favor. He knew he couldn't hope to compete with some Nantucket restaurant chef, but he wasn't planning to compete. Given the amount of cooking she'd had to do, it would be nice for Sophie to come home to any kind of edible meal.

He called Leo into the kitchen. "Let's make a Big Mixed-Up Rice for tonight."

Leo clapped his hands. "Yeah!"

Totally by accident a couple of years ago, Trevor had, out of desperation, thrown into a pot of cooked brown rice everything in his refrigerator and freezer—cooked peas, a can of kidney beans, chopped red pepper, chopped onion, steamed broccoli and cherry tomatoes, and about a ton of grated cheddar cheese. Later, he was surprised to find an entree much like this at a vegetarian restaurant. Leo enjoyed grating the cheese. This puzzled Trevor, plus he was afraid his son would slice the tips of his fingers. He tried to prevent this by carefully enfolding each one of his son's fingers in a Band-Aid. So far, Leo hadn't cut his fingers. Perhaps it was the rhythmic, repetitive nature of grating that Leo liked. The boy had a system worked out: he carefully brought the block of cheese down against the grater, paused, and moved the cheese back to the top of the grater with a grave and exacting deliberateness that took forever and, frankly, *grated* on Trevor's nerves. On the other hand, it was something he and his son could do together. While Leo grated, Trevor prepared the brown rice, steamed the broccoli, and chopped the other vegetables. Finally they tossed the mess together and stuck it into the oven to warm. Another good thing about this excellent recipe was that it would last for days, so if Sophie and her kids weren't hungry, Trevor and Leo could have it tonight and there would be plenty left for tomorrow.

By the time they had washed their hands, Trevor was ready for a beer and Leo was eager to return to his Great Wall of China. It was almost six o'clock in the evening and he assumed his housemates would be home any time. He settled in the living room with a book, rather proud of himself as the welcoming aroma of warm cheddar filled the house. He had acquitted himself like an adult. Go, Trevor.

Suddenly, the front door flew open. Jonah stormed into the house, followed by an angry-looking Sophie, who was trailed by an anxious Lacey.

"Don't walk away from me, Jonah," Sophie yelled at her son. "What you did was just plain wrong."

Jonah turned and aimed a death stare at his mother. "Yeah, and kissing a strange man isn't wrong?"

"Oh, Jonah, it wasn't like that."

"I know what I saw. How do you think Dad would feel if I told him? You're just lucky I didn't call him instead of Grandma."

Trevor's nerves stood on end like a startled cat's fur. "Excuse me, I don't know if you noticed, but I'm here. I mean maybe you don't want me listening in on this conversation."

To his surprise, Sophie sagged against the wall. "What am I supposed to do? I mean, really, *what* am I supposed to do?"

With another deadly eye blaze at his mother, Jonah ran from the room, up the stairs, and into his own room.

Sophie leaned down to hug Lacey, who stood watching with a trembling lower lip. "Honey, don't look so frightened. Everything is going to be okay."

"But Daddy will be mad if Jonah tells him you were kissing another man," Lacey said.

"No, I promise you it will be okay. It was just a European kiss. Really. Now please go upstairs and take a shower—no, take a nice warm bubble bath. That will make you feel better. We're all so tired from so much fresh air and swimming."

Lacey didn't look convinced as she trudged away up the stairs.

Sophie rose and smiled grimly at Trevor. "I'll bet you're curious."

Trevor could only dumbly nod.

"While Hristo was driving us home, Jonah got on his cell phone and called his father's mother and invited her to come stay with us here. He said he hoped she would come soon because I was *cohabiting* with one strange man and I had been kissing another strange man."

"You kissed Hristo?" As the image popped into his mind, a bolt of nausea hit Trevor's guts. "In front of your children?"

"I need a drink." Sophie turned her back on him and went into the kitchen.

Trevor followed. "What *exactly* happened?"

"What *exactly* business is it of yours?" Sophie snapped. Then she sank into a chair and buried her head in her hands. After a moment, she mumbled, "We haven't told the children. I mean Zack and I haven't told them that he's in love with Lila. This time apart is to give him a chance to consider whether or not he really wants a divorce. Zack isn't the most attentive father, but a divorce will upset and confuse Jonah and Lacey. So we agreed not to tell them, not yet, not until we returned from Nantucket."

"Okay." Trevor crossed the room and took a glass from the cupboard. "Let me get you some pinot noir."

Sophie reached gratefully for the wine. After she had taken a sip, she continued, "Plus, I didn't kiss Hristo. He kissed me. He just— kissed me. Then Jonah came up on deck." She flushed a deep scarlet. "Poor Jonah. I was going to explain when we got home, but while I was sitting in the front seat of the car talking with Hristo, Jonah was in the backseat with Lacey, and he called Zack's mother. By the time I realized what he was doing, he had already invited her to come visit, and before I could stop him, he told her he hoped she would come as soon as possible because of—oh, I could just gag."

Pulling out a kitchen chair, Trevor dropped into it and studied Sophie's face. After a moment, he asked, "So tell me about your relationship with Zack's mother. What's her name?"

Sophie closed her eyes a moment before she spoke. "Jeanette. Her name is Jeanette. She's head of human resources at Hubcorp. Her husband's an orthodontist. They have two daughters who are older than Zack, Gayle and Sherrie. They all adore Zack. They're wonderful with Jonah and Lacey. Gayle owns a medical supply company and hasn't married, and showers the kids with presents. Sherrie's married to a geologist who teaches in Arizona, so we don't get to see her and her family often, but when we do, everyone has a great time." Sophie put her elbow on the table and rested her chin in her hand as she reflected. "To be honest, I've always felt closer to Jeanette than to my own mother. My mother is demanding and critical. Jeanette is nurturing and consoling. When my babies were born, my mother sent me books on how to raise good children. Jeanette brought us casseroles and fresh vegetables for weeks. The few times Zack and I have gone off to a conference, we've left the kids with Jeanette and Don. She takes them to movies and lets them eat too much ice cream. They adore her."

Trevor tried to think his way through all this. Finally, he concluded, "So you have a good relationship with your mother-in-law. She likes you."

"Yes, and I like her. I'd even go so far as to say we love each other. But Zack is her son. He is their golden child." Again, Sophie closed her eyes, this time frowning as if to block out a vision of the future. "Of course Zack and I didn't tell Jeanette and Don about our separation. We didn't want to upset them. And I guess it is possible we won't get a divorce." Sophie opened her eyes and shook her head, smiling gently at herself. "Listen to me. My husband hasn't called once in all the days I've been here and I still think we might get back together. I'm pathetic."

"Hey, give yourself a break. You're in a tough situation." Trevor wanted to be—what was it Sophie had said?—*nurturing and consoling*, but more than that he wanted to know exactly what had gone on with Hristo. "So what happened with Hristo on the boat? Did Jonah catch you in the bedroom?"

"Heavens, no! Trevor, don't be ridiculous! It was all very innocent and sort of, well, continental. We were coming into the harbor and we were standing at the stern and Hristo kissed my hand in that European way and then we kissed—but lightly, not in any passionate way."

Trevor wasn't certain he believed Sophie. She didn't meet his eyes as she spoke, plus a blush rose up her cheeks. "That's all Jonah saw?" To hide his intense curiosity, he bent to open the oven. He brought out his casserole and set it on the counter.

"Yes." Sophie wasn't paying attention to Trevor but caught up in her own thoughts. She stood up, and carrying her wineglass with her, walked around the kitchen. "Jeanette is coming here tomorrow. I've got to talk to Zack. I don't want to be the one to call him, but I need to know what he's told his mother. I certainly don't want her to think I'm the villain here." She stopped, tossed back a slug of wine, and murmured, "I suppose there is a chance Zack won't want a divorce. But since he hasn't phoned, I'll bet that chance is slim." She set her glass on the table. Speaking as much to herself as to Trevor, she said, "I'm going to do it. I'm going to call him now." She left the room.

Trevor wanted to slam out of the house and run. When Leo was in preschool, Trevor took the opportunity to run or bike nearly every day for at least thirty minutes, fast and hard, pushing himself and letting the back of his mind deal with any problems while the front of his mind kept a lookout for cars, bikers, and other runners on the path. He wanted to run now, but it was time for dinner. Too bad about this problem of Sophie's, he thought selfishly, grinning at his own egocentrism. Here he had fixed his marvelous Big Mixed-Up Rice and she hadn't even noticed.

He walked upstairs. Standing in the middle of the long hall, he checked the doors on Sophie's side of the house. Sophie's bedroom door was closed and he could hear her murmuring. So she had probably gotten through to Zack. Jonah's door was closed—he was probably playing a video game. Just then, Lacey opened the bathroom door and walked out, wearing her pink plaid pajamas, a cloud of steam surrounding her.

"Hey, Lacey," said Trevor, "I've got a good casserole for you kids waiting in the kitchen. Would you get Jonah and I'll get Leo and we can eat?"

Lacey glanced at her mother's door and back at Trevor.

"I think your mother's going to be on the phone for a while," Trevor told her.

"I'm not stupid," Lacey said defensively.

"Honey, that's the last thing I'd say about you."

"Jonah's not stupid, either. We know something's going on," Lacey insisted.

Trevor looked stern. "Lacey, believe me, nothing is going on between your mother and me."

Almost before the words were out of his mouth, Lacey grinned. "Well, duh, I know that. I mean something's not right with Mom and Dad. It's not just Mom kissing Hristo. It's why we're on this vacation. It's why Dad hasn't even called us to see if we're having fun. I just wish they would tell us the truth."

"I know, it sucks to be a kid. Parents think they're protecting you but they're really driving you crazy," said Trevor.

Lacey looked surprised at his understanding. "That's right."

"Get Jonah and come on downstairs. Things will look better after you've eaten."

Her satisfaction with his depth of comprehension faded. "That's what parents always say."

In the privacy of her bedroom, Sophie picked up her cell phone and tapped Zack's mobile number. Then she pressed "End." She didn't want to be all emotional and pathetic about the situation. She wanted to comport herself with some dignity. She had a pretty good sense, anyway, of what was going on with Zack. If he hadn't called in all these weeks, he probably wasn't desperately missing her.

She performed a few calming actions: used the bathroom, washed her hands, and combed her hair. Her reflection in the bathroom mirror showed a young woman with a glowing tan, and tousled, sexy blond hair. Those pale pink lips? They had just been kissed by a wealthy European. She smooched her reflection in the mirror, and feeling more confident, returned to the bedroom.

When she heard her husband's voice, she lifted her chin bravely and announced, "Zack? It's Sophie."

"I gathered as much from my caller ID," Zack responded dryly. "What's up?"

"Your mother is coming to visit," Sophie said. "I need to know whether or not you've discussed our situation with her. In fact, I'd like to know a lot of things. Why haven't you called? You could at least have phoned the children. This complete lack of communication makes me assume you're going to be with Lila. Are you still leaning toward a divorce? What shall I tell the children? What shall I tell your mother?" She knew she sounded manic, but she was bracing herself, trying to be strong, invulnerable.

"Whoa," said Zack. "If we're going to have this conversation, I need reinforcements." He put his hand over the phone and yelled, "Lila, would you please fix me a vodka tonic? Strong. Just *say* tonic." His voice returned full strength. "Why are you calling like this right now? I thought we were going to have the entire summer before we announced the decision."

"I thought so, too. But I've got to know the situation and what you've told your mother since she's coming to stay with us."

"Okay, but why such urgency?"

Sophie could hear the tinkling of ice and a high soprano voice murmuring in the background. She hesitated, then said, "Jeanette might come as early as tomorrow. What should I tell her? I have to tell her something. Does she know you've moved in with Lila?"

"Not exactly." His voice was cool.

Sophie sat on the bed, arranging all the pillows to support her back. "Zack, I'm sorry to interrupt your evening, really I am. But I don't understand why you're being so secretive and remote."

"Ha! *I'm* being remote? That's a good one. Well, I have to say it's nice to be the remote one for once."

"What do you mean?"

"Okay, all right, if you want to get into this now, we'll get into it now, although it seems kind of unofficial to agree on divorce over the telephone. But then again, that's probably the way you prefer it. Remote, as you said."

Sophie had been expecting this outcome eventually, but to hear the words said so bluntly took her breath away. "You absolutely want a divorce?"

"I absolutely want a divorce." Her husband's voice was firm.

There it was. As cold and definite as a slam of a bat to the solar plexus. Sophie gripped a pillow and pushed it into her stomach as if it could absorb the blow. "Who will tell the children?"

To her shock, Zack laughed, sounding a bit demented. He called out, "Lila, babe, could you please fix me another drink?" To Sophie, he said, "And there we are. I say I want to divorce and the first thing you think of is the children."

"I don't understand."

"Of course you don't. I'll explain it to you. Most women, when told their husband wants a divorce, burst into tears and cry, *I love you! How can you leave me? I'll be lost without you!* But not you, Sophie—you move immediately, unswervingly, to the children."

Sophie was speechless as her thoughts collided in her brain. She started to protest by saying that she loved Zack, but deep in her heart she wasn't sure that was true and she *was* sure that she didn't want to lie. "But a divorce affects the children," she insisted weakly. She wished Lila would bring her a vodka tonic, too.

"There are four people in this family, Sophie," Zack said, and his voice was sad. "But you really only loved the children. It's not enough for me. It hasn't been enough for a long time."

Guilt twisted Sophie's heart. "Zack, I have always been a good wife to you."

"Oh, Sophie, since you want to do this now, let's be absolutely clear, okay? Sure, you've cooked wonderful food and taken good care of the house and given me two great kids. But love, passionate love? That left a long time ago."

Sophie bit her lip. After a moment, she said, "Doesn't that happen in all marriages?"

"Not like it has in ours, and if it has, it's replaced by something else—warmth, intimacy, devotion."

"I—" Sophie began to argue.

Zack cut in. "Anyone can see how warm you are with the children. But with me it's become an act. Wait—I don't mean an act, exactly. An *attempt,* which is worse. You've tried. I know you always tried your best. But come on, honey, that's just sad for both of us."

After a beat of silence, Sophie choked out, "This is kind of a heavy discussion for the telephone."

"Well, Sophie, *you* called *me.*"

"That's true. Still—give me a minute, okay?" Sophie put the phone down on the bed and took a moment to rub her forehead with her fingertips, as if she could calm her thoughts. When she picked up the phone, she said, "Zack, I'm sorry. I'm all confused."

Zack was impatient. "You phoned me to discuss what we should tell my mother about our situation. My mother has always liked you. I think you can tell her the truth."

"You mean tell her about you and Lila? Tell her that we're getting a divorce? I haven't even told the children yet."

"My mother. The children. Your mother. Hey, Angie and Bess! Let's think about them before we think about ourselves. You go right for the peripheral damage, Sophie, because if you're honest, this divorce business is not going to break your own heart." Zack's voice had taken on a hardness.

"You're angry with me," said Sophie in amazement as the truth dawned on her. "You're having an affair and you're blaming me. You get to be good and I have to be bad. You always were a spin doctor, Zack."

Zack's voice became even harder. "Are we going to start calling names? Because I've got some ready and waiting."

"No," Sophie said hurriedly. "I don't want to do that." She rubbed her forehead again. "So I'll tell the kids tonight. Can I tell them to call you if they want to?"

"Sure. I'll be here. You know, Sophie, they won't be as surprised as you are."

"I know you've been too busy to spend much time with them recently. Actually, you've never spent much time with them. But I would think you would want to let them know you intend to be connected to them, that you care for them, that you will not disappear from their lives."

Now Zack was the one to remain quiet for a few moments. "The truth is, to be painfully blunt, I don't particularly miss the kids. They're hard work. They don't care about me, really. They don't even know me. I've never been happier than I have during this summer with Lila. When I'm with her I am my true self. It's like being in a kind of heaven, Sophie, and you know what? I'll bet if you're honest with yourself, you're in a kind of heaven, too, on that island with your kids."

Was he trying to hurt her? Sophie thought so. She wanted to hit back. If nothing else, she wanted to save face. "Yes, heaven, absolutely, and you might be surprised to find that my heaven is a bit more like yours than you think." She hoped this would get some kind of rise from her husband, that he would be jealous or at the least curious.

"Good for you, Sophie," Zack said, sounding genuinely glad for her. "I hope he finds the way to break into that vault you call a heart."

Sophie gasped again. "You kind of hate me, don't you, Zack? I'm so sorry that we spent so many years together when you thought I didn't love you. Do you think a marriage counselor would have helped?"

"Honey, love is either there or it's not. No kind of counseling can change that." More gentle female murmurs wafted through the background air. "I need to get off the phone. Anyway, I think we're pretty well done, don't you?"

"Yes, Zack," Sophie agreed, "we are pretty well done."

After switching off the phone, Sophie waited a moment for the tears to come. Her reflection in the mirror surprised her. She looked younger, less strained.

Dutifully, she went down to the dining room to check on the kids. She found the whole group gathered around the dining room table, Leo on Trevor's lap, all of them playing Monopoly. From the kitchen came the soothing shushing noise of the dishwasher.

Trevor glanced up. "Hey. I left some casserole for you to heat up in the microwave if you're hungry." His smile was warm and reassuring, clearly signaling: *Don't worry. I've got it covered this time.*

"I . . . I think I'd like to have another glass of wine," Sophie told him. "To help me *process*. If you don't mind . . ."

"Your move, Trevor," Lacey said.

Trevor drew a card. "Not again!" he groaned. Glancing at Sophie, he said, "I've got to pass Go without getting any money. Dang." Casually, he added, "Sure, Sophie. Take all the time you need. We're just fine here."

Sophie's smile at Trevor was brilliant with gratitude. "Thanks, Trevor."

Sophie slipped into the kitchen, poured more wine, then hurried back upstairs. How nice it was to have someone to lean on when things got tough. Two parents? Amazing. She had never really had that with Zack.

She shut the door to her bedroom and sat down a moment, sipping the wine, letting her thoughts settle. She waited for anxiety to sift in, for worry to crowd her brain. She was going to be divorced.

Instead, the Pharrell Williams song "Happy" began playing in her head. Humming, she slipped off her bed and began dancing quietly around her bedroom. No one could see her, she was all alone, and music filled her. She smiled at herself, then laughed softly. Anyone who saw her would think she'd gone mad. But she wasn't mad; she was *herself*. She was Sophie, full of music.

23

revor moved the iron five spaces and paid Jonah three hundred Monopoly dollars. Sophie's smile was still inside him, filling him with light. Tallulah had never thanked him for anything he did with Leo; she simply expected it. And all he was doing was having fun with some kids he genuinely enjoyed being around. *Awesome.*

"How did you like the yacht?" he asked, glancing first at Jonah and then at Lacey.

Jonah didn't speak, but his sister politely replied, "It was cool."

"Did you leave the harbor?" Trevor asked.

"Yes, we went out to Great Point, and I went swimming there, without a life jacket!" For a moment, Lacey's voice showed enthusiasm.

"Good for you, Lacey." More silence. "Did you swim, Jonah?"

The teenage boy responded with a grunt that could have meant *yes, no,* or *stop hassling me.*

"Leo and I had a lazy day," Trevor offered. "We made this gourmet meal for everyone. And we took a long bike ride around the neighborhood. We saw some amazing houses."

Dead silence. Lacey and Jonah did not seem to want to hear about those amazing houses. These were not Trevor's kids but they were good kids; Trevor had come to know that much in the few weeks they had spent together. They were in a difficult spot right now and so was their mother.

After the Monopoly game, darkness fell, and Lacey, yawning, said she was really tired and went upstairs to bed. Jonah remained on the sofa, relentlessly clicking through channels with the remote control like someone standing in front of the refrigerator dully looking for something to eat that would satisfy him. Where was this boy's father? Jonah seemed like such a good guy. How could his father keep away from him for so long?

When the phone rang at exactly that moment, Trevor jumped. He had the oddest notion that this was Jonah's father calling, that some-how Trevor's thoughts had prompted the call.

But it was Connor down at the apartment. "I know it's pretty late for you guys," he said, "but tonight the moon is dark and all the con-stellations are out in dazzling form. Back in Iowa, my wife and I used to lie on a blanket and look up at the stars for hours. I'm going to do that now and I thought the kids might enjoy it, too. It's the best show on earth." He chuckled. "Let me revise that. Best show in the uni-verse."

"Sounds like a great idea. We'll be down in a few minutes."

Trevor explained Connor's invitation to Leo and Jonah. Leo was excited—probably because this meant he got to stay up past his nor-mal bedtime—but Jonah only shrugged. Still, he trudged along after Trevor and his son out the back door, over the patio, and down the lawn to the far end where Connor had spread a soft old cotton quilt.

"Welcome, welcome," Connor said. "Lie down and make your-selves at home. Once you're settled, I'm going to turn off all the lights in my apartment and on the patio so we don't have any ambient light getting in the way. This island is an unusual place, so far away from cities, far away from interfering human lights."

The guys lay down, Trevor with Leo next to him in the middle and Jonah at the far edge of the quilt, as if he were certain the other two had cooties. Connor turned off the lights and with a few muttered reactions to his old joints, folded himself down next to Trevor and stretched out.

"Just take a moment to let your eyes get accustomed to the night," he advised.

Trevor took hold of Leo's hand in case the darkness was scaring the little boy. This was a new experience for city dwellers. Beneath the quilt, the ground was slightly uneven, with small bumps and hollows. As they lay there, Connor's apartment and the hedges around the property blurred into looming gray masses. The evening air was warm and humid, without a breeze, yet mysteriously drifting with the perfume of an invisible flower. Occasionally from the trees a bird cried or something rustled in the bushes. The foursome didn't speak but lay concentrating on the heavens above them. Suddenly, Trevor felt as if something enormous had shifted, as if the earth they were lying on was sinking down while the skies above were expanding.

"Whoa, dude." Jonah must have been experiencing the same sensation.

"Okay, now," said Connor quietly. "First of all, easiest of all, see those four stars that make a box, and these stars making a handle?"

"I see it!" Leo cried with excitement.

"Good. That's the Big Dipper."

"What's a dipper?" asked Leo.

At his end of the blanket, Connor chuckled. "People don't use dippers much anymore. It's a kind of cup with a handle you can dip into a barrel of water or apple cider and drink from." He pointed out the parts of the dipper.

"Now see that group of stars over there, beneath the Big Dipper? That's Virgo—the, um, it means 'I serve'—my wife taught me that it's my astrological sign. That ties in with when I was born, and it means earth is my element, five is my lucky number, and I'm sympathetic and faithful. It means I've got a weakness, too, at least one of them. I can be moody."

"What's my lucky number?" Leo was so excited he sat up to ask Connor the question.

"When's your birthday?"

"December twelfth!" Leo shouted.

"Ah, you've got a good sign. Sagittarius. That was my wife's sign. Your lucky number is six. You're a fire sign. You're brave and smart and cheerful."

"And I'm almost six," Leo exclaimed. "I'm four and a half, and then I'll be five and then I'll be six."

"Lots of important people have been Sagittarians," Connor told him. "Mark Twain. Beethoven. Can't remember the others."

Leo lay back down, snuggling close to his father. "My lucky number is six."

"Good to know," Trevor said, wrapping an arm around his son.

For a while the four males gazed at the sky in silence. Then, sounding slightly grudging and embarrassed, Jonah admitted, "My birthday is October twenty-sixth."

"You might be a Scorpio," Connor said. "The scorpion. They say Scorpios are mysterious."

"A scorpion." Jonah's tone expressed satisfaction and even a kind of respect. After a moment, he added, "Of course it doesn't mean anything. It's all made up."

"Everything is all made up in one way or the other," Connor said. "People like to make sense out of stuff. Now what we are looking at, the constellations, are formed by connecting the brightest stars with imaginary lines. But you know some people in different countries imagine figures and creatures and symbols out of the *dark* mass *between* stars."

"Awesome," Jonah said.

Again, they lay in silence, and this time Trevor tried to formulate some kind of image out of the darkness surrounded by a group of stars. Next to him, Leo relaxed into sleep, his breathing like a soft purr, his warm breath barely fluttering Trevor's shirt.

"I've heard that some people can tell the future from looking at the stars," Jonah said hesitantly.

"That's true, some people say they can." Connor shifted around, finding a more comfortable position. "Astrologers say they can look at your birth chart and tell you all sorts of things. Personally, I don't think they know any more about the future than doctors do. No one can predict the future." Roughness edged his voice.

"But astrologers can tell if some people are meant to be together, right?" Jonah persisted.

"You mean like love signs. Like whether or not a Taurus and a Capricorn are a good match."

"Yeah, I guess," Jonah said. "Or like a Leo and a Scorpio."

"Have you got a crush on a Leo?" Connor asked, and Trevor could hear him smiling.

Jonah remained quiet for a minute. "No, that's my dad and mom's signs."

"Oh, well, son, I wouldn't want to weigh in on anything as specific as that."

Jonah didn't respond. Again they lay in silence, gazing up into the heavens. Trevor was not completely surprised when he heard rumbling snores coming from Connor.

Turning his head toward Jonah, Trevor whispered, "Connor's asleep."

Jonah was quiet. Then he blurted, all in a rush, "I shouldn't have called Grandma. Now Mom's mad at me. But somebody had to do something."

Trevor's mind spun like a GPS recalculating. "You mean because your mother kissed Hristo?"

"I guess so." Jonah was obviously struggling with his own thoughts.

"It's not such a terrible thing," Trevor said slowly, feeling his way along. "Nantucket is a romantic place. I'm sure it's fun for your mother to have such an unusual man paying attention to her." He'd gotten himself into a snarl. "I mean, I'm sure lots of men would pay attention to your mother if she weren't married—"

Jonah interrupted. "Dad's having an affair."

"Whoa. What makes you say that?"

"I saw them a few months ago. I decided to drop in on Dad at the office and ride home with him—it was the end of the day—and Dad and Lila were alone in the front office making out. They didn't see me. I got out of there fast."

"That doesn't mean—" Trevor began, wondering why he was trying to plead the case of a man he didn't know and wouldn't like.

Again Jonah interrupted, the words spilling out. "So I followed them. Not that night, but every chance I could after school and on weekends. When Dad said on Saturdays he had to go inspect the site he was working on, I'd bike there and he was never there. So I found Lila's address and checked out her car—a red convertible—and went to her apartment. Dad's car would always be parked behind hers and sometimes I saw him go into her apartment, and twice I even saw them kissing through the window. I'm not *dense*. Besides, Dad's been so happy in the past year. I don't want Mom to be hurt, but I've thought a lot about this and I think they would both be happier if they got divorced."

"Jonah, I hardly know what to say. This is a lot of heavy-duty stuff for a fifteen-year-old to deal with. I mean, you should be thinking about baseball and girls."

"I think about girls. I think about one special girl. But thinking about her gets me all flustered. I stopped going to practice because sometimes she's there and when she is there, my hands sweat and I can't ever hit the ball."

Trevor wanted to take the boy in his arms and hug him or at least, in the way of men, slug him gently on the shoulder. He didn't so much as move his head but lay still, gazing upward, not wanting to spook the kid. "Man, ain't it the devil? I remember feeling that way about a girl when I was in high school. If I saw her when we were walking down the hall in school, I'd become a complete spaz and drop my papers all over the floor."

Jonah made a sound like laughter. "I've done that, too."

"Do you think she likes you?"

"I don't know. Maybe. She smiles at me. I was going to try to be her partner on a field trip, but I got sick and couldn't go." Jonah shifted on the blanket. "That's a lie. I didn't get sick; I used that day when I didn't have to be in school to shadow my dad." Another laugh, this one like a moan. "Listen to me, *shadow my dad*, like I think I'm a private dick. I'm the dick."

"Don't be so hard on yourself. You've got a lot on your plate. Have you tried to talk to your dad about this?"

"Dad doesn't talk much to us kids. He never has. He's always been so busy, and I get it—he's working his ass off to keep us in our nice house, going to a nice school, and having vacations like this one. He's not what you would call a hands-on dad. He never has been. He's an important architect with a reputation to maintain, and that puts a lot of stress on him. Lacey and I aren't supposed to bother him with our kid stuff."

Trevor was overcome with sadness for this boy. Yet he understood the delicacy of the situation and he knew better than to say anything insulting about Jonah's father. "You could talk to your mom about stuff, couldn't you?"

"I used to be able to. But I'm fifteen now. I've got to grow up. Plus, what am I going to say? 'Hi, Mom, I got a C on my algebra test and Dad's having an affair.'" Jonah tried to sound sophisticated but his voice cracked.

"Still, why don't you try talking to your mom?" Trevor suggested. "She's a pretty cool lady."

"She's cool, all right." Jonah's voice was bitter. "She's so *cool* she never played piano for us. We never knew she could play like that. I mean what the fuck, man? Why would she hide something like that from us? I mean that's demented."

Trevor thought Jonah was on the verge of tears. Without turning his head to face the boy, he said in a neutral tone, "All parents have secrets from their early lives. Parents were young once, too, you know."

"Okay, but playing piano? And she's so good! Why keep that a secret? If I were Dad, I'd feel shut out. Hell, I'm *me*, her kid, her first child, she's changed my diaper, and when I heard her play the piano I thought: *I don't even know who this woman is.* It's freaking me out, if you want to know the truth. I can't wait to see what happens when Grandma comes. She likes my mother, but I bet she's never heard her play the piano. I mean, come on, man, this is total science fiction." With that, Jonah jumped up from the blanket. "I can't do this anymore. I'm going to bed." He ran toward the house and a few seconds later, Trevor heard the slam of a door.

The sound of the door woke Connor. The older man made a few transitional snorts as he came into wakefulness. "I guess it's time for bed. Thanks for not leaving me out here to get all covered with morning dew." Knees cracking, he slowly got himself to a standing position.

"Connor, this was a great experience," Trevor told the old man as he got to his own feet. "Thank you for calling us. I hope we can do it again sometime."

Connor swept his arm through the open air. "Any time. Free admission." Bent forward, his hand on his back, Connor limped toward his apartment.

Trevor lifted his son in his arms. Leo murmured and snuggled his head into Trevor's chest. He stayed asleep as Trevor went up to the house and didn't wake up even when Trevor deposited him on his bed and removed his summer clogs.

After seeing his son safely tucked in, Trevor went through the house, turning off the lights and double-checking that the doors were locked—although what he could keep out of this emotionally chaotic household, he couldn't imagine.

Once again, he was awakened by the same four notes from the piano. As he stumbled, half asleep, out into the hallway, he saw Sophie standing at the top of the stairs, listening.

She held up her hand in a "stop" sign to Trevor. "Listen a minute."

Trevor listened. *DAH dum dum dum.*

"They're always the same notes," she whispered. "C-G-G-G."

"What, you think Leo's playing a code? He's working for the CIA?"

"Don't be ridiculous. I do think it means something."

"I think it means he's waking us all up," Trevor grumbled, and hurried down the stairs to interrupt his troubled child and carry him back up to bed.

24

eo's Lego world had taken over the small front room called the library. Both Lacey and Jonah had bought kits for Leo—trucks, planes, and boats that could be painstakingly built to exist inside one of Leo's great walls. Many times during the day as Sophie cooked or read, she would hear gentle murmurs as one of her children gently demonstrated to Leo how certain structures were put together. She knew that Jonah was having a wonderful time—he had always loved Legos.

But today she could not seclude her family in the library for her private talk. After asking Trevor if he would mind doing without the TV for an hour or so, she told her children at breakfast that she needed to speak to them and asked them to join her in the family room.

Jonah slumped in and collapsed at one end of the sofa. Lacey, full of morning energy and curiosity, sat at the other end. Sophie shut the door to the hall.

"Here we go," muttered Jonah ominously.

Sophie heard him. She pulled up an armchair so that she could meet them eyeball to eyeball from the other side of the coffee table.

"Yep, kids, here we go indeed." She looked at the faces of both her precious children. All night she had tossed and turned, attempting to put together the perfect announcement, such a perfect announcement that no one would be sad. But of course, that really wasn't a possibility. "Jonah. Lacey. I have to tell you something that I'm afraid will be hard for you to hear. Daddy and I are going to get divorced." She paused.

Lacey looked quickly at her brother, who did not turn his head toward her but stared stonily at the wall. "Will we have to change schools?" Lacey asked.

This was not the question Sophie had expected. She almost laughed in surprise. "I don't know yet, honestly. Daddy and I haven't discussed the details. I don't know if we'll get to stay in our house or if we'll have to move."

"I refuse to spend the night or any time at all with Dad and Lila," Jonah said.

Sophie stared in amazement. "Jonah! What do you mean? Why are you mentioning Lila?"

Jonah balled his hands into fists and set them carefully on his knees in a sign of forced restraint. "Get real, Mom. I've known about Lila for months. I saw Dad with her. Plus Dad has hardly ever been home."

"Who's Lila?" Lacey asked, looking confused.

"Don't be stupid," Jonah snapped at his sister. "You know Lila. She's an architect, Dad's partner. He'll probably marry her next."

Sophie was baffled. Somehow she had lost control of the conversation. "Jonah, how do you know about Lila?"

"Mom, *why* don't *you* know about her?" Jonah shot back. His left leg was jiggling up and down rapidly.

Sophie recognized this as a sign of stress and knew she had to at least act as if she were in charge. "Jonah, Lacey, I want you to listen to me carefully. Children don't know everything that goes on between their parents. Your father and I have been discussing our future for some time now." Okay, she thought, *some time* was only a matter of weeks, but for the sake of remaining in authority and providing a sense of protection for her children, she was going to fudge the issue. "Daddy and I love you both very much."

"Yeah, that's why we see so much of him," Jonah spat.

Sophie continued as if she hadn't been interrupted. "Daddy and I married when we were awfully young. We were so happy with you children and our family. But things change. People change. It's true, Daddy really likes Lila. I think they'll probably be happy together because they both are architects. So we're going to get divorced, but that won't change the way Daddy and I love you."

"We'll probably get to see more of Daddy now," chirped Lacey.

Who were these children? Where did they get these attitudes? "Lacey, I don't want you to be sad."

"I don't think I am sad, Mommy. Lots of kids in my school have divorced parents." Lacey's face crinkled with worry. "But I totally hope we don't have to move. I want to go to the same school. And maybe the court will force Daddy to spend more time with us."

"Who wants to see more of him?" Jonah said bitterly.

"Have I entered the twenty-fifth century?" Sophie walked around the coffee table and plunked down on the sofa, reaching out to pull her children close to each side. "You two are way too sophisticated for me. I thought you would cry and ask a thousand questions. I'm shocked, frankly, by your reactions."

"Mom," said Jonah, "we're not babies anymore."

Lacey nodded eagerly. "That's true. We are not babies anymore."

"But that doesn't mean you don't have feelings. That doesn't mean you aren't experiencing all kinds of emotions—sadness, even grief, that your family is breaking up. Maybe even anger, but really, this divorce isn't anyone's fault."

"So are you going to date that Bulgarian?" Jonah demanded.

Sophie's head was spinning. "What? Wait. You are moving entirely too fast. Could we focus for a minute on the fact that your father and I are getting divorced?"

Both children went silent. Lacey leaned against her mother, welcoming Sophie's encircling arm. Jonah sat rigidly, neither pulling away from Sophie's embrace nor accepting it.

"I don't know what to say," Lacey confessed. "I always thought we had a kind of funny family. I mean, Dad is nice, and he's there for Christmas and our birthdays, but he really likes his work. Lots of dads are that way. Moms, too. I guess I always thought that when I got older, Dad would be more interested in me."

Sophie's heart hurt to hear her child say such things. "Oh, sweetie, Daddy has always loved you."

"I know that, Mom. Jennifer's dad is like our dad, always working. Michelle's dad is that way, too."

"You kids are being champions," Sophie said. "Still, I think you are going to experience all kinds of feelings about this divorce. You can call your dad or talk to me, or I'll get a counselor for you if you want to talk to someone outside the family. For sure this divorce is not going to happen with a snap of the fingers. It's going to change our lives. You may think Daddy hasn't been there much, but it will feel strange for you when he's not in the house at all."

"There are all kinds of families," said Lacey.

Sophie laughed. "Learned that in a school lecture, did you?" She squeezed her daughter tightly.

"So next you have to tell Grandma," Jonah said.

"That's true. Thanks to you, Jonah, you traitor." Sophie knocked her son lightly on his shoulder.

"Why am I a traitor?" Jonah demanded, suddenly angry.

"It was you who called your grandma. It was you who told her I was kissing another man. She is your father's mother. He should be the one to tell her about the divorce."

Jonah pulled away and stood up. "Grandma likes you. And I like Grandma."

Lacey added quickly, "I do, too. She's all huggy and sweet. Your mother just orders us around."

Another emotional knife wound of hurt stabbed Sophie's heart. "Grandmother is a physician. She saves lives. She's used to giving orders and taking care of people. She works hard and she's sensible. She's quite a different personality from Grandma, but she loves you just as much."

"When is Grandma coming?" Jonah asked, walking a few steps away.

"This afternoon. And since you called her, you are going to ride out in the car with me to pick her up at the airport. And while we're at it, Hristo and I were not making out."

Lacey piped up. "I think it would be cool if you married Hristo. Then Desi and I could be sisters and live in the same house."

"Honestly, kids, I'm astounded. I bet you're both hiding feelings, trying to be all grown up and blasé." Sophie glanced from one child to the other.

"We've had years to practice," murmured Jonah.

Sophie rose and went to her son. She placed her hands on his shoulders and stared into his face. She had to tilt her head back because now he was so tall. "Jonah, you don't have to be grown up. You don't have to protect me. I'm still your mother and I want to protect you. I want you to understand that marriages can last. I want you to know that in a way your father and I will always care for each other. Please don't get all distant and bitter. Promise me you'll speak with your dad about all this. Promise me you'll come to me if you ever feel like it's all too much for you. I'm really okay about all this—I need you both to know this. I'm really okay."

Jonah looked at his mother, his expression unreadable. "I know you are, Mom. I wish you would believe that when I say it. I'm really okay, too."

From behind her, Lacey said, "I just got a text from Desi. Can I go to her house today?"

Sophie threw up her hands. "No wonder there are so many television shows about zombies these days. My children are zombies." But she agreed that their private session was over. Now the day could begin.

Trevor was in the kitchen finishing the breakfast dishes while Leo played underneath the kitchen table. When the Andersons came out of the family room, Leo jumped up and ran to Sophie.

"Can we play piano now?" his son asked.

"Sure," answered Sophie. She took Leo's hand. "Let's go."

"I'm going to get ready to go to Desi's house," Lacey announced as she ran up the stairs.

Jonah didn't speak, but trudged up the stairs with a face like one of the living dead.

Trevor stood in the door to the music room, listening to his son's careful scales. Then—he wasn't sure why—he walked upstairs and stood outside Jonah's door. He thought he heard muffled crying. He knocked on the door.

"Go away!"

Trevor hesitated, remembered their conversation outside the apartment last night, opened the door, and went in.

Jonah was lying on his bed, his face buried in his pillow. Trevor sat down at the end of the bed and put his hand on Jonah's ankle.

"So tell me."

Jonah sat up, pulling his knees to his chest and rubbing his eyes with his fists. "She told us they're getting divorced. Oh, man, I don't want to live with that Lila. She's such a slut. At last year's Christmas party, she kept bending over to serve me punch so she could give me a good shot of her big boobs. I don't want to live with that Hristo guy, either. I don't want to move to Bulgaria." Jonah's shoulders shook as he cried.

"You've moved from point A to point Z way too quickly," Trevor said quietly. "The bad news and the good news about something as enormous as divorce is that you have to go through it day by day. Hour by hour. Somewhere I read that human beings are the only creatures to spend the present driving themselves crazy about the future. Think about today. It hasn't changed. You don't know what's going to happen with your father and Lila. And I'm pretty sure your mom's not going to move you guys to Bulgaria."

"Well, why is Mom teaching Leo piano when she never tried to teach us?" Jonah demanded.

"I guess the time was right. Or maybe the place. I mean," Trevor thought with a spark of inspiration, "did you even have a piano in your house?"

"No. But why didn't she get one?"

"Ask your mother. If she's ready to play piano, maybe she's ready to talk about her passion for it."

Jonah looked up at Trevor with a wry smile on his blotchy face. "You know, dude, you're a smart guy, but maybe you've forgotten no guy likes to hear the words mother and passion in the same sentence."

"Right. Forgot." Trevor returned Jonah's smile, his entire rib cage filling with warmth and pride because this boy was opening up.

"It's all so complicated," Jonah said. "I don't understand. Why do so many people get married only to get divorced?"

Trevor thought about that for a while. "Well, I don't suppose anyone has the absolute answer to your question. But I kind of think people marry the wrong people to get the right children."

Jonah squinted his eyes, thinking about what Trevor said. After a while he announced, "I'm going to wait a long time to get married."

"Good idea."

"But what if I can't wait a long time to like a girl?"

"Geez, Jonah, what am I, a Ouija board? I don't know the answer to everything. You're going to have to figure that out for yourself."

"Yeah, you're right." Jonah got off the bed, grabbed a tissue, and blew his nose. "I'm okay now. I'm gonna go watch TV until it's time to pick up Grandma."

Trevor went to the door. With his hand on the knob, he turned back to Jonah. "One last question regarding the whole thing about you liking the girl. Have your parents talked to you about birth control?"

Jonah rolled his eyes. "Of course they have. Man, you're demented. Go away." He turned away to hide a grin.

Trevor left Jonah's room and walked down the hall to his temporary office. *I'm the man,* he thought, *I'm the man.*

As Trevor was checking his email, his cell phone rang.

"We're on our way!" cooed a familiar female voice.

Trevor froze. The circuits of his brain crashed. Frantically, a luminescent arrow like a computer cursor zipped around inside his head trying to locate the name of the person speaking. A primitive warning system prevented him from asking who was calling and what they were talking about.

"Tell Leo we're bringing him a huge set of medieval Legos so he and Cassidy can build a walled castle."

Cassidy. With that, his brain rebooted and he understood what was going on. Cassidy, a four-year-old girl who attended Leo's preschool and was Leo's best friend, was coming to the island to visit, brought by her mother, Candace. Way back in May, when people were still consoling Trevor and Leo, Trevor had suggested to Candace that she bring Cassidy for a visit. He had foreseen a summer of being alone in a house on the island with his boy and he knew that Cassidy always made Leo smile. It had been a brilliant idea, back then, before he met Sophie.

"Trevor? Can you hear me? I'm not sure this connection is working."

Trevor cleared his throat. There was nothing for it but to go through with it. He had made the date with her; they had confirmed it before he left. "Candace!" He tried to put enthusiasm into his voice. "I can hear you. Great. Leo will be mad crazy to see Cassidy. Are you coming on a ferry or flying from Hyannis?"

"We arrive on the four-thirty fast ferry."

"I'll be there to pick you up. But listen, Candace, the house has gotten kind of full. The other family is here, too, you know. They're nice. But it's kind of a circus."

"Sounds like fun," Candace said. She was as cheerful as she was pretty, Trevor remembered. "See you soon. Huggies." She giggled her trademark giggle because her daughter still used the word for a brand of diapers whenever she wanted to be cuddled.

Trevor hung up the phone and collapsed in his chair in front of his computer. All this information—the date and time of the Halls' arrival—was right there on his monitor, on the calendar he hadn't bothered to look at recently. He had the oddest sense of behaving unfaithfully to both Candace and Sophie even though he hadn't slept with or even kissed either one of them. Back in his bachelor days he had been known to date two or three women at the same time. Candace Hall was a single mom and a rock-star friend. She was widowed, too. Her husband had been killed in Iraq. She had loved her husband. There was no way Trevor could really explain to Candace how his loss was nothing compared to hers. She was an artist, specializing in delicate watercolors, and she'd never been to the island before. Even though she was drop-dead gorgeous, with long brown hair and a willowy figure, Trevor thought of Candace only as a friend. And Leo adored Cassidy.

Everything was going to be fine. Why was he getting so stressed? Why did he want so desperately to assure Sophie there was nothing

romantic between him and Candace? Why did he think Sophie would
even care? All this was doing his head in.

Downstairs in the music room, Leo was sitting on Sophie's lap,
practicing piano. Trevor leaned against the hall door, quietly watching. Leo's focus was absolute. He had a habit of biting his top lip as he
played. It made him look slightly deranged. Sophie was wearing a sundress he hadn't seen before, a lime green that accentuated her tan and
made her blond hair shimmer with silver. The arch of her wrist when
she showed Leo a chord was delicate and elegant. Her instructions to
his son were almost whispered, so lightly spoken Trevor couldn't hear
the words, but he caught the music of her voice.

Was he in love with her? It wasn't simply that she was being gentle
with his son. Lots of women had been nice to Leo. If he was honest
with himself, he knew that he wanted to make love to her. He wanted
to buy a big house and move in with her and Lacey and Jonah and
make everything all right. *Oh my God.* He was a madman.

Sophie noticed Trevor standing there with his mouth open. "Your
son is amazing."

Leo spotted Trevor. "Did you hear me, Daddy? I played 'Twinkle,
Twinkle, Little Star' and I didn't make a mistake."

"I heard, buddy. You really are getting good." He hesitated. "Want
to play the song you play at night? I'll bet Sophie would like to hear
it."

Leo shook his head, slid off Sophie's lap, and skipped to Trevor.
"Can we get a piano at home?"

Home. The thought of leaving this house and this woman and her
kids dropped deep in Trevor's stomach like lead. "Sure. But guess
what? Cassidy is arriving this afternoon."

Leo jumped up and down with excitement, much more like the
happy kid he'd been before Tallulah's death. Out of the corner of his
eye, Trevor saw Sophie stand up.

"Sophie, can we talk a minute, about arrangements?" He picked up his wiggling boy and walked off, dumping Leo on the sofa. "I had forgotten one of Leo's best friends, Cassidy, and her mother, Candace, are arriving this afternoon to stay for a few days."

"How fabulous! This is terrific, Trevor." Sophie seemed genuinely happy at his announcement.

"It is? Why is it terrific?"

"Well, you know Jeanette, Zack's mother, is arriving this afternoon, too. This way, she'll see that you've got—" Sophie glanced meaningfully at Leo, indicating that she was watching her words—"a female friend. So she won't think that I'm your, um, 'special' female friend." She blushed as she spoke.

Did it actually make Sophie happy not to be his, *um*, *"special" female friend*? Trevor wanted to go stick his head in a bucket. "I suppose we need to work out how to deal with extra meals . . ." He was hopeless.

"Don't worry about that. I'll take Jeanette and the kids out to a restaurant tonight so you can have a special time here with Candace and Cassidy. Then you can take your group out tomorrow night. Jeanette is a great cook, and I'm sure the rest of the meals we can take care of together."

"You don't have to take your group out to dinner," Trevor began, his brain creaking along rustily. "Restaurants here are expensive."

"Once in a while won't kill us," Sophie told him. "And it will be nice for you and your friends to have the house to yourselves."

Leo was bouncing all around the room in excitement. Trevor could hardly hear himself think. "About sleeping arrangements—"

"Jeanette is going to sleep in the other twin bed in Lacey's room."

Trevor thought out loud. "Cassidy can sleep in the other twin bed in Leo's room. And Candace—"

"Hey, honey, it's none of my business where Candace sleeps." Sophie grinned at him, a twinkle in her eyes.

Trevor wanted to shake her. "Candace is going to sleep on the fold-out bed in the family room. She's a widow. Her husband was killed in Iraq."

Sophie looked dismayed. "I'm so sorry. I didn't realize."

Trevor was instantly riddled with guilt for making Sophie feel foolish. With Tallulah, everything had been so clear and simple, the train going along a track. With Sophie, Trevor felt like a Labrador puppy chasing after a Thoroughbred jumper. She seemed to fly effortlessly over the fences of their relationship while he ran too fast, banging his head into the posts.

"I think all the towels and linens are clean," Sophie mused. "But perhaps I'd better make a run through the house, especially since Jeanette is coming."

"I'll go to the grocery store and stock up on staples and necessities for all of us for this week," offered Trevor, nearly fainting with relief because he'd come up with an intelligent idea.

"I'm concerned about Jeanette coming," Sophie confessed. "I've got to tell her—gosh, have I even told you? Zack and I are definitely getting a divorce. His mother likes me, but that doesn't mean she won't give me a hard time when she's here."

"Tell me if there's anything I can do to help," Trevor offered.

"Thanks, Trevor, I will." She gave him a grateful smile and headed up the stairs to check the linens.

Sophie had cautioned her children not to bring up any mention of divorce, or the rift between Zack and their mother, to Grandma when she first arrived.

"This is Grandma's first time to Nantucket, and I'd like her to enjoy the town and see it in all its charm. After you kids go to bed tonight I'll sit down and explain about the divorce. Tomorrow you can take all the time you want talking to her about your father or me or the future or whatever."

"Can we take her to the beach?" asked Lacey.

Sophie had laughed with relief. "Of course."

When Jeanette arrived on the fast ferry, they spotted her at once in the crowd walking down the ramp to the dock. Jeanette looked like a very short, very round version of Zack, with beautiful blue eyes and blond hair streaked with white. She hugged her grandchildren and hugged Sophie, too, squeezing them against her ample bosom. She was their warmhearted grandmother and everyone was delighted to be immersed in her vanilla-cookie scent.

"Oh my goodness, Jonah! You've gotten so tall! And look at you, Lacey. You're so pretty. Goodness, Sophie, I don't believe I've ever seen your hair so long. It quite becomes you. And you're all so tanned." Jeanette laughed and laughed with pleasure.

That was the way Jeanette saw the world, Sophie remembered. It was as if she saw only the good and let the bad fade away. No comment about hoping they used sunblock or they'd get skin cancer, like Sophie's own mother would make. No subtle, derisory remark about Sophie's hair looking like it needed a good trim or at least a good brushing. Jeanette had looked at publicity brochures about the island on her way over but unlike Sophie's mother, she had not made a list of must-sees but simply surrendered herself to her family's decisions.

"Let me have your bag, Grandma," Jonah said.

"Oh, dear, it's so heavy, but then you're such a nice big man it will probably be as light as air to you."

Sophie watched with concealed amusement as Jonah took the pink, kitty- and puppy-covered duffel bag from his grandmother and hung it over his shoulder.

It was too late to go to the beach, and Sophie knew Jeanette would be enchanted by the historic town, so for an hour or so the foursome strolled around, Lacey holding Jeanette's hand and Jonah slumping along with his hands in his pockets next to Sophie.

"I'd like to get myself a Nantucket T-shirt before I leave," Jeanette said.

"How long can you stay?" Sophie asked, hoping she didn't sound as if she were really inquiring, *how soon do you leave?*

"Not long, I'm afraid. Hubcorp is undergoing yet again another merger, and that means I have employees to shuffle around. Let's talk about something else!"

They ended up at the Brotherhood of Thieves, a well-known restaurant in a historic building. Tonight, instead of sitting inside the cozy brick dining room, they chose to sit out on the patio at the back. Sophie had suspected that conversation might be difficult as they all tried to avoid the tattletale remark Jonah had made about Sophie kissing a strange man, but Jeanette chattered away happily, seeming as fond of her daughter-in-law as she always was.

After dinner they walked toward Children's Beach, where Sophie had managed to find a parking place. It was still light out, so they all went down to Brant Point to show Jeanette the lighthouse and the Coast Guard station. When they finally climbed into the car and began the drive to the house, the kids and Jeanette, too, were yawning from all the fresh air.

Back at the guest cottage, they piled out of the car and into the house, Lacey tugging on her grandmother's hand. "You're going to sleep in my bedroom, Grandma. I've got two twin beds. This house is awesome. Wait till you see my shell collection."

Sophie had tried to time their arrival back at the house before Leo went to bed so that everyone could meet everyone else and no one would be surprised in the morning to see a strange face. As Jonah and Lacey ushered their grandmother upstairs, Sophie followed the sounds out to the patio.

In the illumination from the patio lights, she saw Leo and a pretty little girl constructing a castle out of Legos. At the round wooden table, Trevor sat with a beer in his hand. Across from him, in what had always been Sophie's chair, sat Kate Middleton. Of course it wasn't really Kate Middleton, but it might as well have been: a beautiful young woman with long brown hair wearing khaki shorts and a pink collared T-shirt.

It took Sophie a moment to catch her breath. She wasn't expecting the sudden rush of emotion—dear Lord in heaven, could it actually be jealousy?—that paralyzed her when she saw the brunette and Trevor sitting there as if they were a couple. She couldn't speak.

"Hey," said Trevor. "There you are. Did the kids' grandmother get in okay?"

"Uh-huh," Sophie choked out. She cleared her throat. "They're showing Grandma the house. Jeanette will be down soon."

"Great. Sophie, this is Candace. And that's Cassidy, over there creating Camelot with Leo."

Sophie took a few steps and extended her hand to the lovely brunette. "Hi."

"Hello, Sophie." Candace's voice oozed with ownership. "Why don't you sit down and join us for a while?"

Why don't I pick up a chair and bash you over the head for a while? thought Sophie, both horrified at her thoughts and insulted to be invited to sit at what was, at least for two months, her own table.

"Thanks," she forced herself to say politely. "I've got to have a serious talk with the children's grandmother, so I think we'll go seclude ourselves in the library—if that's all right with you, Trevor."

When Jeanette came back down the stairs, Jonah and Lacey took her out onto the patio to meet the others and for a while everyone chatted pleasantly. Then Sophie decided she had delayed long enough.

"Jonah, Lacey, I need to talk to your grandmother privately. We're going into the library. If you want to watch TV or go on to bed, that's fine. You can have all day tomorrow with your grandma."

"It sounds like I'd better have a drink with me," Jeanette told Sophie.

"Coffee? Tea?"

Jeanette leveled a gaze at Sophie. "I'm thinking it had better be wine."

Armed with glasses and a newly opened bottle of cold Chardonnay, Sophie led Jeanette into the library and shut the door. They sat facing each other in deep leather chairs on the opposite side of a cold fireplace. Sophie poured them each a drink.

"Okay, here we go," Sophie began. "I know Jonah phoned you to tell you I'd been kissing a strange man and living with another, and I want to address that rather confusing remark. I mean, you probably have guessed by now that Trevor is only a friend. I mean, he wasn't a friend until I met him when we both ended up accidentally renting this house from a pair of daffy cousins. And the strange man I kissed is also merely a friend who I met on the island. But the entire reason I'm on this island with the kids is that Zack told me in the spring that he's in love with his partner, Lila. Yesterday he told me that for sure he wants a divorce." She collapsed against the back of the chair, breathless.

"My. That's a lot for my tired old brain to absorb." Jeanette leaned forward and put her hand on Sophie's knee. "Are you okay, honey?"

The question was so unexpected it sparked tears in Sophie's eyes. "I really don't know. I haven't had a chance to think about it. I'm more worried about the children. I told them about it all last night."

"How did they take it?"

"Surprisingly well. Or maybe they're completely pretending in order to protect me. Jonah is working very hard not to be a child these days. Maybe they'll open up to you more if you talk to them tomorrow."

Jeanette nodded, settling back in her chair. She took a moment to sip her wine. She wore a sundress with a sunflower print. The shape was loose, even baggy, but it still indented below her large monobosom and again below her round belly. To Sophie, Jeanette looked like one of those jolly, friendly Buddhas, or perhaps some kind of primitive goddess. She had the urge to fall on her knees, bury her face against her mother-in-law's comforting body, and let Jeanette stroke her hair, whispering, "There, there."

Jeanette took her time thinking. At last she spoke. "I won't say this is an enormous shock. I suppose I've been waiting for this announcement for years."

Sophie blanched. "Zack's been having an affair for years?"

"No, no, I don't mean that. I guess what I mean is that I never thought the two of you were truly happy with each other."

Sophie's hands flew to her heart. "Wait, what? I had no idea! I thought—" Suddenly she was overcome with tears. "I thought we were an extremely happy family."

"A happy *family*, yes. But not such a happy couple, maybe. There is a difference, you know." Jeanette sipped more wine. "Do you need to get a tissue?"

"I guess I do. I'll be right back." Sophie put her glass on the coffee table and hurried into the downstairs bathroom to snatch up some tissues and blow her dripping nose. When she returned, she entreated, "Jeanette, you have always been such a friend to me. Tell me what I've done wrong."

"It's not a matter of what anyone has done wrong." Jeanette chewed on her lip a moment as she gathered her words. "You know, one generation can only judge the next generation by what we know. In my parents' family, my father worked and my mother kept house and raised the children and there never was much money for us to do family things together. I never really got to know my father. I guess I saw that same dynamic taking place among you and Zack and the kids."

"But we did do family things together," Sophie protested. "At least when the kids were in grade school."

"I know, I know that. And I don't mean I've been spying on you or watching you with a critical eye. I don't want you to think that at all.

If anything, I'm afraid this divorce reflects back on me and the way I raised Zack." She held up her hand to prevent Sophie's outburst. "Remember, Zack came along after his two sisters. He was the baby prince, adored and pampered by three women. Even when he was in college, he brought his laundry home for me to do. And I know that when he was getting his master's in architecture, his older sisters used to send him spending money so that he wouldn't feel that trapped feeling that being poor gives you. Not to put too fine a point on it, Zack is spoiled. When you two first married and I saw the way you kowtowed to him, totally becoming his servant like some kind of geisha, I thought it was a good thing. I thought he would go from a home where he was the prince to a home where he was the king. And that really happened, didn't it?"

Nodding slowly, Sophie agreed. "I did adore Zack. But I was happy, too. You know I'd played piano, and done pretty well, until I failed in a competition. But when I met Zack, oh, the world opened up for me. Suddenly I had this handsome husband and a goal to work for with him, and then our children. My mother was never much of a cook so it was a whole new world for me, learning about cooking. I really love to cook."

Jeanette smiled. "I know you do, Sophie. I've been the lucky guest at many of your meals."

"Jeanette, you are being so very kind to me about all of this. I don't understand."

Jeanette laughed her warm, gentle laugh. "Look at it this way: you are the mother of my grandchildren. I've got a pretty good guess that when you get divorced you will get full custody of them. I can't imagine Zack will fight for half custody. If I want to stay in my grandchildren's lives, I've got to make nice with you." Shifting in her chair, she took a sip of wine, then spoke more seriously. "I don't consider myself an old woman yet, but I have lived a long life and I've seen a lot of friends get divorced. For some of them, it's a good thing, a door opening to freedom. For others, it's heartbreaking. But the worst divorces happen when people fight and snarl and involve everyone in the extended family in some kind of hideous feud. I don't want to see that happen to my grandchildren or to my son or to you. And why should it? You know I've always liked you, Sophie. I think you've always liked me. I love spending time with my grandchildren and I've been thinking about this on the way down here. Over the past couple of years, the only time I've spent with you and the kids when Zack was there was Thanksgiving and Christmas. I had the kids over for sleepovers. I've taken them to a couple of events, the state fair and a ballet, and when I picked them up, Zack was never there. He was never there at their recitals or ball games. I'm not blind. I'm not stupid. I love my son. I love him, faults and all. Exactly like you love your children."

"Jeanette, you are wonderful. I'm speechless with admiration."

"Well, honey, after this heart-to-heart, and traveling all day, I'm completely speechless myself. What do you say about going to bed now?"

"I say it's an excellent idea."

The women rose, carried their glasses into the kitchen, and went upstairs. Jonah and Lacey were already in bed.

"Good night, Jeanette," Sophie said. "I'm glad you're here."

"Good night, sweetheart," Jeanette replied softly. Reaching out, she drew Sophie into a warm hug. "Sleep well."

I will sleep well, Sophie thought as she went into her bedroom, and she admitted to herself that the reason was not simply that Jeanette had taken the news of the divorce so well, but because on their way to the kitchen, Sophie had seen Candace preparing for bed on the fold-out sofa. Alone.

25

Trevor came home from the beach sunburnt and fog-brained. Candace, Cassidy, Leo, and Trevor had spent practically the entire day near the water, swimming, wading, building sand castles, and drowsing on beach towels. While the children played, he and Candace had been able to talk about their lives, their losses, and their children. During their conversations, Trevor had been slightly alarmed by the way Candace displayed her pretty body as they spoke, and by the way she continually touched him on the shoulder or arm or neck. It seemed she had moved on from mourning to the desire for physical consolation. He didn't know what to do about that. Leo was so happy to have his friend Cassidy here. Cassidy was a huge source of comfort and stability in Leo's life. Trevor didn't want to do anything that would endanger that, but he didn't want to build on that, either.

"I thought I'd take you and the kids out to dinner tonight," Trevor said when they arrived back at the guest cottage. "Sophie and I sort of take turns being in charge of dinner and tonight I think she wants to cook for her mother-in-law."

Candace was engrossed in unbuckling Cassidy from her car seat. Over her shoulder, she said, "Nonsense. Restaurants are so expensive. And I love to cook. I'll shower and run into town and buy a few things."

"Oh, uh, let's see what Sophie's plans are. I'd hate for you to have to make a trip into town." He lifted Leo out of his own car seat. "Outdoor shower for both of you," he ordered. "And leave your bathing suits on. You can go play in the backyard for a while."

"I love buying fresh vegetables in August," Candace persisted. "And the farms here are famous. In fact, if you'll give me your car keys, I'll just pull on a shirt and make a quick trip right now."

"Okay," Trevor said reluctantly. After sharing an apartment with Tallulah, who didn't care what they ate or even *if* they ate, being around so many women who loved to cook was disconcerting. He handed Candace the car keys and went into the house.

The delicious aroma of roast lamb assailed him immediately. He stood in the front hall for a moment, breathing it in and practically drooling. He found Sophie in the kitchen, tearing up lettuces.

"My God, that smells good," said Trevor.

Sophie smiled. "Glad to hear it. If you and Candace want to stay here for dinner, I've got more than enough."

"I can't tell you how glad I am to hear that."

Another dazzling smile. "Did you all have a good day?"

Sophie was wearing shorts and a tank top and nothing else. She was barefoot and very tan. Her skin was as smooth as the skin of a grape. After a moment, Trevor realized he was staring at her without answering. "Um, yeah, we had a good day, but I guess I'm kind of stupefied by so much sun."

"Go take a cold shower," Sophie advised.

You have no idea how much I could use one right now, Trevor thought. "Leo and Cassidy are playing in the backyard."

Sophie moved to the kitchen window to look out. Trevor stood next to her. Leo and Cassidy had run to the end of the yard to inspect Leo's Lego fort. Trevor wanted to turn and kiss Sophie's shoulder.

"Where's Candace?"

"Oh. She went into town to get some fresh vegetables."

"I thought you were taking your gang out to dinner tonight," Sophie said.

"So did I, but Candace really wanted to try some of the local farm vegetables. I guess they're famous. She insisted on cooking and eating here."

"That's cool," Sophie replied, but she turned away from Trevor and he had a strong sense that she wasn't as thrilled about this as she had been when the Manchesters had visited. "We'll have even more food to serve."

Women and food. That was a liaison Trevor wasn't even going to try to understand.

"I'm going to go take that cold shower," he said and left the kitchen.

The shower did revive him. He combed his hair, then put on clean shorts and a fresh T-shirt. Only as he was walking into the kitchen did he realize the T-shirt read *Dear Algebra, stop asking me to find your X. She's never coming back and don't ask Y.* Oh, man, he was such a toad. He didn't want to insult Sophie, but here he was in the kitchen and Candace had returned. He couldn't turn around and leave and come back wearing a different shirt. That would be too weird.

His ears alerted him to the tones of a woman in distress.

"A baby lamb? You are actually cooking a baby lamb?" Candace's voice trembled with horror.

Sophie's voice was both amused and testy. "Actually, no, I'm not cooking the entire baby lamb. Just the leg."

"Well, I suppose that is your prerogative. If you choose to eat the flesh of animals, I can't do anything about that. When you are through using the stove, I'm going to make a nice stir-fry of tofu and vegetables for me and Cassidy and Trevor."

Hey! Trevor thought. *I want some lamb, too.*

"Sure," Sophie answered easily, "there's plenty of room on the stove. I've made rice and I'm ready to cook the green beans and I've made a big salad. We can sit at the dining room table and each person can choose what he wants to eat."

Perfect solution, Trevor thought.

"I would really rather not sit at a table with blood on the plates," Candace said, sounding sniffy. "Trevor and Cassidy and Leo and I will eat outside on the patio. I'll wait until your group is all in the dining room before I start cooking."

Trevor stood in the doorway. From the primitive part of his man-brain came the thought: *ME want meat!* But, really, come on, why did Candace get to dictate what *he* ate?

"That's fine," Sophie agreed pleasantly. "There's some cheese and crackers if you will want some munchies while you wait. The lamb's almost ready. Help yourself to a glass of wine."

"Not now, thank you. It's too early for me to drink alcohol. I'll run up and take a quick shower to get rid of the sand and put on fresh clothes." Candace noticed Trevor standing there. "Oh, Trev, could you keep an eye on the kiddies while I shower?"

"Sure," Trevor said.

Candace left the room. Sophie turned back to the stove. Trevor dug a beer from the packed refrigerator. He wanted to say something but didn't know what to say.

"How long is she staying?" Sophie inquired in a low voice. She sounded more amused than upset.

"Uh, I'm not sure." Trevor moved closer to Sophie to be heard.

"Did you know she was a vegetarian?"

"I had no idea. I made our Big Mixed-Up Rice for dinner last night and a salad. I intended to take them out to dinner tonight like you and I agreed, but she wanted to cook here."

"That's fine," said Sophie, draining the green beans. "Dinner's ready for us now. Sorry you won't get any lamb. You look like you'll survive a few days without meat," she added, frankly looking him up and down and then suddenly, easily, without warning, putting the flat of her hand against his chest.

Her touch set off a Fourth of July array of fireworks in his body. He stared at her, speechless and completely aroused and confused.

It appeared she had surprised herself, as well. Sophie stared at him, equally speechless, her mouth open, frozen where she stood.

"Mom." Jonah trudged into the kitchen. "I'm starving."

Sophie took her hand away. She bustled about putting the beans into a bowl, adding a pat of butter to melt over the top. "Call your grandmother and ask her to come in," she told Jonah. "Wash your hands before you come to the table."

By the time Sophie and her family had sat down to dinner in the dining room, Candace had finished showering. She sauntered into the kitchen, tanned and glowing and barefoot, quite the sexy package in a short pink sundress with her long brown hair held up in a ponytail with a shiny pink ribbon. Trevor stayed in the kitchen to help her prepare their dinner—he made a green salad—and they gathered Leo and Cassidy and took their food out to the patio to eat. It was a good decision. He couldn't smell the lamb quite so much out here.

Throughout the dinner, Trevor's mind scrambled to come up with excuses for not having some kind of intimate time alone with Candace after they put the children to bed. Cassidy and Leo were already tired from their day in the sun and fresh air and would go down easily, he knew. Trevor was ready for bed himself, but not with Candace. How many mistakes could one man make with women? Trevor wondered. He genuinely had invited the Halls down for Leo's sake, but it looked like Candace had misread his intentions.

The kitchen door opened and a cluster of people spilled out onto the patio.

"We're all going down to the apartment to look at the stars," said Lacey. She was holding a blanket in her arms.

"Yay!" yelled Leo. "I want to go, too! Can I go, Daddy?"

Trevor didn't have to give it a moment's thought. "Absolutely, dude. Take Cassidy and her mom with you. I'll clean up the kitchen and be down with you in a minute."

"Oh, Trevor, you don't need to clean the kitchen. I'll do that," Candace said, reaching over to put a restraining hand on his arm.

"No, cleaning the kitchen is my part of the renting deal," he told her, in a kind of half lie. "Go on down. You'll be stunned at the spectacular amount of stars you can see. I'll join you soon."

Candace took Cassidy's hand and followed Leo to the dark end of the lawn where Sophie and the others had already spread out blankets. As Trevor watched, Connor came out of his apartment, said a few words, and turned off his lights.

Trevor took a long, long time cleaning the kitchen. He even mopped the floor. By the time he got down to the star blanket, the two youngest children were asleep and the adults were yawning. He carried Leo up to bed and slipped into his own room quickly, shutting his bedroom door and not bothering to say good night to anyone or even to brush his teeth.

Again, around three in the morning, Trevor woke to the clear notes of the piano sounding through the sleeping house. Almost sleepwalking himself, he slipped downstairs.

Candace was there at the bottom of the stairs, wearing a—Trevor didn't know what to call it, but it was short, plunging, and completely transparent. He could see she wore no panties.

"Candace," Trevor whispered. "Sorry Leo woke you. He's developed a kind of obsession with the piano. He does this a lot."

Candace moved close to Trevor, the tip of one breast touching his arm. "Oh, sweetie, I don't mind," she whispered. "Can I do anything to help?"

"Um, thanks, no. I need to get him back to bed before he wakes the household."

"Want to come see me for a while after?" Candace offered enticingly, moving slightly so more of her was visible in the moonlight falling through the windows.

"Uh, no, thanks, I, um, I'll take Trevor into bed with me so we don't wake Cassidy. But thanks, thanks."

Trevor hurried into the music room, spoke to Leo, and carried the boy back to bed with him. Maybe Leo was afraid to sleep alone. Maybe Leo should sleep with him in his bed for the rest of the summer. Or would that set a bad precedent?

Maybe Trevor was afraid to sleep alone. Grinning at himself, Trevor fell asleep.

The next morning, Sophie was sitting on the patio with her cup of coffee and a fresh crossword puzzle when Candace came out to join her. The morning was warm but fresh and dewy. All the children were still asleep. Jeanette was watching her beloved morning show on television and there was no sign of Trevor.

"So," Candace said in a friendly way, "what an odd deal, you and Trevor together in this house when you didn't even know each other."

"It is odd," agreed Sophie. "I suppose if you knew Susie or Ivan Swenson, you'd understand how it all happened. They are sort of hippie-dippies who can't be bothered with hassles like contracts, and I had already made arrangements for my house in Boston and so had Trevor. It seemed like the only solution."

"I hear you're getting divorced," Candace said. She had moved her chair closer to Sophie's and she aimed her eyes at Sophie like a microscope.

"Probably." Sophie didn't want to share with Candace. She didn't like her much and she didn't feel like having an intimate girlie moment.

"*Probably* you could make that clearer. Because in case you hadn't noticed, Trevor and I have a relationship."

You anorexic long-haired lying vegetarian, you can't manipulate me, thought Sophie. Shocked at her hostile reaction, she said nothing.

"It's as if fate meant for us to meet," Candace continued in her sweet voice. "After all, Cassidy doesn't have a father anymore and Leo doesn't have a mother. The children love each other. They are best friends. Trevor and I could meld into a family and everyone would be so happy."

"I hope it works out for you," Sophie replied, nearly gagging on her words.

"Thank you so much," Candace cooed. "I knew you would understand since you're so much older and all. What are you, forty?"

All right, that does it, thought Sophie. "I'm thirty-six," she answered in a perfectly modulated tone. "Now if you'll excuse me, it's my time to play the piano."

In the music room, she began with a soft Chopin sonata so that she wouldn't wake any sleeping children. After a few moments, she lost all sense of other people in the house, emotions she was trying to hide from, and fears about her future. She entered the world of her music with all its order and beauty. Each time she played the piano, she had the sense that this was what life had intended for her all along. Not to be the best, not to be a concert pianist, not to make her parents happy, but simply to play. As if music were a loyal, luminous creature that had been waiting patiently for her to return to it.

Next, a dreamy Debussy fell from her fingertips onto the keyboard. Her entire body surrendered to the music. Everything else fell away—the room, the house full of people, the beautiful island, the complicated, heartbreaking, mysterious world.

"Sophie," a small sweet voice said at her side. "Can I play now?"

Sophie came out of her dream to discover Leo standing there in his baseball pajamas. At some point, Jeanette had come into the room and was sitting on the rose sofa with Lacey snuggled close to her. Cassidy and Candace hovered in the doorway. Cassidy looked curious. Candace looked murderous. Trevor sat with a cup of coffee in an armchair.

"Of course you can, Leo." Sophie lifted Leo onto her lap and they began.

But Candace wasn't the type to be driven away by something as incidental as piano music. She stayed all that day and the next. The weather was so wonderful, she gushed, she wanted to take her daughter to the beach again. Sophie knew it would be ridiculous to hang around the house being irritated, because after all, she *was* six years older than Trevor and it truly would be nice for Leo to have Cassidy in the same house. And why was she even thinking about Trevor and Candace anyway?

"Jeanette? How would you like to go out on a yacht?" she asked.

They didn't go out on Hristo's yacht. Instead, they met him at the yacht club, where he had chosen a sailboat small enough to go through the shoals blocking the inner harbor and large enough for all of them to sit comfortably. No crew was aboard, but Hristo had prepared a lavish picnic lunch that was stowed in the cabin.

The day was warm and sparkling, with a steady gentle breeze. Hristo handled the sailboat with competence—of course he did—and he won over Jonah's reluctant favor by asking him to crew and pointing out parts of the boat offhandedly, flattering Jonah by assuming the boy knew it all. Jeanette and Sophie settled in the stern while Lacey and

Desi lay on the bow looking like mythological goddesses as the boat skipped over the waves, sending a fine spray up over their bare legs and arms, making them squeal and laugh.

They dropped anchor in Polpis Harbor. They swam to shore, not needing life vests because the water was shallow here and full of long shoals. After swimming in the cool, clear water, Hristo led them on a hike through a wild and shady forest populated with huge ancient maples that seemed like gentle elephants and silent giants only pretending to be stationary. The path ended on the edge of Coskata Pond, a small pond open to the harbor by a narrow channel. Here on the beach grass, in the serenity of a world without human beings and their buildings, white herons stood on one leg surveying their domain. Hristo studied the water a moment and informed them that the tide was going out.

"Come with me, and we'll lie down in the water and let it carry us along the channel and all the way back to the boat."

Jonah, Desi, and Lacey were up for such an unusual adventure, but Jeanette and Sophie opted to walk back through the forest and around to the beach facing Polpis Harbor. By the time they got there, the others had already been floated back out into the deeper water. Hristo and Jonah swam out to the boat, climbed up the ladder, lifted the hampers of food and drink above their heads, and waded in chin, and then chest, and then waist high through the water to the beach.

As they enjoyed their gourmet lunch, Hristo entertained them with tales of the Native American ghost, Mudturtle, who roamed this area, mourning his Indian princess lover. It was a Romeo and Juliet story that captured everyone's imagination. As long gray clouds gathered in the afternoon sky, shadowing their small group, Lacey shivered and moved closer to her mother.

A storm drifted toward them from the west, making the trees sway and whisper. The group was glad to return to the boat and sail back to the normalcy of yachts and launches and buildings.

Hristo invited Jeanette and Sophie to dinner, but Sophie could tell her children were tired after the long, adventurous day, and she didn't want to leave them to the dubious mercies of Candace and Trevor. She declined regretfully, and said goodbye.

"I'm sorry you and I had no time for our own conversation," Hristo said, adding diplomatically, "but I have enjoyed meeting Jeanette and it was a pleasure to see the children having such fun."

He walked them to their car, where he kissed Jeanette's hand and favored Sophie with a formal, chaste, European kiss on each cheek.

Sophie was in no mood to deal with Candace and her vegetarian mandate, so she drove her damp and sandy family to Sayle's Seafood, where they ordered fish and chips, coleslaw, and corn on the cob and sat on the porch eating in the fresh air while they watched boats come and go at the end of the harbor. As they drove back to the guest cottage, they were all stuffed and sandblasted, eager to shower and collapse in front of the television or with a book.

They arrived at the house to find Trevor's VW Passat gone. Apparently, Sophie hoped, he had taken his guests out for dinner. After ordering Jonah and Lacey to rinse off in the outdoor shower before entering the house, Sophie and Jeanette went inside.

Sophie stood for a moment in the front hall, gawking at the living room and the steps to the second floor. Was this the same house she'd just left? Candace had clearly taken possession of it, marking her territory in no uncertain terms. Her sandals, beach bag, and sun hat rested in the front hall, while her books and a couple of Cassidy's early readers were scattered on the floor and coffee table. A soft pink sweater was thrown over the back of a chair. On the fireplace mantel, flowers picked from the side garden were prettily ensconced in a vase. A few water glasses and some of Candace's costume jewelry littered the side tables. Cassidy's sparkling pink sneakers were under the coffee table. Candace had done everything but hang a banner announcing "Candace's Room."

Each step to the second floor held an item that needed to be dealt with—wet, sandy bathing suits and beach towels, a plastic bowl filled with seashells, containers of sunblock, more sandals—how many sandals did Candace wear in one day?

"She's a bit messy, isn't she?" said Jeanette in a low voice, as if someone would overhear her.

"That's not the word I'd use," Sophie answered. "But she's Trevor's responsibility." A low anxiety hummed beneath her words: had Trevor invited Candace to stay longer? Had Candace been right—*was* there a relationship between Trevor and her? She really was lovely, and Cassidy's presence made Leo so happy . . .

Sophie and Jeanette went to the second floor and hurriedly took warm showers. Outside the sky was turning an ominous shade of gray and while the temperature was still warm, an unsettling sense in the air made Sophie choose to wear her loose gray slacks and a long-sleeved shirt.

The children had showered and collapsed in front of the television set. Sophie and Jeanette agreed to enjoy a glass of wine on the patio as they watched the storm front roll in. When she poured the wine, Sophie tried to ignore the state of the kitchen. It was chaotic. Several different cheeses had been left out as well as a carton of milk, which she compulsively returned to the refrigerator. Dishes were piled everywhere except in the dishwasher. The jar of peanut butter was open with a knife sticking out of it. This was not Trevor's style, but Sophie told herself to walk away.

On the patio, Jeanette asked, "How long are Candace and her daughter staying?"

"I don't know. We've never discussed it."

"I've always gone by the advice that both fish and guests begin to stink after three days."

Sophie laughed. "Present company excepted."

Jeanette changed the subject. "This was an amazing day, Sophie.

Hristo is an elegant and fascinating man. I can see why you want to spend time with him."

"He is fascinating, and I enjoy his company. But remember, I met him only because his daughter Desi and Lacey became friends on the beach."

"I understand, but he seems quite taken with you. I watched him, the way he looked at you. You don't have to tell me anything, of course, but it seems to me a romance is budding."

Sophie stared at Jeanette. "Jeanette, you must be one of the most unusual mothers-in-law on the planet."

Jeanette laughed. "I suppose I see your point of view, but remember, I want Zack to be happy because he's my son. You've been part of my family for sixteen years now. No matter what happens with you and Zack, you will always be family because of Jonah and Lacey. I think my grandchildren will be happier if their mother is happy. Plus, I care for you, Sophie, and you are a young woman with your whole life ahead of you."

Sophie pondered this as she sipped her wine. By now the sky was dark gray and an occasional raindrop plopped onto the wooden table. "I suppose we should go inside before we get caught in a deluge."

"That's fine with me," Jeanette said. "In fact, I'd really like to stretch my weary old bones in bed and read the mystery I brought along."

"What a good idea. It's a perfect night to read a mystery."

Jeanette said good night to her grandchildren and went upstairs. Sophie, inspired by the weather, settled herself at the piano to play a tempestuous Beethoven piece.

Trevor took Candace and the kids to dinner at the Jetties restaurant, where the kids could jump down onto the boardwalk and play on the beach when they were through with their meals. Because storm clouds were gathering and the wind was picking up, they decided to go into town to browse the local bookstores for some special tale to read to the children. Afterward, they stopped in at the Juice Bar for ice-cream cones. The sugar rush gave the children energy to walk along Main Street, listening to the street musicians playing Irish melodies on their fiddles.

The first time Candace reached over and took Trevor's hand, he actually jumped in surprise. As they walked along the brick sidewalks, he took advantage of other families coming toward him to separate himself from Candace so they could pass by. When they stopped to listen to the street musicians, Candace would hold his hand in both of hers and lean against his shoulder. *Oh brother,* Trevor thought, *what's going on?*

Candace clarified that for him when she giggled and said, "Look. Those people think we're a family. I bet they wonder whether Leo and Cassidy are our twins."

Trevor attempted a kind of laugh that came out more like a choking noise, which was a fairly good representation of his feelings. He liked Candace, he admired her, and he knew she was a babe, but he'd never wanted to take her to bed, forget being a family with her. He thought: *Help.*

Driving back to the guest cottage, Trevor put on an audiobook for the children and kept the volume loud enough to prevent conversation between Candace and him. His mind was working feverishly. He had not invited her here for any romantic reason, but he could understand how Candace would interpret his invitation to have a broader meaning.

Back at the house, no one from Sophie's crew was downstairs. And it was late, not so late for summertime when everyone could sleep till noon, but late enough that Leo and Cassidy fell into their beds the moment their pajamas were on, not even asking for a story from their new books.

In the hallway, Candace moved close to Trevor. "Everyone is asleep," she whispered. "What shall we do now?" Her eyes signaled an offer.

"I've got to go down and clean up the kitchen," Trevor said. "It's an arrangement I made with Sophie when we agreed to share this house. I want to keep my part of our informal contract."

"Quite the little bossy boots, isn't she?" Candace responded. She put her hand on Trevor's shoulder. "I'm going to get ready for bed. Why don't you come into the family room to say good night to me when you're through in the kitchen?"

Trevor said, "Uh." His brain had shut down, overloaded with a screaming mental alarm system.

Candace twinkled her fingers at him. "See you in a minute."

In the kitchen, Trevor moved slowly, loading the dishwasher, putting away the bread, the peanut butter, the box of Cheerios. He wiped down the counters. He considered mopping the floor but he was too tired—or too *something*.

When he finished, he stepped outside onto the patio to enjoy the rush of fresh air and wind preceding the oncoming storm. The breeze scattered over the patio, bringing hints of autumn and apple cider, back-to-school and pumpkins. He had only two weeks left on Nantucket, he realized, and the thought struck something like terror into his heart. It was as if the black wall of clouds passing in front of the moon were a dark magic that would obliterate this amazing summer. A sharp grief stabbed Trevor. It was not a grief for what he had lost but for what he might lose.

"Man up, Trevor," he said aloud in the night and turned to go back into the house.

He found Candace in the family room, curled in an armchair, reading a magazine. She wore that transparent bit of girly nightwear that showed off her lovely body. When she saw Trevor, she stretched and smiled.

"Why don't you lock the door?" she purred.

Trevor shut the door but didn't lock it. He pulled up one of the chairs from the card table and turned it around so he could sit on it with his arms folded on top of the back, with the back forming a kind of barrier between himself and Candace.

The symbolism wasn't lost on her. She tilted her head inquiringly.

"Candace," Trevor began, "we need to talk."

In response, she let the magazine fall to the floor and rearranged herself on the armchair, tucking her long legs beneath her. "Oh? Only talk?"

"Listen, I'm afraid I've been giving out the wrong signals. I'm glad Leo has Cassidy for a friend—and I'm glad to have you for a friend, too." He was struggling to find the right words. He didn't want to insult her.

Candace asked softly, "Friends and nothing more?"

"Right." He held out his hands, as if displaying an emptiness. "You are a gorgeous woman, Candace, and any man would be lucky to be with you."

"But you don't want to be that man."

"No. I'm sorry."

"Do you suppose you're not ready? The time isn't right? I mean, Tallulah hasn't been gone very long . . ."

That would be an easy way out, and for a moment Trevor considered taking it. But no. He wanted to be honest. "It's not the time, Candace. It's—" He hesitated.

"Don't say, 'It's not you, it's me,'" Candace said sharply. "It's pretty obvious you're in love with that Sophie."

Trevor huffed in surprise. "I've only known her for about six weeks."

Candace stood up, her body shimmering beneath her nightie. She walked over to the sofa and sat down on it, wrapping a blanket around her, not looking at him. "You've been honest with me, Trevor. I suggest you do the same with yourself."

He felt the chill coming from her, the anger. "Are you mad at me?"

"Are you kidding? Of course I am. No one likes being rejected. I thought we had a real future, the four of us." Impatiently, she snapped, "Oh, get over it, Trevor; I certainly will. Go away and leave me alone and let me lick my wounds in peace."

Trevor stood up, then waited, wondering what to say next. "Candace, I'm sorry."

"Oh, that makes me feel ever so much better." Her voice was bitter.

He could tell she was going to cry. He felt like a weasel. "Candace—"

"Don't. Shut up. I'm fine. Go away. We'll leave tomorrow." She waited until his hand was on the door to the hallway before adding, "And don't worry, Trevor. I won't get in the way of our kids' friendship. I would never do that."

"Thanks," Trevor said.

Candace didn't reply. Trevor went out of the room, closing the door behind him.

26

Again. Around three in the morning, the notes sounded: DAH-dum-dum-dum.

Sophie slid her feet to the floor and tiptoed down the stairs.

Candace was standing in the living room, looking into the music room where Trevor knelt, speaking in low tones to his son. She was wearing—good grief, what *was* Candice wearing? Something from Frederick's of Hollywood? What if she had to go to her daughter in the night?

"Sexy," Candace whispered.

Sophie realized Candace was being sarcastic as she observed Sophie in her boxer shorts and baggy T-shirt.

Before she could think of a response, Candace murmured, "That poor little boy. Look what you've done. You've turned him into a freak."

Sophie blinked. Trevor was lifting his son into his arms. Leo laid his head on his father's shoulder drowsily. Without responding to Candace, Sophie hurriedly slipped back up the stairs and to her room. She didn't want Trevor and especially Leo to see the two mommies standing there gawking at him. And she was too appalled by Candace's words to think of a response. Anyway, the middle of the night was hardly the time to get into a discussion of Leo's behavior.

As she pulled her door closed, she heard Trevor speaking softly to Candace. Only a moment later, Trevor's steps came up the stairs and turned toward Leo's bedroom. A door shut. The house was quiet.

Sophie sat on her bed for a moment, letting her rattled heart slow to a normal pace. *Was* Candace, in any way, right? Had Sophie somehow added to Leo's obsessive problems by teaching him to play the piano? She didn't think so. Trevor hadn't said anything like that.

A tap sounded on Sophie's bedroom door. Without waiting for a response, Trevor opened the door and let himself in. Before she could speak, Trevor put his fingers to his lips in a signal for silence. Crossing to the empty side of her bed, he pulled back the light summer blanket and quickly got into bed next to Sophie.

Now only the sheet was between them.

Trevor wore only a white T-shirt and his pajamas shorts.

Sophie's eyes were wide. "What are you doing?"

"We need to talk."

"It's the middle of the night. We need to sleep."

"We will in a minute. I need to say some things. Lie down, turn the other way. It's easier if you don't look at me," Trevor whispered.

Sophie did what he said. Trevor snuggled close to her, wrapping his arm around her waist.

"Trevor," Sophie whispered, "you need to work on your seduction technique."

"This isn't seduction. This is a necessary discussion. An enlightenment."

"Yes, well, enlightenment is the right word. I feel like I'm in bed with the Great Point lighthouse."

He was grateful for her good humor and her willingness to accept this spontaneous middle-of-the-night visit. He joked back, "I do have a great point."

"I hope you enjoy it, because I don't intend to," Sophie responded, but not in a cranky way.

"We'll be quiet," Trevor promised.

"Trevor, my mother-in-law and my daughter are on the other side of that wall."

"Sophie, I want to talk. Just talk, about us."

Sophie flipped over, facing him. "Us? Trevor, there is no *us*."

"Okay, that's true, but maybe there should be."

Sophie studied his face for a long moment. "Honey, you are undoubtedly one of the handsomest men I've ever met. You're sexy and—" Sophie closed her eyes and swallowed. She started again. "I want to have sex with you, Trevor, but it would be a huge mistake."

"No, it wouldn't," Trevor replied too quickly.

"Trevor, you and I are both in flux right now. Our lives are turned upside down. It's the wrong time to start a relationship—and before you say anything you regret, for *me* having sex means starting a relationship."

Trevor swallowed. "I want a relationship with you. I think we already have a relationship."

"Please. I'm six years older than you are. I'm a much more serious person than you are. I think you and I have a different definition of *relationship*."

Trevor pulled away from Sophie, sat up in bed, and leaned on the headboard. "Okay, it's probably true, what you're saying. But I don't think it matters, the age thing. Plus, I'm not as immature as you think I am. Maybe I'm just kind of funny."

Sophie grinned and sat up next to him. "You *are* funny and I like that about you. And oddly enough, even though I've known you for such a short period of time, I feel like I can trust you. So I'm going to tell you something I haven't told many people. I've only slept with one man: Zack."

"Whoa. That's radical."

"What can I say? I suppose I'm a freak. But I was all about the piano until I met Zack. How many women have you slept with, Trevor?"

"Um . . ." Trevor grimaced, trying to think of a way to downplay his life before Tallulah. "A few," he finally admitted. "But I was always faithful to Tallulah."

Sophie shifted around to get comfortable. "Tell me about before Tallulah."

Trevor stared at the ceiling. "I was kind of popular in high school. I dated a lot of girls, but I never was serious with any one of them."

"By date do you mean had sex with?"

"Yes, well, sometimes. And in college, too. I'm not ashamed of it, Sophie—I had a good time and I never hurt anyone's feelings."

Sophie looked over at him. "I doubt that."

"Okay, then, I never made promises I couldn't keep. After college, I was busy building my business, and there were a few women I saw, but they were on career tracks, too, and didn't want to get tied down with a personal life. And then Tallulah came along." He paused. "Then *Leo* came along and that changed everything. Come on, Sophie, you have to admit I'm a good father."

"You are. You're a great father. I wish I had had a father like you."

"What was your father like?"

"Distant. Absent. Terribly important. Barely aware that I existed and not particularly excited about it. He was a physician, a scientist, concerned about prostate cancer, and I'm sure he saved thousands of men's lives. My mother was forever telling me I should be proud of him. But it was like being proud of a shadow, a dark, looming shadow that came and went in the house with no connection to me. He died a few years ago of cancer—not prostate—and I tried to be sorry, but I had spent a lot of time attempting to have a relationship with him and then attempting not to feel like a failure because I couldn't live up to his expectations."

"That's sad. I didn't have the best father, either, although it wasn't actually his fault. My mother is on her third husband now. She's quite an, um, *active* personality and gets bored easily. When she married my stepfather we moved to Kansas City for a while and I didn't get to see my dad as much, and then he got remarried and he and his wife moved to Southern California. He died a few years ago, so that's that. But I think if he'd had the chance, my father would've been a good father. He always sent me birthday and Christmas presents and called me a lot and sent me money when I was in college. My mother's second husband and I don't keep in touch. I went to my mother's third wedding, and I suppose I have some stepsiblings somewhere, but they're all grown up so we've never tried to communicate. And Mom, well, she's all about glamour and travel. Although she was good when Leo was born. She did come help me then and she still sends Leo presents and calls him on the phone and Skypes with him."

"My mother's a doctor. Emergency room doctor, busy and stressed. She's completely dedicated to her work. She's not very close to Lacey and Jonah because she's either scheduled at the hospital or exhausted at home." Sophie turned on her side again to face Trevor. "Geez, where did the traditional family go?"

"Maybe it never existed except on Christmas cards," Trevor said thoughtfully. "I remember reading a book about settling the West. Pioneer women used to hang their kids in a bag on a nail on the wall to keep them out of the way while they did chores. I mean, they cut holes for the kids' heads and limbs, but it wasn't exactly all roses for the children."

"Or for the mothers, either. No electricity—forget that, not even running water. It's kind of amazing that human beings have survived as long as we have, especially if you think about disease and germs."

"Oh, yeah, I was hoping we could have a nice conversation about disease and germs," Trevor joked. More soberly, he added, "But if you're a parent, disease and germs are still a big part of your life. I seem to spend one-tenth of my day telling Leo to wash his hands. If he gets an ear infection and I have to take him to the doctor's office where all the other kids are coughing or throwing up, I want to wrap him in sterile cloth like a mummy so he doesn't catch anything. It's pretty terrifying, loving a kid."

"I know," Sophie softly agreed. "If my children knew how much I worry about them every single day, they'd think I was crazy. Maybe I am."

"Jonah is anxious for *you*," Trevor told her.

"What?"

"He told me the night we looked at the stars. He's not a big fan of his father."

"Oh, gosh, this is such a difficult time." Sophie's voice grew heavy with worry. "I don't know what to do for Jonah."

"It's not that bad. Jonah told me he also likes a girl."

"He does?" Sophie brightened. "Rosie?"

"He didn't tell me her name. He said he gets all clumsy when he's doing sports and she watches."

"Must be Rosie. I'm so glad," Sophie said. "Thanks for telling me, Trevor. It's great that he can confide in you. Rosie's a really nice girl. Oh, Trevor, it's all so complicated. Jonah's parents are getting divorced while he's experiencing his first sweet love."

"Don't let on that I told you. I don't know if I should have. And don't worry. We can't control everything."

"Sometimes I think we can't control *anything*," Sophie said, and then she let out an enormous yawn.

"We can try," Trevor said. "We could give ourselves a chance."

Sophie gazed at his face, a soft yearning in her eyes. "Oh, Trevor." She shook her head. "I need some time. I need—I need some sleep."

"Right." Trevor got out of bed and went to the door. "I'll see you in the morning. Think about what I said."

After Sophie heard the door to Trevor's room close, she rolled over to where he had been sitting and buried her face in his pillow, trying to inhale any scent he might have left. She closed her eyes, embraced the pillow, and allowed herself to surrender to the astounding sensations of his body pressed against hers.

So this was lust. It might even be love. She liked him, she admired him, and every time he came into her view her heart did a happy dance. She wanted to hang a full-length poster of him on her bedroom wall. She wanted to carry a photo of him as the screen saver on her iPhone. She wanted to shackle him to her body with chains and locks. She wanted to kiss every freckle, every muscle, even the bottoms of his long, bony feet. She wanted to lie on top of him and fit her body to his, arm to arm, leg to leg, breasts to hairy chest.

Apparently she had finally, at the age of thirty-six, achieved her teenage self.

That he had not pressed her tonight when the desire between them was as strong as the moon on tides, that he had not insisted or entreated, caused her to admire and love him even more. It was one of the few times in her life when she'd resisted the imagined whispers of Aunt Fancy telling her to *go for it.*

If only she had met him instead of Zack, she could have married him. Except then Leo and Jonah and Lacey would not exist.

And if she had met him when she was nineteen, he would have been thirteen. Oops.

She could not be with Trevor, not really. Not in the real world.

She forced herself to roll back to her side of the bed. Closing her
eyes, she fell immediately into a delicious sleep.

It was around seven when she woke. Standing up, she went to her
bedroom window and looked out over the green slope of lawn leading
to the apartment. The morning light lent a soft radiance to the landscape, making it shimmer like a scene from a dream or a storybook.
Could certain terrains be magical? If not, why had stories through the
ages told of such places? In the apartment, Connor Swenson, who had
lived all his life on a farm in Iowa, who had loved his wife and lost her
to death, was beginning his own life again on an unfamiliar island. In
this house, a small boy who had lost his mother to death was learning
how to begin his own life again. And her own son, Jonah, fifteen years
old, part dragon-slayer, part goofball, was learning how to grow into
adulthood with all the emotional growing pains of his physically
stretching bones and hamstrings, and he'd met a man to talk to about
them, man-to-man. Sweet Lacey was having an innocent, happy summer vacation.

Sophie was beginning a new life. She could not explain why it was
here on this island that her piano playing returned to her. She knew
only that it had happened as swiftly and irresistibly as a wave sweep-
ing over her, claiming her, pulling her deep into the ocean of music.
Here, she had awakened.

But like a woman caught in a fairy tale, she knew she had to be
wary. On this island, she was under an enchantment. Who knew
whether, when she returned to the mainland, the dazzling crystal spell
might shatter and fall away, leaving her unable to play piano, allowing
her to see Trevor for his true self, a man six years too young for her.
Allowing Trevor to see *her* as her true self, a woman six years too old
for him.

And what about Hristo? Now there was a fairy-tale prince! Desi and Lacey had become good friends, true, but Hristo was involved in the affairs of an ancient and troubled nation. When she looked at his handsome face, she saw the power and the spirit of a king prevailing there. When she saw him standing at the helm of his boat, she recognized the form of a warrior king, a leader, a troubled and complicated man. She had spent some time researching Bulgaria on her computer. Its history was Byzantine and complex, impossible for her to comprehend without serious study. Its present was turbulent and troubled. Sophie could not even imagine the problems plaguing Hristo.

In a way it was like a dream come true, meeting such a man, a man she might have imagined when she was younger—although she, a fortunate American, never could have imagined the complex and tragic depths of history from which he came.

Noises from the rest of the house reminded her of her life in the present. With her own concerns put in their appropriate perspectives, she pulled on a sundress and sandals and prepared to face the day.

After breakfast, both Jeanette and Candace announced they were leaving that morning.

"What boat are you leaving on, Candace?" Sophie asked sweetly. "Perhaps we could drive you in."

Candace shot Sophie a look that would have stripped varnish off furniture. "No, thanks. It's going to take me some time to get ready." Her eyes narrowed, thoughtfully. "Will your children be going with you to say goodbye to Jeanette?"

"Of course," Sophie answered, silently thinking, *but I don't think it will do you any good to be alone with Trevor.*

As Sophie drove into town, she listened to her children babbling to Jeanette the way they had ever since they were old enough to make noises. Jeanette listened to them with the same adoring fascination. She promised to attend Jonah's soccer games when they started in the fall and to come to the school play if Lacey had a part. When they had almost arrived at the ferry, Jeanette told the children she would love to spend more time with them, that perhaps on Saturdays or Sundays they could come to her house, just the two of them, to go to movies or museums and eat all the foods—mostly cupcakes and ice cream—that their parents didn't allow them to have as often as they wanted. Sophie knew there was an ulterior motive here: if Sophie and Zack had to spend time together breaking up their marriage and splitting up their house, Jeanette's home would be a safe place for the children.

Jonah carried his grandmother's suitcase to the blue luggage rack. They all stood in line until Jeanette boarded the ferry, and then they ran out as far as they could on the wooden pier to wave goodbye as the boat slowly glided out of the harbor toward Nantucket Sound.

Lacey wept. "I don't want Grandma to go," she wailed.

"I don't, either." Sophie wrapped her arm around her daughter and squeezed her close.

Next to them, Jonah loped along with his hands in the pockets of his board shorts, his eyes hidden behind sunglasses. Sophie knew her son was sad, too, but that he would stick himself with pins before admitting it.

What could she do to cheer them all up? The day was hazy and overcast, with a relatively light wind. On the spur of the moment, she rented bikes for herself and Lacey and took them home, where she organized a picnic and filled water bottles for all three of them. They changed into shorts and sneakers, tucked maps of the island into their pockets, and took off.

They hadn't spent much time on the eastern part of the island, so they headed toward the Sconset bike path running straight and easy for seven miles to the village at the end of Nantucket. Jonah, so much stronger than Lacey and Sophie, shot ahead of them, legs pumping, and Sophie let him go. Riding a bike was as good as jogging for clearing the mind and cleansing emotions. They spent the day at Sconset, picnicking on the beach, checking out the Sankaty lighthouse and the beautiful mansions along the bluff, and stopping to view the erosion that recent storms had caused, destroying much of the land between the houses and the ocean. They stopped at the small market and bought ice-cream cones to lick as they strolled along the shady lanes between charming old apartments. On a whim, Sophie returned to the market and bought a cheerful red pinwheel to take back to Leo. Finally, full of sugar, they biked back home.

It was late afternoon by then. When Sophie dropped her bike on the lawn of the guest cottage, her legs practically went out from under her.

"You kids are fixing your own dinner tonight," she warned them. "I need a hot bath and a cold drink."

Inside the house, an unusual quiet reigned. Jonah thumped upstairs to his room and his various electronic devices. Lacey went into the kitchen to fix herself some ice water. Leo was in the garden, rearranging a section of his Lego wall. Sophie opened the kitchen door to the patio. Trevor was sitting at the table with his laptop. He was barefoot. His T-shirt announced: *AutoCorrect can go duck itself.*

Sophie dropped into a chair. "We biked all the way to Sconset and back. I may never move again."

Trevor wouldn't look her in the eyes. "You should've asked me to go along. I could've put Leo on the back of a tandem."

"Didn't you have to take Candace and Cassidy to the boat?"

"Oh, yeah. Right. That was quite an undertaking. Candace couldn't seem to find everything she'd brought."

"I'm sure Leo's sad that Cassidy is gone," Sophie said.

Trevor shrugged. He seemed cranky and unsettled. Shutting his laptop, he asked, "Would you like a beer?"

"I'd love one. And a heating pad and neck brace," Sophie joked, again trying to remind him of the difference in their ages.

Trevor went into the house and returned, handing her a Corona.

"Thanks. What did you guys do after Cassidy and Candace left?" They had two more weeks to live together and Sophie wanted them to live in harmony.

"We went kayaking." Trevor's face brightened. "And we had some excitement. As Leo and I were paddling back to shore, a police boat stopped us. I couldn't imagine what we were doing wrong, but the policeman told us that a boat caught on fire earlier this year—no one was on it, no one was hurt—and it sank to the bottom of the harbor. The police boat was ushering in the burned boat that was being towed to a crane that could lift it out of the water. Leo was thrilled to see the police boat. Plus, the policeman waved at him."

Lacey came out of the house, carrying a pink plastic glass of water. "I can't find anything good to watch on TV."

"Lacey!" From the far end of the lawn, Leo jumped up and began running toward the patio. "Lacey, Lacey! Come see what I built! It's so cool. I made a bridge between my fort and your fairy house."

"Cool, Leo! Show me." Lacey took the little boy's hand and walked with him back down the yard.

Sophie looked at Trevor. "Leo made a bridge."

Trevor swallowed, his Adam's apple moving noticeably. "Don't you see?" he said quietly. "Don't you see how close Leo has gotten to Lacey?"

"Trevor—"

"Don't you see how close I've gotten to you?" Trevor continued, his voice low and shaky. "Last night in bed—"

"Trevor, stop." She reached over, put a hand on his arm, and immediately withdrew it as the chemistry leapt between them. "Trevor, I am too old for you."

He glared at her. "That's ridiculous."

"I'm six years older than you are."

"So what?"

"I have stretch marks. I have a messed-up history and a truckload of complicated relatives. You can choose from any number of pretty young women who would make you happy." She was almost trembling. She held up her hand. "And I don't want to have an affair, a fling, a roll in the hay."

Trevor smiled at her suddenly. "Yes, you do. Last night you were this close—"

She cut him off. "All right, I do. But I don't want only that."

"I don't either. Why would you think that of me? I want the whole thing. You and I almost have the whole thing—the family life, the desire, the—"

"Mom." Jonah stepped out onto the patio. "We're out of tuna fish."

Sophie tore her eyes away from Trevor's so fast her head swam. Touching her forehead, she closed her eyes a moment to get her balance. "Peanut butter," she managed to say.

"Only smooth is left. I like chunky."

Within the calm smoothness of her skin, her nerves were jangling like bells. Her chair should be shaking, her hair should be fluttering, Trevor and Jonah should cry out, "Are you having a seizure?" But it was all in her mind—no, it was all in her heart, a heart that was breaking apart.

She stood up suddenly. "Jonah, deal with it. Make yourself whatever you can find for a sandwich and make one for Lacey, too. The bike ride has drained me. I'm going to bed. I'll see you all tomorrow morning."

She brushed past her son, refused to look at Trevor, went into the house, and hurried up to her room.

It couldn't happen. She was too old for Trevor, too old to live with him, to combine their households, their children, their lives. He wore T-shirts sporting the names of rock groups she'd never even heard of. He was *thirty*. She was almost *forty*. As the tub filled with hot water, she stripped off her clothes—the bathroom doors did have locks, thank heavens—and surveyed herself in the mirror. Lines crept from the corners of her eyes. Stretch marks wriggled over her skin. Her breasts—well, okay, in spite of the fact that she'd nursed both children for a year, her breasts were still pretty good, plump and pointing outward rather than sagging down. She sank into the bathtub with a long sigh of pleasure as the hot water surrounded her. She couldn't even bike all day without earning an aching back and she'd never in her life had an orgasm.

What? Where did that thought come from? Sophie slid all the way under the water, covering her hair, her face, even her nose, as if hiding from a judgmental invisible muse. When her lungs were almost bursting, she slid back up and gasped for breath. For all her intimacy with Bess and Angie, she had never confessed this fact about her odd and uncooperative body. She'd always faked ecstasy with Zack, at first because she had no idea about sex and then simply out of habit. It was one of the things her husband liked about her, he had always said, that she could arrive at a climax so easily.

Perhaps soon, after the divorce, she could find a therapist, a counselor, to whom she could confess her failing, who would help her rather than judge her.

The thought brought her a surge of hope. She vigorously washed her hair with the strawberry-scented shampoo Lacey loved, and soaped her body all over, rinsed and dried and brushed her teeth and put lotion on her body and face. She took two aspirin. She pulled on a fresh T-shirt and undies, then peeked out into the hall—no one there. She hurried into her bedroom and got under the covers.

Sleep refused to come, even though she was exhausted. Her mind was still racing, her heart fluttering around like a sparrow in a box, reminding her of Trevor's words on the patio, Trevor's look, and the bridge Leo had built to Lacey's fairy house.

She couldn't risk letting herself believe that she and Trevor could be together. She had to stop this for once and for all. She had to—

Hristo. He had been so kind to her and her family, taking them out on his yacht, taking her to dinner. It would be only good manners to repay him—she'd invite him and Desi to dinner. She'd invite them to dinner and prepare Bulgarian food! Of course Trevor and Leo could come, too, and Trevor could see how much more suitable Hristo was for her, what a more conventionally appropriate match they were in ages. He would back down. She would be free of this fierce temptation. She slipped out of bed, found her cell, and called Hristo.

He answered. She apologized for such short notice, she said, but their guests had left, and she wondered whether he and Desi could come to dinner tomorrow night. He was most delighted, he replied, to accept.

Back in bed, she opened her laptop and searched out Bulgarian recipes, making her shopping list for the next day. Slowly her senses calmed. She forgot her backache. She forgot her rogue, irrational heart.

By the time she'd organized the menu for tomorrow night, she was genuinely tired. It was only shortly after nine o'clock, but the day had been long and full of emotion, beginning with Jeanette's departure, ending with, well, everything on the patio. She put her laptop on the floor, turned off the bedside lamp, and slid beneath the covers. Her pillow cradled her head like clouds. She closed her eyes.

Her cell rang. She should have turned it off. Drowsily, she reached for it where she'd left it on the bedside table.

"Hi, honey bun!" Angie's voice was bright with affection and good humor. "I thought I might come back to the island for a few days. Do you have room for me in your seaside Shangri-La?"

"Of course, Angie. When are you coming?"

"Would tomorrow work for you? I'd stay two or three days. I've finished a trial—I won, of course—and my brains have melted up here in this heat. Bess and her family are going up to Maine to her sister's. So it would be just lil' old me."

"Tomorrow sounds great," Sophie said warmly. "Text me which boat you're taking."

"I might fly. I'll let you know. You're a peach. Love you."

"Love you," Sophie replied. "See you tomorrow."

Okay. She snuggled back under the covers. *Okay, good.* Angie would be here, and she could flirt with Trevor, she would probably go to bed with him, and Sophie could focus on Hristo and everything would be correct and appropriate.

But now she could not fall asleep.

27

The next evening as Trevor bathed Leo after their long day at the beach, his mind wandered and he only half listened to Leo's chatter. In a minute he'd have to dress his son, and then they'd go down to the special la-de-da Bulgarian dinner Sophie had prepared for her cosmopolitan, sophisticated, wealthy, multilingual, yacht-owning boyfriend Hristo.

Okay, Trevor wanted to say, *okay, I get it. I'm too immature. I wear old T-shirts. I don't have a yacht.*

But Sophie didn't need a yacht, she needed Trevor, and somewhere in that convoluted mind of hers, she knew it. She didn't have to bring Angie down to flirt with him and relieve him of adolescent sexual cravings. He was a big boy. He could restrain himself. It wasn't sex he wanted. It was Sophie.

". . . is dying," Leo said sadly.

The words jerked Trevor back to reality. "What, Leo? What did you say?"

"I said Connor told me he is dying." Leo listlessly pushed a yellow rubber duck back and forth in the bathwater.

"Leo, dude, when did Connor say that?" Trevor tried to keep the alarm out of his voice.

"Yesterday. I told him about Mom dying, and that I wasn't so sad anymore. He told me his mommy had died, and he wasn't so sad anymore, because he was dying, too."

"Um. Leo, I think he meant his wife died, not his mommy. But I'm sorry to hear that. What did you say?"

Leo looked up at Trevor. "I said maybe he'd see my mommy and his mommy in heaven when he got there."

Trevor frowned, trying to remember the last time they'd seen Connor. The summer was flying by so quickly, so many visitors were arriving at the guest cottage, that he hadn't wandered down to the apartment to chat with the old guy.

"Is he breathing all right?" Trevor asked. "Is he eating? Where were you when you spoke to him?"

"I was showing him my bridge to the fairy house. He liked it. He was sitting out on his deck carving something. He didn't seem sad, Daddy. He didn't seem hungry. I didn't ask him if he was hungry." Leo's face crinkled with worry.

"It's okay, Leo, you did exactly right. Old people don't get as hungry as young people. I'm sure it made him happy to see your bridge. It is sad, though, that he thinks he is dying. I wonder if he needs to go see a doctor."

"Oh, Connor doesn't like doctors," Leo said. "I told him I don't either." Leo stood up, water cascading from his chubby, tanned body. "I'm ready to get out."

"I need to speak with Sophie about this," Trevor muttered, more to himself than to his son as he lifted his child's wet body from the bath.

Leo nodded. "Sophie will fix it."

After dressing Leo and combing his unruly hair, Trevor changed out of his damp clothes. With guests coming to this special dinner, he couldn't show up in a T-shirt. He put on khakis and a Brooks Brothers button-down shirt with the sleeves rolled up. He'd been told—even Tallulah had commented—that the pale green of the shirt brought out the green of his eyes. Not that he was competing with Hristo.

Downstairs he found the rest of the party lingering around the dining room table, drawn by the tantalizing aroma of Sophie's cuisine. He shook hands with Hristo, kissed Angie's cheek lightly and warily, and went into the kitchen to ask Sophie if he could help. She was flustered, taking pans from the oven, stirring pots on the stove. Her cheeks were pink from the heat and excitement. Trevor wanted to shove her up against the counter and put his hands down the front of her cute white apron.

Instead, he did as she asked: he marshaled the kids in to wash their hands, then called everyone to the table. Sophie had allocated Hristo, as guest of honor, to one end of the table. She was at the other end, and everyone else could choose a place. Desi and Lacey of course sat side by side, Leo sat next to Jonah, and that left two empty chairs: one next to Sophie, one next to Hristo. With a silken glide, Angie took the chair next to Hristo. Trevor glanced at Sophie to see if she was as amused by this as he was. Sophie winked.

When everyone was seated, Sophie tapped her glass. "Before we eat, I want to thank you all for coming and tell you what we are eating tonight. You know we are having a Bulgarian meal in honor of our guests, Hristo and Desi. First, we will have *tarator*, a cold soup of yogurt, cucumber, and garlic."

"Ick," Leo interrupted spontaneously, and everyone laughed.

"Try it," Sophie suggested gently. "Next, *shopska* salad, which is made from chopped tomatoes, cucumbers, onions, peppers, and white cheese. I used feta. Next, moussaka, which I know my children like, and *sarmi*, grape leaves stuffed with rice and mincemeat. But first, a toast with the Bulgarian rakia Hristo has brought us tonight."

"Can I have some?" Jonah asked.

"Me, too!" Leo piped up.

"No, Leo," Sophie said. "Rakia would burn your throat. Jonah, you may have a sip. One sip, and Hristo is pouring your glasses now. Rakia is clear, so it has the appearance of water but it is extremely potent—that means, Jonah, it could make you sick."

Lacey, thrilled to have her friend to dinner, averted a potential crisis. "Look, Leo—Desi and I aren't having rakia. It stings. We're having ginger ale. Want some, too?"

"Okay," Leo agreed.

Hristo poured, Sophie asked everyone to wait until each person had a glass, and then she held hers high in a toast. *"Nazdrave!"* she said. "To life!"

"Whoa!" Jonah said, swallowing. "I need water."

"We have water for everyone, and plenty of food," Sophie told him, handing him a pitcher.

As they ate, Angie plied Hristo with questions about Bulgaria. Finally he said, "Enough, enough. Angie, tell me what you do."

Angie leaned toward him, showing cleavage. "I'm a trial lawyer. In Boston. We have scores of immigrants from all countries in Boston. I've represented people from practically every nation. Recently . . ."

"Mom. More moussaka?" Jonah asked, holding up his plate.

"More moussaka, *please?*" Sophie corrected automatically.

"Please."

She spooned another helping onto her son's plate. At this end of the table, it was difficult to hear Angie and Hristo because of the children's chatter. Trevor kept an eye on Sophie to see if it bothered her that Angie was attempting to move in on Sophie's beau, but Sophie appeared content, even radiant.

When the meal ended, Sophie said they'd have dessert outside—ice cream and berries. Jonah, in a charitable mood after such a good meal, deigned to play "Statues" with Lacey, Desi, and Leo.

"I'll wait for my dessert," Angie said, rising. "I'm stuffed." She rubbed her hand over her slender belly, inviting them to regard her figure in her restrained turquoise silk dress.

"Go on out," Sophie told her. "I'll clear the table."

"I'll help," Hristo said, rising and picking up a plate.

"No, that's my job," Trevor interrupted—perhaps a shade too sharply. "I mean, my agreement with Sophie is that she cooks and I clean the kitchen."

"But tonight is a special night," Hristo argued winningly, with a smile and a twinkle in his eye. "Bulgarian night."

Angie yanked Trevor's hand. "Come on. Let's go out."

Trevor followed her, feeling sullen. He sat in a lawn chair next to Angie—anywhere else would be churlish—and watched her slowly unbuckle her glittering sandals and remove them.

"Trust Sophie to have men fighting over her to do the dishes," Angie said. She glanced at Trevor. "Honey, I'd say you've got it bad."

He didn't want to discuss how he felt about Sophie with anyone, certainly not Angie. "And how are you doing, Angie?"

"Honestly?" Angie curled up in her chair, tucking her feet beneath her skirt. "I'm lonely. My ex has a serious girlfriend and my kids like her, too, the traitors. Although I know it's a good thing, it's like my kids have even more people to love them, blah blah blah, here I am, all alone in the world, and why? I'm not exactly an old hag."

Touched by her candidness, Trevor agreed, "You're certainly not, Angie. You're beautiful. Smart, too."

"Thanks, Trevor. But do men want beautiful and smart? Sometimes I think I'm too smart, too ambitious, too driven, too argumentative, too flamboyant—and don't say a thing. I know what I am. My husband liked all that until I became more successful than he was; then he became unfaithful and now he's with Betty Boop, all dimples and *gee whizzes.*"

Trevor shifted uncomfortably in his own chair. He wasn't up for this intimate a discussion. "I'm sorry," he said at last, apologizing for men in general.

"Oh, well, don't worry about me. I like my solitude, being my own boss about everything in the house. And I'm getting plenty of carnal knowledge, believe me, and perhaps that's all I need. If I can't get loved, at least I can get . . ." With the children playing nearby, Angie refrained from finishing her sentence.

Trevor focused on the children, who were running over the green grass, freezing into silly positions, falling onto the ground with laughter. Overhead the setting sun struck gold into the edges of the clouds as the sky changed from blue to lavender.

"Remember being that age?" he asked. "The sheer joy of bare feet on soft grass, the excitement of being out at night, the smell of the fresh summer air . . ."

Angie snorted. "Honey, I wasn't ever that age." She put her hand on Trevor's arm. "Move slowly, but look in the kitchen window."

Trevor turned. Clearly outlined by the kitchen light, Sophie and Hristo stood facing each other in front of the sink, so close that Hristo could put his hand gently on Sophie's cheek as he bent to kiss her lips.

"Go on and shoot me now," Angie said.

"He might be kissing her to thank her for the meal," Trevor suggested desperately.

"MOM!" Jonah shouted. "WE CAN SEE YOU!"

The bellow made its way into the house, causing Sophie to jump back from Hristo. She said something Trevor couldn't understand, and then both people disappeared from the window.

"He can't marry her," Trevor said. "He travels all over. Her children need the security of a home base."

"Oh, Trevor," Angie sighed. "Step up to the plate, guy. You're in love with Sophie—go *get* her. Then I'd have a chance with Hristo."

"She told me I'm too young," Trevor protested. "And I *am* six years younger than she is. I don't know what to do."

"If you don't know what to do, you *are* too young for her." Angie snorted. Rising from her chair, she said, "I'm going to play 'Statues' with the kids. At least I'll run off some of my dinner."

Trevor sat brooding while Angie and the kids ran around in the dimming light and Sophie stayed inside, probably making out passionately with Hristo.

A light came on in the apartment, and suddenly Trevor remembered what Leo had told him. He'd better check on the old guy. Skirting the swirling players, he went across the lawn and knocked on Connor's door.

Connor opened it. "Good evening, Trevor."

Trevor quickly assessed the man. Connor seemed perfectly fine, dressed in a white T-shirt and long khaki pants and those handsome loafers with the toe cut out of one side. No doubt, Trevor thought irrelevantly, the man had a bunion. Most old people did.

Quickly, he came up with a reason for knocking. "Um, we're going to have dessert on the patio. Angie is here, and Hristo, the Bulgarian, and we wondered if you'd like to join us."

"Thank you, but I believe I'll decline," Connor replied formally. "I'm in the middle of a good detective novel and I just brewed a fresh cup of coffee."

"All right, then," Trevor said. "I hope the kids aren't bothering you with all their screaming."

"I enjoy hearing their voices," Connor told him. He nodded. "Good night."

Trevor went back up to the patio, thinking that Connor looked all right. He'd have to ask Sophie about him tomorrow. He was glad to see Sophie and Hristo sitting on the patio now, chatting with Angie. Trevor joined them.

"Hristo follows the Red Sox, too," Sophie informed Trevor. "We were just talking about this season."

"Yes," Hristo agreed. "I was wondering why the baseball grand finale is called the *World Series* when it is played only in the United States."

"I don't know," Trevor said. "I never thought about it."

"I'll find out," Angie said. "That's the sort of question that sticks with me."

The conversation evolved into a discussion of players. Jonah left the children and joined the adults to add his opinion of Big Papi and Dustin Pedroia. Not much later, Leo fell and hurt his arm. Trevor consoled his child and carried him up to bed. When he returned, Hristo and Desi were saying good night. Trevor shook hands with Hristo. Hristo kissed Angie on both cheeks, and then he kissed Sophie, politely, on both cheeks. Trevor experienced a whopping great satisfaction at being the one to close and lock the door behind the other man.

"Fabulous meal," Angie said to Sophie.

"Thanks, Angie. Let's talk tomorrow. I'm exhausted." Sophie left to round up her son and daughter and nag them away from the television and upstairs to bed.

Trevor went in to check the kitchen. It was spic-and-span, but he busied himself washing the countertops, hoping to avoid Angie. It worked. By the time he went up to bed, he could tell that Angie was asleep on the pull-out in the family room.

Because of the direction of the wind, the next day they drove out to the beach at Quidnet, where Sesachacha Pond was separated by a narrow stretch of sand that was often breached, allowing ocean water to flood in. Trevor and the kids were at the far end, trying to fly a kite. Angie and Sophie lay side by side on beach chairs, heads back, exposing their necks to the sun, eyes closed.

"You know he's in love with you," Angie said.

"Angie. Get real. He's a child."

"Hardly. He's got a successful business—super successful. I checked it out with some friends in Boston."

"You would," Sophie said with a chuckle.

"You bet. Plus, Trevor's a wonderful father. Oh, and P.S., tell me when it was you ever saw *Zack* teach your kids how to fly a kite?"

"Then why don't *you* grab him? You had sex with him, if I recall."

Angie blew air through her lips like an exasperated horse. "Yeah, because I initiated it. He was capable but not thrilled."

Sophie couldn't help laughing. "You *can* be a touch aggressive."

"Hey, I'm a trial lawyer. I chew men up and spit them out. I need a man who can deal with me." Angie paused strategically. "Like that Hristo dude."

"Angie, Hristo is devoted to his country. He'll always be traveling."

"So? Fine. I don't want to get married. I've been married. I've had my children, my two sweet babies who've turned into defectors, and I don't want any more. I make as much money as I need. I want to travel, too, have fun while I'm still young. I want that Hristo guy. He's mysterious and sexy as hell."

"Take him."

"Get out."

"Seriously."

Angie pushed her sunglasses up onto her hair and sat up to twist around and gawk at Sophie. "You aren't even a small bit smitten?"

"Of course I think he's fascinating," Sophie replied calmly, thinking as she spoke, oddly and very clearly *knowing* as she spoke. "He seems genuinely nice, given how mega-sophisticated he is. And he is sexy as hell, I agree—"

"Have you slept with him?"

"Angie. I'm still married to Zack—"

"Who's sleeping with another woman—"

"Besides, I don't operate on the same wavelength you do. I don't even operate on the same planet as you."

"What are you going to do when this vacation's over?" Angie pressed.

"Return to our house. Get the kids back in school. And, I suppose, start divorce proceedings with Zack."

Angie lay back in her chair. "Are you sad?"

Sophie took the time to consider the question. "I was. I was hurt, insulted, ashamed for myself, and frightened for my kids. Having Zack's mother here helped enormously. And I've learned something I've known all along, or rather I've stopped avoiding the truth. Zack is an absent father. He likes the status marriage and kids provide, but he can't take the reality." Sophie paused. "He hasn't called the kids once."

"Shit."

"I don't think they're too surprised. Or even upset. We're exactly like we always were. And you know what, Angie? I'm sad for the kids about the divorce, but for me? I'm *glad*." She sighed. "Isn't that terrible?"

Angie reached over and held Sophie's hand. "You two had some good times."

"We did. So did you and Spencer."

"But don't you want a man, Sophie?" Angie asked.

Under the hot rays of the sun, hearing her children whoop and run nearby, having her dear old irritating, stimulating friend Angie pressing on her thoughts, Sophie admitted to herself that yes, indeed,

OMG, she *did want* a man. She wanted him so desperately, so unmistakably, distinctly, and fiercely that she was terrified of saying his name.

She hedged. "Not just any man. I don't think I'm as sexual as you are, Angie." They both laughed. They'd been friends since high school and Sophie knew the sorts of escapades Angie had gotten up to all her life. "Sure, I guess I'd like a man," Sophie continued, lying like a rug, "but I'm not in any hurry."

"Well, don't dismiss Trevor simply because he's younger than you are. I think he's a keeper."

Sophie snorted. "You only want me to be with him so I'll give you Hristo."

"Hey!" Angie playfully shoved Sophie's arm. "You don't think I can take Hristo away from you without your permission?"

"I don't know," Sophie teased. "Why don't you try?" She jumped up and ran toward the water, with Angie chasing her. They splashed each other, shrieking as the cold water hit their midsections, then dove in and swam next to each other, racing for a nearby shore. For a while, they were purely girls again.

Later, Trevor dropped into a beach chair next to Sophie and Angie. He got out his water bottle and drained it. "The wind's not quite strong enough to keep the kite up."

"You were good to try," Sophie told him. "Let's let the kids swim a while before we go back to the house."

"I'm getting broiled," Angie said, slowly rubbing lotion on her long, sleek legs.

"I want to talk to you anyway," Trevor told Sophie. "Yesterday when I was bathing Leo, he told me that Connor says he's dying."

"What? That's awful," Sophie said.

"Yeah," Angie chimed in. "That's what Leo needs, someone else dying on him."

"Shut up, Angie," Sophie ordered. Turning to Trevor, she said, "What did Leo say exactly?"

Trevor explained it, working to remember the exact words.

Sophie chewed a thumbnail. "I don't understand. He's always seemed—slow, perhaps, but healthy. His hands are strong; he carves. He picked those berries. But why would he say such a thing unless he believed it was true?"

"He hasn't joined us for drinks recently," Trevor said thoughtfully. "Or come out to watch the stars."

Sophie was startled to find herself crying. "I thought of him as a kind of—oh, this is silly, but a kind of grandfather figure for Leo and Jonah and Lacey. I mean, my father's dead, and Zack's father might as well live on the moon for all the attention he pays to my kids. Grandparents really aren't like they used to be."

"I know," Trevor agreed. "My parents are divorced. My mom visits sometimes, when she's not having cocktails with her third husband, and my dad died a few years ago. As for Tallulah's father—no affection there. When I phoned her parents to tell them about Tallulah's death, they refused to come for a funeral or have her ashes sent to them. They said she was no daughter of theirs."

"Cheese and crackers!" Angie snapped. "Could you two get more maudlin? Come on! It's a fabulous sunny day! We're on Nantucket! Your children are happy. Geez, I'm going back to Boston if you two keep this up." When both Trevor and Sophie shot her the same look, she added, "Oh, no. You don't get rid of me that easily." Laughing, she picked up a plastic bucket, ran to the pond, filled it with water, and rushed back to throw it on Sophie.

Sophie screamed, jumped up to chase Angie, and Trevor rose, too, stretching in the sun, taking in the view: two lovely women splashing in the pond, the sun catching drops of water flying from their skin, for a brief moment flashing with light. Nearby, Lacey held Leo's hands and pulled him slowly in circles in the water. Jonah was farther out, working on a steady breaststroke. Across the pond, a couple sailed a red Sunfish, gliding through the water, and on the far side, a couple of swans paddled together, ignoring the invaders of their domain.

Angie was irritating, Trevor thought, but she was right. *Carpe diem.*

That evening, they sent Lacey and Leo down to the apartment to invite Connor to join them for a simple cookout on the patio, but Connor politely refused. When Sophie grilled Lacey for Connor's exact words, they were: "Thanks, but not tonight, kids." Yet he was dressed and looked fine, Lacey reported. Trevor and Sophie agreed to let the matter lie.

28

The next day Trevor had all the kids with him so that Angie and Sophie could spend a day in town shopping. In the evenings, a slight dry coolness hinted at the approaching fall, and Angie wanted new clothes for work. The women changed out of their shorts into sleeveless minidresses—and sandals, because it was still summer and the sidewalks were uneven brick.

Angie went at clothes shopping as she did at everything: full tilt, fast-forward. She stalked around a shop, eyeing the clothing, spotting a dress here, a skirt there, yanking them from the rack and handing them to Sophie, who carried them over her arm while Angie chose more. In the dressing room, Sophie was the attendant, zipping and unzipping, returning the items to their hangers, handing them to the salesgirl with a request for a different color or size, informing Angie how each dress looked from the back. It was a job Sophie enjoyed. She had never wanted to be a trial lawyer like Angie; she had never needed to care about having a "look." She didn't have the kind of energy Angie had. It would have exhausted her to try on so many outfits, to make so many decisions so quickly, and Sophie found herself watching her friend in action as if Angie were a breathing paper doll. For work, Angie dressed strategically: she had mild, diplomatic, let's-make-a-deal clothes and get-out-of-my-way killer clothes.

This was the woman Sophie had known from childhood, and it was a blast watching Angie with her work mind on. By two o'clock, Angie had bought several thousand dollars' worth of clothes, jewelry, and shoes, and both women were practically limping beneath the weight of the shopping bags they carried in both hands.

As they staggered down Main Street, slightly giddy, laughing, they heard a man say, "Hello, lovely ladies."

"Hristo!" Sophie cried, delighted to see her friend—her tall, strong, capable friend.

"Thank heavens!" cried Angie. "Would you buy us a drink? We're exhausted."

"I can see you've both been diligently assisting the local economy," Hristo said. Without being asked, he reached out to relieve the women of all four shopping bags.

"Only Angie," Sophie told him. "I've been playing handmaiden."

"When I return to Boston, I've got a hell of a complicated case coming up," Angie explained.

"Have you had lunch?" Hristo asked.

"Not yet," Sophie answered.

"Come. We'll go to Cru. We'll eat and drink and you can regain your strength after such a trying ordeal."

At the restaurant at the end of Straight Wharf, they sprawled on soft cushions shaded by blue beach umbrellas, drinking Champagne, eating lobster, and chatting. Angie wore her wild black curls up in the classy chignon she wore in court, and as she talked, Sophie understood how Angie could transform herself from warmhearted friend into elegant sophisticate. From time to time, Hristo sent Sophie a questioning glance, as if checking to be certain Sophie wasn't offended by Angie's dominance. Sophie smiled politely.

In fact, as Angie and Hristo got into a profound discussion about the role of the U.S. in international affairs, Sophie relaxed against her bench and let her mind drift. Being around Angie was always exhilarating and exhausting. Angie was driven, ambitious, cutthroat, determined. Perhaps as a teenager practicing the piano, Sophie had been determined and ambitious, but now she realized she had never burned with the need or greed or hunger or whatever it was that drove Angie and kept her happy and on top of her game even now. It was possible . . . Sophie was just beginning to comprehend this, and she had no pattern or role model for putting it into words, but maybe . . . maybe she'd never wanted to compete. Never wanted to be the best. Maybe she'd wanted to play piano for *herself*. The revelation filled her with a kind of dazzling hope.

"I'm off to the ladies'," Angie announced. "Want to go, Soph?"

Sophie forced herself to the present. "No. I'm good."

"Slide over, then." Angie squeezed past Sophie and headed into the restaurant.

"Ah," Hristo said. With a teasing smile, he continued, "Alone at last."

Sophie returned his smile, but was still swimming her way up from her own private thoughts.

"You do not mind at all, do you?" Hristo asked.

"What? I don't mind what?" Sophie struggled to focus her attention on him.

There he was, broad-shouldered, dignified, and handsome, almost magnificent.

Hristo reached across the table and took Sophie's hand. "You do not mind that your friend Angie is coming on to me."

Sophie blinked. "Oh, I've known Angie since we were girls," she said. "She's always been the show-off."

"That's not really what I'm asking," Hristo said.

"Hristo . . ." She bit her lip, searching for the right words.

"I had the definite idea that you and I would like to see each other after the summer ends," Hristo clarified.

"Yes, of course, but, Hristo—I mean, I'm still married to Zack, even though it looks certain that we'll get divorced—" She was stuttering, tying herself in knots. "And I, I'm happy as a housewife, while you, well, you're so much!" She spread her hands wide.

He released her hand. "I don't believe I have ever been let down in such a complimentary way."

Her hand lay on the table. She knew she could reach for his, she could still bring him back, and she was not surprised to hear Aunt Fancy's exasperated whisper in her mind: *Oh, for goodness sake, child, look at the man! Don't you want some glamour? You could travel to Europe. Plus, please take a moment to imagine what he'd be like in bed. I'll bet he's hung like a stallion.*

"Aunt Fancy!" Sophie said.

Hristo cocked his head. "Aunt Fancy?"

"Sorry. Sorry." Sophie waved her hand in front of her face, as if swishing her aunt away. "I had an aunt who was wildly daring. I adored her. She's not alive anymore, but I think of her often, and I know how much she would have liked you. Liked you, she would have *loved* you! You are—"

"And you don't," Hristo said.

Sophie stopped talking. She could have said, *I don't what?* but she knew very well what he meant. From somewhere, perhaps from the thought of Aunt Fancy, or perhaps from the energy of the summer sun, or perhaps from a muddled but powerful feeling that her life had finally stumbled in the right direction, from all of that came the courage for Sophie to say, with melodic gentleness, "Hristo, you don't, either. If you're honest with me."

His smile was wrenchingly gorgeous. "I could."

"I don't think so. You would become bored, and I would become confused."

To her infinite relief, Hristo burst out laughing.

"What's so funny!" Angie was back at the table, her face freshly and delicately made up, her posture both formal and sexy. *How does she do that?* Sophie wondered.

Hristo, ever the gentleman, rose as Angie returned to the table. "Sophie's protesting that she shouldn't drink Champagne in the middle of the day. Especially in the hot sun."

As if on cue, Sophie yawned. "It's true. And Angie, you have to admit, I worked hard today, trudging around after you, carrying tons of clothing."

"You were an angel," Angie said. "And I'm grateful. I suppose we should go home," she added reluctantly.

"But you haven't had dessert," Hristo said. He shot Sophie one last charming and terribly fond look, then turned his attention to Angie. "Why not let Sophie drive home. You can stay for dessert with me and I'll drive you home later."

Angie would always win at poker. She appeared totally unimpressed with this offer, but she languidly looked at Sophie and asked, "What do you think?"

"That sounds good to me," Sophie told her. "See you later." Rising, she gathered her purse and blew a kiss to Angie and one to Hristo.

Well, Aunt Fancy, she thought as she walked away, *I believe I have just finessed my first and probably only international transaction.* She couldn't stop smiling.

Sophie returned to an empty house. Trevor had obviously taken the three kids somewhere, probably to the beach.

Her lethargy vanished. She went to the piano, took some sheet music from the bench, sat down, and began to play.

She started with an easy Mozart piece, slid into a more complicated Brahms, and gaining courage, attempted to remember her favorite Rachmaninoff sonata. Clunkers flew from her fingers, but no one was there to criticize, no one corrected her timing, no one judged. Each note of music felt like a minuscule, invisible, sterling silver key unlocking the chains that had been wrapped around her heart for years—a fanciful thought, but not untrue. As she played, a freedom rose within her, and a happiness she had forgotten.

Maybe she had never been meant to play for others, but she had always been meant to play for herself. Whoever she was, music was part of her soul, and without it, she was weakened, she was caged.

She played until her arms ached, until they trembled with exhaustion. Finally she had to stop. Alone in the house, sitting on the piano bench, she wrapped her arms around herself in a triumphant embrace. *Hello, Sophie*, she thought, *it's good to see you again.*

All right. Back to normal. She checked her watch. It was after four. People would be thundering in soon, and they would be hungry. And she needed to talk with Trevor about Connor.

In the kitchen she set about rinsing and slicing vegetables, arranging them on a platter around a bowl of hummus so when everyone arrived they wouldn't immediately dive for the chips. She set it on the dining room table. Upstairs in her bedroom, she hummed as she changed out of her downtown shopping clothes into shorts and a halter top and flip-flops. Glancing in the mirror, she decided it was time for a haircut or at least a trim. Or maybe not. Maybe she liked her hair long. Shoulder-length was more practical, but she wasn't sure she wanted to be practical anymore.

As she went down the stairs, Trevor and the kids filed in the door, sunburnt, sandy, hungry, and thirsty, everyone talking at once. She paused on the stairs to listen. Yes, this—childish chatter, sibling sniping, giggling, racing bare feet—this also was the music of her life. Trevor said, "Kids. Look. Sophie's put out snacks."

And Trevor? Sophie thought. He had such a low, pleasing voice. Would he be part of her life, too?

That evening she prepared an easy dinner: meat loaf, corn and tomato salad, and new potatoes in butter and parsley. Leo fussed about the thin red skin left on the potatoes. Jonah said, "Put butter on it. If you put butter on anything, it tastes good." Leo had come to worship Jonah and did what he said. Trevor and Sophie exchanged glances.

"Where's Angie?" Trevor asked. "She can't still be shopping."

"We ran into Hristo in town," Sophie explained. "We had lunch with him, and Angie decided to stay for a drink. Hristo said he'd drive her home."

Trevor's jaw dropped. He wore a faded T-shirt that read: *If you believe in telekinesis, please raise my hand.* His nose and cheeks were fluorescent with sunburn, his teeth gleamed snow white, and his green eyes were wide, almost with wonder. "Hristo is driving Angie home," he said slowly, as if learning a formula for an exam.

"Mom." Jonah pushed back his chair. "I'm done. May I please be excused?"

"You may."

The other kids raced away from the table with Jonah, off to the family room to watch television.

"Trevor," Sophie said when they were alone, "could we talk about Connor? I'm concerned."

"Yeah, me, too. I asked Leo to tell me again what Connor said, but he repeated what he told me, that Connor told him he was dying, but not to be sad."

"I think we should go down and talk to him," Sophie said. "If he's ill, we need to get in touch with Susie or Ivan. He's their grandfather."

"I have no idea how to reach Ivan. He's in India, probably wandering through the desert with a camel."

"I can get in touch with Susie if we need to," Sophie said. "But I hate to worry her if there's no reason." She pushed back her chair. "Let's go see Connor now."

"Wait. Let's take a moment to think about how to approach him. I don't want to tell him what Leo said unless I have to. I think maybe Leo and Connor have developed a kind of friendship. I don't want Connor to think Leo, well, *tattled* on him, or gave away a secret."

"I see what you're saying, but on the other hand, Trevor, is it a good thing for an old man to tell a child he's dying? That's kind of scary, isn't it?"

"Not the way Leo told me. I've been advised that it's good for Leo to talk about death. He doesn't comprehend it, but it's part of life, his mother has died, and I think Connor was only trying to make Leo feel comfortable with the concept."

Sophie nodded. "True. He may not even be dying, now that I think of it. He's an older man; perhaps he merely meant to give Leo a sense of—how do I say it—the *normalcy* of death."

"Do we have anything for dessert?" Trevor asked.

"What?" Sophie blinked at the change in subject.

"I mean that we could take down to Connor, as an excuse to hang out."

"Oh, right. Let me think. We've got ice cream, Popsicles, and the last piece of the key lime pie I made yesterday."

"Perfect. Let's take it down to him. That way we won't have to divide it into fractions."

"Good idea."

Sophie slid the pie onto a plate and covered it with cling wrap. Trevor told the kids they were walking down to say hi to Connor. They stepped out into the evening.

"It's getting dark earlier," Trevor said. "Have you noticed?"

"I have. It makes me both sad and glad. Fall's my favorite season."

"Are you eager to get back to Boston?"

Sophie shot Trevor a wry smile. "I do love the city, but I've got a lot of complicated stuff waiting for me. It's one thing to tell the kids their father and I are getting divorced, quite another to go through with it all. Will we be able to stay in our house? Will the legal bits get messy, dividing up the money and assets, and so on? Not to mention dividing up the furniture, photos, family heirlooms . . ." Sophie shuddered. "I think I'll stay here on this faraway isle forever."

"You'll be okay," Trevor assured her. "I'll help you."

Her breath caught in her throat at his words, but before she could come up with a sensible response, they'd arrived at the apartment.

Trevor knocked on the door. Lights were on, and they could hear the television. But no answer. He knocked again.

"Hello?" Connor called.

"Connor? It's Sophie and Trevor. We brought you some key lime pie."

It seemed a long time before Connor came to the door. They heard the sound of the television muted, and then Connor's footsteps, more uneven than usual, and then the door opened, but only partway. Connor looked out. Sophie could tell that he was neatly dressed in a white collared shirt and his khakis, but he wasn't wearing shoes. *So what?* she thought. She went around barefoot in the summer all the time.

"Hello, you two. What's this? Key lime pie? Wonderful. Thank you." Reaching out, he took the plate. "Sorry not to invite you in, but I'm in the middle of watching one of my favorite old movies."

"That's fine," Trevor told the older man. "Enjoy."

The door was quickly shut.

Sophie and Trevor walked back across the lawn in silence. When they were out of earshot on the patio, they sat down at the table to talk.

"He looked okay," Trevor said. "He had shaved today."

"Trevor, didn't you notice how he talked? He barely moved his lips. He smiled with his mouth closed."

"Maybe he has false teeth and he'd taken them out."

"Well, maybe, although I don't think he has false teeth. Plus he never used to smile or talk with his lips stuck together like that. And he was barefoot."

"Sophie, it's a hot August evening. He should be able to sit in his underwear in his own home if he wants."

"You're right, I know. Still."

"Hi, guys, there you are!" Angie stepped onto the patio. She was glowing.

"So you had a good time with Hristo?" Sophie asked.

Angie slid liquidly into a chair. "He's the most fascinating man! He took me to see his yacht. We didn't go out on it, but if the weather's good, we'll go tomorrow." Innocently, she added, "Of course you all are invited along. I mean, the kids, of course, and Sophie, and you, too, Trevor." She was practically purring.

"Mom." Jonah slid open the patio door and trudged to Sophie, holding out her cell as if it weighed three hundred pounds. "It's Grand-mother."

Sophie accepted the phone warily. "Hi, Mom."

"Sophie. Are you having fun?" Hester's relentlessly sensible voice made the question sound like a schoolteacher asking whether she'd finished her exam.

"I am, Mom. So are the kids. It's gorgeous here. You should come visit."

"I thought I would, actually. I believe you said you have sufficient room."

Sophie almost fell off her chair. She should have remembered that her mother had no sense of polite, good-hearted white lying. If Sophie in any way invited Hester to visit, then Hester would come.

"Um, that's great, Mom!" She forced warmth into her voice. "When do you think you can get here?"

"The day after tomorrow. I've made my reservation on the Cape Air Flight 172 that arrives at twelve thirteen."

"Well! Well, we'll be there to pick you up! I'm so glad!" What else could she say? *The kids will be thrilled?* They wouldn't be, and Hester knew it. If Jonah or Lacey choked or went into anaphylactic shock, Hester could save their lives, but she didn't do cozy.

"I'll see you then."

The moment Sophie clicked the phone shut, Angie said, "When is she coming? Because I'm leaving before then."

Trevor asked, "Is she that bad?"

Angie said, "She's worse."

Sophie said, "Angie, don't be mean. That's my mother you're talking about."

"So I should lie?"

Sophie leaned forward to look around Angie at Trevor. "My mother is practical," she told him. "She's an emergency room doctor, and it's sort of hardened her to normal, everyday problems."

"Yeah," Angie cut in, "she should have been a heart surgeon. She would have loved cutting open people's chests and digging out their hearts."

"Stop it, Angie." Sophie aimed her words at Trevor. "My mother's not warm and fuzzy. But she's not a monster."

"Some people might disagree," Angie muttered.

"Some people are pretty controlling, critical, and demanding themselves," Sophie shot back.

"Only in the courtroom, sweet cheeks," Angie teased, fluttering her fingers along Sophie's bare shoulders. "On this island I'm finding a whole new softer, gentler side to myself."

"You're incorrigible," Sophie declared.

Angie laughed. "I know. That's why you love me." She rose. "Should I find a nice hotel room on the island for a few nights?"

"Angie," Sophie huffed, "my mother won't bite!"

"I know, but your house is full already. I'm on the family room pull-out, which, I grant, is queen-size, but I certainly don't want Hester sleeping with me."

"Mom can sleep in the other twin bed in Lacey's room," Sophie said.

"God, poor Lacey. She'll be told to pick up her clothes and she won't be allowed to read late."

Sophie squinted. "I know what you're doing. You're trying to find a way to escape staying here so you can be in a hotel room in case you want to bring Hristo to your room!"

Angie laughed wickedly.

Trevor rose. "I'm going to say good night, ladies."

"Oh, Trevie," Angie cooed. "Are we scaring you?"

"Frankly, yes," Trevor said, and went into the house.

"Sometimes, Angie, you're too much," Sophie said, pulling her knees up to her chest and wrapping her arms around them.

"No, my sweet, innocent friend," Angie replied, pulling her chair closer to Sophie's, "what I am is Machiavellian. We need to make it very clear, crystal clear, bold print in bright letters, to Trevor that you and Hristo are over, *fini*. Men are dense. Plus, Trevor's nice. He's not going to try to interfere between you and a wealthy guy like Hristo. I've only made it unmistakably observable by the sweetest of men that you are not in love with Hristo. That you are free for what you would probably call courtship."

"Angie, you're kind of nuts, you know?"

"And you're not?"

"Do you really like Hristo?"

"I really do. Of course I've known him for only one day. But I think he likes me, too. I think we're two of a kind."

Sophie eyed her friend. "You speak French fluently, don't you?"

"*Mais oui, ma petite*," Angie answered. "Some German, too. Oh, yes, and now I can speak some Bulgarian." She rose, kissed Sophie's forehead, and said something that sounded like "*Dubro vecer.* Good night."

That night, Leo played the piano again. *DAH-dum-dum-dum.* This time Sophie went down to find both Trevor and Angie standing in the music room, watching.

"Sorry he woke you," Trevor said. He looked exhausted and sad.

"It sounds like something I know," Sophie mused. "A song I've heard before."

"It sounds like bags under my eyes," Angie snorted. "I'm definitely getting a room in a hotel."

"Angie, I apologize," Trevor said. "I'll pay for it."

"Don't worry about it," Angie told him. "You've got enough on your hands. I'll go online and book something." She hurried back to the family room.

Sophie quietly padded into the music room and knelt down next to Leo. "You really like those notes, don't you?"

Leo nodded. "I hear them when I'm sleeping. There's more—there's words—I can't hear it all yet."

"Maybe we can figure it out during the day," Sophie suggested.

"Maybe." Leo yawned and sagged.

Trevor said, "You need some more sleep, buddy." He lifted his son and carried him up to bed. Sophie followed, her mind playing the four notes over and over again, searching for the tune.

29

When River called Trevor to say a client wanted a face meeting right away, Trevor was glad, even though the client was an anxiety-riddled mass of arrogant neuroses who only needed his hand held by the man he considered "the boss." He told River he'd fly up tomorrow for the day. He asked Lacey if she could be Leo's babysitter; he would pay her well. He told Leo he'd be back for dinner, that Leo could spend the day with Lacey, and he prepared to reassure and even bribe his son (big new Lego set) but discovered he didn't have to. Leo was quite happy to spend the day with Lacey.

He dressed for the meeting in the city: jeans, blue button-down shirt, blue blazer. As he drank a cup of coffee and munched a muffin while standing up in the kitchen, Angie and Sophie came in and made a fuss over how great he looked.

"Goodness, Trevor, you set me all atwitter!" Angie gushed. "Now I kind of wish I hadn't booked a room in a hotel for tonight."

Sophie leaned against the kitchen table and scanned Trevor up and down as if he were a bar code. "You do look extraordinarily hand-some," she told him.

"Oh, good. That will impress my client," he responded dryly, but his heart skipped a beat at her words.

As he drove away from the house, along the tree-shaded curving lanes, on to the busier streets to the airport, an eagerness took hold of him. He had to be careful not to speed, and it was easy to speed on this island where forty-five miles per hour was the fastest you could drive anywhere. It was as if he were in one of those time–space continuum bubbles from a science-fiction movie, a sheer, almost but not quite visible glaze of reality that enclosed him while he was on the island, convincing him that life was all beauty, sunshine, beach and ocean, continents of stars, nights of sweet, deep slumber, and days of plea-sure. As he parked his car in the long-term lot and strode toward the terminal, he sensed himself pulling away from this bubble, this fantasy of life, this shimmering existence. He stood in line at the counter to pick up his boarding pass, then stood in line at the gate to board. He walked sedately to the nine-seater Cape Air plane, buckled himself into a seat, and as the plane lifted from the runway over the surround-ing water, Trevor felt himself break free of the bubble.

He stared down at the island, at the shoals lying beneath the water, turning the water turquoise, and the deeper, darker blue of Nantucket Sound. He leaned his head against the window and closed his eyes as the plane rumbled north.

It had been a successful vacation. Hell, it had been a shocking mar-vel of a vacation, more than he had ever expected, more than he could have planned or fantasized. For a moment he pictured himself and Leo in that huge Swenson house alone, without the Anderson family. They would have been okay. They would have gotten to know Connor. Perhaps they would have had more adventures—gone on a whale watch, on a deep-water fishing trip; perhaps Leo could have attended a kiddie day camp. But really, they would have been lonely, knocking around in that big house by themselves. Trevor supposed he could have found a babysitter, frequented a couple of island bars, met some summer-romance women, but really? He was over that scene.

The plane landed. His mind snapped into work mode: briefcase in hand, he walked to the subway, rode to the stop in Harvard Square, and strode through the familiar streets to his office, where he'd go over things with River before his client meeting. Here was reality: college students, university buildings, traffic jams, newsstands, coffee bars, clothing stores, art cinemas, then row after row of streets with triple-decker apartment houses like his own. Some had towering trees and pots of flowers on the porch. Some had barking dogs chained in the yard. Some had children's plastic toys littering the grass. The houses were close together, driveway touching driveway, trash barrels out on the street for pickup, and a slightly worn olive-green armchair sitting on the curb with a sign pinned to it: *Free. Just Take It.* He passed through zones of music, as if he were tuning a radio in a car: rap, then country, then jazz, then a talk show in a language he thought was Portuguese.

He came to a halt when he reached his own apartment building. He took his time to *see* it. Three levels high, an apartment on each level, a driveway, a neglected yard with more weeds than grass—still he was grateful for the weeds; at least they provided some green. The siding was vinyl, it would last forever, which was a shame, because the owner had gotten a deal on a mustard-yellow color that Trevor now understood would never be improved by anything, not by shutters of pale blue or window boxes of geraniums.

But he had to remember: he'd rented it because it was so close to transportation, to the beating heart of the city and its business. In only minutes he could get Leo to day care or over to the Museum of Science or the aquarium or the Children's Museum. And Tallulah—

he must not forget how Tallulah had prized this location with its quick access to so many theaters.

He sprinted up the steps, into the house, up to the second floor, and into his apartment. At first he thought he'd entered the wrong place; then he recalled that River and his girlfriend Nestra were settled there, and that they were slobs, totally and irredeemably, and so the sweaters, shirts, robes, shoes, purses, plastic bags, pizza boxes, dirty glasses, magazines, open DVD cases, empty Cheetos bags, and crumpled candy wrappers were theirs. He checked the small aquarium. The water was clean, nicely aerated, and the fish were swimming normally in and out of their castles.

He found River in the kitchen, barefoot, shirtless, frantically washing dishes. River jumped when Trevor walked in. He said, "Um. Dude. Sorry about the mess."

"It's fine, River," Trevor said. "You've done a great job with work. But better remember we'll return in a couple of weeks and Leo has to go back to school."

"Yeah, sure. We'll clean up. All the info on Butterfield's on your desk."

Trevor went into the office, which, he was relieved to see, was relatively tidy, or as organized as it ever was. He quickly scanned the Butterfield info but he already knew all of it, so he went into Leo's room.

Here it was exactly as it had been. River and his girl had had the sense not to enter. Leo's bed, his small bookcase, the Winnie-the-Pooh curtains and bedspread, perhaps too young for him now. They would get new ones. Leo's dresser, their shrine to Tallulah.

Tallulah. Trevor stood before her framed photo, studying the picture. She had longed to have plastic surgery. She said that symmetry in features was important for the movies. If he scrutinized her face carefully, he saw that one eye appeared slightly larger than the other, but weren't everyone's eyes that way? A person could go crazy thinking about it. The truth was that she was a voluptuous, radiant beauty, a sex goddess, a vamp. He thought he could see in the depths of her eyes a kind of fear, or a fear/hope, that she could be enough to achieve her goals. Loving Leo had not helped with that ambition, nor had loving Trevor, if she had loved Trevor. She had had a one-track mind, one single objective, and nothing Trevor could have done would have made any difference in whether she achieved that goal. Maybe the heroin had made her feel more secure, more successful, more talented. Maybe she had preferred to die with a fellow actor than to live with a normal person like Trevor.

"I tried my best," Trevor said aloud.

He heard no response, not even in the whispers of his mind.

Shutting the door firmly behind him, he stopped in front of his bedroom, where River and Nestra now slept, and recalling the state of the rest of the place, decided the wiser choice was not to open the door.

He went into the kitchen, where River was still washing dishes.

"Okay, man, I'm off to meet Butterfield. I'll go back to Nantucket after our meeting and text you the results."

"Cool."

Trevor paused, really seeing River. "Hey, you've gotten some muscles, guy. You're looking kind of cut."

River turned red. "Thanks. Yeah, I've been working out. Nestra and I are on a health regime. No more pot, less booze; want to get our bodies clear and our heads on straight." Abashed, enthusiastic, he glanced at Trevor. "We're going to have a baby. Nestra's two months along."

"River, that's terrific!" Trevor clutched his employee in a crunching male hug. "I'm happy for you both."

"Thanks, man. We hope we can do as good a job with our kid as you're doing with Leo."

Trevor's jaw dropped. "River, I think that's the nicest thing anyone's ever said to me in my life."

Embarrassed, River turned back to the dishes. "Yeah, well, you can tell we've got a ways to go. But Nestra's working at a Gap—that's why the place is such a mess. We'll have it all good again by the time you return."

"I'm sure you will, River." He glanced at his watch. "I've gotta go meet Butterfield. I'll call you from the airport—I'm flying back this afternoon."

"Got it."

Now his thoughts really were all over the place as he sprinted down the stairs and out to the sidewalk. He stopped again to look up at his mustard-yellow apartment house. Something was different about it—but it had not changed. He had.

He met with Franklin Butterfield at a new fusion restaurant in Cambridge. The meeting went well, as Trevor had assumed it would, because Butterfield basically only needed to have Trevor go through some of the technological steps that baffled the older fellow. Trevor pulled up some graphics on his laptop, calmly explained how the buttons and links would work, and showed him the progress that had been made in building the website, even though he didn't tell Butterfield he'd been doing the work on Nantucket—that might have made the man's head explode. Quite a few really intelligent people couldn't grasp how much mobility Trevor's online work made possible.

He picked up the tab for lunch, which made Butterfield even calmer—it seemed to prove to him that Trevor's business was solvent, successful. They shook hands, and Trevor retraced his steps: subway, airport terminal, ticket counter, plane, flight back to the island. He felt a sense of sympathy for Butterfield as he stepped out of the plane onto the landing strip of the small, almost toylike Nantucket airport;

how could Trevor's two worlds, so extremely different, exist within an hour of each other? It was as strange and wonderful as pushing a button on a computer and seeing a familiar face on Skype.

Driving home, he became obsessed with wishing he'd bought gifts, small presents—Red Sox T-shirts, a book, a toy. But no, that was ridiculous: he wasn't a daddy returning from a long journey; he had been away for only a few hours. Yet it seemed like forever.

The heartwarming aroma of lasagna greeted him when he opened the door. The house was quiet. He went into the kitchen, popped open a beer, and looked out the window. Sophie reclined in a chair, reading a book. Leo and Lacey were at the far end of the yard, making additions to their houses. Jonah had set up a croquet wicket and was playing his own version of croquet/golf, working on improving his aim.

Trevor stepped onto the patio.

Sophie's face lit up. "You're home!"

"Daddy, Daddy, Daddy!" Leo cried, jumping up and beginning to run toward Trevor.

"Hi, Trevor!" Lacey called, running alongside Leo up the lawn. Jonah was more sedately dragging himself up to the house.

Sophie rose. She wore white shorts, a blue T-shirt, and flip-flops. "Dinner's all ready. We were just waiting—"

Trevor interrupted her. Taking her shoulders in his hands, he turned her to face him directly. In a low but firm voice, he said, "I want to marry you."

Her book fell from her hand. She stumbled backward in surprise.

I am a clod, Trevor thought. *I have the sensibility of a gorilla. I should get down on my knees, I should have an engagement ring, we should be alone on the beach . . .*

But Sophie was smiling a great big ear-to-ear smile. "Okay," she said.

"What are you guys doing?" Lacey yelled, skipping up the lawn.

"Okay?" Trevor repeated, amazed.

"Daddy, Daddy, Daddy!" Leo ran onto the patio, crashing into his father's legs.

"Okay," Sophie repeated. "But let's not announce it tonight. We've got to get organized first."

"Organized is not the first thing I want to do," Trevor told her hotly.

"Daddy!" Leo tugged on Trevor's pants.

Sophie's gaze on Trevor's face was like a kiss. "You might notice we are surrounded by children."

"Mom." Jonah stood nearby, arms folded like a high school principal.

Sophie aimed a sunrise of a smile at the children. "Trevor and I are making plans, kids. We'll tell you about them later. First, wash hands. It's time for dinner."

30

should have known, Sophie thought wryly. *We both should have known. This is how life works, without violins and the glorious sunset.* Lying— alone—in her bed, trying and failing to read, she turned off her bedside light for the fiftieth time and tossed over to her side, forcing her eyes closed.

This morning before he left, Trevor had made Leo's cheese-and-mustard sandwich with Leo watching. They'd packed it up with the cold drinks and fruit in the cooler to carry to the beach. Leo had waved goodbye to his father without the slightest tear or whimper. Sophie had driven the gang to Surfside Beach, where they established their home camp in the usual place.

At lunchtime, to everyone's amazement, Leo declared he wanted a hot dog from the concession stand, like Lacey and Jonah. Sophie's heart skipped around in a private little happy dance. They ate lunch, rested, played in the water, played in the sand, came home and showered, then watched television while Sophie threw dinner together.

At dinner, everyone was cheerful, even silly. Lacey told knock-

knock jokes. Trevor entertained them with descriptions of people he saw in the city trudging along in suits, lugging heavy briefcases, newspapers under their arms. Jonah patiently waited for everyone else to eat their fill, then devoured the leftover lasagna, almost half the pan. Sophie noticed that he'd grown at least another inch during the summer.

Whenever she looked directly at Trevor—"Would you like more salad, Trevor?"—he grinned mischievously and Sophie knew she blushed. She couldn't eat, not really; she was too wired, too excited, too nervous.

Then, as they were all carrying their plates into the kitchen, Leo stopped, bent over, ralphed, and vomited down his front, onto his feet, and all over the floor.

"Oh, no, it's the hot dog," Lacey cried.

But as the evening slid into night and Leo continued to retch and hurl, finally and weakly dry heaving, they took his temperature, which was 102, and decided he had the flu. It was going around, Sophie had heard from other mothers at the beach. The good news was that it was a twenty-four-hour flu, intense but short-lived.

So much for romance.

Trevor stayed with his son, wiping his mouth, settling him in bed, rubbing his back. Sophie drove into town for ginger ale and Tylenol. Finally they all went to sleep, Trevor of course sleeping on the other twin bed in Leo's room.

Maybe it was a good thing. *Was* it a good thing? Was it karma? Fate? Was she about to make a mistake, with the goddesses watching over her keeping her from being a fool?

But you didn't tell someone you wanted to marry him unless you were serious about it.

On the other hand, Sophie was thirty-six. Not so very old, but it had been ten years since she'd had a baby, and she hadn't gotten pregnant in those ten years, although she'd always used precautions, and recently she hadn't needed to because she and Zack seldom had sex. Clearly Trevor longed for a family, a complete television-commercial family with the full complement of father, mother, children, and probably a dog . . . A dog would be nice. Jonah and Lacey had been agitating for a dog for years, but Zack said they were too much trouble. They wouldn't have to get a big dog. They could get a West Highland White Terrier, those cute dogs with button eyes and the sweetest faces . . . Jonah wanted a golden retriever, though. But he would be home for only three more years before he went off to college . . . A rescue dog, that would be the best thing, a funny-faced mutt . . .

Sophie fell asleep.

In the morning, Leo's temperature was down and he wasn't throwing up. He'd slept most of the night, but restlessly, and had no appetite. They enthroned him like a small maharajah on the family room sofa, swathed in light quilts, pillows tucked around him, a glass of ginger ale and a handy bucket within reach. Trevor had dark circles under his eyes from lack of sleep and sat on the sofa with his son in case Leo needed him.

Sophie spent the morning doing laundry and tidying the house for her mother's arrival. Lacey agreed to ride to the airport to get Grandmother—Jonah begged off, no surprise. Five minutes before they were to get into the car, Lacey made a giant O with her mouth, bent from the waist, and spewed her breakfast all over the floor.

"Mommy, I don't feel so good," she cried in a wobbly voice.

Sophie sprinted into action, pulling off Lacey's stinky clothes, wrapping her in a towel, and ushering her into the family room to join Leo on the sofa. Trevor hurried into the kitchen, returning with a bucket and sponge. Without a word, he set about cleaning Lacey's vomit. When Sophie saw this, she thought: *Wow. He must really love me.* Lacey had a fever and Sophie prepared a glass of iced ginger ale.

Trevor promised to watch both invalids, and Sophie raced to her car. She was already late to pick up her mother, who would not be amused.

Hester was waiting in the terminal, arms folded beneath her bosom, eyes hidden by sunglasses. Sophie always forgot how pretty her mother was: petite, slim, and blond, with perfect posture and wide blue eyes.

"Mother, I'm so sorry," Sophie said, rushing to hug Hester. "The moment I was going out the door, Lacey threw up. There's a twenty-four-hour flu going around the house, I'm afraid."

"I'm so glad I came," Hester responded dryly, allowing herself to be kissed on the cheek.

"It hit so suddenly—Would you like to go home and return another time when everyone's well?"

Hester shook her head. "I'll be fine. Perhaps I can help."

"Nonsense." Sophie picked up her mother's luggage. "You're on Nantucket. You're on vacation. You're going to relax."

"Yes," Hester joked wryly, "because I excel at relaxation."

It was true. Hester was happiest when she was at the hospital. She preferred to be busy and tidy. Her house could not be called cozy, but it was definitely clutter-free and clean. When she wasn't wearing scrubs or a white coat, she wore jeans, a blue shirt, and a navy cardigan with pockets. Glamour didn't appeal to her; she was all about practicality.

As they buckled themselves into their seat belts, Sophie felt Hester take a good look at her.

"Your hair," she said. "It needs a trim."

Sophie stared at her mother and realized that for years she'd worn her hair exactly like Hester's: short and practical. "I'm growing it out," she said. "Why be a blonde and have short hair?"

"Princess Di was a blonde with short hair and she looked lovely," Hester reminded Sophie.

"Princess Di would have looked lovely in dreadlocks," Sophie shot back.

"Heaven forbid."

Sophie turned the key in the ignition. Two minutes in the car and already they were having a spat. She started over. "I can't wait for you to see the house. It's amazing."

"It must be if you had to dig into your legacy from Aunt Fancy."

"If there were ever an emergency, this is it," Sophie said sadly. "I've spoken exactly once with Zack. He wants a divorce."

"I never liked Zack," Hester reminded her.

Sophie allowed her mother this point. "You were right, as it turns out." She recounted her conversation with Zack, and her talk with her children about the forthcoming divorce. "They seem okay with it, but I'm sure when we're back in our house and they see Zack again and all the hard stuff begins, they'll go through some difficult times."

"Or maybe not," Hester said calmly.

When Sophie drove into the driveway of the guest cottage, the door opened and Trevor stepped out. He came to the car and courteously opened it for Hester.

"Hello, Hester, I'm Trevor Black, your daughter's housemate."

Hester stepped out and shook his hand. "How nice to meet you."

"May I carry your luggage to your room for you?"

Hester glanced at Sophie and a small smile melted across her face. "Excellent service in this hotel," she said. "Yes, Trevor, that would be helpful."

"How are the kids?" Sophie asked as they entered the house.

"Lacey's asleep. Leo's perking up. He drank some ginger ale and ate some dry toast."

"Great!"

"Wait. Jonah's started hurling." With a nod toward Hester, he said apologetically, "I mean he's vomiting."

Hester smiled again. "I'm familiar with the term *hurl*."

Sophie allowed Trevor to escort her mother to her room while she went to the family room to check on Lacey. Her daughter was curled in a fetal position on the sofa, with a pillow under her head, a light cover over her, and a bucket next to her on the floor. Tubee was tucked in her arms.

"I gave her Tubee to make her feel better," Leo explained. He sat at the other end of the sofa, watching television and looking at a children's book.

"That's nice of you, Leo." Sophie gently laid her wrist against Lacey's forehead. "Are you hungry or thirsty?" she asked Leo.

"Nope." Leo thought a moment and added, "Thank you."

Sophie found Trevor and her mother sitting in the living room, talking.

"Jonah's asleep," Trevor informed her.

"Good." To her mother, she said, "Sorry you can't see the children right away. Would you like to go to the beach?"

Hester sniffed. "I've never been crazy about sand in my shoes."

"We could go into town and look at the shops."

"I've heard about the prices here. Besides, there's nothing I need to buy."

Sophie chewed her lip. *What* would entice her mother? Maybe Sophie could bring down her laptop and Google a nice article about the plague.

"Maybe you'd like to hear Sophie play the piano," Trevor suggested.

Shocked, Sophie shot Trevor a "thanks a lot" look. Hester turned toward Sophie, puzzled. "You're playing again? Why yes, yes, I'd like to hear you."

"You would?" Sophie nearly fell off her chair.

"I would. Very much."

Sophie swallowed. "I didn't know when I rented the place, but there's a music room here." She led her mother to the room, gestured toward the rose-covered sofa, and wondered what to play. What would please her mother? She decided on some Rachmaninoff. Her mother hadn't heard her play since that terrible moment at the competition—

well, Sophie thought nervously, *ha ha, Hester didn't get to hear me play then.* Nervously, Sophie began.

When she finished, Hester said quietly, "That was beautiful."

Trevor rose. "I'll check on the kids." He diplomatically slipped away.

"Thanks, Mom," Sophie said. She felt awkward, as if she'd been playing the piano wearing only a bra and Spanx.

Hester stood up. "Let's go for a walk."

"A walk?"

"Yes, where we put one foot in front of the other. We can do it outside on the road in the shade of the trees. It's good for the heart. I do it for thirty minutes every day, rain or shine."

"Let me tell Trevor," Sophie said. She stuck her head in the family room and saw that Lacey was still sleeping and Trevor was working on his laptop. "We're going for a walk," she said, rolling her eyes.

"We'll be fine," Trevor promised.

Her mother had been right, Sophie realized. It was shady and cool beneath the trees, and the lane curved this way and that like a magical path. Houses were hidden behind hedges or tall evergreens or fences spilling with flowers. Her mother walked with a definite rhythm, not too fast, not too slow, and Sophie fell into step with her.

Hester said, "I've always been amazed at your playing. You really have a most exceptional gift."

"I suppose. I'm so sorry I never succeeded."

"Well." Her mother looked straight ahead as she walked, not touching Sophie, not taking her hand. "Maybe it's a good thing. Maybe you've had a better life than you would if you'd continued competing. I know your father never thought he had 'succeeded.' He always thought he should be given *more* fame, more honors, glory, money, academic awards, for the work he did on prostate cancer. I'm not exaggerating when I say there was a time when he thought he would win the Nobel Prize in Medicine. As the years went by and younger men surpassed him, as technology changed, Ken grew bitter. He worked harder; he became obsessed. You remember, he was seldom around as a father, or as a husband for that matter. There was no way I could make him happy."

Sophie only nodded, afraid to break the flow of her mother's words.

"You, like your father, were such a perfectionist."

"Ha. I'm hardly a perfectionist these days."

"No one with children can hope for perfection. No, I'm speaking about your music. For you it had to be all or nothing."

"Mom." Sophie stopped walking. "You and Dad were, too! Dad told me I could either be a winner or a loser! You both encouraged me— you didn't *force* me, but you helped, you pressured, you pushed. It was always clear to me that perfection—total and public success—was the only thing that would make you both proud of me."

Hester stood still, looking down at the ground. "You were extremely talented. We were, naturally, proud of you. We wanted only the best for you."

"You wanted only the best *from* me."

Hester met Sophie's eyes. She nodded. "I suppose that's true. We were younger then, like you are now with your children, hopeful, be-lieving you were capable of excellence."

"You and Dad were disappointed that I wasn't good at science. That I didn't want to go into the medical profession."

Hester continued walking, Sophie at her side. "Yes," Hester admit-ted, "that's true. The need is so great."

"I'm sorry I failed you," Sophie said quietly.

"You didn't fail me, Sophie. You failed only one competition. Maybe you stopped playing piano at that point because you disliked competing."

"I mean I'm sorry I didn't—oh, I don't know—help the world, like you and Dad."

Hester raised her arm to move a low branch away from her face. "But Sophie, you can still help, and in your own way."

"I can?" Sophie chuckled. "I can't envision going to nursing school."

"Can you envision playing piano in a nursing home?"

Sophie stumbled over a branch. "Huh. I never thought of that."

"Music is one of the most efficient mood elevators we have. People in nursing homes, whether ambulatory or even bedridden, whether lucid or not, would be provided with great pleasure by your playing. Maybe they could even dream, return to the best times in their lives, when they were loved."

Tears filled Sophie's eyes. "I've never heard you talk like this."

Hester's posture stiffened. She didn't do sentimental. "I haven't heard you play the piano for years. Why would I think of it?" She glanced at her watch. "We've walked for fifteen minutes. Shall we turn around?"

Sophie waited for her mother to continue, but Hester was quiet. She'd never been one to gush—but she was a good, no, a *great* doctor, Sophie remembered. "I wish I could help Connor. I wish you could help Connor."

"And Connor is?" asked Hester.

Sophie explained about the older gentleman in the apartment, his move from the Midwestern state where he'd lived all his life, his wife's death, his talent for carving. "You'd approve of his worktable," she told her mother. "Everything in its place, all neat as a pin."

"So why do you wish I could help him?"

"When Leo was talking to Connor about his mother's death, Connor told him that he, Connor, was dying. Since then, he hasn't joined us for dessert or even for a chat. He has a limp, and I think he has a bad foot, but his eyes have always looked bright and healthy. Maybe he's just depressed, but it was such a strange thing to say to a child, although he apparently meant it in a consoling way."

"I'll talk to him," Hester said.

Sophie smiled. "Good luck with that." As they turned onto the drive of the guest cottage, Sophie paused. Gently putting a restraining hand on her mother's arm, she asked, "Mother, were you happy?"

Hester pulled back slightly, as if offended. "What kind of question is that?"

"A reasonable one, I think. I never thought about what it was like for you, being married to such an . . . absent . . . man. He was never affectionate with me, and, well—" Sophie stumbled over her thoughts. "It must have been lonely for you."

Hester's face softened. "I don't often indulge in thoughts of the past. It's past. I've learned as an ER doctor to do what I can and get on with it. I've had a *useful* life. That's what's important to me. I've helped heal and save and bring consolation. Your generation is much too pampered, always picking away at the slightest discomfort and whining about it." To Sophie's shock, Hester spread her arms. "I'm *here*. The sun is shining. My daughter is healthy, my grandchildren are healthy. So yes, I'm happy, Sophie. Happy enough."

"I'm—I'm glad," Sophie sputtered. This was as intimate as her mother had ever been.

Before Sophie could say anything else, Hester announced, "And now I'm going down to the apartment to have a chat with that Connor fellow."

"Mother! At least let me come with you and introduce you."

Hester waved a dismissive hand. "You should check on Lacey. I'll be fine."

The afternoon passed in a lethargic preoccupation with the children. Sophie went up and down the stairs, taking Jonah iced ginger ale, carrying down smelly towels, doing laundry, taking everyone's temperature. Leo felt better, restless, and begged to be read to, so Trevor sat on the sofa with a few of the beginning books of *The Boxcar Children* in his hands and read to his son. Lacey curled up on the other side, listening, too, her head resting on Trevor's arm.

Hester was apparently still down in Connor's apartment. At one point, when Sophie and Trevor passed in the kitchen, Sophie whispered, "Maybe they're making mad, passionate love."

Trevor whispered back, "I'm glad someone is."

Sophie quirked her mouth in a grin that made Trevor's stomach flip.

In the late afternoon, Trevor had to make a run to the store for invalid nourishment: ginger ale, chicken noodle soup, graham crackers, frozen fruit ices, and Instant Cream of Wheat, which Leo was craving. He stopped at Sayle's Seafood to buy three seafood dinners: clam chowder, fried cod, amazing French fries, and coleslaw. With the children sick, Sophie wasn't in the mood for cooking, and Trevor snatched any opportunity to eat Sayle's dinners.

By the time he got home, he found Lacey and Leo standing at the card table in the family room, working on a jigsaw puzzle.

"Hey, I thought you guys were sick."

"I feel better, Daddy," Leo told him carelessly.

"Me, too," Lacey added.

From the depths of the sofa, Jonah grumbled, "I don't. But I've stopped puking."

Sophie stuffed clean towels into the dryer and slammed the door. "What smells so good?"

Trevor held up the bags of seafood, already stained with grease. "Comfort food for the adults."

"French fries!" Leo yelled, running into the kitchen.

"No French fries for you," Trevor said. "You've been sick. You're having chicken noodle soup and ginger ale. Graham crackers for dessert." He set about heating the soup for Leo and Lacey while Sophie set up TV trays in the family room for the children. Sophie set the table in the dining room for three, and poured herself and Trevor a glass of wine.

"Honestly? I don't know what to do," Sophie said. "Should I go down to Connor's and drag my mother up here for dinner?"

Trevor laughed. "From what I've seen of your mother, I wouldn't mess with her."

"All right then, let's eat. Everyone else is settled, and I'm starving. I don't think I got lunch today."

They sat at the table, munching the batter-fried cod, moaning with pleasure. Sophie said, "Sometimes I think my dream meal is Sayle's French fries and a glass of Prosecco."

"Sometimes I think my dream meal is you alone in—"

Sophie interrupted. "Don't say it. Don't even think it. My mother will walk in the door and read your mind."

Trevor fixed Sophie with a look. "I doubt it."

Sophie snorted. "You think my mother doesn't know about sex? She's a doctor."

"I'm not thinking about sex," Trevor told Sophie. That was kind of a lie, because anytime Sophie even entered the room he was thinking about sex, but it was also the truth because he was so happy right now, with all three kids in the family room and Sophie here at the table with him in shorts and a baggy T-shirt, her shaggy hair pushed back behind her ears, no makeup, no pretense, all honesty, all real. "I'm thinking about love."

Sophie said, "Oh."

"I don't want to be impetuous." Trevor wiped his hands on his napkin and leaned his elbows on the table. "I've been impetuous, and regretted it—well, not completely, because I have Leo. I don't want to make a mistake. I don't want to seem impulsive, rash—young. I know I'm younger than you are, but I can't change that. But I don't think it matters. You and I seem to—*fit*. Our kids fit. It's been that way since we first walked in the door. We've got something special here, not just you and me, but *absolutely you and me,* and then the kids, too. I don't want to lose it. I want to make love with you, but that's not all I want, and I want you to know that."

Sophie slowly began, "When we all get back to Boston—"

"When we all get back to Boston, it will be horrible!" Trevor said. "I'll miss you. Leo will miss your kids. *I'll* miss your kids." He pressed on, leaning forward in his urgency. "Here's what I want to do. I want to buy a house in the suburbs so Leo has a backyard to play in. Our apartment is too cramped, too full of sad memories. I want to buy a nice big house in your suburb, right next door to you, across the street, something."

Sophie smiled. "Trevor, I'm not even divorced yet."

"Yeah, but you will be. And when you are, you and the kids can move in with me and Leo. I'll buy a house that's big enough—"

Sophie leaned back in her chair, imagining. "Or you and Leo can move in with me and the kids. Our house is big enough, although Zack designed it, and frankly, it's never been my kind of house. Gosh, you'll have to deal with Zack."

"Of course I'm going to have to deal with Zack," Trevor said. "He's your children's father, and I'll just have to man up and be cooperative."

"You've really thought about all this." Sophie's eyes were wide with wonder.

"It's all I can think about. We'll be leaving soon, it's almost September, and hasn't this been great—" Trevor held out his arms, gesturing to the entire house— "all of us here together?"

"Yes, it has been great. It's been an enormous surprise." Sophie toyed with a French fry, dipping it into the cup of catsup and chewing it pensively. "That we've all gotten along so well, I mean. But Trevor, we've been on vacation. Certainly I haven't been dealing with reality. When we get back to Boston, I've got to get the kids ready for school, and go through some kind of grisly divorce proceedings with Zack, and I need to find a way to make money. Zack will pay child support, of course, but I don't know how much, and I'll need to work somehow. Finances have never—"

"You'll teach piano," Trevor announced.

Sophie sort of bounced. "What?"

"You'll teach piano. Plus, I'll bet you could get a lot of other gigs. School musicals. Local theater productions always need accompanists. Private students."

Sophie sat speechless.

Trevor continued in a sensible tone, "Sophie, you know you'll get half of your and Zack's assets when you get divorced. I don't know how much that is, but maybe you'll get the house, plus he'll pay child support. When we get married, you won't have to worry about money. I do pretty well with my business—okay, I do very well with my business. We can—"

"Trevor, slow down." Sophie held up her hand. "We've known each other less than three months."

"But we've lived together, with kids and friends and tantrums and vomit—I'd say that gives us about a year's worth in the familiarity bank."

Sophie looked across the table at him, her face glowing, amused, bowled over, and suddenly mischievous. "Well, there is one problem."

"What's that?"

She peered up at him from beneath her eyelashes, coyly. "We don't know if we're compatible in, um, bed."

Trevor wanted to leap over the table and ravish her right then and there. He restrained himself. "Okay, you're right—we definitely need to test that out, and as soon as possible."

"But how?" Sophie asked, waving her hands in the air. "With three children and my mother in the house?"

Frantic, Trevor suggested, "When your mother returns, you and I can leave the kids with her and drive somewhere, the beach, a hotel—"

"Trevor. We can't leave sick children."

"They're not that sick, and your mother's a *doctor*."

"Still, we're their parents."

"You're killing me."

"I'm killing me, too."

"When does your mother leave?" Trevor asked, as the kitchen door opened and Hester stepped into the room.

"Mom! Hi!" Sophie jumped, so guilty her voice was overly cheerful. "Trevor got a fish dinner for you. We didn't know when you were returning. Is Connor okay? What have you been doing? Would you like a glass of wine?"

Hester pulled out a chair and sank into it. "I would be grateful for a glass of wine. I've eaten with Connor."

Trevor rose. "I'll get the wine."

"So, how is Connor?" Sophie asked. She suspected her mother had already had one glass of wine because her cheeks were rosy.

"Connor Swenson is a healthy male with all the sense of a flea. It took me a while to get him to talk about it, because no male likes to admit weaknesses—thank you, Trevor." Hester accepted the glass of merlot and sipped it.

"And?" Sophie prompted.

"He has an open sore on his foot that won't heal. He's had it for several weeks. Has he seen a doctor? Of course not. He's a man. He's tried to treat it himself. He's used antibiotics and Band-Aids. He's left it open to the air. It's getting worse, so he doesn't go for walks and of course he doesn't do all the physical labor he used to do when he had the farm, and he's depressed because his wife died. He doesn't eat well. He eats too much sugar. I suspect he has diabetes."

"Diabetes," Sophie echoed.

"I called a friend up at Mass General. I'm taking Connor up there tomorrow for blood tests and treatment for his foot."

"How will you get there?" Sophie asked.

"I'll drive us in his truck to the airport. We'll fly." Hester took another sip of wine. "We probably will have to spend the night in Boston."

Sophie's eyes flew to Trevor's. She knew he was thinking exactly what she was thinking: *the apartment would be empty.*

Sophie gathered her wits. "Mother, you're remarkable. Connor must be thrilled that you came along, knowing so much."

"I'm sure he is," Hester replied calmly.

31

Was it too good to be true?

Sophie tiptoed down the stairs, her finger to her lips in a shushing sign, and beckoned Trevor into the kitchen.

"They're all asleep," she whispered, although there was really no need to whisper. Once her kids were down, they were out for the night. Lacey and Leo and Jonah had all recovered from the flu. They'd spent the day in town—a compromise between the more rigorous sun and fun on the beach and more lying around the house.

"They're all asleep. Your mother's in Boston with Connor. Let's go," Trevor said.

"Maybe we'd better give it a few more minutes—"

Trevor gently pressed Sophie up against the wall, put his hands on either side of her face, and kissed her. She put her arms around him, pulling herself against him. His kiss was sweet and urgent.

Sophie moved her mouth away enough to gasp, "Where? Not our bedrooms—too close to the kids. The living room? On the sofa?"

"What if the kids come down?" Trevor whispered.

Sophie nodded. "You're right." She thought a moment. "The music room. We can shut the door and Connor's gone, so he won't be able to hear us in the apartment."

Trevor took Sophie's hand in his and led her from the kitchen, through the hall, through the large living room, and finally through the doorway into the music room. He pulled Sophie inside, shut the door, and took her in his arms, kissing her hungrily on her mouth, her neck, and down the tanned bare skin above her tank top. Sophie moaned and let her head fall back, exposing her neck to his kisses. She embraced him, gliding her hands down the long muscles of his back, sliding her hands around to the front of his jeans, undoing the snap, slowly tugging down the zipper, and slipping her hands inside.

Trevor groaned. "Sophie," he murmured, pulling her to the deep rose-covered sofa.

From the two high windows on either side of the room, a white brilliance gleamed from the moon and stars, striking spots on the chandelier's crystals with light. The shadows seemed to dip and play over their bodies as Sophie and Trevor undressed each other, slowly removing the light cotton clothing so that it trailed like fingertips over their skin. They stood taking in the sight of the other's naked body until Trevor pulled Sophie close to him and for a while they remained like that, naked, pressed together, head to toe, inhaling one another's scent, trembling with desire, allowing the desire, like music, to spiral and climb and build and expand, until Sophie, summoning all her courage, defying any inner voice reminding her that her body was not young, that she might do something wrong, said in a low, urgent voice: "Trevor, *please.*"

He lowered her onto the sofa, pulling a pillow beneath her head. He knelt over her, allowing himself to take possession of her rich, luxurious body with his eyes. Gently, he pressed his knees between her parted legs, rested his hands on either side of her head, and slowly lowered himself to kiss her mouth, her neck, her breasts. Sophie embraced him, nuzzling against his skin, murmuring—inviting. And slowly he entered her and they both closed their eyes to savor the sensation. *This* was perfection.

Trevor set the alarm on his watch for four o'clock so they could sneak back into their own beds before the children woke, but Sophie was awake before the alarm. She lay with her face pressed close to Trevor's chest, which was a marvelous place to be.

The alarm went off. Trevor mumbled, woke up, and stopped the alarm. "What are you doing?"

"Sniffing you."

He pulled back, raising himself up on one elbow to look down at her. "*Sniffing* me?"

"You smell so good. I want to inhale you, molecule by molecule."

His low laugh rumbled near her ear. "You'd better stop. We'd both better get up and get to our beds."

Sophie responded by snuggling closer, pressing herself against him. "Maybe a few more minutes . . ."

"Stop that." Trevor rolled away and stood up. "You exhausted me. I've got nothing left."

Sophie heard herself give out a hum of laughter from deep within her belly. Stretching out full-length and brazenly naked in the gentle light of dawn spilling through the windows, she scanned Trevor up and down. "I can see quite a lot left, actually."

Trevor stooped to dig around in the pile of clothing to find his briefs. He pulled them on. "You're shameless."

"I am? How fabulous." She rose languidly and began to search for her own clothes. As she did, the reality of the day seeped into her mind like the morning light into the house.

Last night, between their first and second times of making love, they had talked about their lives, especially about their children.

They couldn't go frolicking all smoochy and giddy like young lovers in front of their children. That would freak out the kids. Only one more week remained before they left the guest cottage. After that, change would come at them, especially at Jonah and Lacey, like a tornado. Their parents' divorce. Getting to know Lila, who would be in their lives more and more from now on. Realizing that Trevor and Leo were also going to be a permanent fixture in their lives. And for Sophie's kids, the all-important return to school, dealing with new classes, new teachers, old and new friends. This was not the time, Sophie and Trevor agreed, for them to let the kids know their parents were anything more than good, even devoted, friends.

This was going to be hard work for Sophie, now that she had, for the first time in her life, truly discovered what her body could do when sex and love overwhelmed her. She had clutched him to her, weeping. "I love you," she'd sobbed. "Oh, Trevor, I can't help it. I love you."

He hadn't laughed. He had said, "I love you, too, Sophie."

Sophie pulled on her T-shirt and shorts, slid her feet into her flip-flops, and looked around the room. The rising sun sparked rainbows from the chandelier.

Trevor took her in his arms one more time. "You go first. Go up and get in bed. Try to catch another hour or so of sleep. I'll hang out in the kitchen. We don't need anyone catching us sneaking upstairs together."

Sophie smothered a laugh. "We're like teenagers." Then, as her body registered Trevor's body's reaction to her warmth and closeness, she whispered, "Are you sure you want me to go to bed alone?"

He pulled away. "Be good. Go."

Sophie tiptoed up the stairs, unable to stop smiling.

Trevor caught a couple of hours of sleep before he heard Leo bumbling around in the next bedroom. He rose and hurried in for a quick and necessary shower before shaving and pulling on clean shorts. Then he stuck his head into Leo's room.

"Good morning, guy. Want breakfast?"

Leo was, not surprisingly, building with Legos. "In a while," he replied, preoccupied.

In the kitchen, Trevor made a pot of coffee and sat down at the table with his laptop. Pretty soon the rest of the household ambled in, yawning and drowsy. The day had quickly become sticky with humidity, the overpowering kind that seemed to suck the energy right out of a person. Or maybe that was because Trevor hadn't gotten much sleep last night.

Sophie came down, freshly showered and dressed, but looking sleepy. "Morning," she mumbled, heading for the coffee.

Trevor kept his eyes on his laptop. "Morning."

Jonah, Lacey, and Leo were at various spots in the kitchen, fixing toast, gulping down juice, looking lazy.

Trevor kept staring at his laptop, but his mind was on the people around him. *This could be my family*, he thought suddenly. *Sophie could be not just my lover, but my wife*. The thoughts were both terrifying and exhilarating. With Tallulah, even with a child, life had still been more like—well, a play—than the real thing. With Tallulah, there had been no disagreements about what to feed Leo or how to dress him or where and when to put him in preschool. Tallulah hadn't paid attention, and that had given Trevor a freedom that almost felt like being carefree. But with Sophie, who did care about so much, life would be complicated. Trevor would have to man up more than ever before in his life. For one thing, he'd have to be a stepfather. He'd have to engage in these other lives—which meant worry, and sleepless nights, and making mistakes, and getting into heated arguments, and forgiving other people, and forgiving himself.

Trevor said, "I've had an idea. We've only got a week left and we haven't seen much of the island at all. I say we rent a four-wheel-drive Jeep and have a picnic at Great Point. We can see seals out there."

"*Dude,*" Jonah said approvingly.

"Great Point," Sophie echoed, her back to Trevor as she prepared her coffee. "What a brilliant idea."

They prepared a picnic, rented a Jeep, and set off. To get to Great Point, they had to bump over a rutted dirt road between the end of Nantucket Harbor and the few summer houses facing the Atlantic, high on the top of a dune. At a marked fork in the sand, they turned right, the Jeep growling like a tank as it climbed up the dune and dumped them on the long white stretch of beach on the ocean side. Nothing here but sand, more sand, and the blue Atlantic stretching out forever. It was hard work steering the Jeep as it whined through the deep sand, but the kids shrieked with laughter as they tilted and bounced nearly out of their seats.

The Great Point lighthouse rose at the far end of the barrier beach, a tall white steeple to the sky, with a working light flashing at the top. Here was the end of the island, the great point where the Atlantic Ocean met Nantucket Sound in a froth of waves. All along the point, enormous fat seals lolled on the sand, occasionally lumbering in and out of the water, grunting and lounging like a tribe of overfed Roman emperors.

"Can I pet one, Daddy?" Leo asked.

"Forget it. They bite," Trevor warned. "We won't go near them. We'll watch."

"We won't swim here, either," Sophie added. "The water's too rough, and we don't know who's out there."

"Maybe a great white shark!" Lacey giggled, safe inside the open Jeep.

They ate lunch and walked up the path to check out the small white entrance to the lighthouse. As they got back into the car, Trevor said, "I think we'll return via the beach along Coatue. The sand's packed, easier to drive on. Jonah, why don't you drive?"

Jonah was too shocked to respond. He gawked at Trevor, eyes wide.

Sophie said, "Um, Jonah doesn't know how to drive."

"This is the perfect place to learn," Trevor said. "No other cars around, and the beach is so wide I could stop the car if he steers us toward the water . . ."

"*Mom,*" Jonah said.

"Okay," Sophie decided. "You've got to learn sometime."

Sophie remained in the backseat with Leo and Lacey. Trevor sat in the passenger seat instructing Jonah as they lurched down the beach, past driftwood, curious gulls, broken buoys, and seaweed. When they reached the point between Coatue Point and the jetty protecting the harbor, Jonah stopped. They all got out, climbed on the rocks for a while, waded in the shallows, and looked for shells. Trevor stayed away from Sophie, knowing that if he came too near her, he'd give himself away—take her hand, rub up against her arm, touch her somewhere, somehow . . . This was enough, he thought, the way she smiled at him, the way their kids beachcombed together, the way Jonah, Lacey, and Leo teased and chased and carelessly wrapped arms around each other as if they were of the same flesh.

The ride back through the brushy trails of Coatue was long and hot. Leo complained he was getting motion sick. Jonah didn't complain because he was the new king of the world, having driven a Jeep on the beach. When Trevor checked in the rearview mirror, he saw Sophie relaxed against the seat, eyes closed, face lifted to the sun.

That night they went out for pizza at Sophie T's. After showering and cooling down, they all agreed the expedition had been a success. Back home, they spread a map of the island on the dining room table and planned three more explorations. Leo sat on Trevor's lap, yawning. Even Lacey and Jonah seemed tired from all the fresh air. Trevor thought it might be possible for Sophie and him to go to her room tonight, instead of going down to the music room. He'd keep his hand over Sophie's mouth.

"Hello, everyone." Hester walked into the room, pulling off her head scarf. "You all look busy."

"Mother. I didn't expect you back so soon," Sophie said, sharing a quick glance of disappointment with Trevor.

Hester pulled out a chair and dropped into it. "Connor's lab work won't be ready for another day or two. I tried to rush them, but they're backed up as usual, and it's not an emergency. They did bandage his foot properly. He's wearing a walking boot for a few days. When we get all the lab work back, we'll work with a physician here and start him on some kind of medication."

"Grandmother, we went to Great Point today!" Lacey babbled. "We saw seals! Jonah drove the Jeep!"

Sophie's mind was still caught on her mother's announcement. She asked, weakly, *"We?"*

"That's wonderful, Lacey," Hester replied to her granddaughter. "I hope you took photos." To Sophie, she said, "Yes, *we*. I promised Connor I'd stay here for a while to help him start his medication and begin a new cooking and exercise regime."

"That's awfully good of you, Mother, but what about work?"

Hester shrugged. "I've got plenty of leave coming. I've already spoken with the supervisor. I could use a spot of vacation myself."

"But Mother," Sophie protested, "we've only got three more days left in this house. I mean, I'm sure Susie—or Ivan—wouldn't mind if you remained here a couple of days more after that. But I don't even know how to get in touch with them, or whether or not they've made plans for the house starting September first."

"That's fine," Hester said calmly. "I'll go back up to Boston when you do. I've invited Connor to come up and stay with me while he gets a complete physical."

"Stay with you?" Sophie echoed.

"Dude," Jonah muttered.

Hester blushed. It might have been the first time Sophie had ever realized her mother *could* blush. "Connor is a lovely and intelligent man. I would like to be certain he's on a routine toward better health. Also—" Now Hester blushed pinker and *smiled*— "I thought he might enjoy seeing some of Boston."

"Well, Mom, that's awfully nice of you," Sophie said.

Hester shot Sophie one of her looks. "I *do* have a guest room, you know." Softening, she added, "And I do enjoy his company."

DAH-dum dum dum.

Trevor sat up in bed and allowed himself a moment to calm his nerves. He'd awakened from a deep sleep to the notes from the piano and his heart was racing.

Leo was getting so much better. Trevor had thought so, at least. Leo no longer insisted on putting on clothes in a certain order. He allowed Sophie to make his sandwiches. But this was too much, this entire summer of sleepwalking and obsessive, repetitive key-banging. Trevor rose with a sinking heart. What would happen when they returned to Boston? Leo was asking for a piano, but should he have one?

Trevor headed barefoot down the stairs. When he got to the music room, he was surprised to see Sophie already there, kneeling next to Leo. Trevor stopped in the doorway, listening.

"Leo," Sophie was saying, "I think I know what song you're playing."

Leo aimed his large eyes at Sophie and even in the semidarkness Trevor could see the hope in his son's face, in his entire body. "You do?"

"Is it this?" Sophie slid onto the piano bench and placed her hands on the keys. Softly, she played the opening bars to the Irving Berlin song made so famous by Ethel Merman. "There's NO Business Like SHOW Business," she played, quietly singing the words.

Leo nodded vigorously, almost hopping with excitement. "That's Mommy's song! Play more."

Sophie played the song through, singing most of the words, fudging the ones she didn't remember.

"That's Mommy's song," Leo said again. "She sang that to me all the time. She said to remember that song. No matter what happens, she said, go on and have fun."

"That's right," Sophie said. "Your mommy was a smart lady. Leo, would you like me to teach you to play the song?"

"Okay," Leo said, and began to crawl up onto Sophie's lap.

Trevor started to intervene—it was three thirty in the morning. But Sophie took the boy in her arms, settled him, and said, "We have to be very quiet so we don't wake people. I'll put my hand over yours. I'll press your fingers on the keys."

Trevor stood watching. Slowly, and terribly, Sophie and Leo played, "There's NO Business like SHOW Business."

"Again," Leo demanded.

"Not tonight, Leo," Sophie said.

Trevor held his breath, expecting a tantrum.

"You know," Sophie continued, "this song is meant to be played and sung really loudly, as loud as you can be. And we can't do that tonight, can we? We'd wake everyone up."

Leo thought a minute. "Okay. Can we do it tomorrow?"

"Sure, honey-bunny," Sophie assured the boy. "We can do it a lot tomorrow."

Leo slid off Sophie's lap and ran to Trevor. "I'm ready to go to bed now, Daddy. I have my song."

32

The end of the summer arrived with the swift chaos of a wave rolling in to crash onto the shore. Sophie and Trevor had to share a marathon of laundry, packing, organizing, cleaning out the cupboards, searching beneath beds, sofas, and desks for lost socks, filling a box of staples—sugar, flour, spices—to take down for Connor to use. Trevor couldn't find a way to reach Ivan, and when Sophie tried Susie Swenson's cell phone, no one answered. Trevor had to run to the grocery store to find cardboard boxes for all the Legos people had given Leo over the summer. He and Sophie had a conference with the three kids to figure out whether various games—Clue, Monopoly, Ticket to Ride—belonged to one of the families or had been on the shelf in the house.

Sophie assumed her practical, efficient, Mother would help organize and pack, but Hester spent much of her time with Connor, driving him into town for short walks and lunch, or out to one of the beaches to drink wine while watching the sunset.

"I'm amazed at my mother," Sophie said one evening after she and Trevor had gotten the children in bed. They were sitting on the patio, lights off in the kitchen, enjoying some private time being alone to-gether in the dark.

"Why?" Trevor asked.

"I've never seen her so . . . mellow. The Hester you're seeing isn't the Hester I grew up with."

"Speaking of . . ." Trevor lowered his voice. "Look what's going on now." He touched her arm gently. "Ssh. Don't make a move. We don't want them to know we're here."

Following his gaze, Sophie glanced over at Connor's patio. The older gentleman was holding a blanket over one arm, and holding the door open with the other so that Hester could step out onto the patio. Murmuring quietly, they walked down the lawn to the darkest spot on the property. Connor flipped open the blanket. Hester caught one end and helped spread it out on the grass. Then, gingerly, the two carefully lowered themselves onto the blanket and lay down, staring up at the sky. After a few moments, Connor raised his hand, no doubt pointing out a constellation.

My mother is lying on a blanket with a man who is showing her the stars, Sophie thought with wonder. She swallowed the large lump that rose in her throat. When Connor reached over to take Hester's hand, and Hester reached to receive it, Sophie found herself smiling and crying at the same time.

Leaning over to Trevor, she whispered in his ear, "I want to go in-side. I sort of feel like we're spying."

Quietly, like children on Christmas Eve, Sophie and Trevor slid out of their chairs and crept into the kitchen, leaving the pair on the blanket to watch the stars in privacy.

Two days before they had to leave, Hester was absentminded, Jonah
was sulky, Lacey was whiny, and then Leo told his father that he was
riding back with Jonah and Lacey.

They were all sitting around the table, finishing a dinner of leftovers. Leo's announcement brought a stop to the conversation.

Sophie glanced at Trevor. "Leo, honey," she said gently, "we'd love
to have you ride back with us, but I don't know where you live."

"We live with you," Leo told her.

Trevor swallowed. "Leo, on Nantucket, on vacation, we live with
the Andersons, but at home we live, well, at home. In our apartment.
With the goldfish, remember?" Suddenly a goldfish seemed like a pal-
try reason to call a place a home.

Leo's lip quivered. "But I want to live with Lacey and Jonah! Why
can't we live with Lacey and Jonah?"

Trevor was heartsick as he looked at the confused face of his little
boy. "Leo, listen, we'll visit Lacey and Jonah a lot. They'll visit us.
We'll do a lot of cool things with them. But they have their own
house, and we have our own house."

"But that's all wrong!" Leo cried. His self-control fell apart. He
sagged on his chair, sobbing.

Lacey was crying now, too. "Oh, Mommy, I wish we could adopt
Leo."

Hester, trying to be helpful, said, "Lacey, you're old enough to know
that's not possible."

"Oh, Mother, shut up," Sophie snapped. Her own eyes were welling
with tears.

Trevor moved over to embrace his son, trying to pull him onto his
lap, but Leo hit out at him, his face red and wet with tears. "No! I
want to go with them!" Trevor thought he was going to throw up right
then and there. He wanted help, he wanted Sophie to help him, he
wanted Lacey and Jonah to reassure Leo, but Leo was his child and his
alone, and he was the father, the grown-up, and this was all messed

up. He and Sophie hadn't been able even to kiss for the past three days, since Hester returned. Someone was always in the room with them, or about to enter the room. They hadn't had a chance to talk about the future, and while every fiber in his being screamed out that he should stand up and announce right now that he was going to marry Sophie and they would all live together, Trevor wanted for once in his life not to be impetuous.

"Leo," he said, forcing himself to sound calm, to sound in control, to even sound *kind*, "Leo, kid, I know it's hard, but we have to say goodbye to the Andersons."

And then Sophie was there, kneeling on the other side of Leo's chair, reaching out to take the child in her arms. "Leo, we *will* live together, very soon. Your daddy and I have to make some arrangements first, but while we do, we have to live in our own houses. But we'll see each other all the time. You and your daddy can come to our house for sleepovers. We'll all come to your house for sleepovers, too."

"Really?" Leo asked, his eyes wide with hope as tears ran down his face.

"Really." Sophie picked up a napkin and gently wiped the boy's nose.

"Are you my family?" Leo asked.

Sophie nodded. "We're your family. Lacey, and Jonah, and me, and Daddy, too, and you, Leo."

"Oh my gosh!" Lacey cried, jumping up from her chair. "Does that mean we're going to get married?"

"Duh," Jonah said. "*They're* going to get married, not all of us."

Hester, her practicality tempered by her relationship with Connor, asked gently, "But isn't Sophie still married to Zack?"

"Technically." Sophie waved her hand as if flapping away a gnat. "Not for much longer." Gathering Leo into her arms, she slid onto his chair. Now she was very close to Trevor, who remained next to the chair, wanting to console his son, wanting to kiss Sophie passionately, trying not to beam. Leo was snuggling against Sophie, digging his head into her bosom—Trevor wouldn't mind doing that himself right now. But he stood up, gathering his words, thinking how best to apologize to Sophie's children for this bizarre sudden announcement that they were all family, terrified that Jonah would consider Leo a spoiled brat who got his own way by having tantrums, and especially that Jonah wouldn't understand that Sophie and Trevor had been talking about this like adults.

"We intended to sit down with you all—" Trevor began.

"Dude," Jonah said, and shoved back his chair. He walked over to Leo and squatted down next to him. "I have an idea. You can ride back to Boston with Mom and Lacey. They'll take you to your apartment before we go to our house. We can come in and see your room."

Leo's brow wrinkled. "But then Daddy will have to drive all alone."

"Nah," Jonah said. "I'll ride with him and we'll meet you there."

Trevor turned on his heel and strode from the room. Overcome with the first true joy he'd felt since Leo's birth, Trevor went into the bathroom, shut the door, met his reflection in the mirror, and gave himself a big, fat high-five. *This was happening. It was real.*

Finally he pulled himself together, calmed his breathing, and returned to the dining room.

"Goodness," said Hester, "you must have terrible allergies. I have an antihistamine with me you can take."

"Thank you," Trevor said.

Sophie said, *"Mother."*

A knock sounded at the kitchen door. Hester jumped up to answer it.

"Hello, everyone," Connor said, waving. "Are you ready, Hester?"

Hester looked at her watch. "Goodness, I lost track of the time. Yes, Connor, I'm ready." She searched the kitchen counter for her purse and found it, then glanced back at Sophie. "We're going into town to hear a lecture on island farming at the Nantucket Historical Association. Don't worry about dinner for us. We'll eat in town."

"Great, Mom. Have fun, you two," Sophie said.

"Thanks, darling," Hester replied as she went out the door.

My mother called me darling, Sophie thought. Miracles really did happen.

The day before they left the guest cottage, Sophie sat down at the piano. Her mother was at the apartment having lunch with Connor. Trevor was at the beach with the three kids for one last swim. She had remained home to do laundry and pack. Finally, she was organized for their trip back to Boston tomorrow.

She let her hands drift idly over the keys, gliding from one old favorite melody into another, wondering why it was that here, in this house, on this island, she had discovered her music again. The easy answer was that here she was free of Zack, released from his demands, desires, and ambitions. There was some truth in that, but that was not the entire truth. Maybe she had accepted—even needed—the restraints and aspirations of his way of life because she wanted to escape from her own goals. *Yes,* Sophie thought, playing a light arpeggio, *right:* when she had been all about piano, something deep within her had known she also wanted children and family and home and humble homemade zucchini bread. She couldn't have that and become an international concert pianist as well. Professional musicians worked as hard, in their way, as long-distance truck drivers. They had to practice for hours every day. They had to fly all over the world to perform in countries where they didn't speak the language on pianos they'd never used before, the ivory keys holding an unfamiliar and unpredictable response. Not much time for zucchini bread.

She didn't want to believe she had been ruthless when she met

Zack, that she'd only pretended to love him so she could have a family, so she could escape her own obsession. Lightly playing the familiar notes of "Some Enchanted Evening," she remembered meeting him, being enchanted by him, fascinated by his verve and motivations. If she hadn't loved him, she certainly had been swept away by him, and for a long time she had enjoyed the ride.

Somewhere along the way, in the midst of his architectural success and her happiness with her children and home life, she had lost her admiration for him. That was true, and that was sad. It had been a gentle falling off, maybe beginning at a cocktail party when she watched him suck up to some corrupt, unconscionably wealthy banker, in the hopes that the man would ask Zack to design a house for him. Or it might have been other times, all the times Zack didn't show up to see his children perform in ballet recitals and school plays and Little League games. And what had started as a trickle of unrest had built into a river of dislike. She had tried to keep up the façade of loving him. She had thought she was doing the right thing for her children.

Arriving here to find the piano, sitting down to discover that she still could play—not well, but well enough for her own pleasure—had been a revelation. She had recovered a deep and significant part of herself. It was not all of who she was, but it was an important part.

And Trevor and Leo? How could their meeting be explained? Chance, serendipity, fate, the stars in alignment, the universe blessing them . . . a *miracle*. Sophie had always believed miracles existed, and now, for the third time in thirty-six years—the first two times had been the births of her son and daughter—a miracle had happened again. It might be as simple, as incomprehensible, as illogical, as marvelous, as that.

And now she would always have music in her life.

33

One Year Later

"Mom." Jonah hulked into the bedroom, trying not to look pleased with himself in his tux. Today he was going to walk his grandmother down the aisle to give her away in marriage to Connor, the man who had changed her life.

"Jonah, sweetheart, you look so handsome! Grandmother will be thrilled." Sophie crossed the room to inspect her son. She was wearing high heels, and still she had to look up. "Let me straighten your tie. You did an excellent job of tying it."

"Yeah, at this rate I'll be a great butler."

"I think I see you more as a soccer star, sweetie," Sophie told him, reaching up to ruffle his hair.

Jonah jerked his head back. "Don't touch my hair." He had obviously spent some time gelling and arranging it into its ridiculous startled porcupine appearance.

"Mommy, Mommy," cried Lacey, running into the room. "Look at me!" She wore a lavender dress with a full skirt that twirled out all around her when she spun.

"Beautiful," Sophie said. "Come let me put the circlet of flowers in your hair."

Jonah plopped down on the bed, putting his feet in their handsome black shoes right up on the duvet. Sophie didn't scold him. She was pleased that he was remaining in the room to talk to her and Lacey. Obviously he was becoming comfortable with the entire formal, dressy fussiness of wedding preparations. It would be the third wedding he'd taken part in this year.

First, and most extravagant, had been Zack's marriage to Lila. The ceremony itself was held in Trinity Church in Boston, with no fewer than five bridesmaids for Lila, who was resplendent in a personally designed Vera Wang gown and tiara so covered with sparkling stones and pearls Sophie was amazed the woman could stand. Lacey had been Lila's flower girl, and both excited and nervous about her performance, but *totally* enthralled by her own outfit, a black (Lila was nothing if not edgy) sheath, low black heels, and a wide rhinestone headband. The roses Lacey sprinkled on the carpet were blood red.

Jonah had been his father's best man. At first, he had balked, complaining that it didn't even *make sense* for a guy to be best man at his father's wedding to someone else. It was Trevor who calmed the boy down, by saying simply, "Yeah, well, Jonah, I want you to be best man at my wedding ceremony when I marry your mother."

"Dude," Jonah had sighed. "Life is so complicated."

"Dude," Trevor had replied, "you have no idea."

So Jonah had bit the bullet and been his father's best man. Later, he confided to Sophie that he'd found the scale of the wedding and the reception at the Boston Harbor Hotel both overwhelming and boring. "Dad's such a phony," he grumbled, "and Lila is, too."

Lacey, however, idolized Lila, with her fabulous clothes, her coiffed hair and plucked eyebrows, her scarlet lips and heavy gold jewelry. "I want to be just like Lila when I grow up," Lacey told her mother.

"Lovely, sweetie," Sophie responded. "You should try to spend as much time with Lila as possible, don't you think? To pick up clues on how to dress and wear your hair?"

Lacey had eyed her mother skeptically. At eleven, she was beginning to achieve a sense of independence and a brewing need to break away from her closeness to Sophie. Sophie understood this. She'd read a lot of books on child rearing lately. Her sadness at Lacey's changing attitudes was balanced by the surprising knowledge that Lila was nice, and more than nice, caring and willing to be involved with the children. Now when Zack had his children for the weekend, as decreed in the divorce settlement, he actually spent time with them, because of Lila. Zack didn't claim many of those weekends—he often had important business. But Sophie was grateful for Lila's willingness to help Zack build a sturdy relationship with his children. She knew it could have been otherwise.

Sophie, Trevor, and Leo, too, attended Zack and Lila's zillion-dollar wedding extravaganza so they could see Jonah and Lacey in their finery. But Zack and Lila weren't invited to Sophie and Trevor's wedding. That was a much more modest affair, attended by family and a few close friends: Bess and her husband and Cash and Betsy; Angie; River and his wife, Nestra, and their baby, Plum; and Anne, Kyle, and Gabe Manchester. Jonah was Trevor's best man, Lacey was Sophie's bridesmaid, and Leo was the ring bearer. Hester and Connor flew up for the wedding and hosted the wedding celebration—a private dinner cruise on a posh yacht that slowly glided around all the islands in Boston Harbor.

Today Hester was marrying Connor. She had finally accepted a long-deserved sabbatical from the hospital in order to take a honeymoon with him in Hawaii, where, Sophie hoped, Hester would not spend the time trying to find and cure an obscure disease among rare parrots. Connor's softening influence on her mother was amazing, but no one could change the woman completely.

Even so, Hester was going to have a wedding, a real, romantic, sentimental *wedding*, on Nantucket, in St. Paul's Episcopal Church at eleven o'clock. Susie Swenson had happily given the guest cottage to Sophie and her family for the weekend, and the house was nearly explosive with excited people—not only Lacey, Jonah, Leo, Trevor, and Sophie, but in the other wing, Hester and her friends (Sophie had been startled to learn that her mother had *friends*), who were now in the process of arraying the bride. In the family room, Connor's old friends Curt and Marjorie Luber and Sylvia and Donald English were staying. They had flown in from Iowa for the week, and Sophie had been delighted to see how much fun they all had together. *Well*, she thought, *they don't have to worry about how their children do on their school exams or the future economy.* They seemed to have reached the age of freedom—perhaps it wasn't golden, but it certainly seemed like a lot of fun.

Trevor stuck his head in the bedroom door. "Time to head out for the church, everyone."

Lacey, the flower girl, shrieked, sprinting to the stairs and down to the car. Jonah was going to give his grandmother away and Leo was going to be the ring bearer once again, a position he bore with extreme earnestness.

"Come on, Leo," Jonah said, holding out his hand to his stepbrother. "Let's go on down."

Leo was playing with Legos between the bed and the window, but he rose quickly, allowed Sophie to straighten his little blue blazer, and ran to take Jonah's hand.

When the room emptied of children, Trevor stepped inside and shut the door behind him.

"What a crew," he said. "If the kids get any more excited, they'll levitate."

Sophie laughed. She rose from the chair and walked over to her husband. "You look stunningly handsome." Wrapping her arms around him, she leaned against him, allowing them both to share a peaceful moment in their own private world. Her mother had asked her to play the piano for the wedding, and Sophie had happily agreed. She had also made the wedding cake and much of the food for her mother's reception, which would be held back here at the guest cottage. But for now, for a moment, she pressed against Trevor, indulging her senses in the pleasure of his love.

Trevor kissed her forehead and held her away. "Stop that. We'd better catch up with the others." He cocked his head, scrutinizing Sophie. "You look beautiful, Sophie. I mean it. I don't mean you look nice—you look *triumphant.*"

Sophie laughed smugly as she opened the door and stepped out into the hall, where her mother's friends were gathering like a flock of twittering doves.

"Thanks, Trevor," she said over her shoulder. "It must be that pregnant glow."

Trevor's jaw dropped. *"What?"*

Sophie nodded, smiling brilliantly. She held out her hand. "Shall we go?"

ABOUT THE AUTHOR

NANCY THAYER is the *New York Times* bestselling author of *The Guest Cottage*, *An Island Christmas*, *Nantucket Sisters*, *A Nantucket Christmas*, *Island Girls*, *Summer Breeze*, *Heat Wave*, *Beachcombers*, *Summer House*, *Moon Shell Beach*, and *The Hot Flash Club*. She lives on Nantucket Island.

nancythayer.com
Facebook.com/NancyThayerAuthor

ABOUT THE TYPE

This book was set in Goudy, a typeface designed by Frederick William Goudy (1865–1947). Goudy began his career as a bookkeeper, but devoted the rest of his life to the pursuit of "recognized quality" in a printing type. Goudy was produced in 1914 and was an instant bestseller for the foundry. It has generous curves and smooth, even color. It is regarded as one of Goudy's finest achievements.